SACRED SHADOWS
and LATENT LIGHT

Sacred Shadows
and Latent Light

DUSTIN LAWRENCE LOVELL

Foreword by Thomas Allbaugh

RESOURCE *Publications* • Eugene, Oregon

SACRED SHADOWS AND LATENT LIGHT

Resource Publications
An Imprint of Wipf and Stock Publishers
199 W. 8th Ave., Suite 3
Eugene, OR 97401

www.wipfandstock.com

PAPERBACK ISBN: 978-1-6667-3332-7
HARDCOVER ISBN: 978-1-6667-2786-9
EBOOK ISBN: 978-1-6667-2787-6

DECEMBER 14, 2021 2:50 PM

To Amy Grace and Evangeline Locke

Amy,
your support as a wife and judgment as a listener
made this book possible; it belongs to you.

"I do love nothing in the world so well as you ..."
—*MUCH ADO ABOUT NOTHING*, IV.1

Geli,
The only thing that could eclipse this book's publication acceptance
was your birth a week later.

"I have done nothing but in care of thee,
Of thee, my dear one, of thee, my daughter, who
Art ignorant of what thou art."
—*THE TEMPEST*, I.2

"Well, God be thanked for these rebels. They offend none but the virtuous."

—*Henry IV Part 1*, III.3

Foreword

"WRITE WHAT YOU KNOW."
Most writers will hear this in their first fiction writing workshop. Usually, the advice is interpreted to mean that they should submit to limitations. Few consider it an invitation to learn new subjects and have new experiences, or even to observe the world more closely than they have before. I took it as a warning not to write about New York City unless I had actually been there. And at the time, this did prove helpful as it led me to pay closer attention to the community I grew up in and was, with a typically youthful, romantic gaze, looking past.

I don't know that Dustin Lovell was ever subject to the banalities of a fiction workshop. But if he was, writing what he knows would have meant writing about Shakespeare. A little more broadly, I think, it also might mean writing about the influences of reading on character. *Sacred Shadows and Latent Light,* his first novel, had its beginnings in an undergraduate thesis he wrote defending his interesting view of Hal as spending his time with Falstaff in taverns as a subversive way to secure his kingship. His work explores both Shakespeare and the importance of reading to character, subjects of great importance to him. The difficulty here, as some might see it, is that a critical thesis rarely suggests promising material for the novelist, whose concerns with the conditions of existence will be measured in terms of character strengths and weaknesses. Usually, a character's vanity, or vain need for certain privileges like recognition, creates more interest for readers of fiction than the character's consideration of some philosophical premise. The exception to this, of course—those philosophical premises considered by characters in a Dostoevsky novel, where the philosophical can become a pretext for murder—is still mainly a focus on character weakness. Dustin Lovell is an avid reader of Dostoevsky, and in turning to fiction and writing about what he knows, he has transformed his undergraduate thesis into an engaging novel centered on a conflict over Shakespeare on a fictional college campus named Orangedale University.

In the opening chapters of *Sacred Shadows and Latent Light*, one cannot fail to recognize academia in full swing. Mixed in among characters motivated by ambition and politics are those for whom reading and the study of what they are reading—in a word, the humanities—really matters. The characters who inhabit this world are entirely recognizable in their frailty and mistakenness, fully and bodily present in a world of dictates, students like Elliot Fleming and Cora Madison, Ermine Jackson and Smith Ingman, and even Ryder Colson himself, the adjunct professor who is confronted by those with more power than he has as an adjunct, and who must act with integrity. Ryder may seem a little distant initially in his manner and pronouncements, but in the same way that we might with a good teacher, we learn more about his backstory the longer we know him. I find him most interestingly driven, helped and shaped by his reading. He is someone constructed in the humanities. There is an integrity to him. He is deepened as protagonist in his reading of Nietzsche and Dostoevsky, two authors who helped him to navigate a life crisis.

In the thinking and dialogue of Ryder Colson, perhaps, the author's avid reading emerges, which includes much of the classic canon, from Plato and Aristotle to Nietzsche and Dostoevsky. And, of course, most centrally, there are Shakespeare's plays. Ryder's presence in these pages as director of the play and also an avid reader of works of the Western Canon is dynamic and defining. Reading scenes where he interacts with students in their more vulnerable moments, gently guiding them past danger and giving them authors to read (because he has read them and found in them help during his own dark periods of doubt), made me nostalgic for the period of the 1970s when I entered academic life as a student. My memory is still vivid of a place and time I have never been again, where meeting people and getting to know them also meant getting to know the books they mentioned, the books that mattered to them, books that could have the same weight in the academy at that time that dry Power Point presentations and budget reports seem to have today.

Even as a current member of the academy, I miss this. And, as an academic, I enjoy seeing my profession satirized. I am a fan of books like

Richard Russo's *Straight Man* and David Lodge's *Changing Places*. Dustin Lovell's novel is in good company as it shows faculty in all of their posturing, administrators in all of their machinations, and students in all of their momentary conflicts, misleading passions, and love affairs. I should add that Lovell knows the academy. He has been a student, a tutor, and a teacher. So here also, he is writing about what he knows.

I should add a disclaimer: Dustin Lovell is a friend. We have worked together briefly in a writing program and shared drafts in a critique group. Early on, when reading a draft Dustin had shared with our group, I raised questions about the premise of the plot. How would Shakespeare become controversial among academics? However, the further I read, the more it began to occur to me that the conflict that drives this plot could perhaps also be seen as a reminder of affairs from the Bard's own day, when the Globe Theatre faced shutdowns quite regularly in London. Shakespeare was always seen as fair game for the censors, and these echoes can remind us that history is at any moment in danger of repeating, or at least rhyming, with itself. That one of Shakespeare's history plays could be a source of trouble, or seen as a text of controversy, seems, in today's climate, both an absurd likelihood and a strong possibility.

In *Sacred Shadows and Latent Light*, what we have is this: a contemporary work written in the nineteenth-century tradition of the novel. Lovell invites his reader into a world that seems to be fully present, a world where many characters, many points of view emerge, with deans, directors, and students weighing in. It also means that an overarching authorial presence, in the nineteenth-century sense, lurks behind the action. There is no provisional, unreliable first-person narrator or narrators, no fragmentation, no minimalism. We enter the thoughts and rationalizations of everyone.

The challenge for the writer of fiction, in any age, certainly, is to make our current and perhaps momentary absurdities not into polemics, stereotypes, or social media put downs, but instead to somehow give them human faces and the right nuance. Dustin Lovell has done this. Among the students, professors, and administrators he imagines here, I detect the echoes of a Dostoevsky novel. *Sacred Shadows and Latent Light* makes for a rich, compelling work of contemporary fiction.

Thomas Allbaugh
September, 2021
Southern California

Acknowledgments

Sacred Shadows and Latent Light took a few years to complete, and its germination goes back many more. Needless to say, while SSLL's setting and characters are fictional, I am indebted to several people for the knowledge, experiences, and support that enabled me to write it.

As a piece of novelized Shakespeare criticism, SSLL would have been impossible without a solid literary and performance foundation. Professors Judith Tschann at the University of Redlands, who both slogged through the 63-page thesis that served as a distant background to Rydar's interpretation of Prince Hal, was the type of professor who could scaffold students' ambitions and help build something meaningful. Steven Shade of U of R's Theater Department taught me how to bring a scene to life, for which I will be ever grateful. Dan Cork, who managed the U of R stage while I attended, was a great boss; thank you, Dan, for hiring me in the scene shop and for trusting me with building the set pieces. Steven Sabel, previously of the Redlands Shakespeare Festival and currently head of the Archway Theater, introduced me to community and professional theater; Steve, I'll always consider you a brother.

While the bulk of SSLL was finished by the time I met Thomas Allbaugh of Azusa Pacific University, his encouragement and guidance helped me turn my first draft (over twice the final length) into a clear, coherent plot unencumbered by unnecessary backstory and literary discussion. Tom, thank you for agreeing to write the Foreword, as well as for inviting me into your writers group. Thank you, Elena Smith, Gary Wallace, Kristen Schmidt, Anthony Wai, Pastor Martin Smith, and the others for the honest notes and excellent ideas. Tom's eventual suggestion

I submit the book to Wipf and Stock Publishers was, of course, the underscore to all his previous help. I want to thank Matt Wimer, Jonathan Hill, and the others at Wipf and Stock for taking on *SSLL* and for making the printed edition look so great.

The greatest thanks, of course, is owed to my family, first among whom is my mother, Jackie. A fellow English teacher and my primary reader, her suggestions gave *SSLL*'s characters a depth and subtlety they would have lacked otherwise. Mom, thank you for your faithful rereads and suggestions, and for loving my characters so much. Finally, I must thank my wife, Amy Grace, for helping me hash out the themes and theory behind the plot, for telling me when something did or did not work, for tolerating when an idea would strike at 3:00 am and had to be written down, and for agreeing to let me take time off of work to finish the project. Babe, you once asked where you are in the book; you are everywhere, insofar as you made every page possible, and nowhere, insofar as the lessons and admonitions it contains are, for you, moot. You already possess the resilience, patience, and joy to which my characters aspire.

PROLOGUE

"YOU'RE ASSUMING HARRY really cares about Falstaff, the way he acts—and he does, very much! But what if that's still what he's doing: acting?"

Vesta Lloyd looked from the man speaking—adjunct literature and writing professor Rydar Colson—to the half dozen or so men and women seated around the sides and back wall of the room. Inclining forward, reposing back, or sitting still, the members of the central panel did not respond. The relatively young professor seated before them, who, pending the outcome of this meeting, may or may not direct Orangedale University's annual Shakespeare Festival in the Spring semester, ran a hand through his short, blonde hair before sitting back to await a response.

Stifling a smile, Frank Hoegren, head of the theater department, festival producer, and the official authority in the room, spoke up: "So, you're saying you want to turn Prince Hal into a conman?"

"I'm saying he turns himself into one, to some extent," Rydar Colson resumed as if released from a tether. "It's not a new argument, though it's been out of vogue for a while. But it's right there in the text. Harry's surrounded by conmen, and not only in the taverns. At least Falstaff's honest about being one—and he's only an effect of Richard II and Harry's father. If Harry's going to save England from itself, he needs to get past the corruption of the previous two kings and resurrect what the crown used to mean . . . " Taken up by the subject and employing his hands to emphasize his argument, Colson could barely hold back his grin.

Vesta released her breath. She had seen Colson speak like this last semester; his eyes always seemed so focused, as if he were fighting to

1

rescue his listener from something unnamed but nonetheless pernicious. She had never understood why it left her breathless, but it had provoked her to read last Spring's plays not as mere class tasks but as enigmas to be scoured, as if it were crucial she comprehend them, if only to understand why Colson saw them that way.

It was why when professor Colson announced to his Fall classes the previous week that, pending approval, he would be directing a series of Shakespeare's history plays, Vesta knew she needed to be a part of it. Professor Colson had subsequently invited her to this meeting as a prospective costume designer, joking that, "Thesis defenses don't end at graduation, even for professors!" Scattered around the room was a handful of other students. Vesta wondered if Colson had invited them, too. One young man with brown, neatly combed hair met her glance before looking away with a dimpled smile.

"Harry's approach is so subtle it's easy to miss," Colson continued. "Whether by prudence or accident, he never fully gives in to Falstaff's impulsivity, nor to Hotspur's open rebellion. Instead of simply rejecting the previous kings' legacies, like those two knights do, Prince Hal nuances the best of both responses; he paradoxically uses the outward corruption of Falstaff to hide the fact that he's secretly fostering and refining the chivalric honor of Hotspur.

"In other words," Colson raised his hands, palms upwards as if depicting a balance, "to become England's greatest king Harry must first wear a mask of crime—the mask of a conman. But it's just that: a mask."

"So, he's lying the whole time?" William Akron, university treasurer and board liaison, said more than asked. "Even when he obviously prefers Falstaff—whom we've already cast, by the way. What will Ernest Blythe say when he hears he's to play his most inveterate role not as the heroic soul of the common Englishman but as the butt of one big ruse? Our deposit on his flying out here was non-refundable." Contrasting sharply with the other adults' mix of general interest and end-of-week lethargy, Akron's acerbic demeanor had provided most of the meeting's energy.

"I'll repeat what I said before about Blythe," replied Colson. "If he declines the role because of that, he's not who we want. From what I know of him he'd be excellent, but he'll need to follow my lead. He'll need to be a Falstaff about how he interprets Falstaff—he'll need to meet the action to the moment, to improvise like an expert while still looking like a buffoon. I've seen several actors who wouldn't flinch from their interpretations of the fat man for anything. I know I'm new to directing, so I'll be relying heavily on whomever we cast. Our Falstaff needs to be able to manage any unexpected situation without breaking character. I mean really unexpected," the professor motioned with his hand, as if throwing out an example, "like Viola walking onstage naked."

A few coughs and shifting of seats issued from around the tables at the comment, as did a few chuckles. Vesta Lloyd gasped, both from the unexpected mention of her favorite heroine and the nature of the reference. Most of the students were smiling, wide-eyed, at the joke; smirking down at his feet, the brown haired boy shook his head.

"Well," Colson resumed, "maybe not that bad, but you get the point. I'm sure Blythe can pull it off, in his own way. However, Falstaff is still Prince Harry's biggest threat—no pun intended." The man smiled, evoking a chuckle here and there from those sympathetic to his cause. "I mean, a genius knight-turned-drunken-thief, arguably in response to the post-divine-monarch England, must be as tempting for Hal as it is dangerous; it's dangerous because it's so tempting. I have a hunch Blythe will understand. But first he'll need to know that, so far as the core theme of Falstaff's character—and of our whole production—is concerned, it's my way, not his."

"He's a professional who knows the part better than any!" Akron exclaimed. Startled, Vesta found herself noting the shine of the classroom's fluorescent lights on the man's head. She averted her eyes so as not to giggle; this meeting was important.

"Yes, and I worry that might translate into resisting fresh interpretation," Colson replied in an even tone. "The Henry cycle is about reevaluating not only past traditions but also our own impulse to revolt against them. I'd love to work with Blythe, but as for that 'heroic common man' idyll you mentioned, that's exactly the kind of assumption I'll need him to question. I have one word for Falstaff's seemingly democratic, if shortsighted, ethos: nihilism, which in the context of medieval England would have meant regicide, even deicide, at least ideologically."

"Of course, it's obscene to speak of Shakespeare's greatest comic creation so dryly—and as if he were ever meant to be taken so seriously. Besides, I don't presume to think I have Falstaff completely figured out. It would mean I had Shakespeare, himself, figured out, and even I'm not that arrogant."

Some snickers could be heard around the tables, though a few mouths remained stolid. Vesta looked through the windows at the oak trees outside the Hall of Letters; she met her dim reflection's gaze, just as she had often done when taking French 202 in this room the previous semester. Her curly red hair brightly contrasted with the late-August green outside, and the blue of her eyes faintly matched the hazy summer sky.

Colson continued, "Still, for the sake of argument, sometimes it's necessary to take the fat knight's presumptions seriously, all the more so because of humor's ability to make the unpalatable palatable. It's in this sense that Falstaff is a danger to Prince Hal, and it's imperative that Harry not follow the man's example to its logical end, even as he uses aspects of it to avoid his father's and Richard's fates. So, if you choose me to direct next year's Shakespeare festival, that's the reading everyone involved will need to follow."

The table sat silent, though several around the table shifted again. Akron, however, pressed, "We know you're young, Rydar, but we won't let you go off on some freak reading."

Vesta noticed Hoegren tense up, as if about to respond on the young professor's behalf. However, before he could, Colson took a breath, relaxed for a moment with closed eyes, and replied, "I'll submit that it is not a 'freak reading,' as you call it, William, but is grounded in and jejune to Shakespeare's text. It's all there in my prospectus." Colson motioned to the stapled packet that sat unopened in front of Akron.

Everyone had received one upon entering the room. Skimming the abstract before thumbing through the pages, Vesta had seen that the paper examined not only Prince Hal's use of a dissembling act to achieve his ends but also Hamlet's, as well as other Shakespearean characters', establishing Colson's argument first before progressing to how it might translate to the stage.

"But," replied a relieved Hoegren with a wry smile not devoid of affection for Colson, "I think William's concern isn't without merit: it sounds like you're making Falstaff the villain." If Hoegren's relaxed tone was meant to compensate for Colson's apparent cheek, thought Vesta, he was trying too hard. No one but Akron seemed bothered by Colson's premise; indeed, some looked interested.

"I don't think it's me doing it, Frank." Colson's pace and tone grew familiar. Vesta had always enjoyed when he spoke like this—sometimes explicating one line for half an hour and at a pace that often left his listeners striving to keep up. She resisted the habit of reaching for her pen; she did not need to take notes. Just listen—and remember. She glanced at the brown-haired student; he seemed to have been looking at her just the moment before. Vesta felt herself blush.

"In Shakespeare, the idea of rightful kingship is . . . " Colson said, pausing after a moment with his fingers pressed down against his own heavily annotated paper, " . . . no. It's in there—if you care to read it and consider my research and argument. Suffice it to say that Prince Hal must resurrect the crown's integrity and value, which the previous two kings let die. However, in an England where values have been turned upside-down and emptied of meaning—where the 'God' of the realm is dead and seemingly beyond reach—he can only do that by preemptively undercutting how those values are understood. He must play not a king but a fool—in the technical sense of the term."

Colson relaxed back with a patient smile. Vesta still felt as if he could have talked much longer; he already had, she thought, looking down at the packet.

"He is not wrong, William," ventured Nilette Lilledahl, professor of theater and Women's Studies, in her slight Norwegian accent. "Of course, I might not take such a view of the plays, but Rydar's argument is legitimate and sound. I wonder how it might look onstage . . . " Seated at the far corner of the tables, the platinum-blonde woman—Vesta guessed between Akron and Colson in age—leaned her head toward Colson in acknowledgment as she let her words trail off.

"Thank you, professor," Colson said, turning his clean-shaven chin toward the woman, "I can only base it in what I've read in the texts. In fact, I'm very interested in your perspective on producing the plays. It's one of the reasons I requested you be here today—as well as wanting to defer to your guidance as a theater professor."

The woman paused a moment; amidst the wary hardness of Lilledahl's composure Vesta recognized a woman who found herself unexpectedly flattered.

"Well, don't misunderstand me: your interpretation will stretch a lot of people the wrong way, however well-researched it might be," Lilledahl said, glancing at the proposal. "In any case, I won't be able to recommend your production to my students. The best ones will be graduating this year and will already have a lot to deal with, what with our Fall production and their own senior projects."

"I understand," Colson replied, a momentary flex in the jaw his only reaction. Glancing to Hoegren, Colson continued, "I've been candid about my perspective from the start. I won't force or expect anyone to participate who doesn't want to," Colson looked to Professor Lilledahl, who had turned her attention away from him, "though I do ask that you at least tell your students so they can decide for themselves. If you let me direct the plays for Spring's Shakespeare Festival, we'll be presenting Harry with this interpretation," he pressed his fingers to the packet before him, his eyes taking in the whole room, "unironically. Not as a conman, as Frank said, but as that most uncommon man in the history of English royalty: the man who resists impulse and extremism and, instead, earns his own virtue—and thus, his crown."

"By lying to Falstaff," Akron said, crossing his arms with a shake of his head.

Colson sat back and, after a moment's look at Akron, sighed and chuckled to himself. Following his glance, Vesta looked at Grey Maxwell, head of set design and theater foreman; the man had sat quietly throughout the meeting in a corner to the side of the panel, leaning back in his chair and watching his younger colleague from beneath whitening eyebrows. The man's subtle yet unwavering smile seemed to convey the feeling that the answer was simple.

"No," said the young professor, looking Akron in the eye before softening his gaze at the rest around the surrounding tables, "lying—the refusal to admit what's right in front of him, exactly as he sees it—is precisely what Prince Henry does not do. The only person someone can truly lie to is himself, and out of all the characters in the entire dramatis personae Hal's the one who sees, understands, and accepts what he must do, even if all the others would rather not. 'He knows them all, and does awhile uphold the unyoked humor of their idleness . . .'" Colson continued in the articulate voice he always used when quoting lines in class, pressing his palm to his worn copy of Shakespeare's Complete Works, as if simultaneously for support and as a check on himself.

Watching Colson, Vesta felt she understood what their Prince Henry had to be—like justice on a monument, smiling at grief. She giggled at how the lines from *Twelfth Night* might apply to both Harry and Colson; she quieted herself as she realized several around the room were looking at her.

"Yes, Vesta?" asked Colson, smiling.

"Oh! Nothing, Professor Colson."

"What was it you laughed about?" the man pressed, unblinking yet calm. The rest of the tables were looking at her.

"Oh, um . . . I was just thinking of what . . . " Vesta improvised, grasping the first thing she could think of, " . . . what Princess Katherine would think about meeting a man like that—who needs to pretend to be something else in order to hide not his vices but his virtues."

Colson said nothing; he merely looked at her, smiling and tightening the muscles around his grey-blue eyes. A nervous tremor stirred Vesta's stomach.

"'For this,'" said Colson at last, gesturing with his hand to Vesta, "'has he laid by his majesty and plodded like a man for working days.' Ladies and gentlemen, meet Vesta Lloyd, one of my brightest students and, assuming you trust me with your stage and she accepts the offer to occupy it, the first member of our cast: Princess Katherine. Now," he said, returning to his harsher tone as he observed the group, "either you're going to give me this thing or not. What other questions—real questions—do you have?"

Vesta felt her face flush; she shouldn't have covered with a *Henry V* reference, especially when she had only read a synopsis of the play. Designing costumes was one thing, but playing a part onstage? Nonetheless, beneath her nervous self-reprimand was a growing excitement that Colson had relied on her and that her presence had given him strength. Besides, Katherine only really appeared in the end of the *Henry* plays . . .

Vesta looked over to the corner of the room for relief and distraction; at some point the young man with the brown hair had slipped out of the meeting.

"I know it's superfluous, Ry," Grey Maxwell said, relaxing into the irresistible smile he felt when looking at his young friend, "but I think I knew this production was coming. Even back when you were an undergrad there was something you didn't know how to let out. Maybe I hoped it was something like that. Oh well." Maxwell shrugged. "Whatever it was, I think this is part of it."

Looking through the office window at the afternoon light outside, Maxwell slipped his hands into his jeans pockets. He had come to the second-story office often since Rydar's return to Orangedale University as an adjunct. The young man did not mind, and they had enjoyed the ease of colleagues to which the boy's few years of set building in the theater had been a prelude. The younger Colson's precision with a table-saw then was the first of a handful of images that made Maxwell proud of his own life's work. Despite Colson's sharing it with another professor, this office was another such image—as would be, thanks to the board's decision not fifteen minutes previous, the school year's later production of *Henry IV Part* 1, *Part* 2, and *Henry V*.

"Thanks," said Colson, tucking a curl of dark blonde hair behind his ear as he leafed through the production proposal he had submitted two weeks before the meeting. "I hoped for more from Nilette, but it could have gone worse."

"I'd bet Lilledahl will come around—or at least stay out of your way, so long as you stay out of hers this semester. I also think she hates most literature professors on principle; it doesn't help that you're a man, either. You're also young; maybe she feels threatened—though that's only because she doesn't know you. Still, she knows a good show when she sees one, and Frank's willing to trust you with his theater either way. You should really get better light in here, kid."

"I like it this way." Rydar leaned back in his chair and looked out the window.

Maxwell turned to Rydar's bookshelves. The volumes had no discernible order; many were stacked haphazardly and in odd bunches. They contrasted sharply with the neat, alphabetized shelves on the other side of the office.

"Got any Chekov?"

"Third row down, on the left, blue cover," Rydar said without looking. Maxwell smiled, expecting such an answer. He did not bother checking.

"How about Beckett?"

"God, no, check over there." Rydar motioned across the office. The two men shared a quiet laugh.

After a moment, Maxwell sighed. "What's wrong, Ry?"

"It's just . . . goddamn it, Grey, he's such a little bastard!"

"Who? Akron?"

"No. Fleming."

"Ah." Rydar had mentioned Elliot Fleming. "The boy you want to play Harry."

"I want him to grow up. Which, yes, is why I want him to be Harry. Of all my students, he's the one I hope will succeed most, or drop out— which might be the same thing."

"What, so you can tutor him privately?"

"So I can punch him in the face to wake him up, and then buy him a drink; that's probably how it would go if I did tutor him, in a sense. It's ironic—he's read more than some seniors, but just when he's about to say something noteworthy in class or in a paper he undercuts himself with irony or humor at precisely the worst time." Rydar chuckled despite himself.

"I can see why that'd get to you. However, if I remember, you rarely took class seriously, despite everything else." Maxwell smiled, remembering how peripheral Colson's classes had seemed to his life and his private studies—which had often far outstripped his assigned readings.

"Yeah, but I was naive, too, though in a different way . . . " Rydar let his thought trail off. Maxwell looked away by force of habit.

"Do you know what he said in class last semester?" Rydar asked. "Mind you, he was a sophomore taking junior classes. He said the best thing Hamlet ever did was die because it made room for Fortinbras—which is technically true. But he then proceeded to say that for all his brilliant language Shakespeare's plays might lead aliens to think the English-speaking world has a fetish for killing off its heroes."

"Did you correct him?"

"Yeah, but it was the most brilliant thing I'd heard on *Hamlet* all term, even if it completely misses the point of tragedy—which I told him. But he only smirked as if he'd expected it!" Rydar could not repress an ironic smile. "Of course, I can see right through it; he loves the plays, even while he spits on them. That, itself, might make him a decent Prince Hal."

Maxwell watched Rydar, admiring how much he had changed since college and remembering all that had been the price of the change. Maxwell chuckled. "I've never seen you get like this about a student. What makes Fleming so special?"

"I can't say. Maybe it's the fact that he's apparently read some Aristotle. He has a lot to give and nowhere to give it. I'll have to be careful, though: in getting past who he thinks he needs to be he might just cop out and try to be like me."

"A little bastard?"

Rydar uttered an obscenity over his shoulder with a smirk.

"Gonna talk to him?" asked Maxwell.

"He seemed uninterested when I mentioned the production in class. Probably wants me to approach him directly so he can act like he's giving me alms."

"Like when I asked you to work for me."

"You didn't ask. You said if I worked as hard backstage as I did on-stage you'd have a job for me, and I needed cash."

"And here we are."

"Yeah. Whatever—I'll figure it out. Any plans tonight?"

"Since when have you cared?"

Rydar chuckled, slinging his book-bag over his shoulder.

"Say," said Maxwell before leaving the office, "what was all that about Miss Lloyd?"

Rydar shrugged. "Besides you, Frank, and Jonas, she was the only person there who didn't seem bored. That's how she is in class. She's like Elliot, in a way: she gives a damn, in spite of the students around her, only she's not afraid of it like Elliot seems to be. She'll do well."

"Bit of a gamble, recruiting her right then and there," Grey said.

"I've known her for a couple of semesters. She's almost the opposite of Elliot—he expects antagonism when there is none, and she can't conceive of there really being such a thing. However, I'm not really worried about her; her eyes are open in ways Elliot's aren't. But you're right." Rydar shook his head. "I shouldn't have been that weak."

Maxwell said nothing. He sighed as they reached the Hall's west door. He wondered about Colson's unusual preoccupation with Fleming and Lloyd. "Ry, I think if they have what you see in them, then you wouldn't be able to stop whatever happens to them, nor whatever they choose to do. And it'd be vicious to try."

"Probably," said Rydar with a sigh; he squinted as he stepped out into the sunlight. "Y'know what? I hate giving a damn."

"Tell me about it. I never knew I could hate it until I met you. When are you gonna buy a hat, kid?"

"Waiting to inherit yours."

They shook hands, Maxwell turning south toward the theater, Rydar north to the faculty lot.

Chapter 1

E LLIOT FLEMING checked the clock. Fifteen more minutes. After that, only three more classes. Then, freedom.

"And so," continued his philosophy professor, Smith Ingman, "our perception is limited not only by our finite physical senses but also by internalized environmental and cultural influences on our respective consciousnesses. Thus, we can't simply deduce a set of universal human values, as much of Aristotle's work assumes, because, for all his writing on such things, their articulation may have had more to do with ancient Greek culture than with their supposedly objective universality."

Ingman looked at the girl who had raised the topic. "Thus, as it pertains to your point, Cora, we can't just measure differences between people—whether cultural, racial, or the like—against some objective idea of humanity, as such. Despite different presumptions by Aristotle or the Enlightenment of universalism, the standard of measurement would necessarily be bound to the culture of the individual speaking—and, therefore, may be too easily biased in its values, which limit its scope. At least, that's the direction philosophy has gone since the nineteenth century. Of course, provincial though he may seem to us now, Aristotle had his place, however far beyond him we may have moved. Still," the professor shrugged, "I'm never saying don't read something. Thank you for the input, Cora."

Eleven more minutes.

"But, Professor Ingman," Cora Madison asked, apparently unsatisfied with his evaluation of her presentation of the second week's assigned reading, "doesn't the fact that we're political animals presuppose that we can understand other people, even those from other cultures? It seems you're saying we can never really understand each other, individually or culturally, and that we can't choose our own ideas and perspectives."

Elliot smiled. He wondered if Cora had deduced Ingman's distaste for Aristotle from the syllabus, as he had; either way, she had volunteered to lead discussion on the Philosopher's only appearance in the semester, proposing after her summary of his ideas how they could help mitigate modern racial tensions. Elliot found he agreed with Cora. He glanced away to the clock, frowning; he was looking at her too much.

"I see what you're getting at," Ingman replied, checking his wrist-watch. "You're still assuming, as Aristotle did, that perceptions and language can be trusted objectively and pragmatically and that different cultures use language in the same way. For the sake of day-to-day matters, you're correct, insofar as we need a reliable way to perceive the same thing—that we both mean 'mug' when we say the word," the man held up his mug of tea, "but remember that we are both speaking English. That is, we're defining what is real from the same language and, implicitly, culture. A different culture might derive a totally different meaning and value from the mug—and that's assuming they'd even recognize and value it as a drinking vessel. The same goes for Aristotle's logic: even his formalization of it was a creature of his living in the culture of his time . . ."

Elliot sighed, putting away his papers as Ingman pontificated on absurdity. While Elliot would normally fit other students' presentation notes into his bag behind the laptop case—keeping them for a day or two before tossing them—he slipped Cora's into the back of his binder.

" . . . There are, of course benefits to such a shared structure of human relations," Ingman motioned around the room, "but there are also many issues—especially when we start talking about the interaction of fully separate cultures. One culture's idea of a thing, whether something as innocuous as a 'mug'—which notably shares it name with an act of petty theft—or something as abstract as logic, itself, is shaped not by an objective knowledge of the thing as it is but by our place in a society that interprets a certain thing a certain way.

"Of course," Ingman nodded his head to the side, "that's not to say cultures can't or don't exchange, emulate, or, more often than not, appropriate different things and ideas; however, the point is that it's practically impossible for any item or value to be 'universal' to or inherent in humankind. Unfortunately, the assumption of universalism too often obscures the fact that a particular thing or idea is little more than a mere cultural tool—that is, intrinsically not universal."

Cora nodded, but her furrowed brow and closed mouth belied her acceptance of Ingman's words; Elliot did not doubt she would speak more if given the chance. He smiled, suppressing the impulse to chuckle. Ingman had denied the existence of universal human truths with a universal truth.

"Do you have something to add, Elliot?"

Damn. Elliot flinched; he was too expressive for his own good.

"No, you pretty much said it all."

"Enlighten us," Ingman said, observing Elliot over the rims of his leveled glasses.

Elliot paused. He should get better at hiding his reactions—at least in Philosophy 206: Fathers of the Mind. Elliot had predicted on the first day the class would be a waste; had Ingman really wanted the course to deserve its title, he would have assigned no one but Aristotle, with some Plato for context. However, Elliot had grown used to being disappointed by professors.

"A is a," said Elliot, leaning back in his chair.

"Pardon?"

Oh please, thought Elliot. *Posterior Analytics*, book one, section ten, the root of everything. Had Ingman even read Aristotle?

However, rather than casting such a pearl, Elliot quoted from elsewhere: "'That which is non-existent cannot be known.'"

An expectant eyebrow raise was Ingman's only response.

"Before Cora's argument can be either right or wrong culturally," Elliot began, "there first has to exist the concept of being, per se, as well as the dichotomy of 'correct' and 'incorrect.' Her argument can't exist as objectively wrong, as you imply, unless some objective, universal reality exists in which you can know it to be wrong in a way that transcends culture—or else one culture might call it wrong and another call it right, with neither having the final say. Presumably, that goes for individuals, too. I.E., she'd be just as correct in believing she's right as you are in saying she's wrong."

Ingman said nothing. The man's mouth pursed as if tasting something sour. Elliot was disappointed the man did not perfect the cliché of the bested professor by rolling his eyes.

"Elliot," Ingman said, shaking his head, "that's not how culture works; also, you and I can't help being part of the same culture. However,

I wasn't saying Cora was objectively wrong, but that trying to deal with things as being universally right or wrong already assumes a certain perspective. Again, even if there were such things as absolute truth and untruth, we couldn't know if they were universal or merely cultural, since we'd necessarily be seeing them from within culture. Understand?"

Wondering whether it was worth setting a pall over the rest of the semester, Elliot replied, "Do you want my answer in objective or culturally subjective terms?"

A mix of scoffs and gasps rippled through the twenty-odd students. Most, slumped in their chairs and watching the clock and door, merely looked like they wanted to leave. Ingman sighed, checking his watch again.

Prompted by a steady impatience, and aware of Cora's eyes on him, Elliot continued, "Either way, it's you, not Cora and I, who assumed the existence of universal absolutes; you said absolutes do not exist. That is, as you implied, they absolutely do not exist."

Ingman's glance remained fixed; he did not answer. Elliot waited, not blinking. Catching a professor in a slip was one thing, thought Elliot, but explicitly turning his argument back upon itself was another. Elliot regretted saying anything. However, a few of his peers were smiling at the gambit. Cora could barely contain her smile. Ingman would be hard-pressed to appeal to the consensus, at least in this classroom. Elliot swallowed, straightening his back.

"It's late," Ingman said with a sigh, taking in the whole class with a turn of his head, "and we don't have time to fully cover this debate—nor the many philosophers we'll read this semester who contributed to it. No doubt we'll be having this discussion again, Elliot. Not that I'm complaining." Ingman raised his palm with a shrug. "Either way, I'll see you all on Tuesday. D.J. and Erica, please be ready to present on Longinus." Ingman looked at Fleming. "See you Saturday, Elliot," the man said, his voice dropping below the shuffling of bags and chairs.

Standing without response, Elliot lifted his bag strap over his shoulder, smiling at the weight in his bag of the copy of Aristotle, which he planned to bring to every class to spite Ingman. If professors like Ingman wrote the Philosopher off, so much the better. Ethos had a natural inferiority complex compared to logos, Elliot had mused before, and often dismissed logos as simply corrupted or biased ethos—and altogether lacking in pathos. Aristotle's *Rhetoric* had anticipated as much. Elliot suddenly thought he would write his final essay on academic postmodern subjectivity's ironic reliance on Aristotle's a priori axioms; he considered what he would say and whom he would cite. He also imagined how Ingman would react.

The thought, and Ingman's last words, reminded Elliot of what he had been putting off; he would deal with it over the weekend—when he saw Ingman to declare his major. Walking down the Hall of Letters's eastern stairwell, he wondered whether he should petition for a new advisor. Ingman could hardly be trusted to be objective with Elliot, especially once Elliot told him he no longer wanted to major in philosophy.

The sunlight coming through the trees as Elliot left the building soon outshone the worry; apart from a chemistry lab the next morning and his meeting with Ingman on Saturday, his weekend was free. Elliot inhaled, smiling at the clean, bright feeling. Soon he would be alone to read what he wanted and game as long as he liked. He had expected all of college to be like that: a time to spend his effort how he wanted and grow into the person he wanted to be. That he should have to seek outside of classes to realize such an ideal struck Elliot as profoundly ironic.

As he crossed the campus's central street toward the Commons, Elliot remembered the summer after high school. Suffused with the anticipation of college, the authors he had read and the games he had played at the end of high school stood out so vividly compared to those since. He had enjoyed a few classes, all things considered, and he relished feeling he had earned the right to spend his afternoons and evenings gaming with impunity. Yet, overall college had been an anticlimax, and it made him miss high school all the more that he could not articulate the impression's cause—or what cause had evaded him.

An elbow nudged Elliot's arm.

"Thanks for that," said Cora. Had she been behind Elliot the whole walk?

"Don't mention it," said Elliot. "He shouldn't have left himself so open like that."

"Yeah, but you'll have to present eventually . . . " she said as they walked into the Commons. "Who are you thinking of doing, if you don't mind?"

She was staying with him; no grab-and-go lunch today. Suppressing a sigh, Elliot took a tray and walked toward the pizza bar.

"Marx," he said, choosing the most ridiculous and cliche thing he could say.

"Marx?" She gave him a mixed look of confusion and clever interest. "But he's not on the syllabus."

"Oh, yes he is," said Elliot, seeing as he spoke how he really could write the paper, which he had even considered early in the semester. "See, before he and his buddy, Eng-balls, called it 'communism,' they had another name for it: Plato's *Republic*."

"But Plato was last week."

"Yeah, but we haven't seen the last of him," Elliot said.

Cora smirked as she took a piece of veggie pizza. "Where should we sit?"

"Oh, um," Elliot stalled, searching for a table out of the way. Chatting in the Commons hardly fit his afternoon ritual of detoxing at his computer. "How about over there?" He motioned without looking toward a lowered area with tables of only two or three chairs. If he had to stay, he'd be damned if he'd end up in the middle of a crowd.

Elliot sat at the first table he could find, facing the tall windows. Without thinking, he had fit his two pizza slices cheese-sides together and was halfway into his first bite when Cora sloughed off her pack and sat down.

"Do you always eat two pieces at once?"

"Of course. A pizza sandwich beats a pizza taco any day." Elliot fought back a wince. He had never eaten them like this; he did not plumb why he had tried it now, focusing instead on Cora. The girl smiled, leaning forward to take a bite from her piece.

He must have missed something, Elliot thought, if one interpolation of himself into a class discussion was enough to evince Cora's attention. He had seen her look at him in previous semesters, sure, and he could remember a couple of times when she might have tried to interact. Dismayed at her sudden presence, Elliot took a drink and let himself look at her; with her dark skin and hazel eyes containing an inexplicable suggestion of blue, Cora would be called gorgeous by any standard, he thought not for the first time. The bluish glow from the shaded, northward facing windows did not hurt the image.

"So, somehow I would have never plugged you as being into Marx."

"I'm not," Elliot said, swallowing as he met her eyes, "not in the absolute slightest. I don't even hate the guy, though I probably should. It'd be like trying to hate some kind of senseless animal that thinks all humans are bad, and that dogs are the real movers of society, even though humans have kept him safe and alive his whole life."

"Ah, I love Orwell," she said, leaning back and crossing her arms, "though I can understand Marx's perspective."

"Yeah, I guess that was Orwell, though I wasn't thinking of him," Elliot said, noting Cora's tone of critical conciliation. That was another reason he would have to be wary of her, as he was with most other students. He was not sure sympathy could accompany a serious understanding of Marx.

"Anyway, I'll probably contend that Marx didn't exist because his ideas are just Plato, rehashed and demystified," Elliot said, expounding on ideas he had imagined saying to Ingman's face. "You could say the same for basically half of Western philosophy—Augustine, More, Hegel, Rousseau, everyone who envisioned making a perfect society without regard for the actual people they'd force into it. The joke, which I might have to save for my final paper, is that if all they were doing was copying Plato—that is, if none of them contributed anything original, whatever their new vocabulary—perhaps the same can be said of Plato."

"Really? That's a pretty big thesis," Cora said. Her slit-eyed look of practiced skepticism, which usually annoyed Elliot in other students, paradoxically relieved him; she had not yet read a page of the other names on their syllabus, either. "But whom did he copy, then?"

"No one. That's the point—that there's no solid center to any of it. There's nothing real that can be known, to take it back to what Aristotle said. Even Plato said that ideas are just inspirations from the realm of the Forms, which, even if true, he doesn't really prove. But he's Plato, so people took the ideas they liked and ran with them, whether they worked logically or not. And, thus, the spectre of state collectivism has practically had a divine mandate for two millenia."

"What about Socrates?"

"I don't know—and probably can't, since most of what we know about him is filtered through Plato. Honestly, I'd probably like to meet the guy, especially if his ideas had anything to do with Aristotle. I wouldn't say the same for Plato." Elliot took another bite.

"I'm sure Ingman will find who you would and wouldn't like to meet completely relevant." Cora chuckled around a fry.

"By then I'd hope to have the language for why." Elliot wiped his mouth as he glanced at Cora's legs through the glass tabletop. She was only a bit taller than he, but her leanness, as well as the proud way she carried herself—shoulders back and chin level with the ground—made her appear much taller. Her clothes seemed to exaggerate it; even the way she kept her hair up emphasized the length of her neck, as did the loose, low-hanging cowl collar she now wore over her cami.

"So, let me get this straight," she said with a laugh, pulling up Elliot's attention. "You're accusing the biggest name in philosophy of not saying anything original, and your reasoning is that you wouldn't like to meet him? Well, good luck to you sir."

"He's just a man," Elliot replied around a bite. "His ideas were profound, yeah, and so was his rhetoric for them, but more than a little of it was unprovable speculation. I've found I usually dislike being around that kind of person. I merely reversed the equation."

"And if you could meet Aristotle?" Cora asked.

"Weren't you in class?" Elliot pulled the volume of Aristotle out of his bag, smiling. "I have met him—and I've enjoyed every moment of it."

"Do you always use that as your standard of judgment?" a voice behind them asked.

Elliot looked over his shoulder. Rydar Colson, his professor for Literature 319: Shakespeare's Histories, who must have sat down without Elliot's noticing, was leaning back, eyes intent on a page in his old volume of Shakespeare's Complete Works. He held up a finger, finishing what he was reading before turning to them. It was not the first time Elliot had seen him do something like that. Glancing at him from across campus or passing him in the Hall of Letters as a freshman and sophomore, Elliot had often experienced a subtle mix of hostility and intrigue. Taking Shakespeare After 1600 the previous Spring had exacerbated both, though it was different from how Ingman made Elliot feel: whereas he avoided Ingman out of disillusioned boredom, he avoided Colson out of a too curious excitement.

"When I can, professor," Elliot replied, noting the amused smile on the teacher's shaven face.

"Indeed. You know that might say more about you than them?"

"Of course. Surprised?" Elliot met the man's glance; Colson chuckled.

"Not a bit," the professor said, tightening one of his rolled up sleeves. "What surprises me is that you think so highly of yourself that you'd do such a thing unironically." Leaving Elliot to decide if his words had veiled an insult and reaching out his hand, Colson addressed Cora. "Pardon me. Rydar Colson."

Cora shook the man's hand, a wide-eyed focus on her face meeting the man's smile. "Cora Madison. You teach English, right? My roommate has you—Vesta Lloyd."

Elliot separated his pizza slices and took a bite, feeling an inexplicable tinge of jealousy at the thought that Colson had never smiled like that at him. Elliot never noticed how blue were the man's eyes; he said nothing.

"Oh, you know Vesta; yes, she's wonderful. I'm her advisor, actually. What's your major, if you've chosen one?"

"I haven't decided yet," Cora said, leaning forward to reach for a napkin. "I'm between Philosophy and Women's Studies."

Chewing, Elliot looked between the two; he had no idea Cora, too, was a junior between majors.

Colson sipped his black coffee. "Why those two?"

"Well, I really enjoy dealing with big ideas, but I think women's equality and justice are more important, in a way."

"Do you think the two are separate?"

"Well, no, of course all subjects are related, but I actually want to help make justice happen, not just think about it in an ivory tower."

Colson looked at the girl, pursing his lips as if considering a thought. Cora's eyes were slightly squinted, as if she were unsure what to expect.

"If that's what you think about philosophy," Colson said finally, "I can understand why there'd still be a contest."

Smiling in interest, Cora reassumed the skeptical squint she had aimed at Elliot a moment before. "Sorry, what do you mean?"

"I mean," said Colson, shifting toward them in his chair with a resigned sigh, "that if you see philosophy as having no practical impact on the state of women in society—rather than its being not only a possible solution to those problems but also the source of many other problems—then choosing a direction must be difficult, indeed."

Cora crossed her arms and leaned back. She retorted in a hard tone, "Well, one in six women are raped in their lifetime, right? And one in three women in college. If it's a choice between reading stuff from the ancient past or doing something to change those facts, I'm going to do what's right."

Gently holding up his hand, Colson asked, "Would it be too impolite if I contradicted you on our first meeting?" At a nod from the girl, he continued, "I know the study you're referring to; those ratios don't line up with the study's statistics—if unverified, anonymous sampling and unclearly defined terms can be called 'statistics.' Even the authors said it would be inappropriate to use their study to make blanket claims about colleges and society." The man took a slow sip of his coffee. Cora was about to respond, but Colson resumed: "But that's missing the bigger issue: in large part it is philosophy, or what is left of the culture that produced certain philosophies in America and the West, that has given us the conviction that we should keep such numbers on the subject in the first place. I believe much of how we modify our future actions—like how we treat sexual assault—according to successes and failures of previous experience was first formalized many centuries ago by Elliot's man, Aristotle."

"You know he was a rapist, himself," Cora replied, looking away from Colson. Elliot knew which passages she was thinking of; they were a stretch, anachronistic at best and contradicted by other passages. He looked to Colson for his response.

Colson pursed his lips and lowered his head. "Mmm, that's debatable, unless you're referring to Greek pederasty in general. However, if you'll excuse me, the fact that you find what we'd consider statutory rape distasteful when many in his culture did not proves my point about his philosophy's and others' unique effect on our culture and life. Mind you, I'm a lit professor, not a philosopher, but it was with the tools of Aristotle," Colson gave Elliot a terse smile without relaxing his gaze, "and, I'm sorry Elliot, of Plato, that later thinkers and saints would deal with many problems of the past. Often the issue was not in debating or reconciling ideas but in applying them consistently. Nonetheless, it was the continuing conversation of their ideas—and the physical progress of an innovative economy, itself an effect of certain metaphysical conceits—that raised women and children to a level of respect equal to men, especially compared to other places in the world, past and present.

"At least," Colson raised his hands in a gesture of demur humility, "that's one perspective. Still, seen this way, your laudable desire to help women might accomplish more if applied to certain schools of philosophy, or to their prophet, literature. Indeed, Women's Studies, itself, may be an extension of and already contained within philosophy and literature, which I'd argue have been the real tools of cultural liberation."

"Oh my God, that's such bullshit." Cora slid her chair back and grabbed her bag.

Colson reached out his hand. He did not touch her, but the gradual sweep of the motion slowed her just enough. She leaned back, crossing her arms as she looked at the man.

"I'm sorry, Miss Madison," Colson said. "I know it's a touchy subject, and I haven't earned the right to speak into your life. No one is removed from sexual assault; it should not happen in a society that enshrines each individual's right to their own life, liberty, and property, each of which applies first and foremost to one's own body. However, the fact that we punish assault when it's proved to have happened—and that we as a society agree it should be punished—is an achievement. But even the guarantee of rights is just one philosophy, and if its roots are not understood, defended, and rearticulated, how can we expect them to be respected? You don't have to believe anything I've said—professors are often wrong." The man suddenly smirked despite himself. "I'm certainly not advocating you major in anything so monetarily useless as philosophy or literature. But, if you're offended, please allow it to provoke you not to action but to reflection. I only meant to show that your belief that philosophy has anything but a profound effect on society is, itself, a philosophy—one that's debatable at best, and dangerous at worst."

Cora pursed her lips, saying nothing for a long while; her unblinking eyelids were darkening at the edges. Colson met her gaze, his unprepossessing expression ready to accept whatever she might throw at him.

"It must be nice to be a faculty member—and a man. You know I could probably have you fired for speaking to me like that?"

"Will you?" the man asked, finishing his cup of coffee.

"No," she said after a moment, looking away as she exhaled through her nose and crossed her arms. "It was nice to meet you, Professor Colson."

Elliot moved to say something, but Colson put a hand on his shoulder with a barely perceptible shake of his head.

"I'm sorry—I've spoken where it wasn't my place. Nonetheless, please know that I understand what it's like to see a whole, defenseless demographic being compromised because and by means of their virtues. I understand it—and hate it—every day. It's healthy; you can never love something without hating its opposite. But it gets a lot easier once you know what that opposite is."

Cora smiled in exaggerated, dismissive politeness, focusing on her food.

Professor Colson stood, put his book in his bag, and slung his coat over one shoulder. He looked from the girl to Elliot. "Cora, would you prefer a bit of privacy? I need to talk to Elliot about something."

Cora shrugged as she took a bite of crust, lifting her chin and crossing her legs away from the both of them. Colson gave Elliot a look that commanded him to follow. Elliot barely grabbed his bag in time to keep step with the professor. Looking back, he saw Cora lean back to look up at the ceiling, arms crossed. Her shoulders rose and fell with a large, steady sigh.

"She was probably just mad because of our last class," Elliot said as they left the Commons. "Still, what was that all about?"

"That wasn't about either of us, and it's none of our goddamned business," the man said as he turned to face Elliot. "Now, do you believe the things you said in there?"

Elliot paused to think. "Oh, you mean about not wanting to meet Plato?"

"Yeah, and about the others who wanted to force humanity into their own image of mediocrity."

"That's not what I said, but sure."

"It's what you meant, notwithstanding your utter misread of Plato—and, thus, of Aristotle." The man faced Elliot. "You know I'm directing this year's Shakespeare production, the Henry cycle. Three plays, one character. You avoided the topic in class, but if you really want to put your person where your ideas are—and discover what they mean—you'll be on that stage."

Colson turned to walk away before Elliot could respond.

The nerve of not caring about his response—as if Colson both assumed Elliot's agreement and was indifferent to it—incensed Elliot. A moment too late, he exclaimed, "Even if I wanted to, I've never acted before!"

"Oh, yes, you have," Colson said over his shoulder. "Next time don't have lunch with a woman unless you know you want to. It's insulting. Saturday, theater, nine o'clock."

"'Kay, baby, I'll see you tomorrow. Love you too," Ermine, née "Christopher," Jackson said into his phone as Cora Madison dropped her backpack onto a neighboring couch in the Breitlinger Center foyer. Ermine watched as she sat down with a sigh, saying nothing.

There were several other couches, their haphazard placement displaying the whims of the foyer's most recent occupants. As its shorthand Daoist nickname implied, "B-Center" was a safe space where any student could come and rest without fear of criticism or reprimand. The foyer often attracted students who felt they did not fit into their own dorm communities or who needed a refuge from the implicit antagonisms that, sadly, still plagued Orangedale. B-Center residents made it a rule to have as few formal rules as possible; nonetheless, out of the intentional disorder several conventions had formed, one of which being the constant presence in the foyer of a resident who could act as a dorm emissary—as an ally for anyone who might need it.

With a thrill, Ermine knew that, today, Cora was such a petitioner. He smiled; he loved talking to Cora, and the chance to help her in an hour of need was a rare treat. She had come to the right place.

"Darling, what's wrong?" he asked.

"It's nothing; I didn't want to interrupt," she said, forcing a smile as she glanced at Ermine's phone.

"Oh, that was just Sam—he's treating me to dinner tomorrow for my being featured in the art department this semester. You should come to the symposium on Saturday afternoon. It's on the history of un-bodied visual art as the medium of counter-culture gender fluidity," he waved his long, dark fingers in the general direction of the Art building less than fifty yards from B-Center's southwestern corner.

"I'd love to." Cora smiled; still, Ermine recognized a tension behind her attempt to appear relaxed.

"Of course you would," said Ermine, resting his hand on his knee with a flourish, "now tell me what's wrong."

"Just . . . you never know who's a fucking bigot—even teachers!" Cora lifted her chin, swallowing whatever had brought her here.

"Baby, they're the worst," Ermine replied. "Let me guess: he looks and acts nothing like us." Ermine motioned his whole body with both hands. Per his intention, the tan long sleeve, unbuttoned to the middle, emphasized his mauve scarf and dark skin.

"You guessed it," said Cora, "white and probably straight as an arrow—though he did talk about gay sex. Not in a way you would like, though."

"There isn't a way I don't like it," Ermine said with a giggle. Cora smiled, acknowledging his attempt to put her at ease.

"Well, he probably wouldn't. I'm sorry," she said, covering her eyes with one hand as her bottom lip quivered, "can I just be here?"

"Of course," Ermine moved to her couch and motioned her to rest her head on his chest. With a little push, she would feel safe enough to release the tears he knew were waiting to come out. She let out a long exhale through pursed lips as Ermine stroked her tightly tied-back curls. He prided himself on knowing how to make people feel safe.

"It's okay," she said. "I'm okay. It's just, some of the things he said and how he said them. He was so calm and goddamned sure of himself. And what's worse is he might be right."

"It doesn't matter what he said, whoever he is. He's a pig. Anyone who makes someone feel like this is the problem, and they can't be right. You don't need to worry about a thing, sweetheart. Fuck'im."

She was about to protest, but Ermine bopped her on the mouth with a finger.

"Repeat after me: fuck 'im."

She smiled, reaching her arms around Ermine's slim figure. She repeated the words. They sat for a while, neither speaking, he rubbing her back as she nuzzled against him.

"You need some love," Ermine said after a while, picking up his phone to check his feeds. "Sam and I are gonna take you out tomorrow."

"Oh no, I couldn't," Cora said, "it's your big night." Her head still resting on Ermine's chest undercut the earnestness of her words.

"Every night's a big night for us. Besides, Sam would love to have you." Ermine closed his phone to lightly tap Cora on the hip. "If there was ever a femme fox I'd worry might take him from me, it's you. Mm-hm!"

"Okay," Cora relented, smiling. Ermine could tell she was in a better place.

"We'll pick you up at Laramie Dorm tomorrow at six forty-five. But don't try looking better than me."

"You know that's impossible, Ermine." Cora stood up, stretching.

Ermine lifted his palms to the ceiling and shrugged. "Probably true. One last thing: not that he's worth it, but who, pray tell, was the racist, sexist, homophobic bastard who almost ruined your day?"

She looked out the large foyer windows at the quad toward the Commons.

"Just some English professor. Sexist, but not racist," she said.

"Sexism is racism, since oppression is oppression. You know that."

She conceded a nod with a smile, looking back out the window.

"He's young, too," she said after a few moments. "I'd expect him to be more progressive. I just worry about him attracting students who don't know any better."

"We can't all be perfect like you, baby." Ermine shook his head as if in awe. He could tell there was more she had not said, but that was Cora:

more apt to try and figure out problems herself than to burden others. Ermine took it as a good sign; he indulged in a moment of satisfaction—like an unspoken social checkmark—at the fact that Cora had needed him the way other, often younger, students needed her. It was unprecedented, and it gave him a pleasure that proved he had treated the situation well.

Whoever that professor was, thought Ermine after Cora had left, he was why a safe space like B-Center existed. Ermine felt a hot anger against the man, who was probably like every other homophobic white man who refused to support all shades of human life. Against the administration that would hire such a man, however, Ermine felt a continuous, cold ire. B-Center students and faculty generally stood at odds with most decisions of "Ad Hill," as most students called the administration, just as they did against all subtly authoritarian structures, and Ermine felt it his duty to fight the oppression of non-acceptance until B-Center's uncritical solidarity was the norm everywhere.

It was this resentment against regressive social stigmas—which he had thought he left at home with his Filipino mother and African American father, both active members of their Baptist church, only to find them implicitly alive at Orangedale—that had provoked Ermine in Freshman year to leave the traditional, grade-bound English Literature major in favor of designing his own evaluation-based Breitlinger emphasis, "Journalism and Social Progress," and to subsequently join the university newspaper, *The Praesidium*.

Ermine smiled as he remembered the look the paper's faculty head, Smith Ingman, had given at him on his first day at the paper: one of bright welcome, containing all the acceptance that should color every moment of college life. Ermine understood that Ingman was what the administration—and this other teacher—was not. If the Orangedale student body was to have a conceivable future, the university needed to move toward the former; it would, if Ermine had anything to say about it. "As B-Center goes, so goes Orangedale," he had written in a recent article on reevaluating the ubiquitous gender and orientation-based regulations of campus roommate placement. Ermine believed progress should be seen as inevitable and, should some recalcitrant want to hold onto their privileged inequality, compulsory.

Sniffing in distaste, Ermine swiped open his phone to post his thoughts on the topic.

CHAPTER 2

E LLIOT CURSED UNDER his breath. The Hind helicopter had almost seen his avatar—Vexxen—as he leaned out from behind the bushes to take out the last ground member of the player group. One more shot and he could finally hit the chopper pilot through the broken windshield, thereby earning the *"Heli-captor"* achievement, but the past half hour would be wasted if the pilot got a clear shot at him. Vexxen could possibly take a 5.56 from a ground troop, but that Hind would shred him. He crouched behind cover to wait until the pilot circled around.

Elliot smiled. Not long ago this gambit would have been beyond him. Although the massively multiplayer online third-person shooter *Vanguard Pulse* lacked an overarching story, Elliot had enjoyed building Vexxen into a kind of sniper-medic over the past month since renting an apartment off campus. Striking and running had allowed him to work alone and avoid direct conflict as he explored the vast terrains and climates of the game's beautifully rendered open world. Seeing them approaching his favorite jungle ravine by foot and chopper, he had cut off and taken out most of the group where the trail ran along a cliff by the waterfall.

As the Hind turned and its heavily cracked windshield came into view, Elliot reloaded his SR-25 sniper rifle and held his breath before throwing a smoke grenade. As the pilot took the bait and fired at the growing cloud, Elliot crawled Vexxen around the opposite side of the cover and, zooming to scope mode, fired at the cockpit. The glass shattered. Without ceasing his spray, the pilot turned toward Elliot in time to receive a shot to the nose.

Three things happened: a window opened with a slow-motion video following the bullet from Vexxen's prone figure to the pilot's aviator-shaded face, a chime signaled his gaining the gold *Heli-captor* achievement trophy, and Elliot shot his fists into the air with a yell.

Dragging the kill-cam onto his secondary monitor to watch later, Elliot swallowed his elation. This kind of thing should be no big deal; the pros did that stuff every day.

Elliot walked Vexxen to the edge of the cliff to observe the downed chopper—laying beside the river, more or less on its belly—before looting the nearby bodies. Whatever misgivings he harbored for taking out a whole team were allayed by a glance at the chat box; as always, player-to-player communication was most toxic against solo players like him. He merely typed, *"Thanks for all the free stuff XD!"* and closed the chat before they could respond. Elliot caught himself, dropping Vexxen to his stomach and pulled out his binos to check for any vultures—players who waited for others to take out most of a team before seizing the equipment. Seeing no one and reading a clear sonar ping, Elliot walked Vexxen down toward the ravine.

The small cargo area of the Hind held enough ammo to fill Elliot's reserves for a few more fights. He also found a new flak jacket and two new camo patterns—*"Desert Wolf"* and *"Brick Digital."* However, the prize came when he selected the chopper as a whole and, below *"Send to Base,"* Elliot saw *"Modify for Subsistence."*

He had never seen that option, this being his first intact helicopter. A submenu opened with a click.

> *Tail blade → Machete*
> *Fuel → Molotovs x20*
> *Flares → Smoke Grenades x20*
> *FLIR Thermography → HUD InfraRadar (TECH req. 45)*
> *GSh-30 → ASVK 12.7 Anti-materiel Sniper Rifle (STR req. 35.*
> *Upgradable)*

Elliot would have an easier time with the InfraRadar; it would always be on in the upper corner, showing terrain and location of other players—a big improvement over his current sonar's white dots every three seconds. However, a high-powered sniper rifle like the ASVK would enable a more offensive playing method, especially if a suppressor was among the possible upgrades.

Elliot leaned back to think. His clock read 6:53 pm. Scanning his apartment, he saw the open laptop on the couch; the screen still showed the partially typed Longinus notes he had started the previous evening. Considering them left Elliot feeling hungry. The Commons would still be open for another half hour, but he did not want to see anyone.

Despite Elliot's efforts to focus on other things, Cora had been in the back of his mind since the previous day. Elliot kept remembering times he had noticed her on campus over the previous two years, trying to discern memories without constructing more. Getting an unprecedented head start on the next week's reading had distracted him for a while, yet, before he slept around 2:00 am, he had admitted to reading and preparing with the unspoken awareness that she would be a part of Tuesday's discussion. Even his daring gambit against the Hind, he thought with a frown, had not been without the unconscious fantasy of her seeing it. He tightened his lips. Elliot had not trusted his emotions since high school, and he did not intend to start now.

Looking back at the screen, Elliot clicked on the ASVK. Before he could second guess himself, he exited the game, grabbed a light jacket and a book on Longinus, and went downstairs to his bike. There was a pizza shop in downtown Orangedale that had separate booths where one could read over an idiosyncratic but delicious barbecued chicken and mashed potato pizza. Elliot slipped the thin literary journal into his jacket's inner pocket and began to pedal.

The afternoon was warm and comfortable, still holding on to the scents of the desert's late summer air even while growing cooler sooner in the evenings. Elliot was considering how the new rifle would impact his gameplay as he biked south around the chapel, heading under the line of oak trees that ran between the quad and a row of dorms.

Elliot was looking across the quad's green expanse when a red sedan sped around a corner behind him, its occupants laughing over their loud dance music. Elliot just had time to swerve before the car bumper clipped his back wheel, causing him to run his bike into a tree and fall to the ground. The driver, cursing, skidded the car to a stop.

"Oh my God, are you okay?" cried the driver as he and his two passengers opened the doors.

Leg between the bike and a curb, Elliot was about to yell an obscenity at the driver when he saw Cora staring at him from the back passenger seat, eyes startled yet unblinking. He extracted his leg from under the bike, brushing dirt and dried, spiked oak leaves from his jeans before picking up the journal that had fallen out of his jacket. He could expect a bruise on his shin, but he felt otherwise unhurt, if shaken. "I'm fine," he said, looking back at Cora.

Elliot knew he should not notice it in such a moment, but Cora looked beautiful. A jade comb held her hair in place in a tight bun, and dark ringlets escaped to frame her sharp chin. However, it was her posture—tall and shoulders back, as if standing against an unexpected adversary—that kept his eyes on her.

"Elliot, are you okay?" the dark-skinned young man from the front seat asked as he skipped up and put a hand on Elliot's back, examining him with a concerned look. Elliot had seen the young man before—Ermine Jackson. He wrote for the school paper. They had never met.

"Yeah, I'm fine. But my bike . . . " Its front wheel was bent and the chain had come off.

"Sam, get his bike," Ermine instructed the wide-eyed driver, who looked to be in his late twenties or early thirties. "Let's see if we can fix part of it."

"Don't worry about it," said Elliot, glancing at Cora as he inhaled to calm his racing pulse. "It was used when I got it."

"Still, I'll get you another one," asserted Sam, apparently relaxing though still in earnest.

"Yeah," said Ermine. "What dorm should we take it to?"

"I'm in an off-campus apartment," replied Elliot, motioning to the north with his chin, "but if anyone in the administration asks, I'm a commuter."

Cora walked over, arms crossed. A pearl necklace and earrings complemented a shimmering green shawl that hid a black v-neck dress. The shawl, the dress's long slit, and the matching black heels seemed to make Elliot aware of all the lines of her body at once.

"It's fine," Elliot said, turning his face away from Cora. "It was a cheap bike."

"No, I want to pay for it," said Sam, kneeling down to examine the chain.

"Really," said Elliot, placing his hand on the bike and hardening his tone, "I'm good."

"But there's gotta be something—," Sam began.

"Come to dinner with us," Cora said without preamble. Elliot looked at her. She was not smiling, but her eyes were focused in a strange way, as though she both hoped and feared he would accept.

"Yeah, that would be great—then it could be a double date!" Ermine said, putting his hand on Sam's arm. "We'll drop off your bike, let you get dressed up if you want, and you can join us for dinner. Or are you busy?"

"I was just going to Artisan's," said Elliot, remembering his plan for the evening. "Really, it's not a big deal."

"Pizza sounds great!" Sam blurted, nodding at the others for confirmation. Ermine smiled ear to ear in answer, as if to move the scene past the shock they all still showed. Sam would probably be worried all night until he was sure Elliot was fine.

"Okay. Don't worry about taking me home; I'll be faster just walking. I'll meet you here in about fifteen minutes."

"Beautiful," said Ermine, patting Elliot on the arm. "We really are sorry, Elliot," he said in a lower tone. "I don't actually think we've officially met. I'm Ermine Jackson." Ermine proffered a hand.

"Elliot Fleming." He took the hand. Ermine's long fingers, barely giving the token pressure required by the gesture, were cold with sweat. "And don't mention it."

"This is my boyfriend, Sam," said Ermine.

Elliot nodded as he hoisted his bike and turned away, leaving Sam with hand extended, a deflated smile on his face.

"I'll go with Elliot," Cora said, stepping forward after him.

Elliot paused. Her decision to come to his apartment should not surprise him; it would be the second time she had followed him that week. Nodding, he resumed his pace, forcing himself to think past the suddenly prevailing image of her heels—and the length of her calves they accentuated—by trying to remember the state of his apartment.

"It might be a mess," he said as they passed the chapel.

"Don't worry about it. You didn't expect . . . " Cora's voice fell.

"I'm okay, really," Elliot said, repositioning the bike on his shoulder, "not hurt, anyway. How about you?"

She sniffed, smiling but saying nothing.

"You look really nice."

"Thank you."

"Do you always dress up when you go out with those guys?"

"This is our first time, actually. They insisted I dress up. They're trying to make me feel better."

"From what?"

"Nothing," she said, forcing a smile.

"Oh, yeah," Elliot muttered, remembering the previous day and guessing it had to do with Colson. "That guy's a little intense."

"A little." She chuckled under her breath. "What do you think of him?"

"I had him last semester, but I'm still trying to figure him out. He's a whole different kind of animal from Ingman. I can't decide which one I'd rather not have as a teacher."

She stayed silent, her mouth a thin line.

"Y'know it wasn't your fault either, back there. Or in the Commons."

As soon as he said it, Elliot silently kicked himself for stating the obvious. Cora lowered her head, failing to suppress a smile. She said nothing the rest of the walk. However, when crossing the gravel ringing Elliot's apartment, she put her hand on Elliot's back to steady herself; Elliot wondered if she kept her hand there for a moment longer than necessary once on the sidewalk. Her fingers brushed off slowly, like a caress.

"Sorry about the mess," he said as they entered his apartment. He leaned his broken bike against a clear spot of wall and removed his jacket.

"No, we're the ones who imposed," she said, touching his arm in thanks where Ermine had touched him. Whereas Ermine's overly familiar touch had left a prickly feeling even through the jacket, Cora's hand caused a thrill. Elliot found himself wishing she would do it again.

"I'll be out in just a sec," he said, stepping to the closet near the bathroom. He grabbed a different pair of jeans and a button-down with the sleeves already rolled up. Using a wad of toilet paper and water, he wiped off the layer of sweat from carrying the bike through the warm late afternoon; he then splashed some aftershave on his wrists and neck before putting on the shirt. Looking at himself in the mirror, he exhaled, running his fingers through his dark, curly hair. His normally pale cheeks had a mix of rose from carrying the bike. What the hell am I doing, he wondered before returning to the main room.

"I like your apartment," said Cora, observing his computer desk while checking her phone. A program on his computer had automatically loaded a set of screenshots from his kill cam as his screensaver.

"Yeah, I worked the last two summers to save for rent. I have a deal with my family. If I keep my grades up and pay for half of it, they pay the rest."

"Where do you live?"

"Not far. Less than an hour drive."

"Why don't you commute?"

"Dunno." Elliot shrugged. "Just wanted my own place."

Motioning to the monitor with her chin, she asked "What's that?"

"That's me."

"What do you mean?"

"That's my character. It's what I was doing before I left."

She said nothing, just looked back at the screen and then down at her phone. After a moment she shook her head.

"What?" Elliot asked.

"Nothing; Ermine already posted about the accident. Don't worry, he didn't mention you." She sighed, turning off her phone. "Not bad," she said, raising an eyebrow as she examined Elliot's outfit.

"You should see yourself," he deflected in a tone he immediately regretted, remembering her sensitivity from the previous day. However, she merely looked down and smiled.

"I'm sorry," he said, fearing he might have betrayed the unspoken confidence that had settled between them over the walk from the quad. Elliot heard honking from outside.

"No, thank you." She smiled, looking over her shoulder. "It's different when you say it—from Ermine, I mean. Of course, it would be." She winked, turning to the door. "Anyway, let's go."

"Well, I thought it was atrocious," replied Ermine. "I mean, who are they to tell me what I can wear? Especially when suits are just another way of reminding people who are—how should I say?—different of who's in charge."

"Oh come on," Sam contested. "You wanted them to kick you out so you could have a story. You love it when I wear a suit."

"That's because I know you aren't a racist homophobe." Ermine stroked Sam's shoulder.

Elliot traced the napkin's pattern with his fingertips; Ermine had been talking since picking him and Cora up. Elliot had felt the polished wood of the table, noticed the Tuscanesque paintings on the walls, and admired the setting sun's glow on downtown Orangedale's main promenade through the restaurant's window. With a smirk, Elliot knew he would never forget Artisan's Pizza Shoppe. The thought did not thrill him.

Glancing at Elliot, Cora spoke up, "Ermine, we can debate the merits and history of the European suit, but getting mad at a five-star restaurant for requiring one is stretching it. Shouldn't places have standards?"

"Darling, I'm surprised at you, being black and from DC; you know the need for standards merely perpetuates cultural conflict. It's a way for some to exert power over others—ironically with suits made by people who also wouldn't be allowed into that restaurant." His smile and playful tone showed he meant no serious antagonism, but the intentness of his eyes held a sly readiness to continue with less magnanimity. Cora met his exaggerated moue but held her tongue.

Sam turned to Elliot. "So, Elliot, what's your major?"

"Still deciding. Either Philosophy or English."

"Oh, I think that's great," Ermine interposed, missing the shade of irritation on Sam's face, "I mean, literature's just another group of old white guys, but there are some that actually benefited the world. I love Dickens and Sinclair. Who are your favorites?"

Elliot kept his eyes on Sam as if he had asked the question. "Hugo in Europe, Jefferson in America. You know, the ones with standards."

Ermine closed his mouth and widened his eyes, sitting back as though physically pushed. Before Ermine could retort, Sam said, "Oh, I really like Jefferson, actually." Sam placed his hand on Ermine's thigh under the table, as if to keep him at bay. "I mean, of course nowadays people consider him unforgivable, but he really was a great man. It was Kennedy who said at a dinner that at no other time had there been such a collection of genius in the room—except, of course, when Jefferson dined alone. Something like that."

"Yes, well," said Ermine in a mock concessionary tone, "it must have been wonderful to have time to study—with his slaves doing all the work."

"Well, yeah," continued Elliot, forcibly repressing a sardonic response, "I like those writers because things like slavery and oppression are so bad." He conceded a glance at Ermine, which the young man refused to acknowledge. Elliot continued, "The way I see it, most of human history has involved people treating others like animals in one way or another—except for one man over two thousand years ago who said we are not animals, or at least we're a different kind, and that to live as a man means treating people as men—and women," Elliot motioned to Cora, who, smiling, bowed her head in thanks at the inclusion.

"Well, if Jesus were alive in the eighteenth century, he would've been a slave, you know, being a foreigner of color," said Ermine.

"I meant Aristotle," Elliot replied without moving his head.

Ermine took a drink of water, shaking his head with a frown.

"But why group Hugo with Jefferson?" Sam inquired, leaning forward, "besides Jefferson's French connection, I mean."

Elliot thought for a moment; he had never needed to articulate his reason for associating the two.

"It's like," Elliot ventured at last, "Hugo makes me feel the way Jefferson wrote. Like, with the same assumptions, the same worldview of individual rights and choice." Elliot crossed his arms to think. "With all the blood of the French Revolution, Hugo took the ideas of the nineteenth century seriously. His characters' choices matter. Even when they end badly, it's because they could have chosen differently but didn't. While I think the French Revolution was more about revenge than liberty, Hugo's stories are about the same thing as the Declaration, I think, the same experiment: what will people do and become if given rights, if they suddenly have the freedom and responsibility of choice?" Elliot took a sip from his soda, shrugging as if his sudden explication were nothing special.

"Wow," said Sam, leaning back, "I was always depressed when I read Hugo in high school; I should probably pick him back up. I had to study the French Revolution as part of my emphasis on the American. Many back then thought it was the same fight, especially Jefferson, but you're right—it really wasn't. The Americans just wanted to be left alone to enjoy their rights as British citizens; most didn't resent the aristocracy the way the French understandably did."

"Yeah," Elliot said, "that's what gets me about Hugo. Take Dickens," Elliot motioned to Ermine, who still refused to look at him. "His characters are funny and all that, and he's a great narrator, but it's too cynical because of where and how they live. Hugo's different, more optimistic. Jean Valjean lives in ignominy just like any of Dickens' characters, but his circumstances aren't the focus. He is."

Inhaling as though trying to keep himself calm as he patiently stated the obvious, Ermine said, "Well, both essentially wrote about how the upper classes mistreat the lower ones; when that's happening, can—or should—there be optimism about individual agency? Wouldn't that just enable more injustice?"

"Plus," said Sam, nodding with an interested smile, "*The Hunchback* doesn't end much better than many of Dickens' stories."

Elliot thought a moment, raising his fist to touch his thumbnail to his lips. "Maybe optimism isn't the word for Hugo," Elliot said, looking at Ermine before focusing on Sam, "Maybe clarity? I mean, might just be me, but I don't feel bound and gagged the way I do reading Dickens. Circumstances and historical context definitely affect Hugo's plots, but the drama comes from how people choose to act in spite of all that. It feels like just because someone's in a certain class doesn't mean they couldn't make moral choices. The optimism is that you can be virtuous—and, therefore, happy—anywhere. That, to me, is Jefferson."

Sam sat back, smiling openly. "I'll have to get a copy of *Les Mis* and use it in my classes—I teach history at Orangedale High."

Elliot's drink caught mid-swallow. "Dude, try leading with that!" he said after catching his breath. "And I haven't even read that one all the way," Elliot admitted, trying to hide a self-conscious wince, "but I've read an abridged *Hunchback.*"

In an exaggeratedly happy tone and volume, Ermine laughed. "Well, you two white men who needn't worry about circumstances enjoy Jefferson and Hugo some other time. Just warn us; Cora and I can have a movie night. How about it, sweetheart?"

Before answering, Cora looked askance at Elliot, their eyes meeting briefly. Elliot felt the same interloping warmth from earlier—the desire to hold the moment for just another breath. However, by the time Elliot noticed it—and wondered if Cora had—she was speaking, matching Ermine's jovial tone. "Of course, Ermine. I always love our movie nights. My place or yours?"

Ermine smiled wide, leering triumphantly as he began to discuss what movies they should watch. The change in the young man made Elliot uneasy; Ermine had seemed livid, not the least due to Elliot's admittedly rude treatment of him. Sam was sipping his coffee, his motion conveying that the attention was and now should be on Ermine, as if it were to be expected. Resuming his observation of the restaurant, Elliot reexamined their booth's painting; the intricate frame had interested him more than the Tuscan countryside it presented. After a few minutes he found himself dwelling on the happy surprise he had felt when speaking with Sam, whose proximity to Ermine gave Elliot the same feeling as did the painting's frame to its subject. In the next moment he realized he had decided two things: he would not press charges for the accident, and he wanted to be Sam's friend.

He took a drink, listening absently to Ermine and Cora. They had progressed from discussing the relative merits of dramas and comedies to theater and, eventually, Shakespeare. Ermine's elongated vowels in praise of humor contrasted sharply with Cora's direct but smiling disagreements on behalf of drama. Somehow she could respond to Ermine without annoyance, and for whatever reason Sam still chose to be with him, despite his apparent distaste for Ermine's bombast. Elliot had no right to judge Ermine; he was just an extrovert with different opinions.

Elliot was suddenly distracted: in sitting up Cora had let the lengths of her bare arm and thigh brush and remain against his. Elliot felt a warm glow replace the immediate coolness of her skin on his air conditioned jeans.

"But, great as Shakespeare was, and blah blah," continued Ermine, rolling his eyes as he waved away the words, "I don't think we should distinguish between comedy and tragedy, nor main and sub-plots for that matter. In the end drama is just us fooling ourselves into thinking there's some higher order of transcendent values that justifies the norms we've inherited—and which, in reality, only reinforces the status quo. They're all just social constructs that keep those who invented them at the top and those who didn't at the bottom. Humor undermines all that by not giving the hierarchy the respect it thinks it deserves. It lets you be frivolous about the serious and serious about the frivolous. It's a leveler of values—an equalizer, if you will. I'm only sad Shakespeare didn't go all the way and replace Hamlet with Rosencrantz and Guildenstern. But it's okay—Stoppard did it for him."

"So you don't believe in values?" asked Cora, her glance inviting Sam into the conversation. "What about things like adventure, romance, and love?"

"If Ermine believed in love," Sam said with a wryness that clashed with his pensive look of a moment before, "do you think he would have worn that hideous red scarf?"

Touching his hand to his chest in mock offense, Ermine replied, "Any self-respecting gay man would know this is carmine. Besides, I found it in your closet." He let his hand fall beneath the table on Sam's thigh.

Sam smiled, taking Ermine's hand and holding it on top of the table. "Still," said Sam, "I think I'm with Cora and Elliot on this one. There are some things that shouldn't be joked about; They're too precious."

"Well, I'll have to be careful," said Ermine, "or else I'll lose Sam to you, too, Elliot."

"Too?" asked Elliot, turning to Ermine.

"Well . . . " Ermine's eyes went to Cora as he leaned his head forward, pointing his raised eyebrows at their touching arms.

Cora tensed but did not move. Elliot fixed his eyes on Ermine.

"Ermine, don't . . . " Sam said tentatively.

"Oh, relax you guys," Ermine said, smiling with a glee only he displayed, "it shouldn't be a surprise. Cora hasn't thought of anything but Elliot the whole night." He turned from Sam to Cora. "You shouldn't have tried so hard not to look at him, dearie."

Cora's skin, light brown though it was, flushed.

Elliot gritted his teeth. He understood, feeling suddenly vulnerable—less because of what had been exposed than because of who was exposing it. This was Ermine's way of getting him back for the earlier conversation.

"Come on, people," Ermine went on. "You're acting like being honest is wrong. We were talking about love, right? Which, in the end, is just glorified attraction." Ermine winked at Elliot. "Well, Elliot, if I'm right—and I usually am about this kind of thing—then you'd be the first man to ever catch Cora Madison's eye. And to think, I actually wondered about her sexual predilections. You should be proud, Elliot; y'know she was voted one of the hottest girls on campus by one of the freshman sports teams? I'd normally be offended, but they're harmless—and in this case, correct!"

"Ermine, you're an asshole," Cora whispered, her arm and leg still rigid against Elliot's.

"Okay, okay, but when you tell your kids about tonight, don't leave out Uncle Ermine when describing the fortunate coincidence that brought you together."

"You mean the misdemeanor?" Elliot countered.

Ermine's smile fell as his eyes shot to Elliot. Elliot held his lips closed as he met Ermine's gaze.

"Goddamn it, Ermine," exclaimed Sam between closed teeth, sitting back slowly as if hit by a prolonged blow. The man passed his hand over his eyes.

"Don't worry about it, Sam," Elliot said. "I'm not pressing charges. Just help me pay for my bike. Also, I'd like to keep in touch to talk about what we were discussing earlier. However," Elliot resisted the urge to look at Ermine, "just us, okay?"

Ermine was about to respond, but Sam, despite his unprepossessing demeanor, cut him off, "Shut up, Ermine, this is my ass. Jesus, you just couldn't be polite and get through the night. Did you forget I almost ran somebody over?" Sam turned to Elliot. "I'd love to take care of your bike—it's the least I can do. And I think I'd like to meet up, if you wouldn't feel uncomfortable having lunch with a thirty-one-year-old homosexual." Ermine snorted at the last phrase, conveying his thoughts of people who might feel discomfort; to his credit, thought Elliot, Sam's expression remained diffident and guileless.

"Not at all; I'd like to hear your perspective, actually," Elliot motioned to Cora with his chin, "yours too."

"I'd love to," replied Cora, finally relaxing her arm to reach for a drink of water. She kept her thigh where it was.

"Well then," Ermine said pertly, "I'm gonna step to the gentleboys' room." Ermine climbed out of the booth, nose upturned.

The others exhaled a collective sigh when he had gone.

"I really am sorry about that," said Sam. "It wasn't any of his business—though to be honest, I kind of assumed there was something already going on between you two."

"You don't need to apologize for him," Cora replied with a smile.

"He's loud, and loud about it," said Elliot, his sharp tone surprising even himself. "I mean, how insecure is he, really?"

Sam held his hands up in a shrug. "I don't know how much you know Ermine, but I can understand his frustration. Tonight was originally supposed to celebrate his art project. Taking you out was wonderful, Cora, and I think he wanted to play a white knight, to use a phrase he'd probably hate. It's just, I think he had an idea of how the night would go, and I ruined it."

"You're fine, Sam," said Elliot. "I wasn't watching where I was going, either. Don't worry about Ermine. He didn't get mad until you and I started talking. Maybe he's jealous—he said as much."

"You're probably right, but not the way he meant. It's happened before—he feels cornered whenever he and I really disagree about things he's passionate about."

"Yeah, he wasn't mad until we started pushing back against him," said Cora. "He must've felt exposed."

"It's still not okay," said Sam, "and it doesn't give him the right to presume on your privacy, regardless of what is or isn't between you two." The man looked away, as if distracted by the direction Ermine had gone.

"But it's happened before. He'll probably be this way the rest of the night; if you two want to take off, you can."

"Oh no, we don't have to leave things like that," said Cora. "We're the ones who made him uncomfortable." She looked at Elliot; her words and glance implied a question.

"Frankly, I'd rather not deal with him or try to figure him out," said Elliot, irritated at the idea of feeling pity for Ermine rather than Sam. "His issues aren't really my problem. However, I don't want to just leave you with him."

"Thanks, but that should be my line." Sam laughed. "I'm the one dating him. I'll take care of it. Honestly, it might be for the best."

Elliot looked at Cora, who shrugged and nodded with a forced smile. As she gathered her things, Elliot scribbled his number on a paper napkin and handed it to Sam. "Start of semester might be weird, but text me when you're free."

Sam got out of the booth and shook Elliot's hand, tearing a piece off the napkin with a chuckle at the outdated medium and returning it with his number.

"Ermine's probably waiting for me to check on him," Sam said, smiling with a shrug as if such childishness could not be helped. Elliot turned so Sam would not see his involuntary frown. Cora gave Sam a hug and walked out with Elliot.

Without either initiating the direction, they began to move east toward the campus.

"You okay?" Cora ventured after they had walked about a block, interrupting Elliot's wondering how many times he had biked this street alone at night.

"Yeah, of course. Just been a long day. But I'm fine."

"In objective or subjective terms?" she replied with a giggle.

Elliot snorted, smiling. So much seemed to have happened with Cora since the previous day; among all of it, Elliot had not been able to shake the image of Colson and her interacting.

"Listen, about yesterday at lunch . . . " he trailed off, considering whether he should mention Colson's invitation.

"Don't worry about it, Elliot. I was a bit sensitive; Colson probably caught some of what was meant for Ingman. I mean, what he said was awful, about Women's Studies and stuff, but he wasn't trying to fight."

"That's really generous of you," Elliot replied, "and yeah, I think he knew it was a touchy conversation from the start."

Cora made a sound as if catching her voice, then ventured, "But do you agree with him?"

Elliot was struck by the idea. He had contradicted Colson in class the previous year, but it was always in order to match him in some way, to show something clever his professor had not thought of—which he usually had. Nonetheless, the way to best Colson would not be to prove him wrong but to gain his agreement; it was an altogether different provocation than the kind Elliot experienced from Ingman. Colson would have definitely included more Aristotle in his syllabus, were he teaching Ingman's class, thought Elliot. The idea made him want to laugh with sudden glee. He swallowed the excitement.

"Well," Elliot said at length, "I'd really never thought of the things he said. I'm not saying I'm with him, but I can't really speak to it."

Cora crossed her arm across her stomach, saying nothing. Though she did not slow nor speed up, the sound of her heels seemed sharper as they echoed under the oak canopy of the brick sidewalk; it's probably just the trees, thought Elliot.

"Listen," Elliot said; Cora lowered her arm slowly, straightening her back as if readying herself to face some threat. "I don't think Colson meant anything bad. He took the issue seriously, too. You might disagree with him, but I wouldn't confuse disagreement with an attack." Elliot attempted a smile, slipping his hands into his pockets and nudging her arm with his elbow. "Not to speak more than I should."

Lips pursed, Cora looked ahead. Elliot kept his eyes on her, feeling that he needed to do so.

After a few moments she relaxed her shoulders, smirking. "No, you're fine. A is a, right? I'm glad to know what you think. Thank you, Elliot."

She kept walking. Elliot had to step faster to keep up with her. Her tone, so much calmer and steadier than it had been the day before, unsettled him. He said nothing, walking silently to the sound of her heels on the brick walkway.

With a frustrated sigh, Vesta turned off her phone screen to lay back and read *Henry IV Part* 1 for the next morning's theater meeting. Vesta felt herself blush. She was rarely distracted like this.

She looked up at the shadows of branches blowing in the early fall breezes. She considered mimicking her way through some more online videos of Princess Katharine's French scenes. "I don't need it yet," she said aloud.

Deciding she would not be able to sleep, Vesta pulled back her covers and walked to the bathroom joining her dorm with the next. She turned on the faucet and washed her hands, leaning against the sink to let the water wash over her fingers. Just focus on that feeling—clean, cold water running over your hands; there's nothing else. Vesta cupped the water and doused her face, feeling the water envelope her nose, eyes and mouth in a cool safety.

Holding her breath under water still calmed her, just as it had in high school. While everyone on the swim team showered after morning practice, Vesta would stay alone in the pool, submerging and letting out just enough air to slowly drift to the bottom. Laying there as long as she could, watching the early morning mix of stars and sunrise from beneath the surface, had been one of her favorite parts of the day—and well worth smelling like chlorine all day. Enjoying the memory, she impulsively removed her clothes.

Standing in the shower, Vesta tried to recapture how she had felt about that sky above the water. Back then, alone and immersed, it felt as if she were a few precise, beautiful movements away from another world where those stars and sunlight were constants, and where among their light there walked men and women who deserved such a setting. Though foregoing a shower did a number on her already unruly curly red hair, the morning ritual was enough to push her through the days' AP and honors classes.

At some point she realized that she had been anticipating college, and that in reality college felt very different from her expectation. She hesitated to call it disappointing, but she had more often than not found herself returning to the solitude of her dorm to prolong the state of anticipation for the fullness she hoped was still to come.

Until now. Pressing her palms to the tile of the shower, Vesta leaned her face into the water, feeling the cool water rush down her chest, waist, and legs. It seemed more than just Professor Colson, just as the feelings he provoked seemed bigger than attraction. Though in rare moments some people at Orangedale had reminded her of the stars above the silent waters, Rydar Colson exuded the sense of having reached those stars—and of knowing it. If she could be a part of his play, she dared to hope, then those starlit hours of underwater anticipation would be fulfilled, justified.

Turning off the shower, Vesta pictured the image of Rydar looking down at her from the surface of the pool and reaching down to pull her up out of the water and into that world, of which he considered her a needlessly slumbering native. Vesta was dimly aware of the draining water's settling from a trickle to a slowing drip.

A sharp turn of the doorknob brought Vesta out of her thoughts. "Yes?!" she said, startled.

"Oh, sorry Vesta," called Cora from their dorm. "I didn't know you were here."

"I'll be done soon."

"No rush, dear."

Vesta grabbed her towel. She regretted the interruption—she could swear she had been close to articulating something important. However, Vesta liked Cora Madison. With her composed air and affectionate way with the other girls in the dorm, Cora seemed the antithesis of what Vesta had once feared receiving in a roommate. Despite Cora's general aloofness, as Vesta's neighbor the previous year she had welcomed Vesta into a frank but friendly honesty. A mutual intimacy had developed, and their usually checking in at day's end had progressed naturally to their petitioning to be roommates in their junior year.

"It's all yours, Cora," Vesta called, grabbing her clothes from the floor into a haphazard bunch.

"Thanks," said Cora, opening the door.

Cora had removed her dress and had her cami only halfway on. That was another trait of Cora's: often vocal about how women should feel unashamed of their bodies, she was very free with her own. As used to it as she could be, Vesta sometimes thought the girl was overdoing it, and, considering how beautiful were her seemingly unblemished skin and slim figure, worsening the issue. Most girls—at least, Vesta, with her benign but ineradicable paunch just above her beltline—would not dream of taking their clothes off in front of a woman who looked like Cora. Nonetheless, Vesta smiled; the girl's intentions were good.

"How wa' your day, Westa?" said Cora through the strokes of her toothbrush. "You're up 'ate, fo' 'ou."

"Oh, fine," said Vesta as she finished drying off and put on some pajama bottoms and an old Rush t-shirt of her dad's. "Just brushing up on my lines. I'm doing the Shakespeare plays in the spring."

Cora spat and rinsed. "Which plays are you doing?"

"*Henry IV Parts One* and *Two* and *Henry V.*"

"Huh," the girl said, covering her face with cleanser. "Sounds like a lot of work. What parts are you playing?"

"I'm playing Princess Katherine in *Henry V*," Vesta said with a coy smile she imagined befitted a princess. "I'm also Professor Colson's costume designer."

Vesta could not decide if Cora had paused for a moment before turning the water off; she sauntered in, drying her face as she leaned against the threshold.

"Rydar Colson? From the English Department?"

"Yes," said Vesta, trying to determine Cora's tone.

"Hm." Cora bit her lip as she looked away. "Figures." Her arms were crossed, and she was digging the ball of one foot into the carpet.

"What does? What's wrong?"

"It's not your fault—I'm sure you'll do great. That's the problem: that you'll do great and still won't be a main character. I'm not surprised he picked a play with only one or two girl parts—one of which is a helpless princess."

"Well, he's putting on three plays, and there are a lot of parts . . . " Vesta saw Katharine as far from helpless but said nothing. She was trying to see Cora's face, which was an obscure silhouette against the bathroom doorway.

"Full of actors like him, no doubt," Cora said, shaking her head.

"What do you mean?" asked Vesta, perplexed. "I didn't know you knew Professor Colson."

"I met him yesterday in the Commons," Cora looked askance at Vesta, "but it was enough. He's such a man." She walked over and slumped backwards onto Vesta's bed.

"What's wrong with that?" asked Vesta from the foot of her bed. "Did Colson do something, or what?"

"He's just the kind of man who can't help being a male—and trying to keep it that way. The old kind of masculinity, I mean," said Cora. "He tried to correct me on something related to how many women are actually assaulted—as if the numbers were the issue! He basically implied Women's Studies is a joke. He even implied men are being unjustly punished for their virtues—typically missing how that perspective is what keeps men on top. Besides, doesn't he see that, right or not, he shouldn't speak at all on the subject, since as a male in authority he's part of the problem?"

"Oh, no, I'm sure he didn't mean it like that!" Vesta replied; Cora could not be mad, thought Vesta, since, despite her words, she was smiling. "Rydar—Professor Colson—couldn't be that kind of man."

Cora sat up and stared at Vesta with pursed lips. After a moment she placed her hand on Vesta's knee. "You're not the first to tell me that, so you're probably right. I'm probably overreacting. Still, be careful. You're too nice, Vesta, and not a little prone to see men as heroic, if you don't mind my saying. I'd hate to see you disappointed or hurt."

Vesta smiled. "I'll be fine. I really think you got him all wrong—if you don't mind my saying." She patted Cora's hand in thanks.

"Okay, dear," said Cora, standing, "just don't be alone with him. There was something dangerous about him, though he hid it better than most."

Cora's eyes were often very animated, and her actions so precise as to seem affected, if a little exaggerated. Vesta thought it beautiful, as though the movements and expressions of a practiced movie star were being offered for all around to see and enjoy. However, the look she now saw—withdrawn in the next moment—had a strange intensity. It was not the practiced disgust Cora had so often displayed. Had Cora not been criticizing the man, Vesta would have called the look a prelude to interest, or at least curiosity. More confusing to Vesta was a sudden warmth of defensiveness and, unaccountably, jealous worry in her own chest.

Vesta swallowed the feeling and smiled at Cora as the girl stood and squeezed Vesta's shoulder before walking to the door.

"I'm gonna go watch TV in the lobby a while. Sleep well, 'kay?" Did Cora normally walk that fast? No, thought Vesta, she just has long legs.

Despite the previous moment, Vesta felt less restless than before. As she turned off the lights and slipped back into her sheets, she paused. Although Vesta had many times thought her too sensitive and prone to prejudice against men, Cora had ironically given Vesta the right word to interpret her own vexed feelings about Colson, at least enough to sleep: heroic. It was OK to feel strongly about heroes. And though she knew she should consider Cora's warnings—and the feeling they had evoked— Vesta wanted to laugh at the idea of Colson disappointing her heroic expectations, or of his being dangerous. The first seemed impossible, and the last . . . wasn't that part of what a hero should be?

Vesta closed her eyes, pondering how bad it would be if she were a hero-worshipper. She thought again of the stars from beneath the surface of the water. Being such had carried her to this point, and she had felt nothing but joy because of it.

Yet, just before falling asleep, Vesta remembered Cora's look. She would have to watch more closely in the future. She felt without words that there was something Cora was not talking about—that there was something significant about her reaction to Colson, and, though Cora had not said it, though she might not even realize it, she had been talking about nothing but it.

CHAPTER 3

"So, you still need another three-hundred-level course this semester to stay on-track for your major."

Smith Ingman reclined in his chair, skimming the course catalogue on his screen. The clock read 8:47 am. Whether to stick it to the professor or to be cautious at the most precarious point of the semester, Elliot had arrived early at Ingman's office. However, it had been unnecessary: Ingman himself had arrived late, offering token apologies about freeway repairs and traffic.

"Frankly," said Ingman, "I don't understand why you're behind. You're certainly passionate about philosophy. Is there a specific reason you're dragging your feet? I hope I haven't done anything to discourage you."

Elliot scratched his eyebrow to hide the impulse to roll his eyes. However, he could no longer avoid it. Clenching his jaw for a moment, Elliot began.

"Actually, Professor Ingman . . . " Elliot's voice caught.

Ingman turned, eyebrows raised.

Elliot cleared his throat. "I'd like to request a new advisor."

After a pause, Ingman leaned forward, brows furrowed. "Well, that's fine, but why, if I may ask?"

"Well, I don't think I'm going to major in Philosophy." Elliot looked away from Ingman as soon as he finished the sentence, letting himself be distracted by a stack of books tenuously balanced on the edge of a shelf across the room.

Ingman tilted his head. "Elliot, please don't misinterpret our disagreements in class as lack of support on my part. You really are an exceptional student, and I was just pushing you . . . "

The tone of apology—even of pleading—seemed out of character, thought Elliot, from the man's usual conceited dismissiveness. Elliot glanced at his schedule on the screen, focusing on his resolve to sever ties with the professor.

"Thank you, but I've made my decision. I'd also like to drop 206. I hope . . . I'm sorry." Elliot cut short his planned words of parting in good faith. Fleming hated the idea that this man still held his schedule in flux.

However, far from foreshadowing any retaliation at being snubbed, the man looked genuinely disappointed. Shifting in his seat, Elliot continued to examine the bookshelves on the other side of the office. Whereas Ingman had kept his side neat, whoever shared his office had left piles of books on the floor and shelves; even those in the shelves lacked any apparent order.

"No, no," sighed Ingman after a moment, waving his hand and adopting a smile, "it's your life. I'm sure you'll do fine wherever you go. However, who will be your advisor? For the forms, I mean."

Elliot looked at Ingman. He had planned to just contact the administration on another day once he had found a new one. He shut his jaw, which had open dumbly.

"You know both your current and future advisors must agree to the transition," the man said, lowering his chin as he observed Elliot. "Who is to be my replacement?"

"Rydar Colson," Elliot said without thinking. However, after a moment he realized it fit in a way he could not explain. His nostrils flared at the feeling.

"Huh. Majoring in Literature then?" Ingman said, raising an eyebrow as he cocked his jaw under a frown of interest. "I didn't know you and Rydar were that close."

"Yeah. I'm going to meet him now, in fact," said Elliot cautiously; despite considering it as a possible escape plan, Elliot had told himself he would not mention the play. However, he had already stayed five minutes later than he should have. In the stacks across the room Elliot saw poetry, novels, plays, and philosophy books; some he had read, others skipped, and many he did not recognize. On one of the shelves was a tall pile of heavily worn Shakespeare criticism.

"Why? It's Saturday."

"He invited me to do the Shakespeare plays." Elliot jumped on the idea. "That's why I need to free up some credits."

"Oh, Elliot," Ingman began with a slight shake of his head, "are you sure that's a good idea? I've seen the rest of your grades, and you need to maintain priorities. Also, capable as he is, it's Rydar's first time directing, and that often means more work for everyone. Besides, if you can handle it," he motioned to the screen, "you have room for a fifth course, and I'd gladly give you a place on the newspaper, if it's extracurriculars you're looking for."

"No," said Elliot, annoyed by the man's inexplicable concern, "thank you, but I'll be fine."

Staring at Elliot, the professor exhaled and shook his head. "Alright. As your current advisor, I'll convene with Professor Colson and complete the proper paperwork. Colson really is a good professor, if a bit young. That's what worries me; I just hope you don't regret it," he said, nodding with a sigh to the unkempt bookshelves on the other side of the small room. "At least I can look forward to seeing you from time to time."

Elliot's stomach sank. He had forgotten—if he had ever known—that Colson and Ingman shared an office.

"I'll talk to Colson and take care of the paperwork. I actually have to go or I'll be late. Have a nice day, Ing . . . Professor." Elliot stood and was out the door before Ingman could comment further.

Elliot knew he should run to the theater, but he checked his pace. He should sort through his thoughts; with Colson as his advisor he would be unable to avoid Ingman next semester. However, the image of several titles on Colson's bookshelves preoccupied him. He had been encouraged by the Shakespeare, Hugo, and the rest, and he could even understand the Bible for reference, but others disconcerted him. Above all, he had experienced a sour shudder at the crowded line of Germanic consonants he had seen on a worn spine peeking out from under Aristotle's *Ethics*. Elliot began to trot.

Grey Maxwell leaned against the black cinderblock of the stage-left wall, watching the faces in the audience. Onstage, in jeans and a white button-down with rolled-up sleeves, Rydar was outlining his plan for the production.

"Anyone wanting to be involved, even backstage, will need to read all three plays, as well as *Richard II*, by January . . . "

Some students were from Rydar's classes, while others, still in their pajamas, had no doubt seen the blanket casting advertisement on the university website and been curious. Many sat wide-eyed, others bored; few looked confident, and fewer ready. Grey recognized several they would not see in the spring.

However, a handful stood out; they would be the ones Rydar had personally invited—apparent from the marks of alertness and interest Maxwell knew his old employee would look for. Vesta Lloyd, the lightly freckled redhead from the week before, had arrived early and introduced herself to Grey. Observing her as she sat upright taking notes, Grey smiled; Rydar had been right to recruit her.

The young man who arrived a few minutes late would be Elliot Fleming. Rydar had not even noted his entrance—a fact which Grey saw was not lost on the boy, who sat behind the others pouting with arms and legs crossed. Grey chuckled. The arrogant little bastard didn't even know whether or not he wanted to be there. Rydar had been right about him, too, thought Grey; poor kid.

"We're going for a modern look. Think New York, early fifties, economic boom after the war, just before Korea; if you're unfamiliar with it, brush up on your economic history. I recommend Hayek to understand the thematic conflict of the period—the need to understand and undo the unintended consequences of the previous generation's choices before they ossify and endanger the next generation. Gentlemen, get used to wearing ties. Ladies, if you're unaware that you can do whatever men can do, prepare to learn it quick because we're considering recasting several roles—the Dauphin, Harry's brother, the Duke of Lancaster—as women."

"Isn't that a bit anachronistic?" asked a dark-haired girl from a group of especially insulted faces. "Wasn't it a man's world back then?"

"Perhaps—we'll just have to see," Rydar said with a wry smile, expanding his glance to the whole audience. "We'll figure all that out during production. Thank you for mentioning it, Megan."

The girl squinted, nonetheless returning the smile as if used to engaging in reparte with the man; she seemed to know she would get her fill of discussion. However, some other students shifted. Two—whom Grey had already noted were fidgeting on the edges of their seats—stood and left with an urgency that confirmed the act as pre-planned.

We're in for some surprises, thought Maxwell. Convincing Hoegren, Akron, and the rest of the board to agree to the production had been one thing; trying to find students to join it was another.

As he often did, Maxwell let his eyes drift to Colson; the man stood, back straight and hands in motion, a smile and laugh barely contained behind his chronically furrowed brow and brusque tone. In the nine years since a sophomore Rydar had walked into Maxwell's theater, the old man had forgotten how rare a spectacle Rydar's mixture of pride and under-statement must be to most students, especially considering the deviant pleasure the man took in misleading people's perception of him—the real him, whom Grey had seen grow over the years.

"But if it's set in America, what is he going to be king of?" queried Vesta. "Are we going to change all the place names?"

"Oh, it's still England, in vocabulary," said Rydar, "but set-wise and thematically, Harry won't be aspiring to head a country. He'll be taking over the family business: England Royalties, Ltd."

Maxwell saw a mix of reactions. Vesta stared at Colson as if con-fronted by an unexpected and curious riddle. Fleming, leaning back with his feet up on the seat in front of him, lifted his chin.

After a moment, Megan spoke up, "But, Professor Colson, wouldn't that remove all the things you've been talking about—about preserving his greatest possible value by earning the crown in the right way? Making him a part of some corporation would just further remove grandeur from the crown, not restore it . . . " Those had been Colson's words, and, as Maxwell had expected, they had provoked not a few looks of skepticism. Grey shifted his weight to hear Rydar's answer.

"By your premises, you're not incorrect," said Rydar, shrugging and putting his hands up before raising a finger. "However, if true, the as-sumption that business doesn't contain abstract virtues might reveal that the modern world is quite similar to Hal's—thus proving my point. In Hal's England, where not only the value of the crown but of noble ideals, themselves, have been questioned, the highest seats of power have been emptied of grandeur. 'There's honor,' says Falstaff over Walter Blunt's corpse. Hal's is an England where royal authority—whether rooted in divine kingship or democratic politicking—is empty and suspect. Thus, Hal's task is not to revolt against his father's world by reverting back to Richard's idealism, nor to embrace the cynical affectation of his father's populism, but to synthesize the best of both with the examples of the kings that preceded them. He must show that the royal 'we' can still contain the grand office of Richard and the pragmatic public awareness of Bolingbroke. He must resurrect the royal virtues by living them, himself."

"So, I just have to play a Prince who wants to make money and be popular," said a voice from the crowd.

Many heads turned to Fleming; Vesta frowned over her shoulder before turning back to Rydar.

Nostrils flared, Rydar met the boy's smile. Maxwell knew that face—a violent interest held behind a look of indifference. He had seen it every time he asked Rydar to design a set project alone, and many times since.

Rydar chuckled; from his back pocket he pulled a silver money clip containing a few neatly folded bills. "Do you all see this?" he asked, brandishing the billfold like a trophy before tossing it up and down like a toy. "This is the value of my time and person made concrete. It's more mine than are the initials on the clip. I didn't give myself those initials; I did give this cash its meaning. You might consider money a symbol of greed or selfishness, or even oppression, but I—who earned it—can't begin to tell you the meaning I see in these dollars."

Though there were some intrigued smiles, by taking unapologetic pride in his cash Colson had lost several students. Probably intentional, Grey thought with a smirk.

"The same goes for Hal," continued Rydar. "Once the thing that unified his people, the crown has divisively come to mean different things to different people—and, thus, nothing at all. It's Hal's task to reestablish it as the highest locus of value for England, as the value which unifies his people. He does this by focusing not on receiving grandeur from the crown—which is, really, just a crafted lump of metal—but on forming himself into a king who might restore grandeur and meaning to such symbols once again."

"But, still," replied Fleming, "rather than doing something honorable, you're saying you, yourself, just selfishly made money, and you want us to interpret Hal in the same way."

"You said it Elliot," Rydar said, pointing his billfold at the boy. "I made this money. By earning it honorably, I turned it into something honorable—just like Hal arguably succeeds in restoring justice, honor, and magnanimity to the crown by being just, honorable, and magnanimous.

"'I am not covetous for gold,'" Colson continued, slipping the bills into his back pocket while quoting, Maxwell knew, from *Henry V*, "'but if it be a sin to covet honor, I am the most offending soul alive.' Don't be too quick to dismiss this idea of creating value through action. Shakespeare presents kings as human beings, who rise and fall by the virtue or vice of their actions; thus, he played no small part in laying the cultural soil for following generations, even our own. That's why, with textual guidance and consideration, I decided it would not be incorrect to present Prince Hal in the form and attire of one of his thematic offspring, one who must consider how his actions will affect not only his own life but those of everyone else who relies on him: an American businessman." Rydar looked at Fleming on the last word.

"Grey," said Rydar, turning his attention from the kid before anyone could respond, "tell them about the set." Rydar stepped back to lean against one of the onstage tables, arms crossed.

"Sure," said Grey, walking to the front of the group. "We're modeling the stage after New York, as Rydar said. The production will seem minimalist, but don't let that fool you. You'll have to use everyday items as props. Start learning how to hold a pen with your whole body because we want to see a swordfight in written terms from the last row." Grey motioned to the back of the theater.

"Also, what Rydar said about dress will be important. Dressing for business in the twenty-first century and doing so in the mid-twentieth are two completely different things. Young people didn't have social media or job application sites whereon to present their worth. You'd wear your tie like your future depended on it; it often did. I believe that's Miss Lloyd's department." Grey motioned to the young woman, who confirmed with a prompt thumbs-up. "Next year this fifty-foot stage will look like three blocks of precarious, nineteen-fifties New York opportunity, which only your feet—or, at least, your characters'—can secure. Also, on that topic," Maxwell surveyed the group of students, glancing at a few, though without malice, "no sandals or pajamas on my set."

"You can't tell us what to do," snapped a young man who had arrived shoeless and wore a beanie of non-descript color over matted hair.

"Of course not," replied Maxwell. "If our requirements make you rethink joining the production, you are free to leave." Maxwell smiled. "Besides, it's a safety hazard." He did not look long enough to see the student's reaction as he walked to his office.

"I think that's enough for today," Rydar said, suppressing a smirk as Grey neared his office door. "I'll send around some paper. Anyone wanting to be involved, give your name, email, and the part you're interested in . . . "

❊

Grey returned to his office, holding up the paper bag with their lunch. Grey had introduced Rydar to the sandwich shop's excellent corned beef on rye years before; now he shared the meal with the young man whenever he could—always remembering the extra mustard.

"I'm still deciding, Frank," Rydar said over Grey's office phone. "It'll either be England Oil or Electricity Royalties. You think it should just be England Energy, generally? 'England Power' could cover both, except for the obvious . . . "

Grey heard a mumble with Hoegren's cadence from the phone. Rydar did not move as Grey sat down a few inches away; he smiled, enjoying being welcome in Rydar's immediate physical space.

"Oh, you meant was I sure I wanted an energy concern at all? Yes, I'm sure . . . What? . . . Yeah, I know it'll be a problem with some groups on campus, but that only proves my point. Hal must preserve the value that enables the rest of England's values to exist, even as he's defamed all over court; the same can be said about American businessmen, specifically those who deal in energy concerns. They redeemed the economy in the fifties and several times since, despite being reviled by the culture—whose lights they kept on."

Grey chuckled. Frank was on their side, but as Theater Department chair and Shakespeare Festival producer he needed to mediate all the entities involved, including elements of the administration subject to student pressure. Frank understood whose word mattered in the end: his.

Nonetheless, kids were becoming unpredictable, especially with faculty support. Over recent years student groups across the country had started to expand their protests against administrations to target virtually any other department and subject they did not consider valuable. The most vehement among the groups ironically emulated the very strawman of evangelicalism they despised as being too repressively puritanical. If one wanted to see religious fervor in America, one no longer looked to the chapel pew but to the university student's social media app.

"Okay, fine. Thank you, Frank, really. You know I'm no good at that kind of thing . . . What about Ingman? I don't think he'll be so bad . . . No, put it in the actual papers. You want to recoup what you might lose from a student boycott, invite people who have actual income. But I think we'll be fine, Frank; there're more students who'll want this kind of production than we hear about . . . Yes, I know. I'm betting my job, too. You knew I'd have to before you asked me to do this whole thing . . . Hell no I'm not complaining, this is why I'm here . . . Alright, I'll talk to you later. My love to Angela."

Colson hung up, exhaling heavily as he looked down at Maxwell.

"Frank worried about the budget again?"

"Yeah, not unreasonably, either. Akron barely agreed to allow me to direct, and I think Frank wants to be a buffer between him and me. But holding back because we're worried about what some students and faculty might do is the wrong move. He agrees, but his position involves a lot more than mine. I don't blame him for being cautious."

Colson really had grown up. The twenty-year-old Rydar—who assumed all administrators were essentially bureaucrats—would have been much less forgiving. Everything that had happened since college had merely refined the boy. Grey smiled to himself. Rydar had learned to recognize when others shared his values, even when they used different language. Hoegren's battles were not Colson's; his convictions, if not vocabulary, were. Grey had seen seeds of the perspective in Rydar's undergraduate years. Then . . .

Grey took a bite of his corned beef; he preferred not to think of Rydar's last year of college while in the man's presence, feeling it would be a kind of sacrilege.

Grey had to remember that, besides Rydar's having grown up, he and Hoegren had developed their own relationship, too. During graduate school, Rydar had received an invitation to Hoegren's home for dinner. Whatever Hoegren said to Rydar showed him he had at least one friend in the administration. Grey knew that Frank had also vouched for Rydar's hiring; it was the least he could do, after seeing all Rydar had survived and miraculously overcome. "'When you were in the undergrad theater, you thought you were proud, but you weren't. You were just arrogant,'" Rydar had quoted Hoegren to Maxwell. "'Now, you're almost there.'" It had only been a matter of time before Hoegren gave Rydar a production.

Of course, Maxwell thought, Rydar had never really left Orangedale's theater. After nearly a year of silence following graduation, Rydar had returned to Orangedale for graduate work. He attended plays headed by other faculty—including a few by Lilledahl—and often just passed time reading or grading in the theater auditorium. Maxwell had given Rydar freedom of the building, knowing that the boy's love for it had nothing to do with his old boss. Hoegren's vouching for the boy's candidacy as an adjunct was a similar underscore and acceptance of the rightness of

Rydar's silent affection for the campus—and his willingness to face and draw life and strength from tragedy.

"What do you think of our recruits?" asked Maxwell, nodding to the roster he had set on the desk. "See any who'll stick?"

"Fleming's in, whether he signed or not. Vesta, of course. Believe it or not, I think I saw our Dauphin—Megan, the brunette who spoke up a few times. She's sharp enough to ask the right questions, and to believe the answers."

"How about Lancaster?" asked Maxwell.

"I'm still deciding whether to recast him or Poins as a woman. After reconsidering it, I think turning Lancaster into a sister for Harry would make things problematic. However, doing Poins has other problems— how not to have them romantic and all. However, I wonder if we can—or should—gender swap the characters at all, rather than simply casting cross-gender; we can't just rewrite the text." The man sighed, running his fingers through his wavy, dark blonde hair. "The fact that I'm even worrying about it bugs me."

"Any prospects in there for Poins?" Maxwell motioned out the open door to the auditorium seats.

"No. I think I met her earlier this week. I doubt she'd say I made the best impression, but damn it if she wouldn't make a great balance for Harry. She already knows Elliot."

"Would I know her?"

"Maybe. Black with lighter skin, about Elliot's height; she has a knack for making herself seen. I think she had a buzz cut last year, during that campaign against traditional beauty norms."

"I try to stay away from the campus social element," said Grey, taking a cue from the young man as he dipped his sandwich into a small cup of mustard. "Thinking about approaching her?"

"No, not at this point. It was just an idea. There's something too strong about her. Possibly forced. It might get in the way."

"That's the majority of theater students, Ry. Affectation's literally a way of life. Also, your bar for strong women is rather high."

A side of Rydar's mouth lifted with a chuckle. "Yeah, maybe I'm expecting too much. This girl's not Eun-Ji." The man sighed, glancing out the door.

"That you see a comparison at all is the best compliment she could receive."

"She probably wouldn't see it that way. I'll think on it—like I said, we only met once."

Grey considered Rydar.

"You know, I think you see what students could be—good and bad. It's why you seem so morbid and cynical all the time, when in reality you're the least cynical person I know."

"Yeah, yeah," Rydar said, waving his hand and picking up the roster.

Grey smiled, unsurprised by Rydar's diffusal. He knew it was not modesty or discomfort—there was too much between and behind them for that—but rather a respect for others' and his own privacy that Rydar had adopted over recent years. There was only one person from whom Rydar had hidden no part of himself, and Grey Maxwell was not her.

"How about Hotspur?" asked Grey.

"For gender-swap?"

"I meant who to play him, but there's an idea."

"No, Shakespeare wrote him as a man, and he's too big and complex a character just to—."

Rydar stopped. Nothing had changed in the room, but Grey knew something had shifted inside of Colson, like a combination lock clicking open.

"I'll be goddamned." Rydar threw the roster onto the desk and grasped his chin.

"Hm," Grey smiled as he made the connection a moment later.

"Cora would be perfect."

"If something in her reminds you of Eun-Ji, she probably would."

"I'll have to find a tactful way to approach her, but if she does it, she and Elliot would make the play. She could do Lancaster, too, I'd bet, though that'd be tough, scene-wise . . . "

"You never can tell." Grey shrugged. "Sometimes we get what we've earned. After all, you got Fleming. Speaking of which, you said Akron wanted you to present your production schedule to the board of trustees, in-person. Need backup?"

"No, I'll be fine, Grey—I like doing that kind of thing alone," said Rydar, his relaxed tone acknowledging Maxwell's concern. "I have everything I'll need. Still, keep your phone on next week, just in case."

A concession for me, Maxwell thought as he wrapped up his sandwich and slipped it into the paper bag. If Rydar called, it would be for Grey's sake, not his own. Grey could not decide if that made it more or less vicious, but he smiled nonetheless.

"Oh, and keep an eye out for ideas from Jonas. He showed me some preliminary sketches for backdrops; they're good. Anyway," Rydar said, crumpling his sandwich wrapper into a ball and tossing it in the trash can, "busy weekend?"

"No plans yet; I think I'll be keeping things open for a while, just in case I'm needed."

"You're too good for them, Grey."

"I meant by you, kid."

Colson chuckled, turning back to the list. After a moment, without looking at Grey, Rydar said, "Fine. Tomorrow, usual time. Your turn to bring the scotch."

❄

The office door opened behind Smith Ingman; the imperious pace and the faint odor of tobacco smoke made turning unnecessary. Ingman acknowledged Colson with a waive, keeping his eyes on the page.

"Don't mind me. Lessons to plan, you know," Ingman said.

After Elliot had left, Ingman had taken down his copy of Shakespeare to skim the History plays. What had started as an impulsive dip into nostalgia had, in the previous three hours, become a full dive into his long-distant literary past. Perusing *Henry IV Part* 1 and 2, Ingman had found himself smiling, despite his initial—and, if students asked, official—view that the plays eventually ended in soft imperialism.

"Nice play," said Colson with the flicker of a grin as he sat down.

"Yes, I'd heard you were doing it next semester; for all its faults, it really is entertaining."

Rydar said nothing.

Even sitting, relaxed, Rydar still seemed nervous; no, wondered Ingman, that's not it. Ten years ago Colson's intensity as a student had pleasantly jarred Ingman, making him wish he had more classes with the boy, or that his other students would exhibit the same uncanny focus. Now Ingman felt a wary respect and, if he were honest, envy of the man. Ingman had tacitly assumed Rydar would someday relax; he never had.

Ingman looked over to see Colson examining a map of the United States on his laptop.

"Going somewhere?"

"No, just researching." He had scrolled to the midwest and was zoomed in on Michigan.

"What could you find here that has to do with Shakespeare?" Ingman scoffed.

"That's what I'm researching. We're setting the play in early to mid-twentieth century US, or at least in a stylized Britain in that vein."

"Why?"

Rydar leaned back to look at Ingman. With a sigh, as if making a decision, he said, "Because I think the best things Shakespeare put into Prince Hal are what made America."

"What do you mean?" Ingman turned his chair, closing his volume around a finger.

"I mean several ideals taken for granted by early British Americans can be generally found in Shakespeare, and specifically in Harry's character—things like the desire to achieve one's own success, the implicit respect for people in different levels of society, and the willingness to risk sacrificing everything to achieve a better life and country."

Ingman paused his response. Normally he would have countered the idea; however, the rare eye contact from Rydar reminded Ingman that this was not a classroom and that the young man was a colleague, not a student. Ingman considered the idea.

"You know," Ingman said, the sight of Detroit on Colson's laptop further revivifying his interest in the play, "you could go a couple of directions with something like that. Falstaff and company could be union workers, with Henry as the politician who stands with them, and—."

"Hal's going to be a business tycoon," Rydar said, "though that's a good idea about Falstaff. Mind if I use it?"

"Sure," said Ingman, taken aback, "but wouldn't that put Hal in the wrong light? He's trying to undo the sins of his father, not exacerbate them."

"Exactly," replied Rydar, "which is why I don't think he can be a politician. It was his father, the 'vile politician, Bolingbroke,' who put things into the state they're in, to say nothing of Richard, who could easily be recast as a complacent baron who incorrectly believes himself immune to market forces. If Harry's going to be a hero, he needs to be heroic in a heroic profession."

"Heroic?" Ingman shook his head, turning back to his desk; he should have expected it. He had hoped he might connect with Rydar—and was surprised at how excited he had been to do so. However, Colson's conservatively idealistic reading of American history had once again foregone such a possibility.

"Sure," said Rydar, finishing his thought, "though, granted, that depends more on Harry than anything else. Again, it's just stylized, for costuming and sets; there won't be any serious text changes."

"Well," said Ingman, assuming a measured tone befitting the older, more experienced of the two, "that will, no doubt, be an interesting performance; you're the right man for it, I'll give you that. Who else is directing? The other plays, I mean."

"No one else. I'm doing the whole festival."

"What?!" Ingman gasped, looking at Colson.

"Yup." Rydar scrolled his screen from Michigan toward New York.

"But Frank usually uses a different director for each play."

"Mm-hmm. However, this year he asked me to do the whole thing. He probably thinks he's doing me a favor. It's insulting." Despite the words Colson could not suppress his smile.

Ingman swallowed, surprised at his own reaction. "Well, I hope you don't mind if I approach him about it. Again, I'm sure you'll do a great job, but we must maintain a balance of perspectives. At least bring in another director. You understand."

"Of course. I'd be hurt if you didn't push back, Smith. For any other set of plays I'd gladly share the load, though whatever play I'd do would have to be mine." Colson smirked. "Frankly, I'd prefer someone else do the whole thing; I'll probably catch hell."

"Then why not relax your . . . Jesus, do I need to say it? Your r— . . . romantic values?" Ingman had caught himself before saying "right-wing." He could not understand why he was becoming so frustrated. Though Colson scrupulously kept his politics to himself on campus, his small-government conservatism had become a more or less open secret shared by the two officemates.

"Why doesn't Harry relax his? Either way, if I'm going to do it, I'm going to do it fully—if that's what you mean by 'romantic.' What's wrong, Smith?"

Ingman looked at Colson, thinking back to the previous year of sharing an office with him. Colson's take on Henry should not have surprised Ingman. With the same bashful self-reproach at his rereading the plays, Ingman realized that despite their differences he had come to care for the young man; he worried what he, as head of the campus paper, would have to do to his colleague's production. A truism in the paper was that corporations unlimited by unions and democratic regulation were a menace; if Rydar presented Hal as a businessman . . .

As if discerning Ingman's thoughts, Colson chuckled. "I'm not scared of you, Smith. I knew when I accepted the directorship that because of who I am and what I'd do with the play I might be walking into martyrdom—as much as a professor can, nowadays. I want you and *The Praes* to fight me. I plan to produce a show worth fighting for." The man reached out his hand.

Ingman looked at Colson. For just a moment he felt the itch of tears at the unexpected gesture and accompanying smile. He shook the outstretched hand.

"Alright. If you pull this thing off, I'll write the review."

Colson let out a single, deep laugh. Ingman saw in his unblinking eyes an unprecedented respect.

Nothing more was said. Not until twenty minutes after Rydar left did Ingman remember he should have asked about Fleming. However, rather than drafting an email, Ingman leaned back, reopening *Henry IV Part 2*.

An hour later, after finishing the play, Ingman passed off his earlier frustration as merely a prideful reaction to the loss of a promising student and the news that the yearly Festival would have only one director. Still, beyond whatever isolated mania Ingman had, himself experienced—his Saturday having been upended by Elliot, Prince Hal, and Colson, as it were—by the time he reached his car he was resigned to the task of lobbying Frank Hoegren to appoint a co-director. His own emotions aside, as head of *The Praesidium* Ingman had the professional obligation to ensure other departments did not reneg on the University's values of inclusion and viewpoint diversity.

However, as he drove home to the relaxed tones of an NPR discussion, he found himself returning to the pleasant feeling he had received from rereading Falstaff—and from his young officemate's handshake.

CHAPTER 4

D RYING HIS HAIR, nodding to the rhythm of Trent Reznor's distorted voice coming from his phone, Elliot stepped out of his bathroom; glancing at the clock—10:38 pm—he decided to play a few hours before sleep. He could stand being tired for his Monday classes. Wrapping his towel around his waist, he sat down at his computer, reaching for his mouse to wake up the split background of his monitors, a formatted screenshot from the Hind fight stretched across both screens. It had only been a week ago, but the encounter seemed far behind him. That gambit had changed everything.

That whole day had changed everything; Elliot ignored the thought.

Elliot walked Vexxen through Centurion City, one of *Vanguard Pulse*'s few safe zones. Gaining confidence from the new sniper rifle and other materials, Elliot had traveled some hundred miles farther than he had ever gone; now he was returning in personal triumph, having finally accrued the millions needed to purchase a HUD InfraRadar from the NPC market.

Elliot having unequipped all significant items to avoid being marked by other players as worth following to loot later, Vexxen looked as much like a brand new character as possible, his olive drabs incongruous among the many well-outfitted avatars in Centurion.

Crossing a bridge over a green, grimy aqueduct two alleys from the shop district, Elliot heard a hum to his left. A text had lit up his phone screen.

He stood and stretched, running his fingers through his damp hair. It always curled like this if he forgot to comb it; he needed a haircut. He reached for the phone.

Unknown

Hey—on a walk in your part of campus and wanted to see if you'd like to join.

-Cora

Suddenly feeling how cool was his apartment, Elliot tightened his towel before looking back at the phone.

He had tried not to dwell on Cora; still, from time to time an image would surface before he could swallow it back—the line of a calf muscle stepping out of a car, the sound of long fingers tapping the wooden table beneath the drone of voices, the sweep of an elbow and open fold of a blouse turning defiantly to face him. The suddenness of the attraction had scared—no, surprised—Elliot; he had tried to treat it for what it was, a momentary infatuation brought on by their mutual interest in Aristotle and exacerbated by the accident. It was not worth altering his life. Nonetheless, the more he tried to forget the thoughts, the more unforgettable they had become.

However, the evening of the theater meeting, Elliot had dreamed he was back home, and someone he knew to be Rydar Colson was outside, approaching his house. Elliot very much wanted to open the door but had instead walked back through the house to his room where he found a naked Cora, who had been reaching for him the whole time. Even in the dream Elliot thought it odd—that such a thing would never happen, that, were she to learn of the scene Cora would take its every implication as a subconsciously sexist and predatory affront. Nonetheless, in the same blurred, intense awareness of an important presence outside, he had stepped into Cora's arms.

Elliot awoke the moment before their bare chests could touch. Sweating, tangled in his single sheet, and painfully erect, he had felt more than anything an aching wish to return to the dream. In the next moment he was on his feet, pulling on his shorts before going to the bathroom to splash his face.

Though the vividness of the dream had faded over the week, the memory of the longing—like a weight simultaneously resting in his chest and just above his groin—had not.

It was the foggy sense of Cora, naked and desiring him less than a step away, that confronted Elliot now as he reread the text. For the first time since waking that early morning, he let himself think of her as he stared at the phone screen. Snap out of it, part of him told himself. What would she say if she knew you were thinking this right now? She'd probably say you're just as bad as . . .

Elliot could passively tolerate the thoughts of Cora, even the rush of warmth to his pelvis, but the memory of Colson's presence in the dream—whether threatening or encouraging, he still could not say—woke him up.

Be cool. This won't be like high school. A pale face with blonde hair floated at the edge of his consciousness as Elliot began to type.

> *Sure thing. Be out in a bit.*

Elliot exited *Vanguard Pulse* and walked to his closet. Despite the tightness in his eyes and the latent apprehensions of his fifteen-year-old self, Elliot resigned himself to see what might happen, knowing what could happen and wondering what he hoped would happen. Even if things went like last time, he would be OK; he had learned.

Sent: 12:37 am PST 15 SEPT
From: singman@orangedale.fac.edu
To: cjackson@orangedale.st.edu

Ermine,

I hope you had a nice weekend. I hate to trouble you, but I've got a story you might be interested in.

You know the university puts on an annual Spring Shakespeare Festival. As you know, it's customary for the Theater Department to choose a group of directors, each of whom produce a different play for a plurality of perspectives. However, this year the department has chosen to appoint only one director—an English professor—for next year's festival.

Though a fine teacher, this man, Rydar Colson, has no formal production experience, though he did work in the theater as a student—no doubt the source of his pluck. He's also one of our youngest faculty members. These things could be overlooked, were it not for their culmination: Colson has chosen to perform Shakespeare's history cycle through a problematic interpretation. I've emailed the department, but somehow I doubt they'll take my concern seriously.

That's where you come in as a member of The Praesidium. In addition to publishing news, I believe we bear the responsibility of checking the university administration through journalism and advocacy. The plays are excellent, being Shakespeare, but I doubt Colson's performance will emphasize the criticism Shakespeare implicitly directs at monarchy through the plays (if you haven't read them, a spoiled prince inherits a stolen throne and attempts to use legal loopholes and eventually force to take over another country, to the praise of all).

I admire Colson's commitment to his values, but frankly Nixon couldn't have done better than Henry V, either in spin or invasion. I worry Colson will be too focused on his own reading to avoid an overly chauvinistic presentation. I hate to bother you on the weekend, but some student push-back early on might accomplish much toward balancing his perspective. This isn't my fight; it's yours, as a member of the student body. Let me know if you'd like to pursue it; no requirement from my end.

Best,
Smith Ingman
Depts. of Philosophy, Political Science, Journalism.
The Praesidium: Faculty Overseer, Editor
Orangedale University

"So, why'd you come out here and not stay in DC?" Elliot asked as he and Cora walked along the quad toward Ad Hill.

Meeting outside Elliot's apartment, they had walked in initial silence until Cora mentioned the heat and Elliot described growing up in it.

Cora chuckled with a wave around them. "Well, the weather for one thing. Virginia's beautiful, but I wanted a big change—and not just the seasons. I wanted to go out on my own, that kind of thing. I think it was also political; I wanted to see the progressive things I heard happened out here."

"And what do you think?" asked Elliot, suppressing a sarcastic tone. Focusing on his own life, school, and work, he had spent little time studying politics beyond working out some general principles from Aristotle.

"Well, I just feel freer, like it's not so restricted out here. Take Sam and Ermine: my neighborhood would have loved them, would have seen a gay biracial couple as a symbol of how advanced and liberal we were—which is great. But out here it's not even a novelty." She laughed. "Also, really, there's my race. I mean, I love my parents and being half black, but sometimes certain people focus on it too much, and they make it kind of tokeny, as if it's the only important part about me they care about, even when they're trying to help."

"Do they?" Elliot said. Despite having nothing to say, he still pre-emptively closed his lips.

"Some do. My parents don't, thank God. But you don't have to search far in DC to find someone who assumes I think a certain way just because I'm black. I'm not even African American." She sighed. "Y'know my dad's dad's grandfather came here on his own from the Caribbean? I mean, distantly we'd have to be from Africa, but we don't fit the stereotype."

"Hey, go back far enough and we're all from Africa," Elliot ventured. Through several interactions in high school and more frequently in college, he had heard that denying racial differences in the name of fighting racism was, itself, a racist act, since it ignored present inequalities and the power dynamics they contained. He had listened without comment, experiencing a consistent, though undefined, caution as he tried to reconcile the responsibility to respect people's individual rights with modern racial awareness. Above all, he had learned not to speak on the topic. He was surprised by, and curious about, Cora's perspective.

"True." She half smiled, hands held behind her back as she looked up at the sky—which pushed out her chest to distracting effect. Cora continued, "And I shouldn't say we don't fit the stereotype at all, but still . . . From what my grandmother told me—my dad's mom—her grandfather was brought to America as a slave but died free. Supposedly, he was even one of the slaves who stayed to finish building the Capitol as a free man after fighting in the Civil War."

"That's amazing. I'd never heard of slaves doing that."

"Oh, it's common knowledge in DC, part of every tour you go on." Cora snickered. "Though those might be biased."

"To be frank, in high school we only ever heard bad things about that time—like how ending slavery didn't get rid of racism, and how the country was still oppressing Native Americans."

"Yeah, there's definitely that, but is that all you heard? Maybe it's because of all the history there, as well as the optics for tourists, but there were a lot of stories like my family's. My grandma was always stressing how her family was part of the city, and by extension the nation, and how despite our struggles I should be proud of my heritage. My cousins and I never understood why she kept pictures of Washington and Lincoln next to those of Kennedy and MLK, but I never forgot it.

"I think it's from her and grandpa that I got my dislike for people— of any color—who want to co-opt my race for their own views. Like, yes I'm black, yes I'm proud of that, and yes U.S. history is uncomfortable, but it doesn't prove anything about me, personally, especially when you want to make me just like you . . . That, plus my mom's refusal to rely on men . . . well, let's say I haven't fit most people's ideals. That's also why I came out here—so I could redefine myself."

"Are your parents back in DC?" Elliot asked, hoping to steer the conversation to less fraught waters.

"Yeah, but they're not together. They endure each other on special occasions for me, but having me wasn't enough to keep them together. My mom was way too intense for my dad, and eventually enough was enough for both of them. They weren't married anyway, so their breakup wasn't that big a deal, and I was too young to be sad about it. Don't get me wrong, they're good parents, in their own way. My dad's never said it, but I think I took too much after my mom for comfort."

"Well, you're still you," Elliot affirmed, closing his lips.

"You can relax, Elliot," she said, "I hate that they've done it to you, too, though thanks for listening . . . It's not as bad as I make it sound, but it's still annoying. I mean, seventy years ago my parents never could've been together at all. Still, you're always wondering if someone's treating you a certain way because of it—especially those who say they're on your side. Like, I don't have a side, I'm just me. I didn't ask for anyone's charity; I don't need it. I think that's why I liked reading so much—especially the writers who don't talk about race."

"Isn't that the most racist thing you can do, to ignore race?"

"Don't just repeat what they say," she admonished with a softness that bespoke understanding. "Of course we need to look at things as they really are, but it should push us forward, not hold us back. That's how people stay victims. I never felt that way—not with my mom. 'You're gonna meet people who will treat you differently, Corrie,' my mom said, 'they'll treat you special because they think they owe you something special, or because you can't do it on your own. They don't, and you can.' She was talking about my being a woman, but it wasn't hard to apply it to my race. My mom never let me think either gave me an excuse or a pass. She saw the two as synonymous, I think, that treating me special because my dad was black and treating me special because I was a girl was the same kind of insult. It surprised most people, and offended some, but you'd understand if you knew her. Even my dad agreed when I brought it up, though he didn't like to talk about it. I think he was just deferring to my mom—he usually tried to avoid fights, and he probably felt stuck between her and his family. Still, everyone expected me to do things like join black student clubs or support affirmative action, and I was like, how is that different from opening the door for a woman just because she is one? Don't worry, I don't think that's a big deal, and I'm generally pro affirmative action, but you get the point. That's why I read the books that everyone considered the worst. Y'know *The Great Gatsby*?"

"I missed Fitzgerald in high school," Elliot said.

"Nothing but spoiled wasps. Granted, my mom basically was one. The book even talks disapprovingly about racial diversity, thought it's the bad guy doing it. I knew some students who flat out refused to read the book after Tom's introduced; they missed out. It was my favorite book. I think I was in love with Gatsby. I felt I understood him—someone who wants to be allowed in as an equal and has done more than anyone else to deserve it but is sabotaged before he can be. Only I knew the secret, how those whom Gatsby wants to join—Daisy and the rest—aren't worth him and what he has inside. The whole time he's trying to get them to condescend to him, when he was actually condescending to them."

"Did anyone—your family and all—get mad at you? For reading it, I mean. I can imagine some of the stuff they'd say—about just wanting to be part of another culture or race." Elliot bit his tongue. "Sorry, I shouldn't presume . . . "

"Oh, I never told them how much I loved it," Cora said, looking up at the stars, "and it was true, I think I did want another culture, or another understanding of it. But it was an older culture, or what people envisioned back then, however different and oppressive it was in reality. I guess it was life as Fitzgerald presents it, as Gatsby wants it—optimistic, beautiful, romantic, where your origin doesn't have to hold you back. Even he, or Nick, admits in the end that America might not have reached the full potential of that initial promise. But we're a lot closer, now, whatever some people say."

"Isn't that an admission that you felt held back, in spite of every-thing?" Elliot looked at her, enjoying tenuous freedom to inquire about the topic—and about her.

"Yeah, I guess so," she sighed, "but Gatsby's culture—the farm he ran away from, when he was just Jay Gatz—wasn't the one that held him back. I don't know. I didn't really think of it at the time; I just loved reading it."

They walked in silence a while. The heat of the day had dispersed from the asphalt, and a breeze kept the air atop Ad Hill just above a chill. Elliot wondered how empty the campus felt this late at night.

As they rounded the Hall of Letters, Cora asked, "So how'd you get into Aristotle? I'd never read him before last week's presentation, but you sound like you've read a lot of him."

"Thanks." Elliot grinned, taking the unintended compliment and thankful to change topics. "It was in sophomore year. Your mentioning *Gatsby* actually reminded me of it. Everyone was dating around and tak-ing tests and preparing for college, and, while I was, too, I also wanted to find my own ideas, ones others couldn't dream of. So, one Saturday I biked to the library and just wandered around. I ended up in part of the philosophy section, where the fewest books were missing. I figured if the shelf was that unpopular, it must be right. It was Aristotle. Since I was in Honors English, I picked his *Poetics*, then eventually went through most of the rest."

"Where would you recommend someone start?"

"*Nicomachean Ethics.* Technically you're supposed to start with the *Analytics*, but that's a tall, hard mountain. I skipped most of it and look up explanations instead. Besides, the *Ethics* gets into really concrete things, since he's talking about how actual humans live."

"You mean actual Athenians?" she asked in half-mocking correc-tion. She bumped his elbow with hers.

"Nope, humans in general, as much as possible," Elliot said, ignor-ing her gesture. "Of course, yeah, he was limited to Greece, but he does a pretty good job of applying the same systematic approach of his science books to his observations of people. He presents it as a science, and he bases it on several cultures' examples. Despite what Ingman says about everyone's perspective being a result of their upbringing and culture, Ar-istotle tries to base his arguments on abstract logic. When he can't prove something, he says so. I mean, sure there are issues with his works, and the Greek culture's preference for logic probably does prove Ingman's take more than I'd ever admit in class, but take it all in context, like Colson said."

Elliot paused. Thinking of the man in her presence made him uncomfortable. *Probably because I still haven't asked him to be my advisor,* he thought. Nonetheless, he felt sure Cora would appreciate Colson if she really got to know him.

"Don't worry, Elliot," Cora said as Elliot was about to voice the idea, "I know you like him. I mean, sure he's in an unfair power position as a male teacher, and he should be more circumspect about dismissing a woman's views," Cora rolled her eyes, drawing out her syllables with a patient smile. "Still, he's just a teacher, and, like I said before, he apologized. But you never told me what you think of him."

Unlike Cora's previous reactions to Colson, now her tone was calm, almost curious; the change seemed stranger than open belligerence or indifference would have.

"Honestly," Elliot said with a sigh, "I had him all last semester and couldn't figure him out. He usually stuck to Shakespeare—didn't really elaborate personally, besides why he thinks certain plays are still relevant. I'll probably get my fill, though: I have him now, and I'm doing his Shakespeare production next semester." It was the first time Elliot had admitted the decision aloud. However, the moment he said it he realized it had been made weeks before.

"Yeah, I know," she smiled, "my roommate's doing it, too," she said, nodding in the direction of the dorms skirting the quad, "Vesta Lloyd, remember?."

Elliot shrugged. "There were a bunch of people at the meeting."

"Kinda red hair, usually wears it up in a bun, really light skin with some freckles. She probably had a notebook." Cora laughed. "Yeah, she'd write down everything Colson said. She probably likes him."

"Yeah, I saw her. I think she's working backstage or something, and maybe playing one of the characters."

"Princess Katherine, I think."

"Oh, yeah," Elliot replied, realizing the implications for himself as King Harry. "Y'know," Elliot said, still thinking of what Cora had said, "Colson's doing the plays like how you described *Gatsby*—with Harry making his own way in twentieth century America. If you like that kind of character, you'd probably like Colson if you gave him a chance."

She looked ahead along the sidewalk. "Y'know, you might not be wrong." Elliot heard no irony in her voice.

"Would you consider joining? Regardless of Colson, I'd bet you'd enjoy it. And it'd be nice to have someone I know there." Elliot had not planned to ask that—had not even thought about it before the words had left his mouth. He pursed his lips.

She laughed aloud. "No thanks, I'm not a masochist. Don't get me wrong, I'd probably love it—so much I'd hate myself for it. But you guys are doing the history plays, right? I'm brave, but not that brave."

"What do you mean?"

"Of course you wouldn't know . . . " she said softly, thinking for a moment. She sighed. "It's people like Ermine. The mere fact of a pro-British play is going to get a lot of backlash."

"I hadn't thought of it. Yeah, Ermine probably wouldn't like it. And I can't imagine a man like Colson apologizing. You should've heard him describe the play." Elliot chuckled. "He was practically daring students to take issue with it—though I bet he was just separating the wheat from the chaff."

"Yeah, I'd rather not get my hopes up. I'll stick to things where I can't be used by either side—like Aristotle. Still, I'll be rooting for you."

Cora's fingers slipped between Elliot's knuckles; Elliot swallowed a gasp as a weight sunk into his torso. With it flashed images of the dream and imaginations provoked by the past weeks' attempts not to dwell on Cora. Elliot focused on staying beside her without pulling his hand away. Whether to further disconcert him or lend him support, she shifted her fingers to tighten the contact between their palms.

They walked on without speaking, Cora steadily moving her fingers around Elliot's as if sculpting his hand through touch. As he followed suit, Elliot realized he was controlling his breath as rigidly as he was his steps. Exhaling a long breath, he forced himself to relax.

Part of him seemed to be laughing at himself: he had seen this flood coming—and had made it worse by trying to ignore it. That in the end he had been unable to do so gave him a strange pleasure. How else could things have gone? For all his defenses and evasion, he had wanted this. The fact that he had even responded to her text in the first place was proof. Everything after that was inevitable.

At this thought, Elliot turned to face Cora. She looked at him, eyes wide and lips parted in a barely visible smile.

"Do you really want to prove Ermine right?"

"Shut up." She reached up and pulled his mouth to hers as his hands moved past each other across her back.

In the past, Elliot had worried more than he cared to admit whether he performed poorly the few times he had kissed; imagining how to improve had left him apprehensive, his pillow and fingers falling victim more than once to inept attempts at practice.

He remembered and forgot all of it after the first awkward but smiling press of his mouth to Cora's. He was aware of nothing but the warmth of her body, of the weight of her arms on his shoulders, of the softness of her lips against his. It was not just Cora as she was now; images of her stopping him after class, of stepping out of Sam's car, of her pressing against him over dinner, of the walk home, and of all his secret thoughts of her throughout flooded into his consciousness. This was what those moments had meant. At some barely conscious level beneath the efforts to rid his mind of her he had rehearsed it many times, and whatever clicking of teeth or over-wet lips he might note were subsumed. Cora seemed to feel the same urgency and focus, guiding him to improve as her mouth moved to meet his more times than he could count, the arching movements of her neck inviting him to continue. Elliot was dimly aware of a pressure building below his stomach, and without stopping he felt a dull disappointment that they were so far across campus from—.

"Okay, you two, give it a rest," a voice said as a light shone on them.

Startled, Elliot turned to block Cora as she let out a small shriek.

"Relax, you're fine," said the man's voice, chuckling, "though you know you're not supposed to be in the orange grove." He motioned his flashlight to the dark patch of trees off to their right. Elliot saw a Campus Security badge on the man's chest.

"Sorry officer. We'll leave," said Elliot, calming his breath.

"Y'know, I could take you to Campus Safety. I won't—you didn't mean any harm. We'll just assume you both have your campus ID's. Still, I'll need you two to head on home. And no sleepovers in the dorms."

Elliot could not tell if the man had meant that last part as a joke; nonetheless, he took Cora's hand and started down the walkway.

"Um, thank you, officer!" Cora called over her shoulder with a giggle.

After they rounded the streetlight-lit corner of another building, she skipped forward with a laugh, turning to wrap her arms once again around Elliot's neck to kiss him. He returned the kiss, despite his still racing pulse.

Apparently feeling this, Cora looked at him. "Everything okay? Elliot, he probably catches students all the time."

"Still, he could've given us a ticket," Elliot said, relaxing his shoulders and leaning his forehead down against hers. He smiled. "That was fun though."

"It took you long enough," she said, her chin moving side to side against his collarbone.

"We only met two weeks ago," he said.

"I've wanted to do that since I first saw you."

"What do you mean?"

In the coy tone of a confession, she said, "You were sitting at a table reading outside the Commons in February. You were totally oblivious to everyone and everything around you. It made me want to meet you—and see if I could distract you."

"So, you've been watching me."

"Of course," she said. "You think boys are the only ones who do that?"

"How'd you get my number?" he asked, unable to repress his smile at being the object of her cunning.

"Told Vesta I got a new phone and needed numbers. She had it from Colson."

"Pretty unethical," he said, stepping back to look at her.

"It worked, didn't it?" she returned, abruptly taking a step away from him. "Tonight was perfect, Elliot—so perfect I don't want it to be ruined. I do that sometimes—end things that are too good. Besides," her eyes met his, "we have time."

She started to walk away, leaving him to consider whether or not to follow. When she was about ten paces away, she slowed just a step. He started after her. Catching up, he took her arm and turned her around; he saw the expectant smile on her face the moment before their lips met again. This time was different; free of indecision, Elliot ran the fingers of one hand through her hair and pressed their lips even harder together. She hung onto that arm with one hand, doing the same to his waist as he was doing to her head. His belt buckle clicked lightly against the button on her white cut-off shorts. Nonetheless, after a few moments she nudged him away, just slowly enough to convey a tremor of indecision.

"That was good," she purred, taking a long breath, "but it's enough for tonight." Her eyes rose to meet his, her shoulders rising with her breath. Elliot could feel the blood moving through his hands, and he was aware of the air passing over his tongue in short gusts. An unspoken acknowledgment passed between them; the only feeling Elliot could formulate was that things had changed, and both had wanted it.

After another moment, he nodded. The movement provoked a smile—of thankfulness?—on Cora's face. She turned to continue the way she had gone, leaving him to look after her. Before she turned a corner, she rounded and yelled, "Don't call me too soon, Fleming!" At the last syllable she broke into laughter.

Elliot did not know how long he stood there, nor what way he took home. After a few steps, suffused in the memory of her touch, he lost himself in what had happened. All he knew was that he eventually arrived home and was closing the door to his unlit apartment. He looked at his swivel chair and computer; rather than sitting down as was his habit, he walked to the center of the room. Removing his shirt, he slid open the windows, letting the night air slowly replace the evening heat.

Elliot felt as if something else flowed out with the stale air; it was only then that he experienced a foreboding. He forced himself to relax as he considered the last time he had felt this way. Despite having told himself many times that everyone was dumb in high school, that getting one's hopes up wasn't bad, and that he had learned better, the memory—the sight of the girl's platinum hair, which had two weeks before graced the backseat headrest of his family's car on the way to the Homecoming dance, leaning back against the upperclassman's thick arm during lunch, her unshrinking eyes showing that she saw Elliot seeing them—still left him feeling defeated.

However, experiencing the habitual, involuntarily desire to hunch forward at the thought, Elliot straightened his back, unbuckled his belt, kicked off his shorts, and lay down on his bed. That girl had been wrong. Cora proved that. Elliot smiled in triumph, in defiance against the memory, and against the part of him that, upon seeing Cora's text, had begun to laugh ironically at how now the fight against his attraction to Cora would be much harder—would have to be, if he were to be successful in ignoring his memories of—.

Habitually, Elliot thought of the passages in Aristotle about self-control and about being high enough above events that they could not affect him. But that old fight was now superfluous. Even those passages had changed this evening, or, rather, he had. He had moved beyond past events and had found something—someone—to match his ascension, someone worth being so affected by. Defiantly, as if that other girl were watching his thoughts, Elliot let himself imagine Cora in his arms as he waited for sleep.

Chapter 5

L EANING BACK IN his chair, Elliot thumbed through his Collected Works of William Shakespeare, waiting for ENG 316: Shakespeare's History Plays to begin. Students were still trickling into the classroom; Colson had not yet arrived.

In the past few days, Elliot had done little but experienced a lot. Sunday night had left him exhausted. Not knowing where he and Cora stood, Elliot had agonized over how he should interact with her. Elliot could not decide if he regretted or felt lucky for dropping Ingman's class the week before. He had texted Cora a couple of times, but she had not responded. He resisted checking his phone, feeling again the impulse to cover his eyes at his last message—*y'know, avoiding me says more than texting back*. He should not beg. Whatever, Elliot again told himself; in the end, she had contacted him first.

As Elliot turned another page, the entrance door to the building opened and a bright thanks from a masculine voice was exchanged in the hallway.

"Well, you're adding just in time; I'm happy to have you."

A moment later Rydar Colson walked into the classroom; behind him, smiling gaily, was Cora Madison.

Elliot sat up so fast his chair almost fell back. Smiling at those around her as she set down her bag, Cora sat across the square of tables from Elliot. Her eyes met his for the fraction of a second, their only acknowledgment a brief widening before she turned to the front of the class.

From sun or artifice, Cora's hair seemed lighter, and she had teased it out into an afro of golden-brown curls. It contrasted sharply with the loose, baby pink t-shirt that, with its collar torn off, revealed a single bare shoulder. The familiar—yet, here, so unexpected—line running down her jaw to her collarbone and, as she leaned forward to reach into her bag, into the subtle shadow of flesh just behind the loose fabric of her shirt, made Elliot aware that his mouth was open. He shut his lips, leaning back against the chair.

"Morning, everyone," said Colson. "I hope your weekend was good—and I hope you had time to read act three of *Henry VI Part Two*. Now, I asked it on our first day, and I'll keep asking it: why the hell would anyone study Shakespeare's histories?"

Expressions of boredom, evasion, and irony effused the class; others—Cora among them—sat smiling, bemused.

"Because they follow one story over several plays," said Megan Armstrong, the girl with dark, tightly curled hair from the theater meeting.

"One reason," Colson said with a deep nod, "thank you, Megan. Whereas his other plays are generally self-contained, Shakespeare's histories follow one set of characters over eight plays. However, what's one problem with them?"

"He wrote them out of order," Megan returned, smiling.

"Right again," Colson said, hammering a fist forward in affirmation. "As we've seen, Shakespeare started with *Henry VI Part One*, wrote until *Richard III*, then went back to *Richard II* and finishing with *Henry V*. We'll get into his possible reasoning, if he was even giving it a thought, but I tend to think he wanted to save the most important for last, for when his ability as a playwright could do justice to England's greatest king. Which," Colson looked at Cora, "is why we're reading in order of writing and not chronology."

Cora nodded, taking the syllabus the others had passed to her.

"As you may have seen even between Henry Six One and Two, even gods can submit to their faults and learn; indeed, that might be how they become gods." Colson grinned at that. "Also, I hope you're seeing how Shakespeare presents political conflict—whether he's presenting one side of the War of the Roses unconditionally, i.e., as propaganda, or whether he's showing a nuanced understanding of both families' claims and weighing both the benefits and drawbacks of different characters' actions. Now, any questions?"

As Colson spoke, Elliot watched Cora out of the corner of his eye. He had thought he had himself under control, but when Cora walked in Elliot's stomach had dropped and stayed down. Cora was watching

Colson; like the silence of her texts, she did not look at Elliot. Refusing to look at me is an admission, he thought, unsure what admission he wanted from her. And that she was smiling at Colson . . . Perhaps she had mellowed out a bit over the past weeks.

"Yes, of course," Colson answered a student, "the question is always why Shakespeare changed what he did from real history and what it adds to his plays. I believe that's one of the greatest ways Shakespeare contributed so dramatically to the later Renaissance, which birthed an entirely new dramatic genre. Even as he broke several of Aristotle's dicta about comedy and tragedy, he took Aristotle's broader convictions seriously, such as the idea that poetry and literature contain more truth than history—in that, though not being literally real, they can concretize certain universal virtues and experiences more clearly than real life usually does, thus making fiction, in a way, more real than strict accounts of historical events. And that's to say nothing of his presenting virtues as self-reinforcing actions that must be lived to be truly known.

"Of course, as the only member of his company not to attend college, Shakespeare may not have formally read Aristotle, but his world—the still implicitly Catholic culture under threat from the English Reformation—was built by Aristotle, by way of that monolith of synthesis, Saint Aquinas. Though he took many liberties with certain characters and events, it's with generally Aristotelian premises that Shakespeare distilled fourteenth- and fifteenth-century England to make its events universally relevant. He shows not just what those events were but what they meant, for his own time and, perhaps, for our own.

"However," Rydar broke from his somber tone with a laugh, standing up, "how you let the plays affect you, personally, isn't my business. Please turn to act three so we can continue our discussion . . . " On the board he had written "Extended Metaphors," underlining the words to prelude a list.

Elliot opened his book to *Henry VI Part One* and started rereading the lines, listening at times to students naming the weekend reading's comparisons between characters and animals and distracted by thoughts of what he might say to Cora.

Elliot passed between the other students to catch up with Cora, who had been among the first out the door.

"Elliot!" Colson, still seated, waved him over.

Exhaling with a look out the door, Elliot stopped.

"Yeah? What's up?"

" I won't keep you long. You see the email about Saturday's meeting?"

"Uhh, yeah," Elliot stammered, checking his phone.

"Good. I bet you're relieved—though you can still use any *Henry V* lines you've learned for the final speech project in here. By the way, you looked distracted during class; everything okay?"

"Yeah, I'm good," Elliot said, putting his phone away; he would read the email later. He sighed at the resignation that Cora was probably half-way to the quad by now.

"Excellent. See you Saturday." Colson turned to his class roster, crossing out names who had not attended since the start of semester. Elliot could not decide if he felt relieved or deflated that Colson seemed indifferent to his progress learning lines.

Exiting the building, Elliot left the flow of students to go around the Hall of Letters, intending to console himself at a shaded bench he enjoyed. As he rounded the corner, a hand reached out to his neck and pulled his mouth into a kiss.

"Well, that was fun," Cora said, taking a breath. "We should've done this sooner—would've made Ingman's class a lot more entertaining."

"What the—," Elliot began to protest after the fact, but Cora held her finger to his lips, replacing it with her own in the next moment. Despite himself, Elliot felt his hands encircle her back. No, this is right; she had been waiting for this, too.

"Goddamn you," Elliot said with a chuckle, embracing the girl as the previous moment's frustration slipped away like a foolish memory. "You could have warned me you were adding Colson's class."

"But that would've spoiled the fun! Seriously, do you know how hard it was to ignore you? Wouldn't want people to know about us, especially Colson."

"Yeah, what the hell," Elliot said as he reevaluated the past week's emotions. "You were all nice to him when you came in."

"Just trying to make a good impression. Figured I shouldn't knock him until I tried him—as a teacher and everything."

"Well, you owe me. You think just kissing me can make up for ig-noring me?" Elliot's playful tone belied the severity of his own question.

"No—unless it can." Cora winked. "Anyway, are you free right now? If we get some snacks, my dorm's free—or . . . " her tone trailed off as she motioned with her eyes to the north, toward his apartment.

"Absolutely," Elliot said, taking her hand as he made toward the Commons.

"No." Cora pulled her hand from his, smiling slyly. "You get the food, I'll meet you there in twenty. Don't want the wrong people to see." Her eyes flashed to the corner of the building as she backed away from him.

Cora skipped away in the next moment. Remembering how she had left him after their walk, Elliot chuckled as he turned toward the Commons. She was wild, and it was amazing.

Ermine looked up from his computer at the rap on the open door. At his threshold stood Cora Madison.

"Well, as I live and breathe," said Ermine. "Who is this vision that confronts me?"

"Hello, Ermine," Cora said, "I hope your semester's going well?"

"Well, as fine as one could expect, being so recently absent of your presence. Anything I can help you with, dear? You're not finally taking up my recommendation to join the Breitlinger Program, are you?"

"No, sorry. I can't chat long, sweetie, but I felt I should tell you before you heard it through the grapevine: I'm taking Rydar Colson's Shakespeare class."

"What?!" Ermine exclaimed, sitting up straight.

"Yes. I think I already know what you'll say, but feel free to say it anyway."

"If you did and still chose to take the class, then you didn't understand. I really feel I should warn you against it. Cora, I don't know if you saw my article today about sexual inequity in the campus professorships, but you're only giving a teacher like that permission to do the things he does, and worse."

"He hasn't done anything. Call it an effort to learn the opposite perspective, if you can't palate it."

"So over two thousand years of history hasn't been enough to know the enemy?" Ermine spat. "You're either against the oppressor or you're for him. I'd expect you to know that." Ermine motioned to her bare, sun-darkened shoulder, refusing to blink so there would be no question about his meaning.

Cora affected a sly look. "What oppressor do you mean, Ermine?"

"You know exactly who I mean—men like Colson!" Ermine closed his eyes, swallowing his frustration. He assumed just enough of a patronizing tone to convey that he should not need to elaborate such things to one such as Cora. "White men who perpetuate the systematic continuation of their power by teaching white European authors—to the exclusion of women and minorities."

Cora looked sidelong at Ermine, her tone elevated into a parody of Ermine's, "You wouldn't be mansplaining to a woman what she should do, would you?"

"God, no, of course not!" Ermine snapped, shaking his head and leaning back.

"Then drop it." Her tone was hard as iron.

Ermine looked at her, saddened that someone so beautiful, so vibrant, so worthy of freedom should be so possessed by a spirit of complacent self-slavery. It would be less vicious if she were a man, he thought; her race would not be compounded with her gender. He could just call her an Uncle Tom and be done with it. But, no: he was fighting for such implicit victims as her. How would she, whom he had assumed would be a major ally, receive the pieces he planned to write, one of which, per Ingman's suggestion, directly targeted Colson?

"Well, there's nothing more to do, then," Ermine said, assuming a broken tone so as not to burn the bridge between them, as he would have with any other peer. "My door is always open—if you decide you've had enough 'learning the enemy's perspective.'"

"Not my enemy, Ermine. I knew you'd take it like this—that's why I felt I should tell you outright. I'm sorry I should have to."

"Not as sorry as I am," replied Ermine, imagining striking a mark through Cora as he would a line of beautiful but now unusable text.

Elliot walked through the black painted hallway and stepped out onto the stage.

"Good, now we can start," Colson said, lowering his chin to look at Elliot through his eyebrows.

The rest of the cast sat around a square of tables, each with a differ-ently colored folder before them. Elliot recognized a few—Vesta, from whom he averted his eyes after a glance, Megan, and a few he assumed were from Colson's other or past classes. To Colson's left sat a middle-aged man, larger and boasting a dark beard with probably recent graying. On Colson's right sat an older woman who would have looked comically long-limbed were it not for the imperious way she stared at Elliot, resting her chin on her thumb and tapping her horn-rimmed glasses with her forefinger. Despite his smile, Colson wore a look of subtle reprimand. He held out a blue folder.

Avoiding the looks, Elliot walked over, took the folder, and sat be-side the large man in the only open chair.

"Alright, productions usually don't involve the cast this early, but we have plenty to prepare for Spring. With a couple of exceptions," Col-son nodded to a few students probably from his other classes, "most of you are new to Shakespeare. That's fine—it actually might be better; you'll have fewer preconceptions. It goes without saying that you won't be able to authentically and accurately portray your characters without understanding both them and the plot. For the next month we'll be going line-by-line through the plays. If you have a question, no matter how simple, ask it; I want to cut right now through any possible hesitation or embarrassment. One main theme of Hal's story is the sustained willing-ness to look like a fool in order to succeed; if there's one play where folly, recklessness, and mistakes are allowed, it's this. For those who have done Shakespeare, be warned: as good as yesterday's manna might've been, today it's rotten."

"What about interpretation?" Elliot asked, lining up the folder with the edge of the table.

"That'll come later, after we've considered the play and its context, though I'll give you my take in a bit. You'll be free to make choices, and I'll take your ideas into account when it comes to line cutting and block-ing, but for now we're all students before the play, itself."

The woman to Rydar's right raised a finger; Rydar nodded, sitting down.

"If you all don't mind," the woman said in a thick, British accent, her voice more sonorous than Elliot had expected possible from such a thin body, "I'd like you to turn to the end of your scripts and tell me what you find—or don't find, rather."

After a moment of shuffling pages, Vesta, who apparently had not needed to look, said, "There's no *Henry V*."

"Exactly," the woman said, clearly pronouncing each letter with a chuckle. "I must stress how important it is that Rydar has cut Henry's final play from our production. It is Harry in his youth whom we will examine, without the assurance that he will succeed. Without stepping on our director's toes, I exhort you to consider how you, as a young person, might relate to Prince Hal's experience—for he, too, is a novice surrounded by supposed experts. As Rydar said, we will base our interpretation on the text and inform our rendition with many alternative perspectives, but there may be an incredible amount of drama to be found in practicing what the Prince preaches, so to speak, and approaching the old with fresh eyes. Pardon me, Rydar."

"Of course, ma'am," replied Rydar. "Everyone, I'd like you to meet Doctor Diane Pelton. She'll be playing the Earl of Worcester in *Henry IV Part One* and the Lord Chief Justice in *Part Two*. Also, Mr. Ernest Blythe, who will play Falstaff."

The two nodded as Rydar motioned to them.

"Dr. Pelton has graciously agreed to come out of retirement for our production. Some of you might recognize her name: she used to head our English Department, and she taught me everything I know."

The woman giggled at the idea, stifling the musical sound with a touch of a finger to her lips.

For the second time that week, Elliot marveled at the smile on Rydar's face: it was a look of unmasked affection. Looking to Blythe on his left, Rydar said, "Mr. Blythe has been performing Shakespeare for years, and he has mercifully agreed to endure my direction and, hopefully, give our Falstaff something he would not have had without a traditional understanding of the role. Ernest, would you like to say anything?"

"Only," the man said with a wry smile, "that I look forward to working with you all, and that, having wrestled through our differences, I've realized how talented a director you might have here. I hope you will all respect his leadership, as I look forward to doing, despite his age."

"Completely unnecessary." Colson waved away the compliment. "You've been performing these plays since before I was born, after all. Still, thank you, Ernest."

Last semester, Elliot would have expected to hear at least some sarcasm in Rydar's voice, but he caught none; something since had softened Rydar's reaction, he thought. Or was it the nature of the meeting and those in attendance? Elliot felt curious—and, inexplicably, jealous—about Rydar's obvious friendship and ease with Dr. Pelton.

"I do want to know," interjected Blythe, "who will be playing my Harry."

Colson motioned at Elliot next to him, on whom Blythe fixed his gaze for a moment before bursting into laughter, slapping Elliot hard on the back.

"Oh, God, he's perfect! Even down to being late!"

Elliot felt himself blush; fighting the impulse to leave, he looked at Rydar. The man winked, idly rotating in his chair.

"I'm sorry," said Blythe, "I don't mean to make a bad impression, but you don't know how many Hals I've met who were either Hotspurs or Henry Vs! What was your name? Or shall I just call you Hal from the start, my mad wag?"

"Fleming. Elliot Fleming."

"Elliot. Well, my boy, I hope you won't mind my loquacity, at least when it comes to you. Indeed, feel free to push back against me; after all, I'll be the source of your greatest temptation."

"What, pork?" Looking at Blythe's gut, Elliot said the first thing that came to his mind.

Blythe roared. After a moment of shock a few around the table chuckled.

"See? Perfect—though a bit nervous about my reaction, there." He pointed a finger at Elliot. "No, my temptation is what leads to pork." The man stood and leaned forward onto both arms, addressing the rest of the table. "I am pity, I am respite, I am reconciliation, I am laxity and softness, I am the temptation to rest, I am the desire to say 'who am I to rule?' I am—forgiveness, for that for which Hal must never deign to seek forgiveness. And you must resist me, Elliot—Hal—with everything in you, lest this play lose all its meaning."

Bewildered, Elliot pressed his palm against the table, looking around at the others. Despite a few confused expressions, many were smiling wide at the spectacle; a couple, including Dr. Pelton, even clapped softly.

Rotating his chair from one side to the other, arms crossed, Rydar said, "Perhaps that's a little much at this point—though Ernest's not wrong. By the end of today you'll hopefully understand what he means."

"Yes, yes. But, make no mistake," agreed Blythe, sitting, "your director has shown me that in this production I truly am the villain—the worst kind, the kind you cannot help but love, and who loves the hero yet doesn't see he is implicitly against him. I am a 'villain,' in the Middle-English sense, a low character, bound to the villa, the land, and thus unable to comprehend the view from the peaks. When you find your characters faced with a decision, even between a lone greatness or a comfortable equity with your fellow man, I want you to see it as a choice between the crown and . . . " Blythe paused for just a moment, looking askance at Elliot, "and pork."

Elliot huffed a laugh, smiling despite himself.

"What is that racket," called a muffled voice from across the stage. A door opened behind Rydar backstage, and Grey Maxwell leaned out. He dropped his joking grin upon seeing Dr. Pelton.

"My God . . . " the woman said, voicing the look on the face of the man who had stood to step outside his office.

"Is that my one, truly worthy, opponent?" Maxwell asked, his tanned face wrinkling into a wide smile as he walked over.

"You won that contest long ago," Pelton said as she stood and hugged the man, "as any father should." They had separated, but her arms still rested on Maxwell's.

"You two are embarrassing," intoned Rydar, not moving from his chair.

"Cool it, kid; mom and dad are talking," said Maxwell, not taking his eyes from Pelton's smile. After a moment, he kissed her on the cheek, and the two embraced again.

"I take it Rydar didn't tell you I was coming back."

"He probably wanted to see me like this. The joke's on him," Maxwell said; the woman laughed again.

"God, you two are indecent," Rydar said, looking askance at the two. "Everybody, before you jump to conclusions, these two had an informal game of who was more my mentor in college. Ironic, since I was just here for a degree and a paycheck."

"Bullshit," Maxwell chuckled. "Anyway, do let's catch up later, Diane. It's been dull since you left, and the English building's barely worth visiting anymore."

Dr. Pelton nodded, exchanging one last squeeze of Maxwell's arm before the man turned back to his office.

Elliot glanced around the tables; the abrupt display of sentiment—and discomfort from Rydar—had surprised more than him. Vesta, especially, looked stuck between concern, relief, and curiosity.

"Anyway," said Rydar, sitting up and opening his own folder to a page of notes, "as Diane said, we're omitting *Henry V* to better examine Harry's personal reformation as a prince. And, yes, it's not Hotspur or the French Dauphin whom Harry fights, nor is it the others contesting his father's claim to the throne: it's the temptation to stay in the tavern—to not deny Falstaff in the end. So, while Hal is Hotspur's worst enemy, Hotspur isn't Hal's; their opposition isn't mutual. Ernest was right: as wonderful as Falstaff is, he is the real antagonist to Hal's plot, even as he is the prince's greatest mentor.

"While one can read Hal's choice as being between Hotspur's orderly chivalry and Falstaff's chaotic depravity, only the latter actually threatens his core values and goals. In fact, just as Hal's wildness implicitly threatens to invalidate all of Hotspur's values—which Hal ultimately holds—Falstaff's uniquely humorous nihilism threatens to do the same to Hal's. Hal reveres the past and the throne while being willing and resilient enough to critically and playfully examine them in the tavern. Hal's not, as his father assumes, ignoring the present state of the state; he is, in fact, dealing with the deeper issue of undermined values in a very forward-thinking way. Meanwhile there's always the danger that Falstaff's Dionysian chaos will overpower Hal's goal of restoring virtue and order to England's throne—through, as Ernest said, the temptation for Hal is to give in to his own mask of drunkenness and extended adolescence . . . "

Elliot had started to take notes, but, seeing Vesta's intent scribbling, he set down his pen. He'd be damned if he took Colson that seriously; besides, he wasn't stupid. If an idea was important, he would remember it. With a breath, Elliot leaned back to listen as, gesticulating at certain points, Rydar laid out his interpretation of Prince Hal's conflict.

Elliot washed his hands. After the fifteen-minute break they would read through *Henry IV Part 1*'s opening scenes. Elliot had retreated to the lobby restroom, dousing his face and leaning against the sink to check his phone.

They had discussed much besides the play—how Shakespeare had recently come under attack at universities across the nation, how Rydar anticipated such opposition at Orangedale, and how they would prepare for such a thing with optional bi-weekly discussions of Shakespeare and other authors in the Western Canon leading up to and away from him, for which they could receive class credits in literature, philosophy, or history majors, since they would discuss all three subjects.

In their folders they had found a page with three columns—one of authors, one of philosophers and theologians, one of historical works. They would sign up to lead discussions on whichever works interested them. With a smile, Rydar added that they were free to bring in any supplementary works they thought important, especially from other authors and cultures, so long as they presented on the actual ideas in their chosen primary piece. "We'll do what Harry does to the shaken values of his times: consider whether his plays and the surrounding tradition really are as useless, empty, and malignant as people say." As Elliot expected him to, the man had winked.

A few students—Megan, Patrick—had hesitated at the idea of just being told what to think about the Western Tradition, but Rydar assured them they would take criticism of the canon seriously—because he believed it could survive it, and that, "part of the canon's resiliency lies in its native compulsion to reflect on itself." His goal was to help them explore the tradition for themselves and find their own reasons for either reading or discarding Shakespeare. "You can think whatever you want about him and the rest—but only after you've actually read them." After they covered the two main plays the seminar was voluntary; Colson only wanted those to participate who really wished to. "Feel free to critique any work on that list—but back up your view with thought and argument, and show you actually understand their ideas before dismissing them." Megan seemed more willing to humor Colson than did Patrick.

Had Elliot known the production would involve an entire extra course, he might have thought twice before joining. Still, he had known it would be a lot of work, and they had all year. Furthermore, Elliot was curious about reading literature, philosophy, and history in tandem. Perhaps Rydar was onto something. Then Elliot actually read the list of names. Among the several he could understand being there—Aristotle, Hugo—were many he was a bit offended to see with the others. Adjacent Plato and Aristotle atop each column were several books of the Bible, while further down the list was Dickens's *Hard Times* and some works by Dostoevsky, as well as Nietzsche's *Beyond Good and Evil*. Elliot had to look away, feeling as if the few points of light on the page were being obscured and smothered by a cloud of superstition, pessimism, and chaos he had thus far avoided.

That last name, especially, which he had seen in Colson's office two weeks previous, made him cringe now as it had then. He had heard about Nietzsche's goal of undoing Western rationality and his subsequent influence on 20th-century Germany, and he had felt a tremendous relief upon learning the man rightly went mad—taking it as a permission to safely dismiss his work. However, there the name had stood, printed on the same level as others Elliot respected; it unnerved him.

The restroom door opened. Blythe stepped in.

"Oh, Elliot—Hal. Wondered where you'd gotten off to."

"Ernest."

For some reason, Elliot suspected Blythe would be the kind of person to strike up a conversation in the men's room. Grabbing a paper towel, Elliot dried his hands and was out the door before the man could do so.

Sitting on a couch to look out the large foyer windows at the small courtyard of grass outside, Elliot heard Blythe exit the restroom. He was not surprised when the man came over to lean against the opposite side of the couch.

"You don't want to be here," said Blythe. His tone was matter-of-fact but without reproof.

"If I didn't, I wouldn't," shrugged Elliot, not taking his eyes from the bright green grass.

"Fine, fine, but you don't really—really—want to do this play. I know we just met, but you'll pardon me if I confess my first impression. Perhaps I'm wrong; it would be better if I were. Nonetheless, the fault, dear Henry, is not in your stars, but in yourself."

"That I'm an underling?" Elliot supplied the next line from *Julius Caesar.*

"Quite right!" The man smiled. "No, not an underling, per se, but were we actually living our parts—you Hal and I Falstaff—I doubt you'd ever leave the tavern. Call it a hunch I have no right to voice, but I wonder if you'll learn more than just lines from this play. You'll have to, if you're going to really pull it off."

"Thanks for your input," Elliot said, rolling his eyes, "but I'll be fine."

"Okay, okay," the man relented, "your life is none of my business—for now. But I wasn't kidding when I said Hal's temptation is to settle—to take the path of least resistance. Do yourself a favor and don't confuse me with my character. You already know we'll be spending plenty of time together when I come back in the spring. I'm willing to be a resource to you, but if you'd rather be treated like a child, like other students I've had to work with, I can't help you."

Without waiting for Elliot's response, Blythe turned to leave.

It was not until several minutes had passed that Elliot realized the meeting had started up again and no one had bothered to come get him.

CHAPTER 6

ERMINE'S PHONE BUZZED. The number was unknown, but one never knew when one was needed. He leaned back in his chair, letting the flow of late-afternoon conversation on the umbrella-shaded Commons patio wash in after him.

"This is Ermine," he said in a sing-song voice.

"Hi, Ermine. This is Patrick. Janek gave me your number; sorry to bother you."

"Ah, no problem, Pat; what's up?" Ermine cooed, excusing himself from the table of other B-Center students. New to Breitlinger, Patrick might have been among them. Tall, not too uppity about his attire, dull at times—probably a remnant from the hide-bound literature program, Ermine thought—Patrick had a lot of potential. Ermine liked him. His academic emphasis had something to do with theater.

"I wanted to ask your opinion about something. Have you heard about the Shakespeare play being put on in Spring?"

"A more atrocious show I've never seen, I'm sure," Ermine said.

"Oh, uh, really?"

"Well, of course, they'll have to actually put it on, but judging from what I've heard I doubt it will be the kind of thing worth patronizing."

"So, you don't think I should do it then?"

"What do you mean?" Ermine asked, blinking.

"I'm actually in the play—or I was planning to be in it. I'm Poins, the prince's friend. But you think I shouldn't do it?"

Ermine was about to say no—to save the young man not only from an embarrassing flop but also from the moral blackmark the play would carry after Ermine's next article went to press. However, as Ermine was about to speak, he realized a new thought.

"No, I didn't say that," Ermine said, relaxing his tone. "We can talk about it later, but I think you should do it."

"But you just called it atrocious," said Patrick's voice with a tremble.

"Yes, but just because the ship has problems doesn't mean you jump off immediately. You wouldn't want to make it worse by leaving, either; they'll need B-Center students just like you." Ermine was checking his words, aware that saying the wrong thing might spoil the opportunity to get someone on the inside. He'd have to thank Cora for the idea.

"So, you support the play? You don't think it's that bad, the things you've heard, anyway?"

"Whether I support it or not, you are the one who has to act in it. However, we are often called to do some unpalatable things for the sake of social justice. I take it Colson's interpretation worries you?"

"Yeah, it's really romantic and conservative—bordering on fascist."

"Frankly, I'm not surprised. But that doesn't mean you can't do good while you're there—suffer for your art, and all that!" Ermine said, muting his giddiness with a merely cheery tone. "Do the best you can—go along with Colson, if only to resist later. Of course, I wouldn't want you to compromise beyond what your conscience can handle, but when the chips fall, any offense is on him, not on you. Also, I'm always here to talk if you need."

There was a pause, Patrick no doubt considering.

"Okay, I'll let you know. Thanks Ermine."

"Of course!" Ermine jumped, punching the air above him. "Also, Patrick?"

"Yeah?"

"Don't worry about anything you see in *The Praes*. Take whatever I might write as an argument for why you need to stay in the play—to prevent it from being what we both fear it might be. Stand strong, brother."

"Oh, alright," Patrick said slowly, sounding less than reassured, "thanks. Talk to you later."

"Be in touch!" Ermine ended the call and slipped the phone into his pocket, skipping into a spin before hopping the railing to rejoin the others.

"That Sam?" asked a voice to his left.

"No, just a friend I have a project with. Discussing an idea I had for a new direction."

※

"If all the year were playing holidays, to sport would be as tedious as to work; but when they seldom come, they wish'd for come, and nothing pleaseth but rare accidents . . . "

Leaning cross-legged against the wall, Elliot tried to mumble his lines without waking Cora. A ray of mid-morning sunlight hit the tawny skin of her stomach, brightening the otherwise imperceptible hairs into a sheen of gold; Elliot resisted the impulse to run his hand along the rising and falling surface. He pitied Harry for not attracting a woman until the end of *Henry V*, though he was glad he no longer had to learn all the speeches of that play.

Cora yawned, looking up at Elliot as she stretched.

"Good nap?" Elliot asked.

"Yeah. That eight o'clock is killing me."

The digital clock next to the bed read 11:27 am. Elliot pressed his palm to Cora's stomach, feeling the warm spot where the light had been before moving it up under her shirt.

Cora sighed; she still had an hour before her next class. Slipping one hand atop his that held her breast, she pulled him down by his arm to lay beside her.

They had relaxed like this whenever they could, seizing the mornings and early afternoons when Vesta was in class now that evenings found Elliot at the theater and Cora studying. Cora preferred not to talk about their Histories class when together, choosing instead to treat their time as a release from their official lives. Though he was curious of her thoughts about the class and of Colson, Elliot had eventually figured she needed at least some privacy, what with all their extra time together. Whatever, Elliot thought as he moved his mouth along her collarbone, so long as this was where Cora smiled like she was right then.

"Oh!"

Elliot and Cora snapped their attention to the voice; Elliot took his hand from under Cora's shirt as she let out a quick shriek. Vesta had opened the door without their noticing, not seeing them, herself, until she was fully inside the room. Her wide eyes showed a mix of surprise, discomfort, and confirmation. Composing herself, she turned to close the door behind her.

"Sorry, Vesta, you startled us," said Cora, her smooth tone dispelling the fright of the previous moment. "Get out of class early?"

"Yeah," the girl said as she put her bag onto her bed, looking away from the two of them and moving as if unsure of the room, "the professor had a fender bender on the freeway. She's okay, but . . . I . . . uh, didn't know you two were together. I mean, I wondered, but . . . "

"Oh, we're not—not like that," Cora said in an easy tone, squeezing Elliot's wrist under the sheet to keep him from talking. "We're just having fun, just blowing off steam, y'know?"

"If you say so; just . . . I wish you would've said something," Vesta looked around the dorm room, as if to say she lived there, too. After giving Cora a pointed look, Vesta again averted her eyes, standing behind a chair and resting her hands on its wooden back.

"C'mon, we're big kids now, Vesta," Cora said, "but I understand. You weren't expecting it."

"Yeah, but, frankly, I didn't think I'd have to . . . "

"Vesta, we're not drunk, and we know each other. This is totally different from Kyrie." Still propped up on his elbow next to her, Elliot could feel an edge of defensiveness behind Cora's conciliatory tone.

"It is—I'd expect it of her," Vesta stressed. Despite her composure, Vesta could not withhold all sharpness.

Cora closed her lips, apparently reconsidering her retort.

Elliot sat up, avoiding Vesta's eyes. He could imagine her discomfort. He, himself, was vacillating between sharing Vesta's embarrassment and feeling encouraged by Cora's refusal to apologize. Not being Vesta's roommate, he reasoned, he had nothing to be ashamed of; yet, he nonetheless winced as he remembered the hours he had spent watching the girl engage with Rydar and the others at the theater. Elliot wondered not for the first time if he owed her an explanation. He glanced at Vesta, looking away as her eyes met his.

"Listen, I understand you had bad roommate experiences," said Cora, a bit more strongly than Elliot felt necessary, "but it's my dorm, too."

"I know," said Vesta, gripping the chair, "just, I didn't know you were sleeping together."

"Oh, we're not—," Elliot said.

"We're not fucking," Cora cut him off. "We're just two friends, hanging out. Sure we mess around here and there—but it's not a big deal."

"Okay, okay," said Vesta, raising her palms in surrender, "I don't want a fight. You guys do what you want. Just . . . I expected you to tell me. Let me know from now on."

Cora paused before closing her eyes and exhaling.

"I'm sorry, Vesta. It won't happen again. I'm sorry it turned into such a big thing."

Vesta just nodded, turning toward the restroom.

"I should probably go," Elliot said after Vesta closed the door.

"I'll come with you," said Cora, as if the moment were behind her. "We need lunch, anyway."

Casting back the sheet, she swung her bare legs off the bed and grabbed a lavender bra from the floor. As she fit it under her crop-top, Elliot stood, feeling he should keep his back to her while she dressed.

"You aren't mad, too," she stated, pulling on her jeans.

"No, I just . . . hope this doesn't affect rehearsals and stuff."

"I'm sure it won't; Vesta'll be fine. She just had a bad roommate. But you sure you're okay?" She stood to put her hand on his back, brushing her lower waist against his hips.

"Well," Elliot said with a wink, "with friends like you . . . "

She leaned in to kiss him.

"That was just for her. I didn't mean it. Now, let's go get some food. I don't even remember what I had for breakfast."

As they left, Elliot felt the impulse to check on Vesta. He had initially thought her bright agreeableness both haughty and naive. Now, seeing her vulnerable—before Cora, no less, whom he knew better than anyone to be strong-willed—he pitied her. The fact that Vesta now shared their secret made him feel an odd compassion, as if it were she, not Cora, who had been unexpectedly exposed. She had, in a way. Descending the dorm stairwell, Elliot took Cora's hand.

Things with Vesta could only improve, Elliot figured; it might even turn out to have been a humorous start to a friendship. She'd have to get used to such things. Originally cast as Princess Katharine, Vesta had been in a limbo since Rydar dropped *Henry V*. However, soon into their discussions she had impulsively lobbied Rydar to play the extreme opposite of a princess—*Henry IV Part 2*'s comic prostitute, Doll Tearsheet. The thought gave Elliot an odd hope. Either way, beneath the remnant adrenaline of the embarrassing scene, Elliot felt an odd relief that at least now someone knew about Cora and him.

Smith Ingman burst through the door.

"Where's Ermine?" he shouted through gritted teeth, his tone implying an obscenity. His eyes scanned the editorial staff. Ermine sat in their center, legs crossed and hands folded comfortably on his lap.

"I told you not to print that piece," Ingman said, shaking a folded up newspaper before slapping it onto a table. "I spoke with Dodson; he takes a picture of every edition he sends to print. Your article wasn't in it. How did it get there?"

Ermine had not expected that; he had been right not to trust Dodson. His intentionally vague smile wavered, but he did not move until he was sure control—of himself and of the room—was his. When enough of the surrounding group was looking at him, he spoke.

"Simple: I felt justified in including my piece as-is, after-the-fact."

Entitled "Preventing the End by Cutting Off the Means," Ermine's article reasoned that because in hindsight one would not hesitate to kill the baby Adolf Hitler, they also should not hesitate to shut down the return of his ideas, and that these included the yet infant but latently dangerous Spring Shakespeare production, which, considering the *Henry* plays' rationalization of colonialism, may have actually led to European colonialism generally and Hitler specifically.

"I know you did—which is why I told you to change it!"

In his reprimanding email, Ingman had called Ermine's comparing Henry V to Hitler "ridiculous and offensive," and ordered him to moderate his stance. However, reasoning that advocating for merely another director was not enough—and that extending free speech to viewpoints already proven to be catastrophically inhumane was even more ridiculous and offensive—Ermine had ignored the email. Nonetheless, he had prepared himself for this moment; it was why he had gathered most of the other editors with him. Ingman would see that his time was passed.

Ermine raised his chin to speak. "I'm sorry, but this is a newspaper, yes?"

Ingman paused, took a breath, and leaned back against a drafting table, eyebrows raised.

"See, unlike some who write mere hyperbole—no doubt to cover the fact that they are only here for the grade, just another line on their resumes—I actually believe in what I write." Ermine turned his gaze to the others. He chuckled suddenly at the ironic thought that he must look like a patriarch surrounded by devotees; he did not dislike the feeling.

Ingman, however, did not move. Ermine had been prepared for Ingman to roll his eyes, or protest, or offer some other response; he had not expected an unblinking stare.

"This isn't like you, Ermine," Ingman said at length. "I've never heard you openly insult anyone, much less your peers."

"Speaking the truth is always an insult to someone."

Ingman thought for a moment, slowly shaking his head as if not seeing—or not wanting to see—that the words were true.

"But we are here to fight censorship," Ermine continued before Ingman could speak, "not participate in it—even if that means disobeying a teacher who's supposed to be on the side of the press and free speech."

Ingman's eyes widened, but he maintained his crossed-arm stance, saying nothing. After a few moments of looking at Ermine—who, after meeting the gaze for a moment, shifted in his seat, despite knowing himself to be right—Ingman's nostrils flared and his eyes moved to the rest of the group. A few of them swayed in the silent tension. Most of them looked away or at Ermine. Ermine was glad he had warned them that this would happen, and that they had all agreed to walk out with him. The flickers of eyelashes filled Ermine with a dark—no, a just—pleasure.

"You see, professor Ingman," Ermine extemporized into the prolonged silence, "we are not afraid to suffer for our craft, even if it means losing face, or grades, or even credit. We, as student journalists, are the bulwark and highest iteration of speech on this campus, and, much as you have been a mentor to me—to us—we will not allow even your old guard attitudes—one might even say," he paused for brief effect, "your latent conservatism—to stifle what we believe is our duty to speak truth to power, wherever it might be. We are grateful to you and your generation for laying the groundwork for free speech on campus, but it is for us to complete it. We are its product, its heirs, its saviors, and you are either with us or against us."

Somewhere during the speech Ingman had uncrossed his arms; he now supported himself on a desk, one arm braced straight, the other held behind his back. His lips remained tightly closed. However, when Ermine alluded to the Free Speech Movement—a nice touch, he thought—something strange had happened to Ingman's face. While his eyes narrowed and his brows grew stern and more focused, his jaw and white-stubbled dimples began to soften, as if in prelude to a smile; it was not encouraging.

Ingman spoke, in a light, almost mocking tone: "Well, obviously you know what you're doing. I should be proud to have taught you so well.

Personally, if that's the kind of stuff you'll be putting out, I'd rather not be responsible for you from here on. Of course, only *The Praesidium* can use campus printing, and only the official newspaper will carry the university's endorsement, but, if you're talking like that, I'm sure you already have your medium all lined up. Good luck."

If raucous laughter could have a tone of speech, Ermine felt with a sudden chill, that would be it.

More abruptly than he had rehearsed, Ermine stood and stepped toward the door, keeping his back as straight as possible. As planned, the group followed him, though to Ermine's chagrin they hesitated, avoiding Ingman's eyes.

"To the rest of you," Ingman said without turning, "my door is always open—should you realize you've been misled. Keep in mind, I will still need to take attendance and grade what would have been your submissions—meaning, if you follow through with this walk-out, you'll receive zeros for the rest of the semester. But I'm sure Ermine already warned you about that before staging this little coup. Again, good luck."

Even as he exited the room, Ermine felt a shudder of doubt go through the group behind him. The bastard, he thought, trying to hold us hostage via grades. Ermine took a breath to calm himself. Just so long as the others stayed with him. He wiped his sweating palms on his jeans.

It was not until he was at the end of the hall that Ermine turned to address the group. All had followed. He smiled; he had won.

Ermine began in a high tone, "Congratulations, friends: now we all know what it's like to escape from what might have become—or had always been—indentured servitude . . . "

Jonas Templeton continued to draw. Unnoticed, he had listened to the exchange from his drafting table, channeling his reaction into his pencil. Angry as he felt on Ingman's behalf, it was not his place to speak. This was Ingman's fight, and he deserved the right to respond however he would. By the time Ermine left, Jonas had broken four leads, but he had held his tongue.

He waited another moment, steadily finishing a line; when Ingman did not move, he laid down his pencil, stood, and walked to Ingman. Crossing his arms as he leaned against a desk, Jonas asked, "So, what now, professor?"

The relaxed look Ingman had worn as the others exited had turned into a hard frown. The man focused on Jonas, a lift of his eyebrows asking if he, too, planned to leave. He motioned with his chin for Jonas to speak.

"I'm not going anywhere, Smith. Sure, there are things you do that I disagree with, but," Jonas waved a hand toward the door, "I'd never do that. That's just narcissism, as far as I'm concerned, and they deserve whatever they get. You don't need me to insult you by saying I like it here, but I do. I always kind of wondered if you put me on comics because of my beliefs, but I'm proud of my work. I've made some good copy, and you were a big part of that. Whatever your motives, you made me a better journalist."

Ingman looked down, pursing his lips. Jonas looked away, giving the man the privacy to deal with whatever he was going through. He doubted it was just about losing the editorial staff; Ingman really had not seen it coming—much less from his implicit protégé.

"I haven't given you enough credit, Jonas," Ingman said at length, "though once you caught your stride with the strip I really did trust you with it. You always brought a bit of balance; I'm sorry I let you think I was somehow against you all this time."

"Don't mention it—it wasn't that bad, and it made me better. And whatever they say, I know you're actually concerned with free speech and diversity of thought."

"Guess I should've sat in with you and Rydar more often . . . " The man had seemed about to chuckle but stopped, his eyes suddenly widening as they snapped to his copy of the paper on the table. "The article. I need to talk to Rydar!" He looked at Jonas.

"Theater. Want me to come with?"

"No," the man turned to the door, snatching the paper from the table as one might pick up a weapon, "you have a retraction to write."

The tone of contempt in Ingman's voice, and the hard, grinless wink that accompanied it, had the sound of a signature underscoring a contract.

Vesta walked into the theater auditorium. A few were already there, sitting in seats or leaning against the stage. A few rows back from the main group sat Elliot.

After finding him with Cora—not only confirming the suspicion that they were somehow involved but that living with Cora would most definitely stretch her—Vesta had relaxed her opinion of Elliot. Rereading *Pride and Prejudice* over summer had reminded her that one's initial assumptions often needed adjustment, however right they might seem. Besides, she should not expect everyone to have grown up in church as she had. She still thought their actions unwise, but, knowing how Cora could be, Vesta almost felt sorry for Elliot.

"May I . . . ?" She motioned next to Elliot.

"Oh, sure," he said, pulling his feet off the back of the next row.

She lay her bag down next to Elliot and sat in the row's third seat, pulling out her notebook.

"Any idea why Rydar wanted us here today?" A couple of hours ago she had received the brief text calling the cast to an unscheduled discussion.

"You didn't read the article?" Elliot asked, pulling out a rolled up newspaper from under his thigh.

"What article?" Vesta replied, taking Elliot's copy. Any time between class work had been spent researching costumes and reading their plays.

"It's clever. Bad, but clever," Elliot said with the edge of a chuckle.

Vesta found the page and skimmed the article.

"What the fuck?" she exclaimed in spite of herself.

"Wow, Vesta, language," Elliot snickered.

"Sorry," she said. She reread the penultimate paragraph: "*The plot is so biased toward the English that even the king of the aggressed-against country in Henry V agrees with Henry's stealing his land. Can one say psychological colonization? As always, it precedes actual colonization. These plays, I suggest, might threaten to do that very thing here: to prime those who sympathize with such a 'hero' to aggress in his name—and those whom they oppose to let them.*"

"But still," Vesta said, "why would anyone say something like that?"

"Because nothing fun or great can be so anymore. I've been thinking about it. It reminds me of something Rydar said a few weeks ago, about how British Puritan Protestants hated the great art and hierarchy of Catholic tradition. They didn't respond by bringing something greater or more sublime, but by completely reinterpreting greatness, art, even the implicit theology itself, and degrading it. That article seems to do the same, trying to take the highest down to the level of the lowest. There's other examples of it, too, if you think about it. I guess Colson was right about his play, and about how people would react."

"It's unconscionable," said Vesta, creasing the newspaper.

"It's inevitable—probably because it's unconscionable," Elliot said in his same half-laughing tone.

"You sound rather morbidly resigned about it. Excited, even," Vesta noted.

"Don't know how to say it, but it makes me want to fight. Like, if this were a video game I'd be hunting this guy down."

"So you could kill him first?"

"No—so I could let him live knowing he couldn't kill me."

"Hm." Vesta considered the idea. She had always wondered how committed Elliot really was to the play. Despite this being her first time really talking to him, she could tell the animus was new—to him as much as to her.

Rydar Colson stepped out onto stage.

"Circle up," he said, motioning to center of the stage before the living room set of Nilette Lilljedahl's mid-October production of *An Enemy of the People*. The auditorium echoed with wordless shuffling. Vesta saw Elliot and Rydar lock eyes for a moment; Elliot's tightened lips barely withheld a grin as he nodded; Rydar returned the nod and motioned for the boy to sit. A line from *Henry V* came to Vesta's mind—" . . . at his heels, leashed in like hounds . . . " Some tacit agreement had passed between them; it gave Vesta an unexpected courage. She sat next to Elliot.

"If any of you want to quit," Rydar announced once everyone was seated, "now's your latest chance."

No one moved, though a couple—Patrick, Vesta noted—glanced toward the back exit.

Rydar pulled out a copy of the article; he held it up and began to read. There was not a note of scorn in his voice; he read as earnestly as if he had written the article. When he finished he folded the paper. In the silence, he looked at every member of the circle, some briefly, some longer until he was satisfied. Vesta could have sworn he half winked in the twinkling that was her acknowledgment. Colson skipped Elliot.

"Well, what do you think?" the man said with a shrug, stepping into an easy stroll with his hands behind his back.

"I think it's disgusting," Vesta said. "We haven't even started rehearsals, and he's never come to our discussions. He has no idea what he's talking about."

"I think he's right," said Elliot, looking intently at Vesta as if in agreement, "not literally right, but from his premises, he's correct to oppose us. Our play probably is that big a threat to his viewpoint."

"What's the answer then?" asked Rydar, steadily strolling around the group with hands behind his back.

"To correct his premises," said Elliot, "to keep going and prove him wrong."

"But," said Patrick, his voice unsure, "is there something to what he said? I mean, if the play really is fascist or racist . . . "

"And what about that last part?" said Megan, looking around. "I want to do the play, but are we in danger?" Despite his explicitly not calling for action, Jackson had left vague what actions might result—" . . . *for even threatened animals will bite when cornered, especially if it is by the same hand that killed others of their kin.*"

Rydar continued to circle the group, saying nothing.

"But we aren't even setting it in Europe," Vesta said. "America in the fifties was bad, but we're not hiding from that. We shouldn't even have to say it, but it's nothing like Nazi propaganda. For heaven's sake, the US and England had just beaten the Nazis!"

"Someone should invite Jackson to a discussion," Elliot said, grinning.

"Separate our production from the play, itself," said Rydar. "I don't give a damn what that kid thinks; I care about you. Based on the things we've been talking about and what you know of the text, what do you, yourselves, think of Jackson's interpretation of the plays? Is it credible?"

A couple of students leafed through their lines; others looked up to remember.

"Megan," Rydar focused on the girl, apparently noticing a nascent thought, "do you think Prince Hal, as presented by Shakespeare, becomes a colonist?"

Megan leaned back.

"Well, the opening of *Henry V* is all about Harry's claim to France. Harry's not really excited about it until he's sure he has the right to retake it. I mean, maybe he's already decided to invade France and is just looking for a pretext—still shady, but I don't think it's colonial."

"Shady's workable," responded Elliot, who had been fidgeting. "He knows his job is shady. That's why he does it the way he does—to make it less shady. Most of the time he doesn't even want the responsibility he's inherited. But that's what makes him the best one for it. He's no Hitler.

In fact, he spends more time misleading people's support than grasping for it. If it were propaganda, would Shakespeare have shown Hal getting drunk and playing jokes?"

"I agree," said Vesta. "Even at the end of *Henry V*, he could just command Princess Katharine, but he woos her instead. He respects her right to consent; in fact he puts all his work in her hands. If you consider her a symbol of France, you can see Harry's not a colonist, and certainly not a propagandist. He wins by attraction and persuasion, not command. That's what's so bad about the article: it uses things like the French King's respect for Harry as a smear. Like, even if you read that as Shakespeare rewriting history to glorify Henry V, you can't just dismiss the whole play like that."

"If Hal's a tyrant," Megan said, sitting forward and nodding, "he's the least tyrannical one I've ever heard of. I studied actual propaganda last year for a project in my twentieth-century Russia class, and this ain't it."

She looked at Rydar. Arms crossed and leaning against one of the cinderblock walls framing the stage, he nodded for her to continue.

"Propaganda isn't just eulogizing the status quo; it's when the state or other ubiquitous entity tries to artificially replace the organic culture without allowing a counternarrative. Generally speaking, propagandistic states don't have artists like Shakespeare; they can't risk undermining the aesthetic message they're trying to enforce. The fact that Shakespeare even shows the side opposed to Hal makes the plays not propagandistic; it might even make them arguably subversive! Sure, different countries may have different ways of interpreting history, but that's a different thing, and, yeah, like Vesta said," Megan motioned to Vesta, "Shakespeare is pretty generous to the French, just as he's usually generous to the rebelling English in the earlier plays."

"Ermine doesn't know what he's talking about," said Elliot, nodding. "I've talked with him; this isn't the first time he's tried to pass off an important writer with an anachronism. And as for killing an enemy in their infancy . . . you all remember the stuff I said about *The Iliad* a couple of weeks ago and how it can help us understand Hal and Hotspur? The Greeks knew to appreciate the strength of one's enemy; that's why Hal loves Hotspur, even as he fights him, just like the characters in Homer do. The idea of killing an enemy as a child to prevent him from becoming an enemy wouldn't've occurred to either side of the Trojan War—and if it had, both sides would have considered it the lowest you could go."

"Why," Rydar said in the tone of an underscore.

Elliot thought for a moment.

"Because they were men. Not in a sexist way," Elliot held up his hand, though no one had said anything, "the women and the goddesses would have had the same response. I mean, they wanted their enemy to be strong; it made them better and more famous if they defeated him."

"Yes," Rydar responded, "that's excellent, Elliot. You're right: the Greek heroes did not consider defeat something to be feared, so long as they were defeated by someone they could respect. Where else do we see that idea?"

"I mean," Elliot continued, "it's in Aristotle, in his section on picking one's friends; I don't think that's ironic. The Greeks saw enemies and friends in the same way: the greater they were, the greater you were for being at their level."

Part of Vesta had been watching Elliot since sitting next to him; as he spoke he seemed to change—to grow more real—before her eyes, as if someone had turned up the photographic contrast to accentuate the lights and darks of his face. Whereas previously he had offered ironic, disaffected comments during discussions, he now looked as if he were having to hold back a sudden intensity. Vesta felt herself blush as her confusion at his and Cora's relationship gave way to a moment of clarity. If Elliot looked at Cora like this when they were alone, it fit; a girl like Cora could only want someone who would focus on her just like that—who had to watch her with everything in him, either as a lover or rival.

Deciding to consider these things later, Vesta asked, "What do you think, Professor Colson?"

Looking down at the stage, Rydar glanced at Vesta without raising his face. He pursed his lips and sighed.

"No. I could tell you what I think, but it would be superfluous—and demeaning." He shrugged, smiling. "And you can probably guess what I'd say. Isn't it implicit in everything we're doing here? Besides, you already have the sources necessary to form your own conclusions." Rydar pushed forward off the wall, stepping into the circle's center. "That's," he said, looking at each of the members, "what I want you to do as you go home: consider your reasons for being here. I want you to be sure that what you're doing here is good, as good as Shakespeare. If you, yourself, don't find value in being here, then you are free to leave. But, you don't have to fear this article, and you don't have to worry about what people will think, not in any primary way. Worry about what you think; could you be proud of performing these plays? For now, that's all I'm concerned with. Because he who has a why can face almost any what."

He dropped the newspaper on the ground, smiling as if forgetting it in the same moment. Glancing to the back of the auditorium, he paused. Vesta looked over her shoulder.

Cora Madison was walking down the stage right aisle.

"What the . . . " Elliot muttered.

"Professor, I'd like to join your play," Cora said so everyone could hear.

Cora met Colson's eyes as she mounted the stage.

"Haven't you heard?" He crossed his arms and squared his feet. "We're the campus Nazis."

"Please, this isn't *Richard III*," Cora countered.

"You sure?" Rydar said, his voice hard despite his half smile. "You have a bit to catch up with. I still have that part for you, but it's only yours if you're in it for good. You might lose some friends, among other things."

"Why, that's certain," she said in the elevated tone of quoting lines. "'Tis dangerous to take a cold, to sleep, to drink; but I tell you, My Lord Fool, out of this nettle, danger, we pluck this flower, safety."

Vesta recognized Hotspur's response to the cowards who refuse to join his rebellion in *Henry IV Part 1*.

Rydar pursed his lips, withholding the full smile Vesta saw unmasked in his eyes.

"Okay." Rydar turned to the group, ushering Cora a step forward with a hand on her back. "Everybody: your Hotspur."

Vesta cheered; a few people clapped, though a few still looked uneasy. As far as Vesta was concerned, through their discussion and Cora's unexpected appearance the earlier air of dread had given way to a feeling of victory.

"Catch Cora up to speed," Rydar said. "No more discussion today; use the time to really consider what we talked about. If you encounter a question, take it seriously—and don't be afraid: you have the whole of Western tradition behind you. Use it. If you need anything, ask me. I'll be in my office, or text me. But if you do, be ready for more reading." Rydar walked backstage.

Feeling like nothing could stop the play—nor want to—Vesta jumped up and hugged Cora. Elliot paused a moment, looking from where Rydar had gone to the small group greeting Cora. Vesta assumed

Elliot had convinced Cora to join, but though he tried to hide it he, too, looked surprised—and, Vesta thought, slighted—by her appearance.

Vesta ignored the hesitant feeling Elliot's look gave her. She remembered what he had said earlier, that the writer of the article, Ermine Jackson, could not kill him, Harry, or their plays. That Cora had joined— undoubtedly because of the article—proved it; Vesta was almost thankful to Jackson. As Vesta breathlessly explained aspects of their production she had thus far withheld from Cora, the optimism she had always felt while in the theater returned. Only Elliot's stern, wordless face rubbed counter to the feeling. He's probably just miffed Cora didn't tell him she was joining today, Vesta reasoned. She encouraged herself with the thought that for a while Elliot had seemed as unperturbed—and almost as gleeful—as Rydar.

The sidedoor to the theater opened as Smith reached for the handle.

"Oh—Rydar!"

"Afternoon, Smith," said Colson as he stepped out of the building. "You don't normally come this way. Need something?"

Ingman eyed the young man suspiciously, unsure whether or not he was bluffing ignorance.

"It's about the paper. I just wanted to . . . "

Rydar grinned. "A bit strong for the first volley, no?"

"That's what I came to talk to you about," Ingman said, perplexed and relieved by Rydar's easy tone. "I told Ermine to rewrite that article, that we were only pushing for an additional director. You have to understand I'd never have allowed such a thing to print."

Rydar sighed, looking toward the campus. After a moment, he said, "That makes more sense. You don't need to apologize to me, Smith; I know not to believe everything in print, though I appreciate it. Frankly, I'm relieved. You're not responsible if a student goes behind your back. Is discipline in order?"

"Ermine is no longer a part of *The Praes*, though if you ask him he'll say he quit in the name of integrity—his respect for free speech, he said." Ingram shook his head. "I'm out most of my editorial staff, who went with him."

Rydar scoffed quietly, as if unsurprised. "I wonder what will come of it. Poor kid. He's opened himself up with this. He'll have a lot of support, but he showed his cards too early. He's put his face and name on the opposition to this play."

"I have Jonas working on a redaction now. We'll have it on the front page in our next issue. Are you going to fight back?" Ingman asked, glad that Rydar showed little sign of censure. He had expected to have to at least plea for Rydar's understanding, but he found himself being spoken to as an equal, as if Rydar assumed they were on the same side of the issue.

"If by 'fight back' you mean continue with the play, then yes, but I don't think I'll respond directly." Rydar gave Ingman a nod. "That's for others to do. I'm glad you're letting Jonas write. You'll need him. Ermine might not have thought about these issues, but Jonas has. You should ask him his perspective on free speech. You know his grandmother survived the Holocaust?"

"He usually keeps to himself," Ingman said, realizing with growing guilt how little he really knew Jonas. "I don't blame him—he was the only open conservative on the paper." Ingman smiled. "I guess I'm thankful for it, after all."

"Well, if you don't mind my saying, you're a bit of a conservative, too, Smith."

Ingman almost took a step back at hearing the word applied to himself for the second time that hour. At Ingman's shock, Rydar continued, "Or, rather, there are conservative things about you. Politics and culture have moved in recent decades. Things once sacrosanct to all Americans—like the need for free speech, or civility despite disagreement, even the value of classical art and Shakespeare—are now considered conservative, and, therefore, verboten."

Ingman was dumbfounded not just by the words but by the relief they elicited. Expecting Colson to vilify him, he had been met with a smile and inclusion as an ally; he had certainly not expected to learn something about himself—which he would have never uttered but which, he now realized, he had suspected for a long time. He exhaled, feeling as if more than just this day's frustration were sloughing off with the breath.

Showing no recognition beyond an initial moment of eye contact and a quick aversion of his glance, Rydar had continued, "Though, granted, this is a private university, so the First Amendment doesn't really apply, its having been written for the federal government. Ermine will have to learn that there is no such thing as an unrestricted right—that one must be responsible for what one uses it for. He's free to say whatever ideas he wants; he's not free to escape the consequences of doing so.

Wondering if Rydar were speaking proverbially or if he were thinking of something specific, Ingman left it alone, not wanting to spoil the feeling of camaraderie he had regained with the man.

"It's ironic, too," said Rydar, in a different tone, "had Ermine thought it through for two minutes he might've seen that by comparing Henry to Hitler he wasn't bringing Henry down but Hitler up, making him less evil by the comparison—which might be the worst part of it all."

"Why, that's so obvious I didn't even think of it!" Ingman said, putting his palm to his forehead; he wanted to laugh as if the idea were a triumph. It was, he thought; it showed that Ermine had not succeeded in degrading the play.

"Listen, I don't want to tell you how to run your paper—and I fully expect you to continue your critical tack against me—but you should talk with Jonas. He knows more than he says, and thinks more than he knows." Rydar reached out his hand.

"Thank you, Rydar," Ingman said, accepting the handshake.

"And don't worry; I know that kid's on no side of yours, Smith," Rydar said, Smith knew referring to Ermine. "You and I may differ on several things, but we agree on many more. Don't feel you need to apologize or warn me about anything again. Frankly, it's insulting. And who knows—I might know what's coming better than you do."

Ingman merely nodded, intending to ask what he meant in the future but feeling he knew what Rydar meant—and that he was right.

As the director walked toward the campus proper, Ingman took a long way around a nearby park to consider the things Rydar had said. Culling through the memories that might support Rydar's claim about him, Ingman unexpectedly savored the feeling that, regarding at least that part about the conservative perspective—that pertaining to literary tradition—the roles of teacher and student had been reversed. A semester before, Ingman would have balked at the idea that Jonas and Rydar might have something to teach him. Now, having received an undeserved magnanimity from them both in the same hour, Ingman felt reassured in a way he had not felt in years.

❉

Continuing Vexxen down a side path that branched off from the main supply road, Elliot heard in the distance an explosion marking the helicopter's crash. A sidescreen opened up showing his stats for the base attack. After twenty minutes of sneaking, he had impulsively switched to offensive tactics, using his ASVK as a close-range cannon to clear the base of NPCs, eventually dispensing with the helicopter automatically called in when one's avatar was discovered on a base. Sure enough, because he had been seen and had needlessly killed so many guards, his stealth score had dropped. Hiding Vexxen behind a thicket of dry brush, Elliot leaned back, taking a drink of water.

That had been stupid, Elliot thought. If Vexxen had died he would have risked losing most of his gear if another player were nearby; however, the map had shown he was alone in the area. Still, it was not good to be reckless, however rote his stealth tactics had become. Elliot did not consider why he had savored exposing Vexxen to death; he just wanted to relax. Setting his glass down, Elliot turned Vexxen toward a nearby outpost where he could find a jeep to commandeer, hugging by force of habit the side of the cliff against which his camo blended in.

There was a light tap on Elliot's door. He knew the knock. A second later, the key he had given Cora turned in the lock. Elliot did not look in the door's direction as it slowly opened. Cora's scent—a light, rosy perfume she wore—entered the room with her. In spite of his mood, Elliot was taken aback by how much he had come to associate with the scent.

Cora walked through the room and, setting a bag of food down in the kitchen, sat on Elliot's bed. Had she made a noise—a sigh, a word—Elliot would have exited the game. However, she made no sound, instead merely watching him move Vexxen through the brush, with the comfortable silence of taking for granted her being welcome as something more than a guest.

"Goddamn it," Elliot said under his breath as he saw a bright glint off to the south denoting the scope of another player's rifle. Elliot dove Vexxen to the ground, rolling him behind a dilapidated wall. Cora merely watched; Elliot felt he knew the smile she was wearing—the one that was not a smile, that was meant to look as if she did not know or care whether it was seen. Elliot still could not decide if it signaled interest or subtle disdain, nor if he thought it more attractive or more unnerving.

"Jesus—Cora, just give me a minute," he said.

"Take your time; I'm enjoying it."

Equipping his thermal goggles, Elliot peeked around the wall. There was no one in the grass where he had seen the glint; scanning, he saw the female avatar sprinting around the crevasse's perimeter. Elliot rolled Vexxen out, took aim, and fired. Running erratically, the other avatar ran through the small plume of dust made by his bullet. Then, their heat signature disappeared.

Elliot cursed. They must have activated some cooling buff. This player knew how to fight other snipers.

"You got this, baby," said Cora.

"Just . . . " Elliot started but bit his tongue. He removed Vexxen's thermal goggles and went to equip his smoke grenades—which he had run out of at the previous base. He rolled back behind the wall to call in a supply drop. Though Cora had done nothing to prompt it, Elliot felt he should explain and excuse his present distress.

Suddenly, Vexxen's avatar was lifted off the ground and slammed on his back. In an instant, the small figure was visible. She had used optic camouflage, turning herself practically invisible for up to twenty seconds; Elliot had considered buying it the few times he had had enough credits. He wished he had.

The avatar wore desert camo similar to Vexxen's, with a black balaclava, which, due to a certain game mechanic, also hid her identity. She aimed a pink 1911 handgun at Vexxen's face, but rather than pull the trigger before the knockout timer above Vexxen ran out, she did a skipping dance. In the chat read the message, "*Lol, get good, noob.*" With that, the other avatar disappeared, having either teleported back to her base or logged out.

"What was that about?" Cora asked.

"Oh, that kind of thing happens all the time, though it usually ends in being totally looted."

"Huh. Cute."

"It's probably a dude," Elliot said, shutting his mouth at the slight snap of his words. He did not look at Cora's reaction.

Elliot exited the game, unable to process his luck and humiliated that he had been ambushed by one player.

"I take it that's a relief?" Cora slipped her hands onto Elliot's shoulders, feeling down his chest as she rested her chin on his head.

"Yeah," Elliot said, feeling sheepish at how worried he had gotten. However, he fought back the feeling; he was right to have been worried, even if Cora would not understand. He might not even have lost had she not shown up when she did.

"Shoot me a text next time before you come over, 'kay?"

Cora's hands paused; Elliot felt her swallow against the top of his head. As he put his computer to sleep, his monitors went blank. In their reflection he saw what he had expected: a light, knowing smile on her face.

With the same reckless feeling that had made him tempt fate with Vexxen not ten minutes before, he said, "Sorry—I guess I shouldn't expect texts from you about your plans."

Cora merely exhaled a single chuckle as she stood up and removed her arms from around Elliot's neck.

"What's wrong, baby?"

"That's just it: I'm not your baby, Cora."

"Oh not this again . . . " said Cora, turning and putting her hands on her hips.

"Yes, this again," Elliot said, rotating his chair around and speaking as much to himself as to her, "and you should have told me you were thinking of joining the play. But then you just walk in, just like you walked into Rydar's class, and in here . . . " He stopped, needing to speak but knowing that with the key and the past few weeks' late nights and lazy afternoons he had given her every right to walk into his apartment.

"No, no, I didn't earn this. You've never complained when I showed up like that, and our not labeling things never seemed to stop you from jumping on me when I did. And you're right, I didn't tell you I was joining because I didn't decide until that day. Besides, you didn't seem to have a problem my being there every other day this week. Are you just mad you lost at your game?"

"Oh, whatever," Elliot said, feeling backed into a corner of his own making, "since when do you care—I mean really care—about me? You just do what you want."

"I wouldn't be here if I didn't; I care because I want you," Cora said sharply before closing her eyes and taking a breath. After exhaling slowly, she said, "I'm not talking to you like this. You know what I think about labels, and getting mad at me for doing what you wanted is stupid. Text me when you're over it and ready to hang out."

Calmly, with the same air as before, Cora turned, took the bag from the kitchen floor, and moved toward the door.

"Wait, Cora—," Elliot stood, about to apologize and ask her to stay.

"No, Elliot," she cut him off, "not tonight. The worst thing you could do right now is beg. I don't want an apology; I'm not even mad. When you've thought, slept, or jerked your way past all this, let me know."

Cora leaned in and pecked him on the cheek before she succinctly pushed past him. The door's shutting was as quiet as had been its opening.

CHAPTER 7

"GODDAMN IT," FRANK Hoegren said, stifling a greater curse as he stood up from his desk. The door to his office was open, and he did not want to startle Marcie, his elderly secretary. Rubbing his beard, he thought a moment; he resisted glancing at the text on his computer. Impulsively, he called to Marcie.

"Yes, Frank?" she asked, leaning into his doorway.

"Get Grey Maxwell up here."

To her credit, the old woman merely widened her eyes, the edge of a smile on her lips. She disappeared back to her desk. Frank listened to her, hearing the dial tone on the other line. When the other end picked up, Hoegren stepped out from behind his desk, turning away from the blog article on the screen.

Walking over to the window, he opened one of his glass-doored cabinets and pulled out a decanter of gin and two glasses, pouring the clear, juniper-scented liquor into one. Swallowing the sharp drink down, he kept his eyes on the blue sky outside, not trusting himself to say anything; it would have started eventually.

The Orangedale IT Department, ever finding new ways to attract prospective students, had the previous week unveiled the new inter-campus social media site, "*Orangeware*." It functioned like many social sites, providing students the ability to build their own profiles, friend each other, and blog ideas. The site had a phone app so students could easily contribute to the campus community while on the run; they even had the option of linking it with other social media sites.

Browsing Orangeware, Hoegren had found, among the other burgeoning student forums, the blog, *The Homefront*. The blog's inaugural article—*"An Open Letter of Introduction,"* by Ermine Jackson—lay open on his desktop; Hoegren kept his eyes on the sky outside. Sparse clouds were gathering, and the temperature had been growing colder. Hoegren put his hands in his pockets, leaning his shoulders back as he forced a steady breath.

Expanding upon the *Praes* article that had allegedly caused some trouble at the newspaper and prompted the founding of *The Homefront*, Jackson had this time called not only for the cancelling of the Spring production but also the removal of Shakespeare from the Orangedale curriculum. Calling Shakespeare's popularity, *"an innocent error of cultural centrism at best, a self-reinforcing assumption of racial dominance at worst,"* Jackson wrote that, *"the default fame of Shakespeare's work—notably given him by people of his own race and culture—should decrease so that others' might increase . . . by self-defensive, liberating force, if necessary."* Hoegren had to fight not to take personally Jackson's claim that their appointing only one director was indicative of, *"the authoritarian tone of the History plays."*

Hoegren sipped his gin, considering Ermine's next line: *"This should not surprise us; for once, we see the intolerance of their monochromatic perspective on art."* Admitting to himself his personal preference for pre-twentieth-century drama, Frank could nonetheless think of nothing more monochromatic than a theater without Shakespeare.

However, Jackson had saved the worst for the final paragraph: *"Until the oppressive weight of the tradition represented by Shakespeare is directly overturned and replaced by previously repressed—because more diverse— plays, then no excuses of 'historical context,' 'artistic tradition,' or 'tolerance of perspectives' can mean anything. 'Freedom of expression' only reinforces the power imbalance of the status quo, whether we're talking about political discourse, historical narratives, or prominence of artistic figures—even Shakespeare."* It read like the mid-nineteenth century Russian revolutionary pamphlets Hoegren had assigned years ago when teaching Chekov; he shuddered as he considered where those pamphlets had led—and that the sublimity of Chekov and his contemporaries had not been able to stop it.

A while later Hoegren heard a patient step behind him.

"He's here, Frank," said Marcie.

"Thank you, Marcie," Hoegren said, turning to see Maxwell at the door. Hoegren merely greeted him with a nod, holding up an empty glass in the next moment. Maxwell looked at Hoegren for just a moment, then nodded, smiling. As Hoegren poured him a glass, he heard Maxwell relax into the chair.

"No," Hoegren said, motioning to his computer screen, "read this."

Maxwell stepped around the desk, accepting the tumbler of gin as he looked down at the screen. Oddly, Hoegren felt embarrassed, aware of the contrast between his dress slacks, button down, and tie and Maxwell's jeans, flannel shirt, and ball cap. He often felt this; it made him miss his office in the theater. He knew it was part of why he had called the man up to Ad Hill.

"Oh, that," said Maxwell.

"You've read it?"

"Yes."

"And?"

"At least now the kid's being honest; it'll make it easier to deal with. I'm kind of relieved Ingman kicked them out. He's a good man, Ingman, or at least not a bad one. Wouldn't want this kind of thing sticking to him."

"I suppose you're right. But damn it, I'd hoped it wouldn't get this far. I knew it would—from the beginning, I knew!—but . . . Has Rydar seen it?"

"You didn't need to call me up here to know he'll be fine. You did your part, Frank. This," Maxwell motioned to the screen, "is for Rydar and the rest to fight. By the time production really starts up next term, they'll be ready." The thin man walked to one of the chairs and sat.

"I suppose so," said Hoegren, sipping his gin.

"Not that I'm worse for the walk." Maxwell waved the hand holding his glass, extending one finger to the room. "You've done well for yourself."

"It's a waste of time and space."

Maxwell chuckled. For a while they just sat, Maxwell in the chair, Hoegren leaning back against the low cabinet, neither speaking.

Hoegren knew Maxwell; he was a perennial optimist. It was what often infuriated Hoegren about the man; it was also why they got along—why they had produced so many successful plays over the years. They had not worked together directly for the most recent of them, not since Hoegren had been promoted to Ad Hill. Nonetheless, he was familiar enough with Grey to know the man would sit there until dismissed—not as an employee, but as a friend.

"You know," volunteered Maxwell, his voice low and unassuming, "the first Shakespeare play I worked on was *Measure for Measure*? I was fourteen," the man chuckled, "no fourteen year old should read that play. Anyway, it was a community theater out in Chattanooga. I was supposed to help change the sets between scenes—had these tall, wooden cutouts. Beautiful." The man smiled, grasping the gin between both hands, his elbows propped up on the chair arms. "Anyway, there I am, dressed all in black, and somehow I trip, and my pant leg gets caught up in one of the wheels. End up twisting my ankle really bad. So, the lights go up, and I'm rolling around, whimpering and trying to get off stage, when the man playing the Duke comes out badly disguised in an undersized priest's habit and lifts me right up on his shoulder like I was a twig.

"That was part of the humor—they'd cast the biggest, most unmistakable man as the disguised Duke, and he was a truck. Anyway, he was already giving his lines to Claudio—it was the prison scene at the beginning of act three—and he doesn't take me off stage. Instead, he goes through the first quarter of his speech trying to find an empty cell to put me in among the line of background convicts we had onstage. Eventually he got me offstage by just handing me to the convicts, who, taking his cue, carry me off to prison."

Maxwell started laughing steadily to himself, his watery, blue eyes looking down into the wood of Hoegren's desk. Hoegren smiled with the man, knowing that if he gave Maxwell time, he would not regret it. Through his noiseless chuckles, Grey continued, "There was ice ready for me offstage. I don't remember the pain—just the sound of the Duke's voice. There was never a break, never even the question of what to do. Sometimes I doubt if he knew I was injured, though I can't see how he could've missed it. But it didn't matter: the show went on, and people eventually laughed."

"So, why tell me that story, in particular?"

"Well, I've seen a lot since then, and a lot of Shakespeare, with more bad productions than I like to give gossip. But something I've seen is you can't beat him—Shakespeare. You can't ruin him. You think there's something in the way, you think there's a problem, but he's already ahead of you. He's the Duke in priest's clothing, if you'll pardon the expression, and he's the biggest one on the stage."

"I know, I shouldn't worry," Hoegren said, suddenly exasperated as he looked back at the screen, "but what happened, Grey? How did students come to—."

"Shut up, Frank."

Grey said the words without ire or guile. Hoegren took a breath, closing his lips sheepishly.

"You need to let them figure this out. You aren't the one onstage." Grey's voice was slow, but hard, like an old stereo that crackled from time to time under the weight of its own current. "I wonder, sometimes, what would've happened if they'd stopped that scene—they should've, by today's standards. That man would be sued, nowadays, for more than just my ankle, and the production would have been shut down," Grey pointed to the computer, "just like what that little son of a bitch is trying to do. I'd still remember it, but I'd've learned a completely different lesson, which I'll reserve the pleasure of not naming so as not to waste your courtesy and your gin. But if our kids are going to learn what that man taught me—that sometimes there are more important things than avoiding even the worst pain—they'll need to risk twisting their ankle."

Hoegren nodded. He had only heard Maxwell speak harshly a few times over the years; he was both sad and thankful that Maxwell had felt the need to do so now.

"Thank you, Grey. I wish it hadn't started so soon, and I wish Rydar hadn't been so right. Still, I need to remember he has more tricks up his sleeve."

"Shakespeare, too." Grey reached his hand forward to place the empty glass on the desk, standing up and stepping to the door. Turning around in the doorway, he looked hard at Hoegren. "It had to be this way, Frank. Greatness attracts enemies. That kid thinks he's the main character; in his world, he is. But what he doesn't see is that by taking on an enemy, especially someone like Shakespeare, he's made himself a side character, a foil. He's only going to make the show bigger and better—if it's as worth putting on as Rydar thinks. I know it is, you know it is, and he knows it is. And I think, at some level, the boy who wrote that blog knows it is. Don't you worry, Frank. You're not wrong, but we have more allies than you think. A lot of people will want to see this play, once all is said and done. Truth will out."

Maxwell tipped his ball cap as he left, not waiting for Hoegren's response, knowing he did not need to. After a moment, Hoegren turned around to look outside.

Slipping the gin back down into the cupboard, he thought he would relax tonight—take Angela to a movie or something. He had been right to trust his impulse to call Grey, if only to remind himself that he did not need to worry about being without allies. Hoegren did not dwell on the fact that it was not himself whom he worried would be caught defenseless and alone before the noxious wave the blog seemed to forebode.

Vesta was noticing Jonas more often. She had caught him looking at her, now as in that first meeting in August; it often left her smiling.

Vesta had first met him a couple of weeks ago. Since walking in on Cora and Elliot, she had found in the costume department a quiet haven where she could read or study in peace. However, arriving early one day to work on an essay, her quiet was interrupted by a high-pitched whine, followed immediately by an industrial shriek. After a few repetitions, Vesta had gotten up in frustration. Vesta's steps flagged halfway across the stage; she knew she was being foolish and that, in reality, she was the interloper. Besides, Vesta liked Mr. Maxwell.

However, rounding the corner, she did not see a head of gray but of dark brown. The young man was at the wall, easing a circular saw down a vertical piece of plywood. Covering her ears, Vesta observed him. He was relaxed, comfortable even, taking his time as the blade steadily ripped through the wood. The smell of sawdust was not unpleasant.

Finishing the cut, the boy lifted the wood from its stand on the saw and, turning, paused upon seeing Vesta. Smiling, he set the wood down, removed his gloves, goggles, and earplugs, and looked at her expectantly.

Vesta had only intended to ask him to postpone the work, yet they talked until people came for the day's classics discussion, pausing at intervals for his continued cuts. To his credit, Jonas did not make Vesta feel as if she were interrupting. She realized only later that she had not introduced herself.

Vesta had kept coming to the costume shop early, but now it was not merely to be alone or avoid her dorm. If she did not hear Jonas working, she would find some excuse to go into the main theater. At first their brief interactions left her berating herself, but Jonas's consistent smile had encouraged her. She had even heard him walk past the costume shop a couple of times—and she had noticed her noticing it.

Now, Jonas sat on a floormat in the backstage workshop, wearing his usual safety glasses and earbuds. Vesta wondered what he listened to. He never bobbed his head—in fact, when he was working he hardly even blinked. Above him across two sawhorses lay the stack of variously shaped plywood Vesta had seen him cut the previous week. He was reviewing some papers; another glance told Vesta they were sketches.

Jonas looked up. His smile curled, but he did not stand. Vesta motioned to the papers. Still seated, he paused his phone and removed an earbud, motioning her over with a movement of his chin.

"Skyscrapers," he said. "I'll be painting soon, and I'm just getting them in order." He had added colored pencil to the sketches, varying the buildings between a brick-brown to steel grey.

"Are those the colors you're using?" Vesta asked, considering an idea.

"More or less. What's up?"

"Well, what if we coordinate a bit? When you pick out the paint, I mean," she said, standing above him yet suddenly feeling like a child.

The young man looked down at his sheets, thumbing through a few. Stacking them neatly, he looked at her full-face. "That is an excellent idea."

He reached out his hand for her to help him up. She took it, feeling the sudden tightness of a laugh in her chest as he stood; he did not need her help to stand.

"So, when are you free? To go pick out the paints with me?"

"Oh, um, I'm free now, if we're back by five." Vesta looked up at the wall; the clock read 3:45. She realized she had come to the theater for no other reason than to see Jonas.

"We'll just about make it," Jonas said, checking his wristwatch. "Let me get my stuff. Want to bring any color references?" He motioned toward the costume room.

"No, I'll be fine. Just let me get my bag."

"Good. Oh, and," he said, lightly touching her arm as she turned, "we haven't formally met; I'm Jonas."

"I know," she smiled, trying to swallow a sudden hiccup. "I'm Vesta."

"I know," he returned the smile, his wink reminding her distinctly of their director.

❋

"He doesn't seem like he'll stop the play," Gemma said to the rest of *The Homefront* writers seated aroun Ermine's dorm room.

"Well, of course not," Ermine said, ignoring Gemma's pleading yet insolent tone, as well as her stating the obvious. "We haven't pushed back enough. Colson's been unthreatened so far. Has everyone been promoting *The Homefront*?"

Nods of different depths all around; Ermine noted those who seemed unconvinced or hesitant.

The Homefront had taken to meeting like this, sharing their pieces and discussing ideas for future ones. Some who had left *The Praes* with Ermine had returned to the paper, earning nothing but scorn from the remaining *Homefront* members. However, with their dereliction there had come others.

"Well, we need to step it up," Ermine said. "Ingman's kept *The Praes* going somehow. He finally moved online, and he's been accepting op-eds from other students and faculty. Even gave Jonas a shot." Ermine wanted to spit at the idea. "God, they're pathetic; we should have their readership!"

"Plus," said Gemma, "they've backed off on fighting the play and are even implicitly supporting it now. Really shows you we were right to leave; Ingman was just a puppet, after all."

Sounds of general agreement. Ermine bit back his response—that their agreement meant nothing without more popular support. They needed solidarity, too.

"We should do the same thing," Carl said, "have people start writing for us. Even if we overestimated how many people would read us, it's just a testament to the university's unfair perspective on free speech. They don't give us a voice on campus equal to *The Praes*, so we have to take it. Start getting students and faculty to push *The Homefront* in their classrooms."

"Yes," affirmed Gemma, "and push to condemn *The Praes* for taking so long to move to paperless. It's an atrocity that they were still printing physical copy until recently—a crime against the planet and humanity. Maybe have the university put us side-by-side with them on the campus website. Then we'll see who gets the most readers."

"And," said Carl, "we could make them limit *The Praes*' readership— like if they get a certain number above us it'll block them so people will have to read us."

"Not a bad plan, though I doubt the university would agree to that much equality," sneered Ermine; a few snickers met the comment.

"What we really need," said Skylar, "is someone who can sabotage the play—or, better yet, that director, Colson. What do we know of him, besides his being a parallaxophobe?"

Transferring to Orangedale a month into the semester, Skylar Evans had almost immediately found their way into *The Homefront*, declaring themself as being of non-binary gender and interested in, "outing others who refuse to admit they are, too, as well as those who have a problem with it." As such, Skylar's rhetoric was as sharp as the jet-black spikes combed sideways on their head, which contrasted with the foundation-enhanced whiteness of the face beneath them.

Skylar had decried in their first post how oppressively onerous it was to have to name each sin of those who did not believe in sexual, gender, and racial rights, and how in the more refined Eastern European world of the 20th century there had been a now lost term that contained all perspective shifts a society or individual needed to make to reach final, singular equality: "synthetic parallaxis." Ermine had noticed that the word, as well as the reverence with which Skylar had first introduced it, had spread throughout the comments, as had its corollary, "parallaxophobe," which usefully contained all the social phobias *The Homefront* sought to combat.

"As for sabotaging the play," Ermine said, smiling, "I've got that covered—I have an ace-in-the-hole, possibly two, if another cast member wakes up. I wouldn't be surprised if she's playing a deeper game, too. Colson, though," Ermine paused, frowning, "I'm sure he can't be squeaky clean. Men like him rarely are."

"Do some digging?" asked Gemma, flexing her upper lip into a grin.

"Sure, though I haven't found anything online, just an obituary from a decade ago in a Korean newspaper in LA; we might need to wait for an opportunity. Anyway, speaking of sabotage . . . " Ermine stood, his tone brightening as he reached into his mini-fridge and pulled out a bottle of sparkling rosé. "Today is November fifth!"

"So?" asked Carl, wiping his chronically leaking nose.

"Many years ago today," Ermine assumed a gentle affect, "around the same time Shakespeare was reinforcing the plague we are still fighting, a lone man was willing to put everything on the line and risk death to blow up British parliament, and the king with it. Would that we might have the courage to risk capture and torture to stand thus against the status quo—the patriarchy, the military-industrial complex, and the fascism of modern capitalism—even as Guy Fawkes stood against the brutal Protestants. Although one shouldn't yearn for the strangling Catholic hierarchy he hoped to return to power, he is a symbol of our fight—which is the same fight against all oppressive states, both visible and invisible."

While speaking, Ermine had passed around a stack of red, plastic cups which he subsequently filled.

"Cheers, everyone, to the last honest man to enter a body of ruling white men."

They all raised the rosé in toast and drank quietly, some assuming a thoughtful aspect, others looking bored.

"Yeah, but torture," said Carl, "I hope it doesn't come to that."

"Oh, I doubt it will," returned Ermine. "We're in the right, and we have more numbers than Fawkes did. We've had enough oppression; it's time we have a turn at power."

"Yes," said Skylar, "that gives me an idea. We need to accompany our words with actions; we knew it would come to it. Frankly, when I came here I was surprised you weren't already putting physical pressure on the school. Nothing violent yet, but if there are Nazis on campus we need to aggress before they do—and if history tells us anything, they will. They need to know we won't just roll over this time."

"I'm all for protesting," said Carl, avoiding eye contact with Skylar, who seemed to scare the freshman, "but really? Nazis? I don't like the Shakespeare play either, but—."

"It's either or, Carl," Skylar snapped. "Either you're with us, or you're against us—and, in the end, if you aren't with us, then you want the same kind of things the Nazis wanted. Even Shakespeare is closer to fascism than he is to parallaxis—which is why he must be sacrificed if we're ever to experience equity. Reread Ermine's article; it's what made me know I could respect this group."

Skylar gave a hard nod to Ermine, to which Ermine gave a token bow and smile. Carl leaned back against the wall and quietly wiped his nose, eyes still wide.

Ermine had recognized Skylar's usefulness immediately—the junior could do things Ermine could not, and their blunt-force presence would leave Ermine free to pick up and arrange the pieces with finesse. Skylar would make everyone grateful for Ermine; Ermine could safely become the more palatable alternative.

Ermine sipped his rosé, letting Skylar bring the group into align-
ment in ways that they could not see but Ermine could. Literally, they
were discussing which friends they could call up, from campus and other
areas, to form a protest outside the theater building. However, implicitly,
Ermine could see in Skylar's filtering of their ideas a game of cat and
mouse—or sheepdog and sheep, though Ermine resented the metaphor's
negative connotation for those willing to follow the right ideas. Nonetheless, Ermine found the similarity between Skylar's hair and face and the
black and white of a border collie's face amusing—as well as the way the
young person's eyes would suddenly focus should a group member accidentally reveal a deficiency in their position or passion for it.

There were moments when Skylar shocked even Ermine; Ermine
would just shrug, thinking that no one was perfect and that he should
be thankful for someone who could finally help him prevent colonized
perspectives in those around him.

Elliot saw the crowd before he heard it; yet, behind his idle conversation
with Cora a murmur had already set his jaw on edge. After the tension of
their fight had subsided the next day in an afternoon of apology that was
more physical than verbal, Elliot and Cora had regularly walked to the
discussion group together. They rarely saw anyone on the way; now they
paused. Perhaps twenty people stood outside the theater's main entrance.

"Here, let's go this way," Elliot said, retaking Cora's hand as he
turned toward the nearby street. Staring as if looking for someone, Cora
followed.

Walking down the opposite sidewalk, they avoided glancing at the
crowd. A few voices rose above the din, speaking in a half-belligerent
tone to no one and everyone.

Past the building, Elliot and Cora crossed the street, keeping an
even pace to avoid drawing attention. It reminded Elliot of sneaking past
a guard checkpoint in *Vanguard Pulse*.

They were crossing the back parking lot when some men Elliot did
not recognize came around the building.

"Oh shit," one of them exclaimed behind him, "they're going in the
back!"

"Go!" Cora cried, pushing Elliot toward the door. He pulled her inside, locking the door before the men slammed against it. With muffled curses they kicked and pulled ineffectively at the door's deadbolt.

"What the hell?" Elliot uttered.

"I didn't recognize anyone in that crowd," she said. "Some looked too old to be students."

"We need to tell Colson," Elliot answered. "You okay?"

"Mm-hmm." She still seemed as if she were still trying to discern something from the crowd. Elliot would ask about it later.

They walked past the green room to the stage. A few people were already there; Rydar was on his cell phone, pacing.

"Alright, Frank . . . No, I can deal with it. Still, get campus security down here . . . Looked like fifteen to twenty. A couple heckled me as I came in, but more have arrived, and my group's a bit shaken up." Rydar winked at Elliot and Cora. "Two just had to sneak in the back. I know this kind of thing—they'll get worse the longer there's no response. Campus security can check their ID's, but if they refuse to leave I'll need you to call the police . . . Alright, sounds good." Rydar closed his phone, eyebrows raised at Elliot.

"We tried to get in the back without their noticing," Elliot said, "but they chased us to the door."

"You did fine. Okay, everyone, circle up. We'll get this taken care of, but in the meantime, are any of you reading Dostoevsky?"

A couple raised their hands.

"*Devils*, or *The Possessed*?"

Only Megan's hand remained up.

"You might be the bravest one here, today, Megan." Rydar smiled, releasing some of the tension in the group. "How far are you?"

"Only about a quarter through. It's hard keeping the names straight."

"Yes; are you using summaries—enough to understand what's happening and where the plot's heading?"

"Yeah, a bit."

"Then tell the rest of them. It's not irrelevant today. You, you, and you," Rydar pointed to a few people, landing on Elliot, "come with me, and be ready to record with your phones. Jonas!" he yelled, his voice booming through the theater rafters.

"Yup?" called a voice backstage, followed by a face marked with paint and wearing safety glasses.

"Give me a hand."

Jonas went backstage and, after a few moments, returned, drying his hands. Rydar had pulled a red dry erase marker out of his bag.

Cora joined the small group as they left the stage. Rydar nodded.

Looking back at the stage, Elliot noticed Patrick sitting next to Megan, who was speaking. His wide, unblinking eyes were fixed on Rydar's back; making eye-contact with Elliot, Patrick turned his glance away.

"Here they come—racists go home, racists go home!"

Fist in the air, Skylar only needed to yell a couple of times before the crowd took up the chant. The fuse was lit; Ermine would not need to worry about the play from now on. If calling them racists was not enough, the crowd could easily be pushed to call the theater group fascists, Nazis, anything Skylar wanted. It was true, Skylar thought: they were those things. If they refused to recognize it and back down, the protest could easily move to the administration building.

Skylar knew many of the individuals in the crowd—had called them from other, state-funded colleges to aid in the protest. When it came to ensuring the voice of progress would not be ignored, they were professionals. Many were people of color; they had been called specifically by design. Some Skylar knew from other protests, fighting the same oppression then as today.

Allowing the more vociferous members of the crowd to take the lead, Skylar had faded to the side to watch the small group of males—probably all cisgender, Skylar thought with a sneer—stream into the lobby behind the glass walls. However, Skylar was suddenly distracted by a young woman of color, whose gaze scanned the crowd and apparently found what it was looking for in Skylar. The two held each other's eyes; by the time the girl broke her glare away, her nostrils flaring in disgust, Skylar knew to remember her face. She was the most dangerous person in there—because the greatest unknown quantity, and the least expected.

The bearded, blonde man, who must have been Colson, had rolled out a dry erase board from a lobby wing. On it, in red marker, he had written, "*Be formally advised: you have created an unsafe, threatening, and oppressive environment for Orangedale students.*" Disgusted at the man's attempt to spin the situation, Skylar watched as Colson periodically cast a look of disapproval at the crowd from beneath his furrowed brow. He continued to write: "*Campus security and Orangedale City police have been called. Anyone without Orangedale campus ID will be removed for trespassing. Your blocking of entryways and pursuit of our students can be considered acts of physical aggression and may be prosecuted as such.*"

"Aw shit," yelled a large black man with a red and white shemaugh tied around a bundle of dreadlocks, "they want to suppress our right to speech! Fascists, go home!"

The crowd roared; Skylar smiled. The disappointment at Colson's not opening the door to negotiate had turned to glee; he had still played into their hand. Who was Colson, a white male professor, to talk—or write—about oppression?

Skylar felt relieved. Despite their chants, the crowd had flagged as they first read the whiteboard; they had not expected to have their own language usurped and used against them. The large man with the shemaugh—a veteran protester—had known what to do. Now the crowd was jumping, yelling righteous obscenities at the glass. Many had their phones out, recording, as did a few in the lobby. More had joined them. Good, thought Skylar, it would only make the protest stronger.

Nonetheless, his piece written, Colson stood, observing the crowd from behind crossed arms. For just a moment—a second for which Colson would never be forgiven—Skylar balked at his intransigent face. He was staring down each member of the crowd, and where his eyes went the crowd quieted. They skipped over Skylar. This man, Skylar realized, would not be cowed.

Skylar grabbed the sleeve of a woman near the back of the crowd. "Do it," they said beneath the din.

In the next moment, even as Colson saw it coming and yelled to those with him, the woman let fly a brick at the glass window. The window burst, and the crowd pushed forward as those in the lobby scattered.

Skylar realized something was wrong; large, hanging shards still dangled from the upper window frame. Unlike windows at other colleges where Skylar had protested, this glass was not tempered. In the next moment, those in the second row of the crowd were trying to pull back, crying out in dismay. In the spaces between the bodies, Skylar saw flashes of blood.

"Fuck, somebody call nine-one-one!" yelled a voice in the chaos. The crowd had already started to scatter, shocked out of their offensive by the need to both avoid the large, precariously dangling icicles of glass and pull to safety those who had been cut by the window's stalagmites.

Directing his students to stay back, Colson dialed a number on his phone and handed it to a thin boy with dark, curly hair. He then leapt forward to cautiously help up those who had fallen.

From amidst the still-lit embers of the back half of the crowd, the large man in the shemaugh stepped forward, as if to protect those crying in front from the unwanted help. In his hand was a pistol. Before Skylar could yell to stop him—that they were already beaten, that sirens could be heard, and that such tactics should be saved for later—the man's wrist was in Colson's hand. Apparently, the director, too, had seen the gun, and, stepping forward, had grabbed the arm before it could raise the weapon. With a shove, Colson pushed the wrist against the side window frame. Skylar saw the remaining glass shards sink into the arm; the big man howled as he stumbled back, shredding the back of his hand as he pulled it from Colson's grip. Beneath the yell Skylar could see rather than hear the thud of the pistol against the carpet. Its black metal was spattered with red.

Preparing to evade the scene at the approach of the police and paramedic sirens, Skylar was stopped cold. The bearded man's eyes had found him; next to Colson stood the black girl who had accompanied the group. She was pointing at Skylar, speaking into the man's ear. Skylar could not hear her words over the sirens and the wailing of injured protesters, but it was unmistakable: now Colson knew who had really been in charge of the protest. The man's unwavering glance, as well as the sudden lack of a surrounding crowd, left Skylar feeling naked and withered—and deeply afraid in a way they had never felt before. Without thinking, Skylar broke into a run, sprinting toward a field of dry grass that bordered the university's southern edge just beyond the theater parking lot.

Halfway through the lot, Skylar was dimly aware of a police car pulling up. It did not matter—anything to get away from the sight of those eyes and the surety and judgment they contained.

CHAPTER 8

"Student Protest Ends in Injury"
—Sybil Braitwaithe, University Liaison, Orangedale Daily Root

Wednesday, November 12th:
  A weekly discussion group at the Orangedale University theater became more than many bargained for yesterday as, accusing the director of the Spring Shakespeare Festival of racism, a group of protesters broke through a panel of untempered glass, leading to several injuries. One student said they were just trying to prevent the spread of unacceptable ideas on campus: "As a person of color, I find it demeaning and offensive that we're still having this fight. We won't sit in the back of the bus, and we won't tolerate a play that wants to put us there."
  Apparently set in the 1950s, the production of Henry IV Parts 1 and 2 deals with how young people should respond to a shaken and unreliable world, said cast member Cora Madison. According to Madison, who will portray the first play's antagonist, Hotspur, the choice to set it in the '50s was intentional: "The England of Shakespeare's play had changed, and the younger generation had to figure out how to survive and deal with the problems their fathers left for them. In the same way, 1950s America was still shaken by World War II and Korea, and they were trying to figure out how to live, even while still dealing with the long-term social effects of southern-state prejudice. I think we're presenting the ideas that led to the Civil Rights Movement, which allowed me to be at this college in the first place. If self-respect, patience, knowing who you are and want to be, and respecting the past with a view to the future are racist, then not much isn't."
  Madison was behind the glass when a brick thrown from outside broke the window, causing several minor injuries to those in the front of the protest who fell on the glass. Most experienced cuts

and were bandaged at the scene, while one protester experienced abdominal injury. He has gone through surgery and is reportedly on the mend. Police recovered a gun from the scene, apparently carried by one of the protesters. The director, English professor Rydar Colson, was unavailable for comment as he helped paramedics with students and gave statements to police.

We contacted the University regarding their plans for the future, but according to theater head, Frank Hoegren, the show will go on. "We might replace the rest of those panels with tempered glass, though. Never know—one forgets how easy it is to mistake a brick for one's student ID when coming to campus these days."

—Sybil Braitwaithe
@thebraiway
University Liaison
Orangedale Daily Root

❧

"Mr. Hoegren, your two o'clock is here," Marcie's voice sounded over Frank's intercom.

Frank tapped the response button. "Thanks, Marcie; send them in."

The name on Hoegren's schedule had been John Atwater, with the note "*-has an interesting offer from members of the city.*" Frank had been intrigued, but Marcie could tell him nothing else. She had seemed as if she knew more than she would say, but Hoegren had been too distracted by dealing with the fallout from the theater protest to query further.

The door opened; in walked two figures: a middle-aged, slightly overweight man wearing jeans and a loose, pastel yellow polo, and, in a red suit and skirt with matching leather bag, Hoegren's wife Angela.

"Dearest, what are you . . . ?" It was the middle of the week, and Angela should have been teaching.

"Frank, I'm here on business," Angela said, the pride in her eyes belying her even tone. "John, go ahead."

The man stood up straight and, extending a manila envelope, said, "Mr. Hoegren, I'd like to volunteer my property to be used for rehearsals of next semester's *Henry* plays. Furthermore, here's a petition signed by over two hundred local households in support of the play, pledging not only to attend but to pay double admission as a sign of good faith in support of your leadership of the University's theater program and of your choice of director."

Angela winked as, eyebrows furrowed, Hoegren removed the papers from the envelope. Behind the cover letter stating all the man had said was a printed and signed list of names. Hoegren went back to scan the first paper; at the bottom were three signatures: the local state representative, the mayor, and finally "*John Atwater, Vice Mayor.*"

"Good God!" Hoegren said, extending his hand.

"Apparently," Atwater said, returning the handshake, "you aren't the only fighter in your family. My office has received all but physical threats from your wife—though once we saw what the real issue was and what all was at stake with that protest, we agreed to get involved however we could. Oh, um," the man said as Hoegren kept shuffling through the envelope's other papers, "you'll also find that the core members of the Orangedale Shakespeare Company have underwritten the petition, volunteering whatever resources they can offer, even offering their open-air stage in Macwhorter Park."

"Mr. Atwater, thank you. I really appreciate this; you can't know how much of an encouragement it is," Hoegren began, sitting back as he took in all the papers in his hand, "but I'll have to consider it. There would be legal issues with moving students off-campus for official classes and university activities. But don't worry. We're in the process of figuring out how to deal with future protests in the safest way possible."

"With all due respect, Mr. Hoegren, a man who is not a student brought a gun to your theater, and a window was broken by a brick. I doubt the campus on that afternoon was safer than my property—which has security cameras, my dogs, and is not," the man emphasized the word, "a designated gun-free zone." Hands on his hips, the man could not resist giving a slight smile from beneath his mustache.

"Oh, I appreciate the offer, don't get me wrong," said Hoegren, looking at Angela, "but despite my position there are many other factors. Others would have to approve, and unfortunately there are some who think the protest was justified. However, let me see what I can do; perhaps there's something we could work out with campus safety to make practicing off-campus unnecessary."

"Alright, fine." Atwater smiled, raising his hands with a sigh of understanding. "Just know that technically my orange grove is city property that I only maintain, and thus you would not be dealing with a private citizen but with the city, itself, which has historically had a good relationship with the University—at least, with its administration."

Catching the leading note in Atwater's voice, Hoegren asked, "Pardon me, but what do you mean?"

"You see, Mr. Hoegren—may I call you Frank? I've been in Orangedale for twenty years, though I was only elected a few years ago. My wife and I always enjoyed your theater department, and we weren't alone. However, in recent years some of the productions have been a bit much. Don't get me wrong: my wife was a high school English teacher, so we know about social critique in the arts, and we know how to appreciate a production even if we personally disagree with its message. But lately . . . Also, are you aware of how the students speak of those of us in the historic section of Orangedale?"

"A bit—we've been here for a few years, too," Hoegren said, nodding to Angela as he leaned back. He was well aware of how students—and some professors—spoke about Orangedale proper.

"Yes, well, we appreciate legitimate criticism provided by the younger generation, and no one is surprised at students resenting wealth, despite its being earned and lawfully possessed, but recently the resentment has only seemed to grow. It's unfortunate—many who live in Old Orangedale were alumni who haven't bothered anyone on campus, and some I know have pulled their funding from the University because of the general feeling we get from the student body. Many of the people on that petition feel that way—and they're hoping there's a way to moderate the University back from such one-sided, and, frankly, ignorant perspectives. They want to fund the University, but not if their money will be used to shame and antagonize them. Frank, please consider letting us help you. I understand bureaucracy, so take as much time as you need. But I think—and your wife has helped me understand—that we, the city, have an investment in what goes on at this campus. How did you put it, Mrs. Hoegren?"

"How goes the university, so goes the city," Angela said with a pert smile.

"That was it. I think I agree with her, Frank, and if supporting a play is what we have to do to help Orangedale U. reestablish some order, it will be worth it. Better than sending police to every rehearsal—which I've considered offering, by the way, though that would incur budget concerns, for either the school or the city, and would no doubt antagonize certain elements."

"No, I wouldn't feel right doing that, though I agree that the way we treat this situation may have positive or negative repercussions. I'm not sure we could just move rehearsals off-site—responsibility to parents and security concerns, the play's being a university project, you understand. Nonetheless, I'll hold onto your offer. Just knowing we have the city's support will do a lot for morale." Hoegren laughed to himself. "Or it will turn even more students against us. Either way, it's nice to know good people are behind us."

"Of course," said Atwater, apparently still considering Hoegren's penultimate comment. "Feel free to hold onto that petition—in case you need a little administrative muscle. If you find any way my office can help, please don't hesitate. Also," Atwater eyed the glass window of the cabinet beneath the window, "my wife and I will have to have you and Mrs. Hoegren over for dinner one of these nights. I'd be more than happy to exchange comments on whiskey and—what is that, gin?"

"Yes—for days like today," Hoegren said, checking his slight embarrassment behind a smile of irony aimed at Angela; the woman merely rolled her eyes, smiling in spite of herself.

"Hehe, of course. Speaking of which," said Atwater, catching the exchanged look, "I'll not take up any more of your time. Thank you very much, Frank. And send my best to that director. I know Sybil, the one who wrote the story; she's fair—and she rarely gets so complimentary. It's easy to tell who was the real hero at the theater. I hope he keeps it up."

The man shook Hoegren's hand and left the office. Angela remained, leaning against the armchair. After a moment's glance out the window, she walked over to the cabinet and, pulling out the bottle, poured herself a glass. Turning to lean back against the wood, she finally looked at Hoegren over the top of the glass. His eyes had not left her.

"Marry me," he said.

"Sorry—I'm a bit too busy nowadays to run off with just anyone."

"Darling, you arranged all that?"

Angela chortled, raising the glass back to her lips. "You fight for Ry in your way; I do it in mine." Her words echoed into the glass before she took another sip. "How's he doing?"

"Recalcitrant as ever. Look at this email he sent me," Hoegren chuckled, reaching over to the mouse. Angela leaned over his shoulder to read; her pearl necklace graced Frank's shoulder.

Sent: 8:57 pm PST 11 NOV
To: fhoegren@orangedale.ad.edu
From: rcolson@orangedale.fac.edu

Frank,
         sorry about the glass; the university can take it out of next
semester's contract pay, if you want.

         R
         Depts. of English, Writing
         Orangedale University

         P.S.—I told Ingman he doesn't have to fight my fight, but I
don't think he'll listen. If you can, try to stop him from taking a
bullet for me. God, I hate martyrs.

Angela laughed aloud, nearly spilling her drink as she stood up.

"He's saying he loves you, Frank."

"Seems so. You know, while what I just said was true," Hoegren motioned after Atwater, "I wasn't thinking about the administration: I was thinking how Rydar would react to the idea of moving everything to a more secure location."

"Let me guess—he'd say it was running, or playing into the protesters' hands."

"Probably, though I think whatever we do will be like that. You should read what students are writing about the protest."

"Is that what Rydar meant about Ingman?"

"No—that was something different; Ingman's article came out on Rydar's side, on account of free speech's including one's ideological opponents and violence having no place in the realm of ideas. No, I meant on private student blogs. I won't put you through reading it right now, but the group that was ousted from *The Praes* have their own site, now. Their article on the protest is the best piece of linguistic manipulation I've seen in a while. Just about the opposite of both the news article and Ingman's reaction."

"Send it to me," Angela said, her voice hard.

"I will, dearest. But for now," Hoegren said, looking at his watch, "would you like to have an early lunch?" The revelation that people besides him were working to support Colson's play had lifted a weight off of Hoegren, and, though remembering Skylar Evans's blog had brought him back to the day's earlier overcast feeling, he felt the unexpected desire to show off the campus to Angela. She could not drive home at present either way, and she deserved to be treated to lunch for her work—it was the very least a proud, enamored husband could do.

"Fine," Angela said, smiling despite the smoldering Frank knew was still behind her eyes on Rydar's behalf. She knocked her head back and finished the gin, slamming the tumbler down on the wood countertop with a wink. Taking Frank's arm, she left her bag on his chair, its bright red contrasting sharply with the dark brown leather and brass of the chair's upholstery.

❊

Sam

> Ermine, c'mon, text me back. We need to talk.

Ermine closed his phone screen, rolling his eyes as he approached Ad Hill. He could have met up, as Sam wanted, but the amount and tenor of the subsequent texts had made him pause. Their growing frequency and tone had come off as too needy. Besides, Sam's requests were ill-timed: while still managing the groundswell from their last protest *The Homefront* had been planning their next. Ermine just did not have time.

They had only the previous hour advertised the Pride Rally to accompany Ermine's recent article, "*Ostrich*," his response to a query from an anonymous student—"Prisoner No. 24601"—of whether homosexuals like themselves really were as oppressed as *The Homefront* claimed. Of all things, Ermine had recounted an exchange with Sam, who had said he "*didn't go in*" for things like Pride parades, calling them "*shabby*" and, as Ermine recalled, "*a mere pretense at pride—an 'arrogance covering an implicit shame.*" "*This is America*," Ermine had quoted Sam, "*and he didn't care to, in his words, 'maintain an inferiority complex' when most people didn't care either way how he lived his life.*" Ermine closed the article by tapping one of the more puerile tropes of the religious right: "*It's those who believe there is no oppressor who have swallowed the oppressor's lies most deeply.*" Though he thought the article effective on its own merit, Ermine had nonetheless agreed with the other writers to hold a protest against those who believe no protest is needed.

However, there were fewer students on Ad Hill than Ermine had hoped for—only between ten to fifteen. Last-minute rallies had worked before, he reassured himself. They had all morning, and more students would come.

Skylar stood on a chair, yelling through a megaphone over the rainbow-flag-waving crowd, who had taken up the chant: "We are pro-pride, Colson step aside!" Ermine swallowed a chill of apprehension; the point of the article had not been to protest the Shakespeare play. However, steadily becoming Ermine's partnering editor at *The Homefront*, Skylar knew how to do this kind of thing better than he. Ermine tightened his scarf. They really should use every possible opportunity to oppose the production.

A hand took Ermine's arm. About to swing his elbow around, Ermine saw Sam next to him.

"Come with me," Sam said, releasing Ermine's arm and stepping toward a set of tall hedges that lined another walkway up to Ad Hill.

"Sam! What are you doing here?" asked Ermine, following the man away from the rainbow-flecked crowd in spite of himself.

Rounding behind the hedge, Ermine looked at Sam. The man's face was hard and focused in a way Ermine did not recognize.

"What do you want? I'm working."

"Have you checked your phone today?"

Ermine sighed, rolling his eyes. "Yeah, but we were really busy."

"And yesterday? How about every weekend this month?"

"Sam, I don't have time for this—if you can't see, we're in the middle of a rally. You should support—," Ermine stopped, suddenly struck by the fact that Sam should come to the very rally that accompanied his being anonymously referenced in *The Homefront*.

"You're right—I don't usually come to these. But you know that already; I read the article, Ermine." Sam broke into a mirthless smile. "God, it's sad; but I guess you wouldn't know, would you?" the man said to himself.

"What?" Ermine narrowed his eyes.

Sam held up his phone, which was open to the Orangeware app. "You answered Prisoner Number 24601 with the words of Prisoner Number 24601."

It took Ermine a moment to realize Sam's meaning.

"That was you?!" spat Ermine, cringing at the idea that Sam would toy with him. "What the fuck, Sam, you know I have a lot going on. I thought those were serious posts; I don't need you trolling my blog." Despite wishing he had never done it, Ermine fought back the memory of how much closer they had been when he had shown Sam how to make a clandestine Orangeware profile the month before.

Sam stood looking at Ermine; it unnerved Ermine that he did not look hurt—that he seemed as if he had expected this.

"I wasn't trolling you. It was a serious message. Ermine, I've tried, but I'm tired of you hating people for having different opinions. Behind all your irony and hyperbole, you're the only person I know who actually seems to want to hurt people, or to convince them that they're hurting. Newsflash: people just want to live their lives, and they don't care if you and I are gay! But I can't do this anymore; I'm tired of trying to figure out you and your inferiority complex."

The man's tone had not changed through the whole diatribe; near the end, Sam had even smiled—and had possessed the gall to look relaxed. In the next moment, he was walking back around the hedge.

Ermine stepped after him. "Don't you walk away from me!" he yelled. "You aren't gonna fucking leave me like that!"

The man did not slow in his steps. Ermine was about to catch up to him—to give Sam what he deserved, to say what Ermine felt with sudden relish that he had wanted to say for a long time—when someone from the crowd approached; the underclassman's pace showed he had been waiting for Ermine.

"What!" Ermine exclaimed, trying too late to suppress the anger and still trying to ignore the absence in his chest.

"Umm, sorry for interrupting, Ermine," the young man said, glancing helplessly at Sam, who had turned at Ermine's outburst, "but a guy handed me this and told me to give it to you. Said you might need it." The boy held out a folded piece of paper; opening it, Ermine saw it was a filled out permit for holding a political rally on campus.

"Who gave this to you?" Ermine snapped.

"He was older—had a beard. I think that's him walking." The boy pointed.

Ermine saw the silhouette of a man strolling with hands in his pockets toward the theater; a ray of light reaching through the oak branches revealed a shock of dark blonde hair.

Suddenly growing cold, Ermine examined the paper. At the bottom, under *"Faculty advisor responsible for event,"* was signed *"Rydar Colson."*

A laugh arose beside Ermine—a joyous, unexpected, triumphant laugh. Sam had apparently walked up and seen the form. Ermine crumpled the paper, gritting his teeth as his anger returned.

"That's your oppressor?" asked Sam, his laugh distracting some of the protestors who were curious at the sound. "He just enabled you to be here. Good thing, too." Sam motioned.

A line of security officers—including a few policemen and women—were approaching. As the crowd hollered at the guards, Skylar looked at Ermine. Seeing Ermine's concerned look, he got down from the steps and came over.

"We have to leave, now," said Ermine.

"Don't worry, we can stand up to them."

"No, we have to go," Ermine said sternly, handing the form to Skylar. Skylar read the page.

"Who cares? It's just a fucking piece of paper. If he's stupid enough to help us put nails in his coffin—."

"No, you don't get it!" Ermine shrieked, shocking Skylar. "We can't let him claim credit for this—it would be handing him a victory!"

Skylar looked at Ermine, silent but with nostrils flaring in disagreement.

"Tell them all to go home," said Ermine. At Skylar's hesitation, Ermine shouted, "Get rid of them or you're off *The Homefront*! I'll be damned if I let Colson co-opt another protest and come out looking like an ally!"

Ermine turned to meet the approaching security guards. He crumpled up and dropped the piece of paper.

"Hi officers. Don't worry—we're almost done here," preempted Ermine in as diplomatic a tone as he could muster.

"Oh," said an older security guard, "good. You know you need to move this to the free speech zone."

"I know," said Ermine, careful not to eye the other guards and officers who had formed a half-circle around him, "I was just telling them that." Sam let out a brief chuckle, but said nothing. Behind him, Ermine could hear Skylar speaking through the megaphone, telling everyone to go back to their dorms. Some quieted down and, seeing the officers, began to disperse, but a few—the ones who had been most visible in their chanting and waving of flags—started to yell back at Skylar. At that, the policemen among the group began to approach the crowd, provoking sudden cries from those who remained.

"Shit," muttered Ermine under his breath. He turned and picked up the crumpled ball of paper. Flattening it out across his thigh, Ermine held it out to the security guard, who had begun to direct his other guards to support the policeman and women.

"Here's our permit," said Ermine, hating his words, "it should be filled out."

"That's fine, but unfortunately your event has moved beyond that."

As the police began to patiently move around the crowd, palms held up in peace, more students relented, backing away from the crowd with arms raised in surrender. Eventually only a small group of students remained—among whom were a skinny student who, having taken his shirt off in the frenzy of the crowd, was yelling about his right to free expression, a black girl clothed all in black who lay face-down and mo-tionless on the pavement, and a girl with unkempt hair still shrieking on the ground next to her.

Ermine turned to the approaching Skylar. "Let's get out of here," he said, looking uneasily at the few remaining students before turning toward his dorm.

"Who's this?" asked Skylar, eyeing Sam with open suspicion.

"Nobody," said Sam, emitting a last chuckle before heading down the hill.

Vesta sipped her Sprite, smiling around the straw at Jonas across the table.

"God, what?" she asked.

"Nothing—I just like looking at you," he said, arm resting along the leather cushion of the booth.

"Shut up." She threw a paper napkin at him.

He shrugged. "Alright, fine," he said, flicking the menu up between them.

He had often done that—assume a veneer of overt indifference to make her laugh; it often worked, especially as she learned how much humor and levity Jonas's usually respectful, even demeanor obscured. Discovering a vein of silliness in him had given Vesta a relief she had not known she wanted, and remembering it had often made her giggle at unexpected and inappropriate times. However, rather than removing the grown-up seriousness she had thought his trademark, Jonas's humor seemed to cleanse it, as if he were so confident of the future's value that he could have fun at its expense without fear.

"Nice place," Jonas said over the top of the menu.

"Begging for compliments," Vesta said. "God, you're arrogant."

"I try," he said, smirking at the antipasti page.

The next day Vesta would drive to Sonoma for Winter Break, and Jonas had insisted she save tonight for him; convincing her had not been hard. Now, they sat in Orangedale's nicest Italian restaurant. Though average by Napa standards, Romeli's prices and quiet atmosphere, and their requiring reservations for larger parties, placed the restaurant outside the list of go-to student eateries, lending it an aura of class. Vesta knew Jonas was trading on this; he had even asked that they dress up. His transparency was so blatant it undercut itself, yet it left Vesta utterly charmed.

After ordering they sat in silence. Vesta knew why Jonas had brought her here, but she would not help him. She merely stared back at him, waiting for him to make his move. However, after a few moments, Jonas's even smile showed he knew what she was doing, and Vesta broke into a smile, hating and adoring him for wordlessly calling her bluff.

Rather than concede a preemptive broach of the evening's main event, she deflected: "Did you hear what Hoegren was telling Rydar before discussion last week?"

"No, didn't see him."

"I only caught a bit of it, but I think he's worried about more protests. Rydar seemed distracted, but I think it was because Hoegren came to see him."

"Yeah, I can see that." Jonas chuckled, leaning back to observe the ceiling, "They're closer than just administrator and teacher—like Rydar and Maxwell but not as close. Rydar would definitely take more issue with people worrying about him than people attacking him."

"But what about us? I want to do this play, and I trust Rydar. It's the protesters I don't trust," Vesta said, adjusting her shawl to cover her shoulders. "I can't help but feel like, for all that's happened, I still can't imagine what they might do. I mean, we've been talking a lot about terrible things people did in the past—in Solzhenitsyn and the rest—but that's just it. Now I'm aware there's a lot I don't know. It's not a nice feeling. Not that I need to feel nice all the time, but you understand? I mean, look, even now I'm bringing it up and ruining our date."

"You're fine," said Jonas, smiling, "so long as you're still here, you couldn't ruin it. But I wouldn't worry: Hoegren and Rydar have more up their sleeves than they show. You can trust them. Grey, too. Still," Jonas's eyes focused on her as his smile sobered, "I wouldn't walk around campus alone at night."

"Sexist," Vesta met his eyes and cocked the edge of her smile up.

"I'm serious, Vesta. When it comes to your physical safety . . . and that's the irony: they think they're setting you free by fighting things like the play, when in reality they're reinstating an implicit curfew, like college in the fifties, or worse. You're right—we don't know what the opposition will do. I'd rather not think about it, but I do. They're out for prey; not all of them, but some of them, which is enough."

Vesta felt his foot rest against her calf. She smiled in thanks. Despite herself she felt touched that Jonas was so serious on her behalf.

"I'll be fine—I've been a girl my whole life. I'm not stupid. How about you?"

"Well, you know I live right across the street from the theater, and I'm usually home when not in class or backstage." Jonas winked. He had still not taken her to his place, blaming the fact on his roommates. She had not pushed, comfortable that he would eventually invite her over.

"I've never asked," she said, changing the subject, "but how do you know Rydar? You two seem closer than just director and set designer."

Jonas smiled. "One day in sophomore year I got a random email from a teacher saying he liked one of my comics and wanted to meet me. The first time we met—it was in the Commons—he didn't even ask about the comic. He wanted to know my thoughts on some recent political articles in the paper. We eventually talked for two hours on the relations between American and ancient Jewish law. I was brought up Presbyterian, you know, but my mom's mom was Jewish, and she came here after the war. So, I had pretty good foundations in Scripture. Rydar seemed to already know it; his questions were more like confirmations. It was the weirdest meeting, though now I'm used to it. He was one of the first teachers I'd met to take that part of my life seriously, even more than I did, in a way." Jonas laughed. "You can imagine it—you know Rydar."

"Yup, I definitely can. I didn't know you were Presbyterian, too."

"Born and raised," replied Jonas, stroking her foot in acknowledgment of learning one more thing they shared. "Though I've broadened my perspectives on other denominations and church history. You can thank Rydar for that."

"He does have a way of doing that." Vesta laughed. "Well, my family will definitely enjoy hearing you're a Christian."

"Oh, you're gonna tell them about me?" Jonas said with mock embarrassment.

"I don't know—depends on whether tonight's worth telling about."

"I'll do my best," Jonas said, bowing his head.

Vesta chuckled. As the waiter brought their food, she decided she would play along with whatever he had planned.

"Just a few more steps," Jonas said as he led Vesta, eyes closed, across the dark stage. "Okay, don't move." He squeezed her arms before jogging offstage.

Unable to help herself, Vesta peeked through her fingers. In the stage's dim backlight a silhouette with clean, vertical edges towered above her. Something perpendicular split the structure halfway up.

"Alright," Jonas called from the back of the theater, "open!"

Vesta heard the abrupt snaps and shudders of spotlights. Opening her eyes only to put her hand back up to block the sudden spray of light, Vesta saw a model skyscraper, its sides lit by a combination of colors that produced the illusion of an even sunset across its facade. With each side facing a third of the audience, the structure's dimensions gave the sense of seeing a panorama of the building and the surrounding three blocks. A giant marquee circled the building, proclaiming in white, capital letters, "*Vesta Lloyd, will you be my girlfriend? - Jonas Templeton*."

Vesta laughed aloud. She knew Jonas had planned to make things official tonight and that he knew she planned to accept. Nonetheless, to have done it so brazenly, especially when they had kept things so understated so far . . .

"Well?" Jonas said, hopping up onto the stage. "What do you think of England Royalties?" He motioned up to the tower's summit, which extended past the theater curtain. "I had some trouble getting the colors right. Believe it or not, I only have the orange lights on; the paint, itself, is what makes it seem to fade from yellow to red."

Vesta put her arms around his neck. "Of course I will."

"You'll what?" he asked, his expression confused.

"Oh, whatever," she said, rolling her eyes but not moving.

Still looking lost, Jonas glanced back to the building; his eyes finally landed on the marquee.

"Oh, that! Good." Relenting, he returned her hug.

They stood there for a few moments, holding each other longer than they had thus far.

"It's so dumb," she said, putting her face against his collarbone as she gazed up at the gesture, all the more more affecting for being so gratuitous.

"It's important," Jonas said. "We can make it dumb or meaningful. I prefer meaningful—and you deserve it. 'We are the makers of manners, Kate,'" he said, quoting, Vesta knew, the end of *Henry V*, where Henry had to woo Princess Katharine into kissing him to mark their engagement. "'Therefore, patiently and yielding,'" Jonas leaned her chin up, pausing just a moment, as if still giving her the chance to withdraw.

Vesta put her hand on the back of his head and pulled him down the fraction of an inch needed for their lips to touch.

They kissed for a while, easily, not rushing what they both knew was Vesta's first time; Jonas was relaxed, as if allowing himself to rediscover the action along with her without pushing farther. Nonetheless, he still seemed to be holding back. Vesta hoped so; she was worth prompting something that needed holding back.

For a moment, as Jonas ran his fingers through the hair around her ear, Vesta felt she understood why a woman might try to tempt a man—that, far from what most girls on campus said, it was a tribute not to the man's power but to hers. She thought, again, of Princess Katharine, then of Cora. Vesta had often wondered why, with her advocacy of female independence, she led Elliot around as she did rather than simply staying single; this feeling must be part of it. Vesta smiled against Jonas's lips; Jonas would never be led around like that.

Suddenly, Vesta saw motion out of the corner of her eye. "Oh!" she cried before realizing it had been Grey Maxwell sneaking back into his office. An old, wizened hand reached out from the light of the doorway, waving before motioning a thumbs-up and closing the door.

Jonas laughed. "Confession: I had some help. Told you we can trust them."

"Listen, all I'm saying is we might want to be cautious," said Hoegren.

Rydar stood leaning on Hoegren's desk with one arm, frowning.

"We won't have Lilledahl's play to hide behind next semester," Hoegren continued. "Nothing will stop them from attacking the theater again. We were lucky you only had a core group there last time."

"Yeah, but in the end they're going to do what they're going to do," said Rydar. "I understand avoiding unnecessary antagonism, but caving usually just encourages more. They're not here to play fair, and they aren't making demands in good faith."

"I understand, Ry, believe me," said Hoegren, measuring the professional need to let Rydar do his job against his personal desire to keep his young friend safe—which he consciously subsumed into trying to ensure student safety. "But you have nothing to prove. Besides, I doubt I'll be able to get funding to reimburse police presence if something happens again. Not everyone on the university board is behind the play, and some are worried about the growing lobby against it."

Rydar looked at Maxwell, who was standing at the window, hands in pockets, observing the light of the setting sun on the mountains to the north.

"I get all that," Rydar said, "but I don't like the idea of hiding when we're doing nothing wrong—really, when we're doing something right. I don't want you to set that precedent—certainly not with me and my production."

"I'm not telling you to hide, damn it," Hoegren said, resisting the desire to slap the desktop, "but we have other options. The city—."

"If the city has to step in, then as far as I'm concerned the university is lost. I appreciate Angela's work and Atwater's willingness to help, but the university needs to be its own parent. Relying on the city should be the last resort."

Hoegren sighed, resisting a shake of his head.

"Rydar, what is *Henry IV* about?" Maxwell asked, still looking outside.

Rydar closed his mouth in a tight line, taking a breath with closed eyes. "It's about a prince restoring his nation's highest values during a time of chaos and conflict."

"And how does Hal do that?"

After a pause, Rydar paced away from both men, putting his hands on his hips. "Goddamn it, Grey."

"Yes," said the man, turning his chin to speak over his shoulder, "he goes underground. He hides," Grey twisted the word into the young man, "until the time is right—not in spite of but because of what he's trying to defend."

Rydar crossed his arms, keeping his back to the other two. As much as he, himself, relied on Maxwell, Hoegren nonetheless felt a familiar jealousy. Though he saw Rydar like a son, it was not himself who was his mentor.

When Rydar finally spoke, Hoegren heard a vulnerability he could have never evinced from him. "So we should just let the mob veto win?"

Grey chuckled, stepping behind the desk with Hoegren. "Win? Sure, if practicing on-campus is your goal—reaching performance be damned. I'm just saying we keep other options up our sleeve; you don't beat a juggernaut by charging it head-on."

Rydar nodded, turning around to sit in one of the chairs facing the desk. He rubbed the stubble on his lips, thinking; his eyes were rimmed with red.

"What is it?" Hoegren asked.

"It's just . . . you know, this time of year." Rydar waved his hand, dismissing the thought, "And when we start talking about self-censorship like this. You guys know how insulting this semester has been to me, in particular. I'm sorry," he said, putting his face in his hands and leaning back to stretch, "it just has me thinking of her more than usual—and what she'd say about it all."

"We know, Rydar," said Grey, "but they're children. They're playing with dangerous ideas, but they're far from North Korea."

"And," interjected Hoegren, "we have a larger support structure, should we need it. That's all I'm asking—that we be willing to roll with the punches next term and use the resources we have."

Rydar nodded, his mouth a tight line as he watched the glow pervade the unlit room through the window. A tear threatened to fall from the young man's right eye; Hoegren looked away, suddenly feeling a desperate desire to hold Angela.

Chapter 9

Hey kid—wanted you to know I was thinking of you. I'm so proud of you; she would be, too.

—G

Rydar Colson

Thank you, Grey :'-)

G REY MAXWELL SET down his phone and reached for his Christmas Eve cigar, fighting back the tightness under his eyes as he looked up at the night sky. He should not cry, not when the man for whom he felt the tears was probably not crying, himself, sympathetic emoji notwithstanding. Hell, Rydar was probably celebrating—either with a whiskey or a batch of Dickens's Smoking Bishop punch he sometimes made. Enjoying the thought, Grey moved to his back porch to enjoy the clear night sky.

It was not that Colson was untouched by mourning, but to mourn would be silly compared to all he had endured and to the joy he took in remembering. It had been nine years since, whether by bittersweet coincidence or self-torture, Rydar Colson and Eun-Ji Ri had married on their final Christmas together. Surrounded by extended family, Grey had received a call from Ry. "Grey. Sorry to bother you, but will you be my best man?" After a pause and a smile at something long-hoped-for, Grey excused himself from Christmas Eve dinner and sped through the empty streets to Eun-Ji's hospital.

After learning about her cancer in late spring of their senior year, Eun-ji resisted simply pushing Rydar away to spare him, knowing they would need each other. However, as her condition worsened the next fall, the tension grew between wanting Rydar's presence in her last months and wanting the best for him. He had already paused his life piece-by-piece to be with her, foregoing summer work and grad school, neglecting the few friendships he had made in college, even going into debt to rent a nearby apartment in which he rarely slept. Even then, Rydar had not balked from his choice to be with Eun-ji.

It came to a head on Christmas Eve, when Eun-ji finally stopped resisting Rydar's resolute compulsion to pour himself into her hopeless situation. Grey did not know what Rydar had said—probably something about forgoing what they should do for what they actually wanted. Grey laughed softly, imagining as he did every Christmas Eve the scene of Ry chastising Eun-ji for trying to spare them both an avoidable but worthwhile pain. "You have no right to insult me by being selfless—by trying to escape what we mean to each other."

She had intended to break off their relationship to spare him. By midnight, surrounded by Grey, Eun-Ji's teary-eyed father and couple of cousins, and the orderlies on rotation that night, the twenty-two-year-old Rydar and Eun-Ji were pronounced husband and wife by a hospital chaplain. Grey could not remember Eun-ji ever smiling so much, despite her pain; she looked the way Christmas Eve is supposed to feel: a night where all suffering, worry, and guilt are rendered powerless by a radiant, contagious affection for one's own existence and that of those one loves.

Grey drew on his cigar. Even then Rydar was developing that look of his, as if while alleviating another's pain he secretly wanted to increase his own to see how much he could take. Rydar knew that night's decadence would cost him.

Four months later Rydar delivered Eun-Ji's eulogy. "I couldn't help wanting to be with Eun-Ji; she was the kind of woman who could never succeed at self-denial. She was too honest and her love of life too great . . . " Rydar might as well have been describing himself, however far from such things he seemed to descend shortly after losing Eun-Ji.

A soft breeze chilled Grey; glancing once more at the stars, he walked inside. As he did every year, he reached for his paperback of Dickens's *A Christmas Carol*, lay back on his couch, and started to read in the warm light of an old lamp.

Having divorced a decade before meeting Rydar, Grey had long ago married his work and lived more or less as a bachelor. He could call Diane; the two had had dinner several times during her September visit. However, she would be celebrating Christmas morning with family, and he preferred to be alone on this most personally sacred of nights.

Though he enjoyed being nothing more than a sleeping dog left to lie in his personal life, he still experienced a muted bitterness at the idea of Rydar doing the same. It was tolerable, by most people's standards, for Grey to be alone on a holiday, but a young man like Rydar?

Yet, Grey knew his younger friend was not alone. Colson was like Scrooge, in a way, and his love for Eun-Ji was his gold. The first year after her death his isolation had been a mania, as if the masochism of memory were the only way to preserve what she meant to him. Grey had stayed in contact with Rydar as he stoically attended grad school the Fall after Eun-Ji's death, respecting the young man's grieving process by not bringing it up.

However, somewhere in autumn of the second year—when he was, no doubt, once again reliving both his early and final months with Eun-ji—Rydar had succeeded in overcoming the depths of whatever had led him to isolate himself in his depression. Grey had not asked, content just to see Rydar smile and start to reach out again and trusting he would tell Grey whatever he needed to know.

Then, on a walk together around an empty campus about a week before what would have been his second wedding anniversary, Rydar finally brought it up, in his own way. Noticing Maxwell's cautious wordlessness, the boy smirked, merely saying, "It's okay, Grey; it was worth it." In his eulogy, Rydar had said his love for Eun-ji was synonymous with his love for himself. Grey's proudest moment was seeing his young friend's posture then, as he admired the mountains to the north; he stood as one who finally believed the words he had said.

Grey turned a page, careful not to let the inch of cigar ash touch the yellowing paper. His eyes ran along the familiar lines, but it was not Dickens's words he was mulling over. In subsequent years, during the weeks leading up to and away from their anniversary, Rydar's countenance still steadily deepened in its characteristic stoicism, but Grey knew that Christmas had once again become Rydar's favorite time of year. After growing up virtually alone, Colson had finally learned to love his solitude—no small achievement. Grey would no more impinge upon his young friend's privacy than he would were Eun-ji still alive and living with him. Besides, Rydar knew Grey was there, and that was company enough. If Colson did not reach out, it was because he was no longer in a nadir but on a zenith, upon which it would not be right for Grey to presume.

Grey smiled, starting the page over with a sigh. He drew upon the cigar. They would talk when they talked.

❋

Rydar Colson hit "*Send.*" Grey never failed, the bastard.

He stood, refilling his bourbon from the decanter behind the couch. He enjoyed the tinkle of ice settling in the tumbler and the whisper of the embers collapsing in the fireplace.

He added another log to the fire; after a glance up to the right of the fireplace, he walked to the bedroom. Under the bed were two safes; one he opened only once a year, on this night. From it Rydar took a thin, purple cardboard box wrapped like a present. Sliding off the twine ribbon, he removed the small bundle of papers housed inside and returned to the living room. Before lying down on the couch, he paused to again admire the picture that took up most of the facing wall beside the fire.

A woman in a crimson dress stood under a latticework of white wood and green vines; sparkling from the lights expertly hidden among the surrounding bushes, the dress outshone the few stars in the night sky. The woman's long, dark hair cascaded down her back in a motion that stressed the daring nakedness of her shoulders in the cold night air. A shade darker red than her dress, her upturned and smiling lips were open as if forever taking in the breath just before a kiss.

Into the woman's steady, dark eyes looked those of a suited young man whose lips had met hers the moment after the photograph was taken. With a sigh, Rydar Colson took a mouthful of cold, bitter liquid.

They were attending the annual Orangedale University holiday concert. While smiling but somber students and families comprised most of the audience, he and Eun-Ji had treated the concert like every other moment of their relationship, with a proud joy. Dressing how they felt the season deserved, they had stood out from the crowd as starkly as the poinsettias adorning the university chapel outshone the clean but faceless stone of the building.

Rydar preferred to spend their anniversary alone like this. The memory of that night—and of every other moment with Eun-Ji—was effused with a clear, unyielding, radiant glow that suited the uplifting spirit of Christmas more than did the sentiments others associated with the season.

He often experienced distaste at how some people would wish merriment at the season while glorying in mankind's supposed lowliness and ineptitude and descrying its materialism. The ideas tarnished the core theme of and reason for the season—that the cold dark of winter could not ultimately suppress man's joy at his own existence. The attitude of Christmas was not one of kneeling but of the uplifted glance, of magnanimity made flesh, of suffering rendered ultimately impotent by the birth of the apogean man. Rydar smiled; of all the characters, the shepherds had gotten it right.

Of course it had taken years and a certain fictional Russian wouldbe priest for Rydar to understand such things without scorn. Yet, he wondered if despite his scoffing and indifference he had not understood and believed it even then.

He usually considered such ideas on this night. It allowed him to savor his next act. Emptying his glass, Rydar lied down on the couch, unfolded one of the papers, and began to read.

"*It was your chin that did it. You held it as if it contained everything about you . . .* "

Though he would have rephrased certain parts, this was one of his favorites; in it, a younger Rydar recounted his first sight of Eun-Ji being led around campus on a Spring tour. Noting the pride behind the girl's posture and filling it in with the understanding he gained of her the next fall, he had given himself a rarely-indulged freedom to elaborate.

Rydar shook his head as he reached his own quote of Aristotle's take on pride—"*Pride, then, seems to be a sort of crown of the virtues; for it makes them greater, and it is not found without them. Therefore it is hard to be truly proud; for it is impossible without nobility and goodness of character . . .* " That Eun-Ji's unapologetic posture came out of North Korea seemed to prove not only Aristotle's contention that virtues are inherent in the human creature but also the inability of all other opposing, degrading perspectives to completely snuff out such virtues. And that Eun-Ji had learned it without the comforts and resources Rydar had had . . .

Rydar skipped to the end of the letter, only half reading as he remembered.

I have never known prayer, but I knew then a helpless desire that might lead one to it. I could tell you and your family were only visiting and that you might not attend here, that the woman I knew I must meet might be gone forever in just a few steps. But when your eyes met mine in the next moment I knew you would choose this place, as I knew you must choose me for the same reason—by the virtue required to see it and each other as we do: with the joy of a desperately earned pride.

When next we met, it was only fitting that you did what you did. The permission had been granted in that first look.

R

Rydar folded the letter, inhaling the soft scent that still remained on it as he recalled his and Eun-Ji's second look.

The only person at the theater, he had been sanding a set piece for the Fall production. He did not know how long she had been watching him, but even with the audience lights off he recognized her immediately. Standing in a yellow summer dress with white lace, she slowly approached him. After a moment's pause, as if confirming that his were still the eyes she had seen, she reached her hands to his neck, pulled him close, and kissed him. His sawdust-covered hands were grasping her back before his sandpaper reached the ground.

Rydar looked over at the wall. The photo showed the same daring, inviting look Eun-ji had worn in the theater. They had not known their picture was being taken. A girl had contacted him the next week to ask if she could use it in advertisements for the show. Looking at Eun-Ji, asleep in the bed next to him after an afternoon spent together, he had politely refused, but not before asking to see the photo first.

After hanging up, he had just sat and looked at Eun-Ji; her hair splayed across the pillow contrasted perfectly with the brilliant skin of her uncovered torso. Despite its being winter, a warm, sunlit clarity had broken through the week's cold snap. As they had done many times the previous semester, they were stealing an afternoon alone, letting the light hit them through Eun-Ji's dorm blinds as they dozed between intermittent bouts of violence and exhaustion.

Rydar remembered he had then thought of the people who would see the copies of the photo, which shortly arrived in an email. They would probably enjoy it as a memento advertisement for the concert and then with the same eyes go watch the newest family Christmas plot that tritely reiterated the spirit of the season while lamenting the commercialism supposedly spoiling it, forgetting that the latter often enabled and was ennobled by the former.

They could not know the season as did he and Eun-Ji, just as they would know nothing of what the photo meant and against which it was both an effacement and triumph. The light, the dress, the flowers, the music, everything that had brought joy to the previously unforgiving cold of winter was enabled by that commercialism. The younger Rydar could not bear the thought of someone looking at Eun-Ji and then thinking Christmas's value was an inverse of a culture's material success. The woman sleeping soundly next to him had come from a place devoid of such consumerism—and where there had been no Christmas.

Nonetheless, Rydar and Eun-Ji both later admitted the photographer had captured the right moment; the photo deserved to be saved and seen by anyone who truly enjoyed the season. Thanking her, they had paid the student to delete all remaining copies, retaining their copy until it could be printed. The sum they paid the girl would have scandalized Eun-Ji's father as much as the night that followed the show would have, had he learned about either.

It had been worth it, Rydar thought. Every time he considered the photo—the only decoration in the otherwise unadorned living room—he experienced the pleasure of owning it completely. That kiss and everything it represented belonged to none but Eun-Ji and himself, as did everything that had come afterward. He had not possessed the words, then, to express what had made them refuse the student. Though his views had acquired more nuance since then, he now understood they had wanted to keep it, and themselves, safe from the sacrilege of mediocrity.

The image of a thin, straggly-haired man seated in a dark room with a bottle in front of a TV flashed into Rydar's mind. The thought did not rankle him as it would have the young man in the picture; he had progressed far beyond either anger or pity. The love between him and Eun-ji and the subsequent depths he had traveled after her loss were beyond such people. Considering how far he had come filled Rydar's chest with a deep, pleasant warmth.

Setting down the letter, he stood and took a wizened, black pipe from a stand next to the decanter; packing it with some cavendish, he walked to the sliding glass door. Striking a match, he leaned against the cold metal of the doorjamb. Rydar tasted the sweet smoke of the false light, letting the top embers cool before relighting and drawing in a mouthful. A cold breeze wafted past him into the house.

He would have a New Year's Eve party.

The inkling and the decision were simultaneous, and, after a moment's puzzlement, he relaxed into the thought that it was right. He had rarely, if ever, had more than a few people over since buying the house; he wondered that he should want to open it up now.

As he gazed through the smoke at the fire, the clear night sky, and the photo between them, Rydar considered how the same sacred pleasure that had prompted him to keep the photo from indiscriminate eyes had caused him to mount the photo as an indispensable part of the home. Yes, such personal sacraments, and the joy he took in them, deserved to be shared—with those of his choosing, from whom he had asked so much and to whom he had already opened himself up in unprecedented ways.

Exhaling a steady cloud, he felt the cold night air on his bare arms as he considered whom to invite. Some filled him with a sense of rightness—"They will enjoy it"—and some with curiosity—"What will they think?" He knew he would need to plan and prepare, but he felt no urgency. The plan, the guest list, and everything else would flow from the initial decision. For now, he could enjoy considering the things that made worthwhile the idea to host a celebration here, in his world, with her.

"Morning, Elliot. It's Ry. Will you be in town Wednesday night?"

"Oh, hey," Elliot said, clearing his voice as he lifted his head off the pillow. "Yeah, I should be."

"I'm having a party. If you're not busy, I'd love to have you here." The man's tone was the audible prelude to a smile.

"Yeah," said Elliot as Cora rolled over to face him, "we'll be there."

Elliot could not tell if there were a pause at the other end. He glanced over at Cora.

"Good. I'll see you on New Year's. I'll text time and address. Merry Christmas."

The call ended.

"Where are we going?" Cora yawned, stretching her arms out from beneath the sheet and blanket.

"Rydar's having a New Year's Eve party, and we're invited."

"We, or you?" Cora chuckled. "I'll wait for my call."

"C'mon, he knows we'll be going together," Elliot said, laying his head on her chest as he ran a finger along her ribs.

"Well, I'll check my schedule and get back to you," Cora said.

Elliot chuckled. Elliot had hoped Winter Break might mark a more public and official phase of their relationship, but such hopes had been subsumed into the cold, overcast winter days of relaxing together as they had through the previous semester. Officially staying in the dorms over Winter Break, Cora had spent most of her nights at Elliot's apartment. However, she said she would spend Christmas with friends Elliot did not know, so Elliot had driven to spend Christmas Eve with his folks. They had been very interested to hear about the play, and an exasperated Elliot soon regretted saying anything. He did not mention Cora; their unique relationship would just concern his parents—and provoke his kid sister to annoy him.

Nonetheless, the thought of Cora alone on campus, waiting for him, had preoccupied Elliot. After finishing Christmas lunch the next day and throwing his cardboard box of presents in the back seat of his car, Elliot had rushed back to his apartment. Now he luxuriated in the contrast between the cold air from the cracked window and the warmth of Cora's legs. It felt like the day after Christmas should.

The feeling gave him courage to broach the subject he had not brought up for a while.

"I think we should go together . . . like, together together."

Cora sat up, sighing. "What?"

"Come on, you know what I mean," said Elliot, rolling up onto his elbow. "I mean everyone knows we're a couple. I just want to make it official—it's been almost half a year!" He grasped her hand.

"Yeah," she said, withdrawing it, "and we've been fine. I thought we were past this, Ell."

"Cora, I like what we have," Elliot said, putting up his palm as he nonetheless prepared to say what he had mulled over while driving back. "Being with you is better than anything I've ever felt. That's why I want to finally make things official. We wouldn't really need to change anything—we're already practically boyfriend and girlfriend."

Rather than respond, Cora stood up from the sheets and picked up her pile of clothes.

"I mean, what are you afraid of?" he asked, more sternly than he had intended.

"Oh, I'm afraid?" Cora widened her eyes as she pulled her head through the neck of a shirt, ignoring her shiver at the still-cold though sunlit apartment. "If anyone's afraid, it's you. Why can't you just trust me? Why do you still need to define things?"

"Still? I haven't brought it up in months!" said Elliot, sitting up and crossing his legs, "Come on, consider it a Christmas present to me . . . "

"I already gave you your Christmas present, Elliot," Cora said, enunciating each consonant.

"Hey, you enjoyed it, too, if I remember," Elliot nearly shouted, remembering the sight of the top of her head at his waist, which he had reciprocated. Despite the tension, he had to resist chuckling; it all seemed so silly. "Baby, won't it be a relief to finally have it in the open? And it's not just affecting me; Vesta and everyone else still feel they have to tiptoe around us. I mean, it's been great in class and onstage to pretend like we're having secret liaisons, and all that, but it's kind of exhausting. Don't get me wrong!" Elliot hastily amended his tone as Cora shot him a look. "I love this game we have, but I want us to eventually move to the next stage." Elliot failed to stifle a smirk at the irony that in any other relationship their roles might be reversed.

Arms crossed and hips cocked to the side, Cora considered Elliot. Her lips pursed. Smiling, Elliot met her gaze, but a ray of gold sunlight reflecting off her thigh drew his eyes down the length of her body.

She sighed. "You're pathetic. I can't believe after all this time . . . " Cora reached down to pick up the jeans Elliot had pulled off her not three hours before. "It just shows you're not brave enough for a real relationship, after all. I thought you were a real man, but you're still that boy in high school who's scared of being led on."

"Hold up, what?" Elliot said, frowning. "No, don't turn this around on me anymore. We're in a relationship, Cora; I just want to call it what it is. I've done my time, and I deserve something real from you—besides your ass. I've let you take the lead, but just 'cause your dad didn't like dealing with your nagging bitch of a mother doesn't mean you have to worry I'll leave you."

"Fuck you, Elliot," she whispered. Putting on her boots with only one sock on, she grasped the rest of her things to her chest and opened the door.

"Cora," Elliot sighed, closing his eyes; he had not meant to say it.

Cora turned to look at him. Her expression was obscured by the sudden brightness silhouetting her form.

"I don't know who's the greater masochist," Elliot ventured, "you, or me for loving you." The words had occurred to him as he mused over her sleeping form a few nights before; they had sounded charming then.

Cora closed the door, leaving Elliot sitting in his boxers in an empty apartment.

❀

"Okay, really, I gotta go," said Jonas, slipping on his leather jacket as he leaned in to kiss Vesta again.

"Thanks for breakfast," she said.

"Of course—I'm sorry I couldn't take you out last night."

"You mean this morning. I was beat." Vesta yawned; after a final dinner with her family she had driven back from Sonoma, arriving after 2:00 am. Cora had not been there.

"Dinner tonight?"

"Of course. Should I wait for you at your place?" Vesta asked.

Jonas winked. "Nah, I'll pick you up. Dress comfy—and get some rest today."

"Fine," she said, rolling her eyes, "have fun working."

"I will; the set's almost done. I think Grey's bringing some Christmas leftovers, so it might be an easy day." He blew her a kiss before closing the door.

Vesta stretched back on her bed. Despite the coffee, she still had a dull headache and a sting of fatigue around her eyes. She had nothing to do but enjoy the day resting and reading.

Standing, she walked to her blinds, dimming the sunlight breaking through the gray. She took out Jonas's Christmas gift: a copy of *The Awakening*. Jonas had called it "a love story—in a manner of speaking."

Vesta was about to climb under her sheets when the door opened.

"Oh, hey," said Cora, smiling after a pause. "I didn't know you were coming back today."

"Yeah, last night actually," Vesta said, propping herself up. "I was really late though. Was just gonna take a nap. You come from Elliot's?"

"Mm-hmm." Cora walked to the restroom. "I just passed Jonas on the stairs," she said as she began to wash her face, omitting the obvious question.

Vesta's phone vibrated. "*Got out just in time ;)*," Jonas had texted. They had not told anyone, deciding after Rydar's earlier calls to both of them that they would attend his party as a couple. But Vesta had to tell Cora; besides wanting to share her excitement, Vesta wanted to break the ice around Cora and Elliot's own relationship. It had always seemed odd how Cora denied they were anything but casual, and she wanted Cora to know she would listen. Vesta was also tired of avoiding Elliot's pained eyes at the subject.

"Now," Cora said, toweling her face dry as she walked in, "Do you have something to tell me?"

"Well," Vesta said, sitting up, "Jonas and I have kinda been seeing each other since before Thanksgiving, and," Vesta drew out the word, wiggling her shoulders with contained mirth, "he made things official right before Winter Break!"

"What a wonderful surprise," Cora said evenly. "I'm very happy for you. I wondered if something was percolating there." She winked over her shoulder at the closet. "I guess I'll have to knock from now on."

"Oh, please." Vesta rolled her eyes, nonetheless feeling a bright and now familiar jolt of adrenaline. "We're not sure how serious we are yet, and both of us want to wait for marriage. But yeah, it's great. Jonas is really fun! Now we can double date . . . if you guys want."

"You still might need privacy," Cora said, "but that won't be necessary. I don't know how much Elliot and I will be hanging out anymore."

"Oh?" Vesta asked, "no . . . "

"Don't worry about it. It just didn't work out, 's all. We were just friends anyway." Cora's tone was relaxed, but she kept facing away as she put a few things in her shoulder bag. "Anyway, I'm gonna go get some coffee at Talbot's. Need anything from town?"

"No, I'm fine. I'm . . . here if you want to talk later," said Vesta, still processing. Despite its undefined status, Vesta had grown used to Cora and Elliot's relationship.

"Thanks," said Cora, smiling as she stopped in the doorway, "have a nice nap."

Vesta could swear she saw tears welling in Cora's eyes before she closed the door.

Vesta leaned back onto her pillow. She would try to get more out of Cora later; she would need to, if only to ask what she planned to do about Rydar's party. Vesta did not want to meddle, but if she could do something to keep the party from becoming awkward . . .

She blinked, yawning. She would deal with it later. Opening Chopin, she began to read; she fell asleep before reaching the end of the first page.

CHAPTER 10

E LLIOT LIKED COLSON'S house. Had he been asked to imagine where the professor lived—for he had imagined it—he would have guessed one of the old Victorians tucked away in the non-grid streets of Old Orangedale. However, after entering behind a smiling Rydar, who had taken Elliot's jacket and given him a brief tour, Elliot recognized that this place fit the man much better. With only a main living room and kitchen, a master and guest bedrooms, and an office, it was understated yet complete; Polonius's "rich, not gaudy," came to mind.

Grabbing a root beer from the ice chest, Elliot sat on the nearest couch to await the others; wondering if Cora would come, he took in the room. It was all angles, straight lines, and curves; the couch, a muted dark gray, was much more comfortable than it looked. The tables—a tall round one near the sliding glass door, a low rectangular one by the couch, and a shallow one running along the back of the couch—were a mix of black glass and steel legs. Beneath the vanilla-mint scent of a large Christmas candle on the coffee table Elliot could smell a heavier, deeper essence of smoke—less sharp and sour than cigarettes yet not as sweet as incense. It was not unpleasant.

The flickering candlelight drew Elliot's eyes to the portrait. On the wall across from the couch was a large, frameless print of a young Rydar— possibly in his early twenties, with no beard and in a black suit—and an Asian woman in a dark red dress. They seemed about to kiss. Elliot found he desperately wanted them to, as if the photo, itself, made one wish it.

It was a good shot, thought Elliot. Rydar had beautiful taste, though the girl was a bit thin. At first glance she surprised Elliot—completely different from the tall, severe blonde CEO of some sort that Elliot had imagined as Colson's type, no doubt influenced by gleanings from his abortive attempt to read *Atlas Shrugged* the previous semester. Though not immediately attractive, the girl did have a mark of severity to her. Elliot was surprised when he saw it—a hardness in the neck and jaw muscles that underlied the joy and unmasked desire in her eyes. Her left arm, falling back and holding a small, black clutch, had a similarly tensile strength, as if beneath the frail muscles was a skeleton impossible to break. Her carefree posture tempted one to imagine trying—and dared one to have pity on her seemingly frail form.

Elliot shook his head. It was just a photo; however, as the piece around which Colson had built the room, Elliot knew, it was much more than that. The couple seemed insolent in the pleasure they took in each other and in their utter indifference to everything around them—including the one taking the picture and, by extension, Elliot, himself.

Elliot imagined whether he and Cora would have looked like that if photographed. Could they? It would probably feel staged, a mere pastiche trying to mimic the unaffected, blissful rapture of the real thing—or, at least, of Rydar and that woman.

Elliot felt encouraged: just a few weeks ago he would have never admitted that. Would Cora have? Elliot doubted it. He sipped his drink, wondering that the previous week's break should have already changed him so.

"Finally," said Rydar's voice, followed by the voices of Vesta, Cora, and, oddly, Jonas. After being shown around the small house, they were escorted to the living room.

"Hey, Elliot," called Vesta in a higher tone than usual, "you should've driven with us, it's cold out there!" She sounded nervous; Elliot could guess why.

"No, I'm fine. I'd rather bike anyway," he said, thanking her with a wide smile. They were behind him greeting the other cast members and adults, but Elliot could have sworn she and Jonas were holding hands. Hanging back from Vesta, Cora made brief eye contact with Elliot. After a smile of token acknowledgment she looked away.

"Wow, who's that?" Vesta had seen the picture.

"My wife," said Colson, emerging from the coat room.

Elliot looked back at Cora; she had seen the picture, too. Elliot could not believe it: despite her tightly held jaw, she looked frightened, as if she wanted to look away but could not. It was the same look Elliot had seen after Sam ran him off his bike.

"She's so beautiful," Vesta cried, sitting next to Elliot and pulling Jonas down next to her, "I didn't know you were married! Why haven't we met her?"

Jonas discreetly put a hand on Vesta's arm. All the adults ceased talking.

"She passed away a few years ago," said Rydar with a smile, raising a hand to calm Vesta's suddenly horrified look. "No, don't worry, Vesta. You didn't know. But yes, that's my Eun-Ji." The man's voice had no trace of sadness, other than the slight magnanimity of passing over Vesta's gaffe.

Elliot glanced back at the picture. It was as if a veil had been removed from understanding his professor: if that young man had lost that woman and had stood back up, the result would be Rydar Colson. Elliot felt an inexplicable, yet slightly shameful, relief in the realization, as if a weight of expectation had been removed. He fought the impulse to look at Cora.

"I'm so sorry—," Vesta began, in a genuine tone.

"Hold on, Vesta," Colson interrupted with a raised hand, calm but with an unmissable firmness. "I have very few rules for my house, since I have very few rules for myself, and almost none on language. But 'sorry' is one word I don't allow here. Outside it's fine, but here I don't let anyone spare me like that—not regarding the things I love."

Despite Rydar's directness, the twinkle in his eye was like a lifeline to Vesta, who just nodded, smiling. Colson had not looked at the picture, but Elliot had the feeling that even now he wanted to.

"Well, obviously you'd like to tell us more," chuckled Grey Maxwell, seated beside Frank Hoegren, who was accompanied by an attractive Hispanic woman Elliot assumed was his wife.

"I guess it's not the most conventional way to kick off a party, though not the worst," said Rydar after a moment without looking at Maxwell. "Some of you have been here before, but this is the house Eun-Ji and I would have had. We were together in college," Rydar said, winking slyly at Vesta and Jonas, who respectively winked and saluted back, "and she was the strongest woman I'd ever known—or have known since. However, because of her . . . rough childhood . . . she developed cancer. We were married for only a few months before she passed, but I wouldn't undo it—and I'd murder the man who'd suggest it be undone." Rydar laughed to himself, looking to Grey. "Maxwell'll tell you the rest." Rydar leaned back against one of the walls, taking a sip of dark liquid from his tumbler.

"What's there to say?" Maxwell said, eyes fixed on Rydar. "Eun-Ji came here from Japan after escaping North Korea, you saw something in each other, and you squeezed as much life out of it as you could. Oh, also," the man said as if in an afterthought, "I had the pleasure of being their best man."

A mix of gasps and knowing smiles filled the room. Noting that none of it seemed to surprise the adults, Elliot realized with a start that Rydar Colson had friends.

"If I might be permitted," Hoegren spoke up, "you all see Rydar at practice and in class. Believe it or not, that's the tavern Rydar, if you understand me. This," the man motioned around the room, his eyes landing on Colson, "is Prince Rydar. Any hardness he's shown toward you at school masks one thing: joy. Insolent, self-sufficient pleasure at being alive—of which he knows the value better than most. I hate to risk spoiling it by naming it, Ry, but you did invite us to your hermitage."

"You couldn't spoil it if you tried. Anyway, enough of all this." Rydar raised his glass, looking pointedly at Hoegren. "Welcome to my monastery. Thank you all for the past year; I look forward to spending part of the next with you."

Several in the room raised their glasses, laughing. It was infectious, Elliot felt, all the more for being so uncharacteristic of Rydar and the others. He turned to Vesta and Jonas; Jonas seemed to know most of what Rydar and Maxwell had said. He began filling in the story for them—how Rydar had worked in the theater, how Eun-Ji had joined theater to better learn English, how in North Korea the movies, however edited and propagandistic, had been her window to another world, and how she had apparently always wanted to be onstage, herself. Elliot wondered at the story, asking questions along with Vesta. Elliot looked for Cora, but at some point she had left the living room.

"I wanna see the study," said Vesta after a while. "I'd like to know what's on Rydar's bookshelves." She patted Elliot's knee in invitation.

"You've seen his bookshelves at Uni," said Elliot, standing nonetheless.

"Yeah, but what do you think he has here?" she replied, making her way through the living room. As they went to the hall, Elliot looked back; Rydar had joined Maxwell and the others. Glancing at Elliot, he nodded his chin forward toward the office.

Inside the small room was a wooden desk, a wall of books, and a small cabinet with bottles of different alcohols and mason jars of what Elliot guessed was pipe tobacco. Atop the cabinet was a wooden box with a glass top housing cigars of different sizes and a stand with several pipes. The source of the smoky scent, much more pungent in the office, was now plain.

"Who's that?" asked Vesta, looking at the wall. A black and white portrait showed a bearded man in a snow cap looking up, as if in surprise. Elliot thought whatever the man was seeing must be important.

"I think that's Aleksandr Solzhenitsyn," said Jonas, "after leaving the Soviet gulag."

Vesta just looked at the man, apparently sharing Elliot's unspoken question of why it should be in Colson's office.

Elliot abruptly stopped surveying the room. On another wall, staring off to the left of the painter, was a face he had not expected: the mustached profile of Friedrich Nietzsche.

"Why's he up there?" asked Elliot, aware of the distaste in his voice.

"Ask Ry," said Jonas, smiling, "and take it as a compliment if he tells you."

"Tells you what?"

Cora had slipped into the office to join them. Elliot held his breath.

"Why he has a portrait of Nietzsche," answered Vesta. "Cora, relax—put your bag down with the coats."

Elliot noticed she was clutching her bag closed with both hands; it did look unnatural.

"I'm fine," Cora said, "but you're right." She left the office; when she returned, rather than stand in the open place next to Elliot she moved to the opposite corner to observe the bookshelves. Trying not to notice and failing, Elliot looked back at the portrait of Nietzsche, recalling the things he had read about the man—and how his own philosophy of welcoming madness had caused him to go mad. Served him right, Elliot thought.

"So, you've found my sanctum," said Rydar's voice from the doorway.

"It suits you so much it's obscene," said Cora, not turning from the bookshelf.

"Thanks," Rydar said, smirking. "I hope you're not disappointed. Anything you want to know about?"

"Yeah," said Vesta, "what's Solzhenitsyn looking at?"

"Frankfurt Cathedral," Rydar replied.

"Why have a picture of him and not the cathedral?" asked Elliot, hoping to move the question to the other picture.

"Because this was taken right when he got off the train after escaping Soviet Russia. Want to know what a cathedral can mean? Don't ask someone who grew up around them; instead, look at the face of someone who hasn't seen a building designed to uplift one's glance for many years. He'd just come out of hell, mind you, where the rule of architecture was to push the individual down. That," Rydar pointed at the portrait, "is the face of psychological salvation and rebirth."

"And why that one?" asked Elliot about the Nietzsche.

Catching Elliot's tone, Rydar just leveled his eyes at him. The pause made Elliot feel small.

"For the same reason; you'll notice Nietzsche's looking over at Solzhenitsyn. Nietzsche may not have lived through the same gulag, but he saw it coming. Like I've said in discussion, he and Dostoyevsky," Rydar motioned to a smaller portrait atop one of the bookshelves of a bearded, bald-foreheaded man with hands folded in his lap, also facing left, "were the prologues trying to prevent the things that happened in the twentieth century; Solzhenitsyn was the epilogue."

"But I thought Nietzsche caused the Germany of the twentieth century."

Rydar just smiled at Elliot.

"I think I know who you need to read next," said Rydar after a moment. "Frankly, I'd hoped you would on your own. I won't make you; on principle, I don't assign Nietzsche unless I'm sure the other person has already read enough Scripture, philosophy, and Shakespeare to understand him in context, and even then I'd suggest Dostoevsky at the same time, if not instead of. You're right to be cautious. You need to be ready for Nietzsche, and you need to be good at extracting the meat from the bones—which are explosive! But he wasn't a Nazi, like the story has unfortunately gone. Far from it; he was a physician who cut into his century in order to prevent cancer in the next. In fact," Rydar paused, thinking for a moment, "here, let me show you something." He waved them after him.

Rydar walked across the hall to his bedroom, the door of which was already cracked. After they all came in, he turned on the light. Above the bed's headboard was a wide print Elliot knew—Raphael's *The School of Athens*, with Plato and Aristotle surrounded by all the other major thinkers of antiquity. However, Rydar was directing their attention to a painting on the facing wall.

A pool divided the scene into two contrasting halves. On the top half, in bright whites, blues, and yellows, stood a throne with a bearded man seated on it, with other smaller thrones seated beside him.

"Is that heaven? Christ, I mean?" asked Vesta, examining the painting with wide eyes.

"No—heaven would have two thrones," said Rydar. "It's actually a scene from literature. Anyone know it?"

"Dante's *Inferno*," said Cora somberly, "that's Limbo, and on the throne is Aristotle."

"Yes—excellent, Cora," said Rydar, nodding at her. "'The master of those who know,' as Dante succinctly calls him, not needing—or presuming—to speak his name."

Elliot noted how Cora's eyes stayed on Rydar a long moment after he turned his head back to the wide mural. Elliot looked back to the painting; he should have known it was Aristotle.

Beneath the bright scene above the pool was not a reflection but a single, upside-down chair, its wood tinted green as if underwater. On it, resting his head on his hand, elbow to his knee, was a suited man with a large mustache.

"I commissioned this painting a few years ago, from someone in LA whose work I enjoy. You see, for all his ridicule of those around and before him, there's one philosopher whom Nietzsche does not explicitly criticize: the Philosopher, Aristotle. Tell me, how was Aristotle different from those around him?"

Those in the room thought. Vesta shifted her arm up and down in the crook of Jonas's elbow as she leaned closer to him.

"He looked at this world, and at humans as such, as ends in themselves," said Jonas, a knowing smile on his face.

"You're taking that from one of our conversations, of course," said Rydar, smirking, "but yes. Let that be your jumping off point for Nietzsche, if any of you choose to approach him. If I commissioned it now I'd probably have Dostoevsky standing behind the chair, or seated in it alone—though he doesn't really fit as a reflection of Aristotle, and he certainly doesn't look merely at this world." Rydar shrugged, smiling. "In the end I think he's the better read."

"Or, if we want to just look at this world, we could just read Ayn Rand," said Elliot, annoyed and looking away from Jonas and Vesta. Jonas snickered.

"Of course," Colson said, moving to the door, "but why play with toys when you can learn to use the actual tools?"

Elliot tried not to react, despite feeling defensive, disgusted, and yet curious.

"You can take the cat out of the jungle . . . " said Cora with a sigh, "he's even a teacher here."

"He's himself," replied Jonas, with an edge of correction, "especially here. If we find there's something to learn, all the better. C'mon—I think Blythe just arrived." Jonas and Vesta followed Rydar.

"Yeah, I'll be in there in a minute," said Elliot, feeling despite the slight that he needed to consider what Rydar had just said. Cora remained for a bit, leaving after a few moments of silence from Elliot.

Despite his admittedly unexamined distaste for Nietzsche, Elliot stayed to consider the painting. He imagined cautiously climbing upside down and stepping into the water, surmounting the impassable river between the painting's hemispheres not by picking his way across but by completely submerging himself into it. The musing left him feeling the excitement and confidence he usually only knew in dreams.

Elliot suddenly wanted to laugh, though he could not articulate why. He did not need to; he could figure it out later. For now, he would just let it work on him. He went to return to the party.

"Had enough?" said Rydar, leaning against the wall beside the hallway as Elliot nearly skipped past him. "I was about to come get you—wouldn't want you snooping around my room too much." The man winked.

"Anything valuable I took out I brought in with me," said Elliot.

"Now, that's the language I like to hear," said Rydar, "and, hey, I probably wouldn't say this at practice, but I hope you know I'm never trying to break you, yourself, down. I wouldn't challenge you so much if I didn't think you could take it. You're a lot stronger than you think you are, Elliot."

"Oh, uh . . . yeah," Elliot nodded, bewildered by the compliment and its timing, "thanks."

"Don't mention it. I think Blythe wanted to see you," Rydar said, pointing his tumbler at the man.

Not until long after he had approached the adults and Blythe—who, after giving him a bear hug that lifted him off the carpet, handed him a six-pack of craft beers with a small red, green, and gold Christmas bow— did Elliot realize he had not felt his usual impulse to be sarcastic. Indeed, whether because of the place or the people, an aura of excitement and levity, as if he had shed a heavy, stuffy jacket, suffused the rest of the evening. Suddenly not caring about what had passed between them, Elliot wanted to tell Cora about his feeling and lift her up as Blythe had him; however, in the same moment he remembered she might not share the sentiment he realized she was nowhere to be seen.

" . . . so, I just want to talk, when you're ready . . . "

Cora held her phone up so Ermine could hear.

Ermine had stayed in Orangedale over Winter Break, having finally told his parents he did not believe in celebrating Christmas, claiming also that he needed to work on things for the newspaper. He had not told them about leaving *The Praes*; besides, *The Homefront* was essentially the same thing, if more honest. Nonetheless, when his mother started to berate him— her Filipino accent becoming more pronounced as she tried, Ermine knew, to cover her sadness with anger—he had hung up. His parents had not called since.

"Elliot just needs to accept that he can't have whatever he wants," said Ermine when the voicemail ended. "To be honest, sugar, I think it's good. It never really felt right, you two together. I didn't like what he brought out of you."

"You just didn't like that Sam and him got along," retorted Cora as she leaned back against Ermine's bed.

"Yeah, and look how that turned out. Just goes to show . . . But it's okay—Skylar and I are a much better fit." Ermine shrugged.

He dipped a chip into the platter of assorted hummus and salsa they had opened the night before. Of course, he had seen her and Elliot peacocking around campus, flaunting how she was siding with the production despite its supporting the very cultural status quo that was stacked against her. However, when she had texted Ermine, he had been careful not to be too immediately vindictive. After all, though temporarily confused, Cora was a comrade-in-arms, and her reaching out over this rupture with Elliot might be her way of returning to the side where she belonged. Ermine leaned back, glancing at the workaday sitcom they had been bingeing over the last two days.

"It's ironic . . . " she said.

"What?"

"I thought I'd like it if he stood up for himself, but when he did it was just annoying, like a pretense. I don't even really have anything against defining relationships, but when it came to ours it just felt wrong. Like arbitrarily caving to others' expectations too late. I'd thought we could work things out, but seeing that picture . . . " She shut her mouth abruptly.

Ermine turned to face her. "What picture?"

"Oh, Colson has this picture—a big portrait of himself and his late wife, when they were students here. It captured what I hoped it would be like with Elliot, if he'd been what I first thought he was."

"Which was?"

"A man. Sorry, I know idealized masculinity isn't your thing, Ermine, but, perhaps to my discredit, it's mine. You know, I was a sucker for books about strong or smart men, despite being told it was all toxic. Maybe it was because I was told that. My mom never let me think it—she was a feminist, but she didn't hate men, only weak ones.

"When I first saw Elliot, and when I heard him talk back to Ingman in class last semester, I thought, there's a man I could be proud of attracting—and of beating with his own attraction. Of course, I didn't think it in those words, but I think that's what the feeling between my legs meant. If Elliot could look at me how he looked at his books, it would be worth me. But as I got to know him, I found that wasn't the case. I had to lead him too often. I mean, it was fun, and when we were . . . "

"Fake fucking?" Ermine supplied the euphemism he had given to what Cora had described in the things she and Elliot had done. Ermine still smiled at the term, surprised that Cora was so needlessly and trivially bashful about asserting her and Elliot's maintained virginity; he took pleasure in pitying her unexpected—and he thought unfortunate—chastity.

"Yeah, when we were doing that he was almost the man I thought he could be. But there was always something that wasn't living up to that first image of him. I attributed it to his age and my possibly expecting too much. And he started standing up like I wanted as we did the play, but it's weird—the more he did so, the more meh I got. Then I saw that picture at Rydar's, when Colson was Elliot's age. It was the exact look I'd wanted to see from Elliot—one of focus, and worship, and pride. It looked so sure of itself, Rydar's face. I realized Elliot could never look at me like that, and that I no longer cared if he did . . . "

Ermine bit his tongue; he had been watching Cora the last couple of days, wondering what was the combination to understanding her. Now, he glimpsed something closer to her center than he had ever seen: she wanted Rydar Colson. Cora's use of Elliot, her sudden joining the play, and her disillusion with both suddenly clicked into place. Ermine needed to be careful how he reacted if he were to best use the discovery.

"Well, that fits, dearest," Ermine said. "A woman like you deserves a man who doesn't question himself. You know I've always thought you were a cut above. There aren't many of us, really, with the constitution to face down traditions and the conservatism of others who lack daring and prefer inertia. I'd never tell them, but most of my staff is not nearly as progressive as they think; without Sky and me they'd be lost. You won't mind my telling you that—you understand. You aren't a sheep, even if you do support people and ideas that feed off of them." Ermine winked. Cora smiled and looked away, as if considering what he had said.

"You know," she said, taking a book out of her bag, "I've been reading Nietzsche over the past week, and you sound a bit like him."

"Purely accidental—I've never had the pleasure, myself. However, I wouldn't wonder at it. He's one of the forefathers of modern protest criticism and culture, after all. Breaking down the church and finally saying, 'God is dead,' and all that. It's unfortunate how he caused the Nazis and all, but from what I've heard of his rereading of history we can forgive him for how others used him."

Cora chuckled. "So if people misuse Shakespeare, it's bad, but Nietzsche's okay?"

Ermine looked at her dryly. "Don't let's be cute. You know that's purely political; I don't mean half of what I say about Shakespeare. It's Rydar I'm against, which, in Orangedale, now means Shakespeare. Which is ironic, considering . . . "

"What?" Cora said, still smiling as she looked up from the book.

"Well, in print I revile the man, yet now I'm seeing one of my favorite people fall in love with him—and I find I'm not unhappy for her."

Rolling her eyes to hide what Ermine knew was sudden embarrassment, Cora began, "Ermine, I'm not—."

"Now, now, dear, I don't mean to speak out of turn," he said, knowing he must be careful at this moment, "you know better than to think I'd have a problem with it. Indeed, if there's anyone I know who could handle that man—who was as great as him—it would be you. More importantly, he could handle a girl like you. Besides, who can say where love will bloom? Look at Sky and me. I think it was always there, part of our shared cause, but it feels as if I finally have what I always needed from Sam."

"Or it was a rebound," Cora said, eyes half-closed in a lilting glance.

"Don't be cynical; I'm happier than I've been in a long time. Skylar understands me, perhaps better than anyone I've ever known. I only want that for you. What you thought you were attracting in Elliot, the manliness you wanted from him," Ermine tried to say the word without too much irony, "well, what if it's been within your grasp all along, just in the person of someone else? It's a risky, scandalous thought, I know, being attracted to your teacher, but really, how much older than us is Colson? From what I've heard he goes out of his way to spend time with students, and he seems to reserve a special attention for you. I'd say part of him probably wants to attract a student, subconsciously; he's a hunter, no doubt. Wouldn't the best thing be a student who isn't prey, who's mature enough to want him like that, as a predator in her own right? If anyone could stand up to him—because that's the kind of woman a man like him needs and wants, a hard target—it would be you, Cora. And, after all, he's not unattractive . . . "

"No . . . " Cora said, her brow furrowing slightly.

Ermine smiled to himself; he had planted the seed. Now he just needed to keep from saying too much and to watch her. He would work out later how to use whatever happened.

"Anyway," Ermine said, "I feel like doing something. Let's go into town! It's a pretty day, and we've been cooped up in mourning for too long. You should be celebrating your freedom! We won't get another chance to see the town when it's empty."

Cora nodded. As Ermine pulled on a sweater Cora slipped the book into her bag and swung her scarf around her neck. She said nothing.

A walk would be good, thought Ermine as he opened the door. It would allow him to forestall any second-guessing he feared was on the edge of Cora's thought. Above all, he had to keep her optimistically romantic. Despite their mutual railing against the plastic and materialism of Christmas, seeing downtown Orangedale still decorated with lights, garlands, and wreaths, along with the sunlight on the puddles from the previous day's rain, would make her believe she could have all she wanted. Ermine needed her to think that desire, joy, and romance were possible in life—for the sake of the yet unformed plan steadily taking shape in his mind.

❄

Elliot had been walking around campus since lunch. He had assumed Cora would return after punishing him with distance, as she had done before. However, Cora's distracted demeanor at the party had struck Elliot as different from her usual affected disinterest.

However, Elliot, too, was changing. His semester-long worry over Cora's refusal to commit—which he had interpreted as a chronic threat to leave, if not an indifference to what he might need beyond the physical—had given way to a latent indignance that seemed to gnash against any regret he might feel. Vesta and Jonas's sympathy at the party had calmed him for a while, but the part of himself that seemed to have known things would end like this left Elliot restless and frustrated. Nonetheless, he told himself he still wanted to be with Cora, but it would have to be on equal terms.

"Elliot!" called a man's voice from across the quad. It was Rydar.

"Hey!" Elliot waved back, turning toward the man who was apparently out for a walk, himself.

Upon seeing Elliot's face as they shook hands, Rydar's brow furrowed. "Nice day out."

"Yeah, it is. What are you doing on campus?"

"Just enjoying the cold," Rydar said, surveying the dim mist rising from the grass in the sunlight. "I like it when there aren't too many people around. Lets me remember when I went here."

Elliot thought of the portrait; he tried to imagine the link between the young man in the suit and the lonesome yet smiling professor now before him. Elliot wondered if the man really was lonesome.

"It's funny," Elliot said, "I was just thinking of you."

"Oh? Why?"

"Well . . . more about your party." Elliot regretted mentioning it, yet part of him felt spurred on, as if he suddenly and desperately wanted to talk to the man. "It's actually about Cora . . . "

Rydar pursed his lips and sighed as he did in class when discussion went off-topic. "Everything okay? I noticed you two didn't show up together."

"It's just, I haven't seen her since the party, and even before that we had a fight."

"I noticed something was different."

A lift of the man's eyebrows implied a question. Any attempt at equivocation would be superfluous.

"We broke up."

Rydar observed Elliot; he tightened his lips. Looking away across the empty quad, Rydar adjusted his scarf as he considered something.

"Doing anything today?"

"Uh . . . no, not really." Elliot unconsciously padded his pockets, feeling his keys, phone, and wallet. He had figured he would eventually go home to read or play until Cora returned his voicemail.

"Let's go over to my place. We'll talk it out." The man nodded toward the chapel parking lot.

CHAPTER 11

"TAKE A SEAT."

Rydar motioned to one of four stools at the tall, circular glass table. From the kitchen he brought two tumblers with ice and a decanter.

"Oh, no, I'm okay," said Elliot.

"Bullshit." Rydar poured the drinks and sat down. He leaned back and stared out the back window into the muted light of the overcast afternoon.

Elliot felt as he had while Rydar was driving them to the house—that, peripherally, the man was watching his every move. Elliot took the tumbler and smelled the amber whiskey.

"I'm not asking as a teacher or director, but as a friend and as a man: what's wrong, Elliot?"

Sighing, Elliot took a drink, trying to resist the cough when the whiskey hit his throat. Rydar was looking outside.

"It's just," Elliot began after catching his breath, "I think Cora and I are really breaking up."

"You think?"

"Yeah; I mean, we never really defined things, but we've been together since September."

"Yes," said Rydar, turning in his chair to take his whiskey and face Elliot. "Wasn't my business; still isn't, really, since whatever's going on between you two hasn't affected the production so far. But, to be candid, I hoped you two would realize sooner that you weren't a good fit."

"What do you mean?" said Elliot.

Rydar looked at Elliot; his eyelids tightened after a moment.

"Relax, Elliot. I'm sorry; under different circumstances you two would be great together, but you're not ready—definitely not for what I assume you've already jumped into. You weren't wrong to like each other, much less to want each other, but two halves don't make a whole."

"What do you mean? How much have you thought about us?"

"Enough. Just because it's not my business doesn't mean it doesn't concern me. I care about you two, and I hate to see young people playing grown-up—which usually ends up distracting them from really growing up."

The way Rydar leaned back calmed Elliot. That the man had needed to spend any time considering Elliot and Cora's love life seemed less of a presumption against the two of them than against Colson, himself. Elliot looked over at the picture on the wall.

"That's the thing," Rydar continued, "you were almost there in summer. I think you might be there now, at the cusp of creating yourself, of becoming your own person. Frankly, you could be a lot farther—and happier, I think. Not to make Cora sound bad," Rydar said, looking outside over his shoulder. "Neither of you are bad; you're just young. You see greatness, but you have no idea what it really requires—or what it even is."

Elliot gave a dry chuckle. "That's the problem—I'll try to stand up for myself, but she'll say I'm just caving to others' expectations. We had a fight a few days before your party. I wanted to come as a couple, like Vesta and Jonas, but she said I was a coward."

Rydar nodded. "Did you think you were?"

"No—I said she was the one afraid of a real relationship. She didn't take it well. I don't blame her."

"You were right—though Cora's perspective in all this is probably just as defensible as yours. There's definitely a place for the privacy of wordlessness early in relationships—the risk of desire without narrative defense—but it's childish to want that forever. Frankly, I'm amazed you two lasted so long; I'm proud of you for standing up for yourself, Elliot, especially in the face of the inertia behind you."

"Thanks," said Elliot, taking a drink without coughing. "It just seems so petty, now, even though it's only been a few days. Like, sometimes I miss her and want to work it out, but other times I get defensive and angry at how she treated me."

"Have you talked to her?"

"No. I called, but she didn't pick up. I think she'd still act like I'm the problem."

"Well, you probably are, for her," Rydar said, sipping his drink. "And you said it: it's petty. Despite whatever you did together, if it couldn't survive your first fight—your first real act of definition—then as far as I'm concerned it wasn't a real relationship. Relationships are only as strong as what they can survive; that's because they're made of people. You want to know why the last few days have been different? I noticed it at the party; even then you'd changed. I'd say it's because you saw you could survive a fight, even if your relationship with Cora couldn't."

"Yeah, things feel really different now," said Elliot, ignoring the part of him that still missed Cora. "Lighter, brighter, that kind of thing. It's ironic: I just want to share it with her. You know when you want to see someone and share some new thing with them because you know they'll understand it? That it'll relieve the problem you've both been fighting, but you can't because they're part of the problem?"

Rydar chuckled. "Every damned day." At Elliot's look he motioned with his forefinger to the tall picture as he sipped his drink.

"Oh shit—I'm sor—."

Smiling, Rydar cut off the word with a glance. Elliot just nodded.

"But," Elliot continued, "you understand what I mean, right?"

Rydar stood and walked over to the table behind the couch. The pipe stand Elliot had seen in Rydar's office had been moved to the living room; the man pinched some tobacco into a large, gnarled pipe of raw wood, packing it down with his ring finger before dropping and packing another pinch. The black band on the man's ring finger, which Elliot had never seen, matched the dark wood of the pipe. Walking to the back door, Rydar struck a match, lit the pipe, let the small flame go out, then lit another and drew in a long mouthful. Leaning against the sliding glass door's metal doorframe, he let the smoke out into the yard. Elliot took a sip of whiskey.

"If I had one wish," Rydar said, "it would be that before she died, Eun-Ji could have known how much joy I'd take in our relationship, in the end. It was worth it—because it was difficult. The abyss we both knew we were jumping into—and which she knew I would have to climb back out of—became a source of joy I could've neither named nor foreseen. It would have been cheap—petty," Rydar looked at Elliot, "had the stakes been less. Sometimes I wonder if at some level she knew that the pain

I'd go through would ultimately increase my joy. One thing I'm certain about: she would have understood."

Elliot did not know what to say. His situation seemed silly by comparison; however, for his part Elliot felt as if he had avoided cheapening things with Cora. Indeed, he realized it had been against the picture on Rydar's wall that he had unconsciously weighed the past few days' thoughts and emotions.

"Why'd you stay, if you knew she was going to die?" Elliot asked.

Rydar chuckled. "How much do you want to know?"

Elliot shrugged, relaxing back. He ran the arch of his shoe along one of the stool's crossbars; despite its metal and glass aesthetic it was comfortable.

After puffing a long cloud outside over his shoulder, eyebrows furrowed, Rydar said, "I think our relationship was, in essence, a triumph over the impotence of need we'd both learned from our childhoods. She was from North Korea, see. Her father, a Japanese POW, married a Korean woman, who died when Eun-Ji was real young. She was a miraculously hard kid—harder even than the life she was born into. She grasped early on that the expected worship of the leader's portrait on the wall and the rhetoric of brother- and neighbor-love from the radio were directly related to the limits on her every attempt to have fun. However, rather than stifle herself under her society's wishes, she decided it was the society that was wrong."

Rydar laughed, a shot of smoke accompanying the sound. "Eun-Ji was exactly the kind of person state collectivism rightly warns its members about. Her dad soon realized he'd never be able to make her obey, and that he didn't want to. So, against all odds, he got both of them out. I think it was in the nineties, but her dad foresaw the problems of Kim Il-Sung transferring power to his son. He got them over the northern border only a couple months before the famines started. They made their way down to Hong Kong and were able to contact his remaining family in Okinawa. Eventually, they came here for a fresh start. Eun-Ji was young, but not too young to forget North Korea and to recognize the difference in her circumstances. She had learned enough English between Hong Kong and Japan to understand some, and one of her dad's nieces came to interpret. But even that wasn't necessary."

"What do you mean?" asked Elliot. Rydar's growing smile had peaked at the thought. The whiskey had filled Elliot's head with a clear lightness, and he was enjoying Colson's story.

Rydar beamed. "It might sound unbelievably cliché, but when we first saw each other we both knew what we were looking at. Through our individual circumstances we'd both developed a heightened sensitivity to need—not practical need, mind you, which when it can't be relieved can be borne with dignity, but real, willful, existential weakness, the kind of needy victimhood that tries to justify itself. I think it was her contempt for such things—and the insolent pride such contempt requires—that I recognized." Rydar shook his head. "Eun-Ji just refused to thank the poor sophomore leading them on a tour of Orangedale. Of course, she was experiencing the pleasure of being in a place where one didn't bow. I saw it in her eyes, and, however incomparable my experiences were to hers, she later told me she saw the same in mine.

"So, I'd say it was that in us which wanted to stand, eyes forward and shoulders back, that made us fall in together—and stay in."

Elliot wondered that this—and the smile around the pipe stem—was what had always been behind Colson's terseness. Hoegren had said as much.

"What did your friends say, after?"

Rydar shrugged. "Few understood, though they can be forgiven their pity. Nonetheless, soon after the funeral I became a hermit. Hiding your light isn't always cowardly, Elliot; at times it can be magnanimous and considerate for others—and for the light, itself. Not for nothing did Christ say to withhold one's pearls from swine. To see no difference between pearls and mud—and to avoid the responsibility of learning to—eventually turns everything to mud." Rydar chuckled, drawing a long draught of smoke. "If he had only said that, he would've already been the redeemer of mankind, besides all the rest.

"Those who knew me—Grey, Frank, Angela—understood it. They didn't try to reduce or escape the meaning of the situation." Rydar laughed, looking back at Elliot; tears had come to his eyes. "They were just with me, y'know? Like Job's friends before they opened their mouths. They looked out for me, but not in any ignoble way that would degrade Eun-Ji's meaning. If they did show pity, it wasn't so I or they might escape the pain but so I could endure it. They gave me the greatest gift you can give a man: they let me suffer the cup I'd chosen."

Elliot looked over at the woman in the portrait, which seemed now to have been set up in defiance of the portraits of the Kim family Elliot had heard annointed every North Korean home. He could recognize what Rydar was talking about; he had seen it on New Year's Eve: the smiling insolence of one too lofty to care whether others looked on. Elliot found himself considering, as he had the last few days, how close Cora had often come to looking that way—or had tried to.

"I guess it really puts my situation in its place," Elliot said with a chuckle. He took another sip of the whiskey; it was burning less, now that he knew what to expect. He enjoyed the light lucidity that seemed to connect his vision with the warmth in his stomach.

"I wasn't putting you down," said Rydar, knocking the pipe against the sole of his shoe before coming in. Leaving the door open—the smell of smoke was still heavy—he replaced the pipe on its stand, licking and inserting a pipe cleaner into the stem. "I just want you to know where I'm coming from, and that I'm not without my college relationship—however rare it may've been." Rydar chuckled. "We made it rare." He went to the kitchen and turned on the faucet, dousing his face.

Loudly so the man could hear it over the water, Elliot asked, "You said you both had 'individual circumstances.' What were yours? What made you sensitive to need, and all?"

Rydar remained silent, drying his beard on a red hand towel as he walked in to sit down. Accepting the whiskey Elliot had poured with a tip of the glass, he smelled it; his nostrils flared for a long time.

"My dad was a drunk. Not the bad kind; he never beat me or anything. Sometimes I wish he had. It would've been something tangible to see and hate, and to forgive. No, he was the weak kind; his was a very different and craftier psychology than the usual stereotypes. The drunks in Dostoevsky were once proud men; my father never was. Rather than compulsively maintaining a pretense at self-respect by trying to excuse his drunkenness, he wore it like a kind of badge, as if any response but pity would be a presumption. I don't even think it was the alcohol he was addicted to, either: it was the pity he could extract from people with it. He fed off of it, and whenever people pushed back and placed expectations on him—when they'd expect a modicum of pride from him—he'd just debase himself even lower to make them feel guilty for it. Degradation has its own virtues, too, Elliot, and often the first dog to show his belly survives longest, however contemptible his method."

"Then why do you drink?" Elliot had started to mimic the way Rydar swished the liquid around the bottom of his glass as it hung from his fingers.

"To ensure he has no power over me—because it's my life, not his. Back in college, though, I was a monk." Rydar smirked, taking a sip. "I was so zealous about my water. Of course, one could say that even avoiding the drink was letting my father influence me; I can live with that. Honestly, I've gone through so much by now that I don't think of him much. But after emancipating myself in high school I was dead set on putting myself as far I could from his weakness. Still, even then I was accidentally learning the dignity alcohol could have—from reading."

"Wait, you emancipated yourself?"

"Yeah. I was sixteen; it was actually over college that I did it. I'd always gotten good grades, and whenever I'd mention college there was a whine in his voice, even as he agreed that I should stay in school. He'd always put in some comment about wishing I could stay closer to home, or wanting me to commute rather than live at school so he could still see me. Of course, in his way and from his perspective, he probably loved me. I was the one thing worth loving in his life. But I started to suspect that if he had his way, without all the bromides of education being important, then I'd just stay at home indefinitely, joining him in his mental coma of TV, booze, and self-pity.

"By talking about college I think I provoked whatever violent reactions lay beneath his pallid demeanor. Again, he'd never hit me, but he'd 'forget' to sign documents or get really quiet and sharp. Drawn over months, every day, that's a whole other kind of abuse, all the more vicious for seeming—and needing to seem—innocuous and hard-to-pinpoint. When I'd talk back he'd always retreat, acting like I was creating problems and was paranoid. Still, within the hour he'd start right back up talking about me to himself, while I was in the room, about how high and far I was gonna go. When I'd call him on his sarcastic tone he'd say he really meant it. He was a master of evasion. Any conflict and he was already the victim before the first word. Wasn't long before every issue became the same issue, all summed up in the same weak, disconsolate sigh of how even his sixteen-year-old son was abandoning him."

"So that's when you left?" Elliot asked, considering how a man like Rydar could come out of such a situation. Elliot realized he had seen no television in Rydar's house.

"Yeah; the night before a class trip to a college he drank much more than his usual chronic stream. I woke up and found him with vomit all over his chest and barely breathing. I called nine-one-one and had to stay home to take care of it."

Rydar's mouth flexed into a tight line as he shook his head. "I felt so embarrassed as the police and ambulance dealt with him. They were professionals with hard training to help actually injured people, and it was beneath them to have to enter my dad's world and deal with a problem of his making. Also, over the course of that day I realized he would rather the same happened to me—that he'd rather I become what he was in that moment than prove it was possible to leave his world."

Rydar took a breath, running his tongue behind his closed lips to soften the dimpled frown on his face. His dry, open eyes looked into space; they did not move when he steadily, deliberately lifted the tumbler to his lips.

"The whole time," he continued, "a voice inside said, 'this is what cannibalism looks like.' The more I tried to force it down by consciously pitying the man and being the good son, the more it grew from a whisper to a statement to a scream. By the end of the day, when I was supposed to be coming home from the campus I'd been looking at pictures of for weeks, I was ready to listen to that voice. Soon a social worker helped me move in with a classmate's family for the rest of high school."

Rydar chuckled. "I haven't seen or heard from my father since. He could have found me—I have the same cell number—but he probably preferred to stay in his little world, licking and secretly adoring the wound of my leaving." Rydar shrugged. "Or he died—though they probably would've contacted me."

Despite the man's smile, Rydar's eyebrows had furrowed. Elliot realized Rydar had remembered all this for him, and that however comfortable the man seemed he still felt sadness at the memory. Elliot imagined the hardness with which Colson would have treated the subject were it to come up anywhere else; Elliot thought of how easy his life had been by comparison.

"It's okay, Rydar," Elliot said, responding as much to his own feeling as to Rydar's. "You've come a long way." Elliot pressed his palm to the table, letting the motion stand for the impulse to pat Rydar's arm.

The man lifted his eyes to Elliot's, grinning in the next moment. "Don't worry, Ell; I know. But thank you."

"What did you do after you left? Are you still close to the friend you stayed with?"

"We haven't talked since starting college. It really was an imposition, and I tried to keep my footprint small. I felt his parents still associated me with my dad, though that might have been my own embarrassment. Either way, they weren't the relief I soon found."

"Eun-Ji?" Elliot asked.

"No, she'd come later," Rydar said, smiling at Elliot's pause of disappointment. "This shouldn't surprise you by now, but once I opened my eyes I started reading as much as I could about great men. 'Til then I'd resisted reading them, in the way that sometimes you avoid something you know you need because of how it'll affect your life. 'God, make me chaste—but not yet!' St. Augustine said. But after I'd done it—after I admitted what my father was—I went full in. George Washington, J.D. Rockefeller, Philip Marlowe, Jean Valjean, Mr. Darcy, Howard Roark, Aragorn, anyone that might teach me how to be a different kind of man. If I saw a writer fundamentally sympathize with and try to excuse the pitiable—Dickens, for example, or Dostoevsky or Marx—I'd finish the book but never reread it. Then I found Shakespeare and Prince Hal—and it was like meeting a brother who'd gone before me."

Rydar looked sidelong at Elliot. "Of course, the heroic, itself, is undergirded by a vast structure of human tragedy and greatness I still wasn't ready to see; one serious look at *Hamlet* or *The Brothers Karamazov* or Dickens would've told me that. But I wouldn't realize that until after college. At the time I had enough to catch up on. Sure, my interpretations were biased, but I wasn't reading to learn: I was reading to survive, to make war on what I had been given, and to discover a new continent I felt had been intentionally hidden from me. Then I met Eun-Ji and, well . . . " The man shrugged, unable to keep himself from looking to the portrait and smiling with pleasure.

"I read Aristotle in high school," volunteered Elliot in the glow of the alcohol. "It was after another break-up. Not even that—a girl led me on . . . " He paused.

"Don't be bashful," Rydar said, motioning with his glass, "go ahead."

"It would've been my first relationship," Elliot continued. "Ends up she was just using me to manipulate her boyfriend—a big jock upperclassman. I was small in high school, and I've always been thin, so there's no way I'd confront her with him around. I probably wouldn't have even when he wasn't. So, there was this big hole of expectation, just gone, failed before it could start, and I thought it was my fault. It was horrible. I didn't know who to trust; I was so embarrassed, especially in front of my friends, who just watched me make a fool of myself."

Elliot paused to take a sip. Caught up in talking, his throat swallowed a moment too late, resulting in a sputtering cough that almost made him spill his drink. He put up a hand to stop Rydar from getting up, managing the burning tickle with further coughing and clearing of his throat.

"I needed to do something to stop its happening again," Elliot continued over a wheeze, "So on impulse I biked to the library and wandered around until I found a shelf I figured no one from school would visit—philosophy. I picked up a copy of Aristotle's *Poetics* and just sat down. It was dry, but I found I could understand it. So, I checked out a beginning primer on him, and soon got my own copy. By the end sophomore year I'd read *Poetics* and almost half of the *Ethics*." Elliot looked from his empty glass to Colson. "I mean, it wasn't that big a deal, the girl and everything, but in the end I came out better for it."

"You're right," Rydar said, standing to go to the kitchen, "and good choice. You literally could not have picked a better book to start your self-definition. Because that's what you were doing—you were redefining yourself in a crisis so you could never again be shaken by such a minor defeat. You should be thankful to those two, since in the end they did you more good than they could know."

Rydar returned with two glasses of ice water.

"Yeah," said Elliot, taking the water thankfully, "but in the end I think I overreacted; it didn't really mean that much—everyone gets rejected in high school. Besides, in this whole thing with Cora I've found I didn't put that girl as far behind me as I thought, nor, apparently, did I learn my lesson."

"First off, it did mean much—you made it mean much by discovering Aristotle out of it. You turned an unfulfilled expectation into a minor teleology from weakness to purposeful strength. Why do you think I've invested more attention and time—and, now, bourbon—into you than I have almost any other student, perhaps besides Jonas? It's because, despite still having a lot to learn about him, you'd read Aristotle before leaving high school, and that, for all your disdain for the man, you engaged in what Nietzsche called 'self-overcoming' without even being taught."

"What do you mean?" Elliot asked, taken aback and, his throat cleared by the sharp cold of the water, openly curious for Rydar's explanation of his venerating the philosopher Elliot had always considered with trepidation and disdain.

"I mean you didn't just discover something already in you: you created something new, mixing the broken mortar of your previous self-perception with the iron of the Philosopher. In a sense, you went from the accidental suffering of unrequited teenage attraction into a purposeful and much harder suffering. Because that's what Aristotle, and every other difficult and worthy book, can be at times: an act of controlled, constructive suffering with the end not of merely understanding it but of synthesizing it and your experience of it as a part of yourself, of growing by surviving it."

Sipping his water, Elliot got the sense that Rydar was not just talking about the high school Elliot, but of all his students—and of how he saw education in general.

"As for this thing with Cora and whether you're still dealing with that other girl, that's for you to figure out and come to terms with. For now, you need to admit what you really need and want, as close as you can stand. This is the time for it: when who you've been with Cora is cracking. Let it happen—in fact, shatter it faster!—and do your best to stand up taller afterwards. Like I said—significantly, on New Years'—you're stronger than you think."

"But do you think I'm wrong? To want things to be defined between us?"

Rydar put up his palm, shaking his head. "That's for you to decide, Ell, but I'd say it's looking down the mountain, not up. I could count many wonderful reasons a man might want to be with Cora, but none of them are worth derailing your own growth—though being with her might be a bluff you had to climb."

Elliot wondered a moment that Rydar might be able to better understand the situation because of his distance. The thought comforted Elliot.

"I don't really know why I was with her," Elliot said. "I just—I guess I just got swept up in how attractive she is and that she liked me. It took me a while to recognize and admit, but I was and really am into her. But part of it, the part I think matters . . . I think after studying Aristotle so much and refusing to be attracted by the next girl to bat her eyes at me I felt owed something. I think that's part of why I fell in so suddenly with Cora." Elliot laughed, relieved to say it out loud and yet imagining what people would think. "I mean, I know it's still just a shallow, long-term rebound in its own way, but there it is."

"Can I be honest?" Rydar asked.

"Please."

"Well, like I said, I've thought this was a distraction for a while—for you, if not for Cora. I don't mean from the play or your studies, but from the part that matters. I've hated seeing how you each corked your growth in different ways rather than face your individual trials. Even last spring I worried you were looking for some way to avoid seeing what you could really do. It's ironic, though not unsurprising, that what might have been your greatest attempt to avoid maturity would be what finally provoked you to stand up on your own. Not much, but enough. For that, this whole thing with Cora might, in the end, be the best thing you could have done if you end up stronger and more resilient because of it. Good or ill, I wouldn't wish it undone, though that's for you to ultimately chew on."

"But," Elliot protested, "if she's able to just end things, and push me around with no say, doesn't that make me weak? I mean, what if she's the weak one? Seems she's the one refusing to grow up." Elliot watched Rydar's face, ignoring the whine in his own voice.

"Like I said, I'm not here to talk about Cora. Don't worry about who was wrong or right; focus on rising above the need to be right, which, frankly, sounds like just another attempt to avoid the growth at your doorstep. Besides, begging by worrying about it demeans both of you." Rydar softened his tone at Elliot's wince. "But as for your being weak, what happens to you doesn't make you strong or weak; your response does. Besides, being able to withstand prolonged weakness or indignity often requires more strength and self-respect than open revolt would. Revolt is easy; you want resilience, Elliot."

Amidst his anxiety, Elliot felt an uncanny excitement he needed to resist—to not let whatever was being provoked in him rise too quickly.

"But I wasn't complicit, was I?" Elliot exclaimed, "I mean, I liked it, and, sure, I kept seeing her, but God! It was so embarrassing how she'd pretend nothing was going on, even though everyone knew. Why couldn't she just be my girlfriend? Open and clean, like Vesta and Jonas, without all the clandestine bullshit? I would have been okay with walks and all the gradual stuff, but we jumped right in, almost as far as you can go, without any commitment. I mean, I definitely pushed things, too, but eventually I felt used, like she was manipulating me with my own attraction—which she initiated!" Elliot cleared his throat, sniffing as he covered his face with his hands. Rydar turned his head to look outside.

"It's okay, Elliot," said Rydar. "You don't need to say more—not to me anyway. You'd do well to process it, yourself." The man looked at Elliot. "But you can do that later. After all," Rydar laughed suddenly, "you're free, Ell! Or you can be. Not from Cora—you two still have to work together, and she might be laboring under her own weights, which you should respect. Don't try to excuse or defend yourself by blaming her. Whatever the circumstances of your implicit arrangement, you were a willing participant; you were complicit, even if passively so. But even that's part of it! You're free from who you had to be to keep all of that going—and out of whom you haven't been able to grow. Maybe that's why it was hard to leave: you needed her to justify your not standing up taller. By letting her go, you've taken a step toward agency and self-respect. I'm proud of you; don't waste it."

Elliot did not respond. Rydar sipped his whiskey, turning in his chair to look outside—Elliot realized to give him some privacy.

After nearly a minute of listening to the faint beat of Rydar's wristwatch, Elliot asked, "How did you get over Eun-Ji? I don't mean over, and it's completely different, but, y'know . . . how did you deal with it?"

Taking a deep breath as he looked at the portrait, Rydar Colson smiled.

"I didn't get over her," Rydar said. "Actively, intentionally. I dug my heels in. I died with her, like a kind of psychological sati. The parts of me that survived did so the way you got past that other girl with Aristotle, only with Nietzsche and Dostoevsky."

The mention of the moustached philosopher again prompted curiosity, and, in his present vulnerability and lightheadedness, Elliot felt ready for anything.

"Is that why you don't talk about Nietzsche much? Because he reminds you of Eun-ji?"

Rydar smirked. "I don't talk about him because it's so easy to misunderstand him; I don't even claim I understand him, his effect on me notwithstanding. There's a lot of bones to pick through, but the meat's worth it. However, finding it needs a lot of context—the Bible, all of Greek philosophy, Shakespeare's corpus, eighteenth-century history, et cetera. It's the same reason you don't start the Bible at Lamentations. In fact, it might be impossible to understand Nietzsche without context. Which, yes, is like my relationship with Eun-ji, in a way. But I'd rather keep those pearls to myself—and you have your own to focus on." The man winked.

"Fine," Elliot said, sitting back with a smile. He watched himself draw a circle on the table with the bottom edge of his tumbler. He chuckled, remembering his reaction to seeing the name in the office at the beginning of Fall.

"Hm?"

"I was just thinking of how triggered I was when I first learned you liked him—Nietzsche; less so Dostoevsky, though I still didn't get it."

"Well, 'like' isn't really the word," said Colson, standing with a sigh and stepping toward the kitchen. Emptying the grounds from a coffee maker, he continued, "It's definitely not big enough. To my dismay—and, oddly, relief—I found I already knew them: Dostoevsky from my own life, and Nietzsche from the ignored and unseen places of the people I'd read. Like I said, I'd avoided Dostoevsky, not understanding why he insisted on choosing such degrading subjects. I'd started *Brothers K* a few times during college but found the characters either so weak or contemptible I couldn't get through the first hundred pages. Perhaps I needed different sustenance then; I'd had enough Fyodor and Smerdyakov from home, and, with the absolute clarity of shallow perception, I felt nothing but contempt for Alyosha. Nonetheless, Dostoevsky's was the humbling—though in the end so therapeutic and morally consistent—world I needed."

Rydar leaned back against the counter as the coffee brewed.

"Without getting too specific, things got bad after Eun-Ji. I'd sit most nights with a bowl of ice, a bottle of whiskey, and a gun on the table, hearing but not listening to jazz on the radio. I'd set it all out but wouldn't touch any of it. I think I was daring myself to say the pain was too much, that the memory of her smile, words, and body wasn't worth it, that I'd rather not exist than live in a world where we're born alone and where the most beautiful gods can die. And yet, even though I found an odd comfort in the option of killing myself, there was something deeper than the despair that said 'no,' something that would rather regard the pain as sacred than obscure or degrade it with whiskey or gunsmoke. To use the bottle or bullet would betray every joyful moment with Eun-Ji, and all the anticipation that had led up to her. Such things had, by then, become sacrosanct to me. I would have killed the man who said they were otherwise—and every night, I tested whether I was that man."

The coffee maker beeped; Rydar carried two mugs, the carafe, and a hot pad to the table. Elliot took a mug, holding it out as Rydar filled it.

"Thanks," he said.

"Sure." Rydar said, filling his own mug as he sat. "Anyway, once the ice would melt completely I'd put all of it away and go to bed. However, soon it risked becoming too ritualistic—which, to my naive understanding of such things, meant affectation. So, with the resigned, curious, pleading impulse of conscious masochism that covered the season, I picked up Dostoevsky, figuring I had nothing to lose."

Rydar blew the steam away from his mug but did not drink. He smelled the coffee for a moment before chuckling.

"Reading through his works—*Crime and Punishment*, then *Devils*—was a necessary humiliation, and a long time coming. Surviving it is my greatest source of pride. What similarity I initially refused to admit between myself and Raskalnikov became too blatant to ignore when I met Kirillov, the erstwhile apologist for suicide as salvation from God, as proof of His death. By making Kirillov a natural philosopher and an unwitting fool, and, thus, a danger to be taken seriously, Dostoevsky made me examine myself with him, watching in suspense whether in the end I'd sympathize with his nihilistic escapism, his malignant romanticism, or whether I'd admit I was just as puffed up a fool.

"Dostoevsky helped me face my nemesis: the nihilism that lay not just in his characters, not just in my father, but, beneath all my effort to throw myself into creating a new world of meaning with Eun-Ji, in myself. And that forced me to really consider it, to learn with horror that part of me wanted to say yes to suicide, to forget everything in the athiest's death of non-existence—and more, that I didn't hate myself for wanting it! But, thank God, through the course of Dostoevsky's skill I had already said no."

"You told us a bit about him when Megan presented on *Devils*," said Elliot. "He was Dostoevsky's image of the human will taken to its extreme. I think you said 'so much for the death of God.'" The smirk Elliot remembered Rydar concealing at the remark now shone as an open smile on his face.

"Yes. Dostoevsky's characters may have missed the point, but I hadn't—and I wasn't even conscious of it! When I read Kirillov's atheistic rationale for suicide—how he'd replace God by destroying the fear of death, how his suicide would make him the Christ of atheism—I laughed. I laughed and cried as I'd never been able to, as I'd never let myself. Despite his pretension to greatness, Kirillov sounded so small and naive—and I had sounded the same. Like him, I was a tragedian stuck not in a tragedy, but a comedy. In fact, it was much worse; *Devils* is a burlesque! Doesn't that make it infinitely more vicious? And to find, in the most critical time of my life, that I was similar not to a hero but to a blind fool! Much more than plot tension released that night. It was the last time I brought out the gun and the first night I opened the bottle—not out of escape but celebration. Dostoevsky saved my life, Elliot; I mean that literally."

Rydar sipped his coffee, smiling as Elliot imagined he had when first drinking that whiskey.

"Of course, if someone in the same situation came to me, I'd tell them to get help and not tempt themselves. But part of me would hope they could beat it; that part would have them read Dostoevsky."

"So, how did Nietzsche enter the picture?" asked Elliot, sipping the black coffee.

"Yes, yes," Rydar said, "after Dostoevsky, I was ready for Nietzsche. With a morbid irony as my only source of laughter, I still maintained that my gun was still there for me, should I decide I couldn't endure. Mind you, my experience—my war on myself, my testing of Eun-ji's effect on my life—was by this time mostly internal. By day I was getting my life together; I'd applied to grad school and started tutoring. But behind my eyes, in the night and isolation, this whole process of realizing what all was packed into my experience continued, though by summer the intensity had dulled into an odd lacuna, like a 'perhaps tomorrow—but after I finish this book.'

"As with Dostoevsky, except by then knowing it explicitly, I think I wanted Nietzsche to prove me wrong. But it wasn't his revolt against the past that got me—which draws on a much greater knowledge of that past than many of even his worst critics possess; instead, it was his case for hardness, for standing alone, for facing truth unfiltered, and for self-mastery.

"That's how he helped me: by teaching me that resilience was superior to purity, that I didn't need to run from my dad's example, that it and the joy Eun-ji occasioned in me could coexist. Indeed, the former had made the latter possible. Of course, though I wasn't yet ready to see it, this is essentially Dostoevky's thesis in *Brothers K*—that the existence of pain and degradation does not negate the possibility of joy, pride, and love, and might even be necessary for them. Either way, like a ladder from and, paradoxically, up to Dostoevsky, I still needed Nietzsche to articulate it. If in my first read Dostoevsky taught me not to be surprised or dismayed by pain, Nietzsche taught me that, rather than being a mark of moral failure, suffering was necessary for growth, and subsequent readings of Dostoevsky showed that it proved the reality of values. Far from being cursed by chance I had been blessed with a door of difficult, ennobling experience. I no longer had to fear psychological suffering; I would never again be seriously tempted to kill myself in defense against—and, really, submission to—my father's cravenness and Eun-Ji's death."

Rydar looked at Elliot over the top of his mug. Swallowing, he refilled the mug before extending the carafe; Elliot put his hand up, taking the half-filled mug for a sip.

After a few quiet moments, Rydar said, "Of course, I could've learned all that from Dostoevsky, but I still wasn't ready to meet the true hero.

When I eventually reread *The Brothers Karamazov*, I was ready to understand the secret to Alexei Karamazov—and to Aragorn, and Jean Valjean, and Darcy, and Prince Hal. It's with his least openly heroic hero, Alyosha, that Dostoevsky articulates the significance of the Incarnation—the rebirth of the supposedly dead God in the individual who redeems even the deepest, most degrading abysses by finding in them not only what is useful, but what is lovely, and fellowships with it. All the steps that had helped me survive the death of the God I didn't even know I believed in led me to Alyosha." Rydar smiled. "Perhaps I only needed Nietzsche and Dostoevsky because I hadn't really read Shakespeare. So much for that." The man waved his hand, shrugging.

"Huh," Elliot said, looking out the window as he considered the idea. The clear color of the January day was fading into the cool shadow of late afternoon. "And what do Dostoevsky and Nietzsche say about Shakespeare?" he asked.

Rydar's laugh echoed through the room. "What don't they say? Especially Nietzsche. Of course, he only briefly references him, but it's like a syringe—just a pinprick, but so much meaning gets through, such that it's almost impossible not to read Shakespeare differently afterward! But, again, that's only because what he points out is already there in Shakespeare, as it was in Aristotle: the great-souled man, though made wiser by the distillation of years. Consider a man of perception who's willing to face suffering and his fellow humans' evasion of it, who tries to raise people above it by seeking to harden them as he's hardened himself. What would he do after being treated not as a hero but as a social criminal? He would start to hide his truth, saving it for those who are ready and protecting it from those who would cry out for protection from it; that is, he would become Shakespeare's fool."

"Falstaff," Elliot said, remembering their literary discussions in the theater and realizing in retrospect how much of the past afternoon's revelations he already understood because of them.

"Precisely. The genius hiding behind the wine bottle—or in the tavern, or behind a veil of madness. Falstaff, Hal, and Hamlet are all different answers to the same challenge: will we evade psychological suffering or dare to wrestle with it, even if it kills part of us, even if we're made unrecognizable, even if we limp ever after from the encounter? However, like Hal to Falstaff, Dostoevsky showed, in Alyosha, the answer to European nihilism before Nietzsche even identified it."

Rydar took a long breath, as if savoring the thought. Though the man was silhouetted against the darkening glass door, Elliot thought he could see tears forming in his eyes; he was beaming.

"Is that why you reference him so much, rather than Nietzsche?" asked Elliot.

"Yes. Of all my pantheon Dostoevsky had the greatest effect on me, especially after the first couple of years, though I'll always be thankful to Nietzsche for preparing me to better understand him—in the sense that starvation can make one all the more thankful for and able to appreciate real food. From Nietzsche I learned method and courage of thought, but in Dostoevsky I found its substance—and life! But it wasn't until my life as I knew it ended, Elliot, that I could recreate myself. It was by reaching back to seemingly dead values through Aristotle, Shakespeare, and Dostoevsky, and forward to make them new and living through Nietzsche, that the Rydar you know brought himself into being, piece-by-piece and page-by-page, choosing books over a gun." Rydar laughed. "The jury's still out on which was more dangerous to the college Rydar. One thing's certain: he had to die to survive his wife's death."

Elliot finished his mug of coffee, which he had forced himself to drink black like Rydar. His eyelids were heavy, the lightness of the whiskey having calmed into a dull fatigue. He checked his phone; it was barely 6:30.

Smiling, Rydar set down his mug. "I should get you back to campus."

"Don't get me wrong," replied Elliot. "It's just been a long week."

"Don't mention it," Rydar said, shrugging as he stood. "You'll forgive me if I presumed more than a little on your captivity. I don't usually talk much about all that; I hope it helps."

Rydar disappeared into the hallway as Elliot stood and checked his balance before donning his coat. He decided against following Rydar.

Reemerging from the hall, Rydar extended a book to Elliot. Elliot guessed it before he saw it: *Crime and Punishment*.

"Thank you—for trusting me to be ready for it, and for bringing me here and everything." Elliot motioned to the bottle of whiskey and the mugs on the table.

"Don't mention it; you needed a distraction."

Elliot realized with a start that he had forgotten his earlier dismay over Cora, though it underlay the whole afternoon. However, rather than return, it seemed still, smaller now, and less pressing—whether from the languor of the whiskey, the book in his hand, or the new understanding of Rydar he could not say.

"And thanks for telling me all that. I'll be discreet."

"No problem; it's not really a secret, though thank you. It's always there." Rydar shrugged, holding open the front door. "It's me."

Elliot nodded and stepped outside.

Chapter 12

Cora shook her head, putting up her hand as she sighed, "I'm sorry ... Line?"

"If he fall in," said Vesta from the front row, "good night, or sink or swim."

"Yeah—If he fall in," Cora took up the words, turning back to Dr. Pelton, "Send danger from the east unto the west, so honor cross it from north to south, and let them grapple ... crap, line?"

"O, the blood more stirs to rouse a lion than to start a hare," Vesta supplied, trying not to cringe.

Cora's post-Winter-Break Hotspur was very different from her pre-Winter-Break one. In the few scenes they had initially blocked near the end of Fall, her Hotspur had been fiery, sure of himself, and daring to take on the highest levels of England Royalties. However, now Cora's first long speeches were dry and without passion, as if the character's "spur had grown cold" prematurely. He seemed cowed and subdued. Cora kept missing lines, and even the lines she knew—which Vesta had heard her recite before—wavered. She seemed distracted. Vesta was not the only one noticing it; onstage the others found it hard to keep character. To her credit, Dr. Pelton merely glanced at Rydar. Her Worcester was meant to talk Hotspur down from a growing delerium of rage—the opposite of what Cora was showing. Quietly pacing the same eight feet before the first row, Rydar climbed up onto the stage.

That Cora had even come to practice had surprised Vesta. When Cora had returned to their room after New Year's Vesta could tell she did not want to talk. Though not impolitely, she had turned inward in a way

Vesta had never seen. Even the way Cora dressed had changed; Vesta had wondered at how the new cardigans and turtlenecks complemented her body as much as camis had done.

Rydar had sent out an email before the first week of semester announcing they would finally begin rehearsals. Before the previous day's all-cast meeting Vesta saw Elliot go up to Cora to exchange a few words, but the girl had politely demured. Elliot walked to the front row and sat a few seats away from Vesta, exchanging a token smile before waiting for Rydar. Their director had proceeded to describe their practice schedule.

Despite her latent excitement to officially begin production, Vesta had felt an involuntary check on her anticipation since Rydar's party—and since whatever had happened between Cora and Elliot; she had swallowed the feeling, reasoning there was no cause to worry.

However, as she noted how much longer Cora's scene was taking to block than the previous two, Vesta felt the apprehension return. Vesta had grown used to seeing Cora's eyes go to Elliot during previous production meetings and discussions; however, then her focus on the young man had seemed to spur her on in discussion and the couple of scenes she had blocked. Now, Cora seemed distracted by Rydar, and rather than provoke her to greater vociferousness, the glances were nervous. Vesta marked one more mistake on her script that she would need to mention when Rydar gave Cora his notes after the scene.

"Guys, let's take a break," Rydar said, interrupting the scene during yet another awkward pause, showing no other emotion beyond his crossed arms. The other students onstage relaxed; tight-lipped, Dr. Pelton looked impatient. Rydar approached Cora. Leaning in, he cocked his head to the side to make eye contact under her uncharacteristically downcast brow. Vesta could guess what was being said, punctuated by nods from both of them. She saw Cora say, "No, fine, that's fine," as she hugged her arms across her chest and stomach.

"Vesta," Rydar turned to the audience, waving her over. As Vesta approached, he said, "Cora's going to take the afternoon off to get herself together. Could you stand in for her so we can at least get the scene blocked?"

"Oh, um, sure," Vesta said, exchanging a look with Cora, "but I'll need someone else to take notes."

"I can do that, no problem," said Cora. "I can stay; I'm just feeling off. I'm sorry." She looked to Rydar.

"We all have bad days—though please come ready to work next time. About the rest, we'll talk later. Vesta, you remember Hotspur's blocking so far, or do you need Cora to walk you through it?"

"No, I was watching." Vesta handed her script and pen to Cora.

"Good. Alright everyone, let's go again."

Handing her own script to Vesta, Cora took the seat next to Vesta's. Pausing to orient herself in the scene, Vesta joined the others backstage for their entrance. She took a breath.

"Alright," said Rydar, checking his wristwatch, "when you're ready."

Cora sighed, crossing the still unlit street between Ad Hill and the quad; as she thought about practice her mouth tightened into a frown. She had thought she could do it. Elliot would not be needed tonight, but even if he were there, she had told herself, it would not matter. She was not there for him; not anymore.

She tried to ignore the name of who she was really there for, as well as the thought that she had embarrassed herself in front of him, his patient demeanor notwithstanding. She quickened her pace. She would have to thank Vesta for covering for her. She had tried to get into Hotspur, but so much had changed over Winter Break—so much had been realized—and with it had changed her conception of the character. Of course, the words were the same, but her gumption to say them . . . Cora smiled bitterly at the thought that perhaps this was when the real acting started. Last semester, and perhaps long before, she had really been Hotspur, in a way. However, now she just felt a restless, though depressed, clarity. What an irony, she thought, not for the first time, that consciously admitting one's ideal could cause such discomfort. Having always striven to be comfortable in and with her body, Cora had felt over the last couple of weeks as if her skin were too small for her, and the result had been unprecedented bouts of nerves.

As she was about to unlock her dorm room door, Cora's phone buzzed. A text from the name she had not thought of appeared on the screen.

Rydar Colson

> *Cora—re today—I know you're going through some stuff right now. I don't mean to pry, but I spoke with Elliot last week. I'm not taking sides, just making sure our show won't be held up. Also, want to make sure you're ok. If you like, I'd be happy to talk, either about Ell or about the role. Feel free to send me a time or see me during office hours—Ry.*

A rush of pleasure accompanied the image of her being taken into Rydar's arms, followed closely by a cloak of wary pain. She should not think that; things like that didn't, shouldn't, happen with teachers. There was too much of a power difference, and it could put her scholarships and his job at stake. However, deeper than the external worry was a conviction that she could not allow to become conscious.

Yet, even in that instant she felt the same invisible, subterranean connection growing between her and Rydar, that may have always been there. People such as they—great ones, Gatsbies—were rare, rare enough that they could overlook certain rules if it meant reaching an end that would befit their persons.

Cora locked the door behind her. Going to her bed, she reached under the wooden frame and pulled out the thin, purple cardboard box and black journal that had been there since New Year's. She had read many of the letters in the box; they had revealed a side to Rydar that she had only suspected might exist but had come to adore. Rather than provoke jealousy, the letters made her feel an immense sadness and pity for the man, all the more for their being so different from the way Colson seemed to present himself to everyone else.

They were unlike any mealy-mouthed love letters Cora had read and immediately hated. Whereas professional courtly love poems of the past had left her feeling inert and indifferent, Rydar's letters were triumphs of love laced with awe and respect, all the more passionate for being direct. Rather than attempt to uplift and elaborate upon his feelings with a potpourri of cliché's, the college Rydar had been frank and unapologetic about his desire for Eun-ji's body as the medium for their love. He did not seek to justify his desire by lifting it out of the physical; instead, the desire to physically possess Eun-Ji, and to persuade her to want to be enjoyed in precisely that way, was treated as its own highest justification, with

Rydar's elaboration and argument articulating all the meaning implicit in their mutual physical attraction.

Instead of a shallow fling into temporary but soon disillusioned sex which then needed to be artificially kept alive with poetry, Cora saw the psychological and philosophical backdrop of two people, eyes wide open about their individual experiences, with their desire as both reward for all that had come before and engine for all that would come after, with the letters being merely an excess and frame of a relationship primarily not of words but of sight and touch. The letters often left Cora weak, and she would now only read them before bed or before taking a shower—and always alone.

Remembering the ravishing look the young Rydar had given the Eun-Ji in the portrait, Cora had experienced a growing thrill at suddenly understanding Colson's hidden passion and grief. Fearing she would feel small compared to the petite Korean woman who had so enthralled him then and since, Cora was instead left feeling greater and encouraged, as if by understanding what Rydar had seen and wanted in Eun-Ji Cora could better show him that she, too, could embody what he must still want in a companion, secret and sublimated beneath his hard passion for Shakespeare and the rest. Just as Rydar had described his and Eun-Ji's attraction as the appropriate expression of their lives up to that point, Cora had steadily recognized how her own attraction to him, too, was a manifestation of her having risen above the expectations and stereotypes of others into being worthy and capable of desiring—and of satisfying the desire of—a man like Rydar Colson.

At first, Cora had experienced a tinge of guilt when she thought over the letters and her desires, and it came in the thought of Elliot. She did feel sorry for how long she had tried to want him the way he deserved, the way she had wanted to want him. He was a good guy, but Cora had recognized upon reading Rydar's first letter that Elliot could never have written something like it. It was ironic, she thought, that on the same day she had maneuvered herself to first meet Elliot after class, in the same hour, she had met his replacement, of whom Elliot was, after all this time, still just a shadow. Cora remembered what Ermine had said. Elliot's words before their first kiss had been right, and, yet, now she was proving Ermine right again. Her longing had never been about Elliot, she thought, and it would have eventually ended like this—with her reaching for the man she now knew she deserved.

Most of the letters had been written nearly ten years before; Cora had not yet touched the journal. She reached for it, opening its soft leather cover to the latest entry at the ribbon.

11/7
    -dream
    -high school auditorium—remembered the architecture; turned into a non-denom Prot church
    -sword next to bag; assembly/service starts; take sword to car, apprehension at being arrested/told to leave
    -in assembly/service—sanctuary full, people having to sit in foyer
    -popular; people singing together; ignoring me; food on tables in back
    -ppl from my past; a few recognize me, happy to see me, been waiting for me to come; they look relieved I'm finally there, though they immediately forget me and keep singing; all is smiling and light
    -foyer floor turns into deep pool in middle; at the bottom I see food ppl have dropped; meatballs and spaghetti, savory/salty foods; I mean to pull the food from bottom back up to the air; feeling of "hey, you didn't get all the nutrients out of this!"
    -I swim down to get it; only one comfortable swimming down; at bottom I think "my ears don't hurt"
    -can hold breath indefinitely; swimming comfortably down to bottom where others can't reach
    -can still see them in their seats above; pool ceiling expand to whole auditorium/church floor, as if watery ceiling of glass beneath all their feet; food everywhere, still preserved by being underwater
    -people oblivious to waste down below; just want to stay at the top talking/singing where it's comfortable, sweet, safe; bright colors
    -what really need to do is go to bottom, to the deep, to pull out nutriment
    -don't know it's useful because no one has tried
    -walking around back at top; leave school/church

Health comes from the abysses we fear to consider but which may become clear only after we go into them. God/meaning/sustenance is not in the light, but in the food, underwater, waiting to be uncovered not by congregations, but by individuals (Prov 25.2).
    Singers treat food as mere refreshments, rather than the purpose of both school and church (self-mastery, sanctification,

etc). Seeking mere safety with no way to deal with the (unnamed)
danger they fear beneath their feet. Would any of them ever leave
the school/church to be their own people?
     Where haven't I? What's next, after Hal?

Cora reread Rydar's terse notes, trying to decide what was mere record and what was interpretation after-the-fact. Either way, she could imagine Rydar having such a dream; she really did understand the man in a way the others simply could not.

Cora closed the journal, holding the soft leather between her two palms. The few times Rydar had brought up Nietzsche to the group could not have prepared her for this. What else could this be than a dream and interpretation that followed a Nietzschean schema—complete with the confidence, pleasure, wisdom, and circumspection which Cora had seen in the philosopher's work over the last few weeks? She marveled at how Rydar's entering the dream's water echoed Zarathustra's descending from his mountain to interact with the misled masses, or Nietzsche's examining "abysses" to wrestle with questions heretofore ignored. The reversal of values—with light being implicitly dangerous and the depths below being the place of safety and health—showed Rydar's having truly moved beyond traditional expectations of good and evil, acceptable and unacceptable. That he should think and even dream in such ways, thinking himself alone . . .

Cora replaced the journal and box of letters under her bed. She looked at her phone, resisting the urge to touch it in the next moment. She would respond to Colson's text only after she could trust herself not to speak too soon. However, she thought as she began to slowly, consciously remove her clothes, I will respond. Maybe later tonight, she wondered as she grabbed a towel and stepped toward the shower.

Cora tapped on Rydar Colson's open door.

"Oh, Hi Cora," Rydar said, waving over his shoulder. "Come on in."

Focused on what looked like a rehearsal schedule on his laptop, Rydar did not notice as Cora pulled the door closed behind her.

"I'm almost done with this. Go ahead and relax. How are things going?"

"Oh, they're fine," said Cora, turning the free chair to face Rydar as she sat, inching it toward him a bit. She crossed her legs, letting the cut in her skirt fall across the top of her thigh.

"Any classes you're excited about?" Rydar turned to look at her. She saw his eyes flash immediately to her legs; it seemed the man tensed, though to his credit he showed no clear outward change as he returned his eyes to hers, besides perhaps a certain tension in his jaw, which relaxed in the next moment. Cora smiled. She had picked the right outfit.

"Do me a favor and open that door," Rydar said.

"Oh, I won't be here too long," said Cora.

"Uh-huh. Alright." The man shrugged, picking up his phone. For a moment Cora worried she had already overplayed her hand, but after apparently checking something, Rydar set the phone back down.

"So," he said, clapping his hands together, an expectant look on his face, "how is semester starting for you?"

"Like I said, everything's fine," Cora said. "But we both know I'm not here to talk about classes."

The man looked to the side for a moment before returning his eyes to hers with a nod and sitting up. "Yes, I did want to check in about other things. I know things aren't going well with Elliot. I'm not taking sides, but like I said in the text, I had a talk with him and I wanted to check that you're doing okay."

"Oh, don't let's talk about that," Cora said leaning forward. "I'm over it. And don't worry about our play—I'm sure Elliot is mature enough for it."

" . . . Yes," said Rydar, as if trying to understand what Cora had hoped would be obvious. She would have to lead him past his professional inhibitions a bit more. After all, she could not just say it outright. Even Daisy's affair with Gatsby had required tact, though nearly everyone knew what was at play.

"I mean he's mature enough to keep working with me. I just won't be going home with him," Cora said lightly, pressing her lumbar against the rounded back of the chair and stretching into a yawn. Rydar pursed his lips at her emphasizing her final word. His light stubble accentuated his terse dimples.

"Speaking of home," Cora said in the next breath, "I loved seeing your place. A real temple you have; I especially liked the library—and your choice of artwork. That was your wife, right?"

"Yes, Eun-Ji," Rydar said flatly, crossing his arms. Cora repressed a chuckle at his attempt at coyness.

"She's beautiful," said Cora, deepening her tone and widening her eyes sympathetically, "How long were you married, if you don't mind?"

"Three months," Rydar said. His brow furrowed as if trying to discern her intention. Relax, thought Cora.

"You got married when she was in the hospital, right?"

"Yes—how did you—?"

"Just inferring. Does that mean the marriage was . . . unconsummated?"

"That's hardly any of your business." His tone was cold metal.

"You're right—I'm sorry. I've just been really curious since the party. It was like looking into a whole world I suspected was there but never dreamed of entering. I'm just trying to understand the man whose world it is, who I've been working with," Cora said, cocking her head to the side to lean her cheek on her hand, "and who I hope to keep working with."

"Cora, if you'd wanted to know more about me, you could have just asked during practice. But, frankly, bringing up my wife isn't the best way . . . "

"Oh, I know—you're right, I'm sorry. I'm just so curious about what . . . " Cora looked to the side shyly, bringing up her hand to bite the first knuckle of her index finger, just like she had read in a Raymond Chandler book. Don't give in, she thought, he's just as afraid of it as you are—which means he wants it just as much.

" . . . What?" Rydar asked.

"What a man like you saw in a woman like her."

"Oh," said Rydar, as if he had been expecting something different, "what do you mean, 'a man like me?'"

"A man of reason," she murmured, looking away as she continued to speak, "a man who can stand up, who's not afraid of suffering, who's not afraid of risking his reputation for his passion. A man who doesn't worry about things like background or race, or what society or the mob says, or good and evil. A real man," Cora said, adding to the list she had already partially prepared, were she presented with the opportunity to say what she saw in Rydar. "I've been reading *Thus Spoke Zarathustra*, and I already read *Beyond Good and Evil*. I know I didn't get most of it, but even though you don't talk about it I see a lot of what Nietzsche describes in you." Cora laughed, trying to ease things back into coquetry. "It's really vicious of you to teach the group every writer except the one that would most help us understand you."

"Well," said Rydar, narrowing his eyes cautiously, "the point wasn't to understand me but yourselves and how Shakespeare and the rest are relevant to you."

"See, even that's from *Zarathustra*! You try to hide it, but I see it— the confidence behind diverting every conversation off of yourself. It's not humility, but the worst, and best, kind of pride, all the more because it's secret."

"Wow, you have been reading." Rydar crossed one leg over the other, leaning back with a smile despite the concern still on his face.

"Oh, I have. After the party I thought, he only has pictures of two people in his house—his wife, and this writer. So, I set out to read him. And I found I recognized a lot of his ideas in how you've worked with us. Not the easy polemical ones—you weren't looking for an excuse to rule us, like others who read only one part of Nietzsche and want to play online edgelord against others' traditions, missing the fact that Nietzsche is laughing most at them from beyond the grave. He was as opposed to mobocracy as he was to theocracy. I think people who want such things commit the same error, to him, by masking an excuse not to examine themselves or their motives."

"Yes, that's right," said Rydar, taken up in the unexpected topic; it had been right to hold this pearl until now, Cora thought, as Rydar assumed the tone of their afternoon discussions. "What Nietzsche was committed to was stopping whatever might stop thought. It's ironic: be- cause he polemicizes so much of traditional philosophy, people assume he must be against reason, but they miss the fact that he was, as he saw it, using his reason more ruthlessly than many philosophy and theology students of his day . . . "

Cora started to relax, letting herself admire the man as he spoke. The corner of his jaw had always struck her; she had imagined slapping the jaw many times, feeling a sudden guttural pleasure at how the act would probably break all the bones in her hand. She hoped it would. She considered what he might do to deserve the slap—and what would come after the token gesture of feminine defense was proven impotent.

"By rejecting what he saw as articles of faith—that reason was some- thing above the physical human person, transcendent, irreproachable, Platonic, and beyond honest inquiry—he presented himself with perhaps a larger problem than they had made: how to understand philosophy and divinity in non-faith terms, which he eventually identified as the will to power and the overcoming within oneself of traditional interpretations of good and evil—and the psychological safety such things contain."

Cora seized on the phrase, which had already fascinated her as a possible set of keys to release Rydar from his own inhibitions. "That's what reading him made me feel—power, and the feeling that I could overcome the preconceptions that were weighing me down. I didn't understand everything, but it wasn't even about that: it was how his writing made me feel—daring, free, unrestrained from sacred cows and social limits." As if coming to herself out of her own emotion, Cora smiled and, returning her attention to Rydar, leaned forward, letting the collar of her shirt open, "And capable of meeting a world where people like you and I can make our own values." Despite the sudden flexion in the man's neck to pull his face toward the bookshelf, Cora had seen Rydar's eyes drawn down the line of her neck and past her collar before flashing back to the closed door.

"Don't worry about how they've applied to me—I can tell you later, perhaps. I just had a talk on the subject the other week with . . . But how do they apply to you, Cora? Explicitly?"

"But don't you see, Rydar, that that's what I've been describing? When I asked what a man like you saw in a woman like your wife, I was also asking if you still might want a woman like her . . . and like me."

Rydar tensed. "What?" Rydar turned his chair to face her fully, at the same time backing it up against the desk. His right hand, Cora saw, was gripping the arm of his chair. Even now, she thought, he's holding back his reaction. He should throw me out, but he isn't.

The man was about to speak, but instead he closed his eyes and shut his mouth. After taking and exhaling a breath, he spoke: "Cora, I know you just had a break-up—no, don't try to call it anything other than what it was—and you might be really vulnerable in this season. However, this isn't the right way to cope. It goes without saying that the kind of women I may or may not like is a wildly inappropriate topic."

"Am I really that vulnerable?" Cora said, shifting her weight to let the loose collar of her shirt fall just so, revealing, if the man had missed it, that she had worn no bra. "And I didn't say 'like,' I said 'want.' Come on," she said, looking up under his brow, "rules are just a narrative, anyway, to keep safe those who aren't brave enough to question their morality. I'm a consenting adult; call it my trying to exercise my will to power. Nietzsche would do it." She let her hand fall on Rydar's knee.

"No, he wouldn't." Rydar shifted his knee away from her hand. "If you want to use him to justify doing whatever you want, then you've misread him as much as the edgelord you mentioned earlier—and you haven't heard a thing I've said about him, or myself. Please, don't do that with your skirt." Seeing his eyes drawn yet again to her skin, Cora had stretched her legs so her skirt would ride up her thigh. "I am not okay with this," he continued, abruptly standing up and, as if against a great weight, turning to face the window. "It's thoroughly inappropriate, and I do not give my consent."

Cora smiled in spite of the sudden hiccup of fear and anger she felt growing in her stomach. "You don't need to be so formal, Rydar. Don't use their excuses. I've seen how you look at me; you gave me the part, you held your tongue while I wasted my time with that boy. Elliot's great, but he's just an imitation, an actor of the kind of man I want."

Rydar said nothing, looking between the blue sky outside and, oddly, his phone.

"Please," Cora whispered, her voice breaking, "don't you be weak, too. Not now. I did all of this for you . . . "

Rydar turned his head to speak over his shoulder, causing his sharp profile to silhouette against the blue sky outside.

"You know me better than that. I'm sorry you think someone can give you whatever it is you need; I do care about you, Cora—which is why I wouldn't give it to you even if I could. Now, I really think you should go." Rydar inhaled calmly, as if he had passed some inner task, and sat back down, still facing the window.

Shaking, Cora stood, holding onto the fact that, despite his words, everything Rydar had done over the months had implied a special atten-tion—an implicit connection—to her, and that, even the moment before, his eyes had been drawn to her body, which, despite the crying of feminist bromides about the male gaze in the back of her mind, she had wanted and loved. He was obviously attracted, and his eyes and actions spoke more of his subconscious—his real—desires than his words ever could.

Desperately, with a flourish worthy of such a gambit, Cora removed her shirt. The sudden coolness of the office made her hesitate as tight-ening skin met the sudden rush of adrenaline at her own daring. She let her shirt fall to the floor as with a determined step she put her arms around Rydar's shoulders, pressing her breasts to the cool, thin fabric of his button-down. Even as he went rigid, his hands gripping the front edge of his desk, she felt the warmth shared between her breasts and his shoulders—those shoulders she had so often imagined in recent weeks as someday being above her on his bed as she looked up past him at the painting of the philosophers on his wall.

"Cora, put your shirt back on and leave. Now." The voice was hard and lacked any hint of the fear Cora read in the white splay of his fingers on the glass desk top. A fog of sweat had spread between the knuckles of his hands. Feeling the man's voice resonate through her torso, she began to move her hands across his arms and upper chest, feeling the muscle beneath the shirt.

Suddenly, as Colson flinched his shoulders to stop her, one of his hands slipped off the glass. As he stumbled to the side, he caught himself on one of the nearby book shelves, which broke under the sudden weight, spilling books over the desk and floor. In the same moment, even as she was smiling at the man's obvious but unnecessary discomfort—and at the electrifying fact that he had torn the shelf in half—Cora's eyes saw his phone on the desk. Above a red dot read "15:45," with the number rising steadily.

"What's that?"

"Cora Madison," Rydar said clearly, facing her but keeping his eyes on the ceiling as he motioned to a section of his bookshelf near the door, "per the notification you read when coming in here, I reserve the right to record any exchange between myself and students, whether for educational purposes or otherwise. I am not angry with you, and you are in no danger from me, but you have ignored my requests to leave and I have proof. As one of my students and a member of my cast, you do mean a lot to me, but I'm sorry if you have misinterpreted our relationship. I have never intended anything untoward when interacting with you. I will not use this against you any more than necessary, though your actions here are serious. Now please put your shirt back on and go."

Having in a panic already picked up her shirt to cover her chest before reading the placard on the bookshelf, Cora choked out, "But Ryd—."

"Now," Colson said, finally looking at her with eyes wide open and jaw muscles strained.

Cora let out a wordless sob. Fighting the sudden impulse to hunch, she put her shirt on quickly, causing Rydar to look away again. Taking her bag, she impulsively slapped his face before striding out of the office, slamming the door behind her.

Not until she was in the stairwell above the bottom floor did Cora realize she had put her shirt on backwards; pulling her arms into the shirt and turning it around, she still felt the blood pumping hotly in her hand, the scruff of his shallow beard still grating against her palm. In the next moment, she dropped her bag and sunk against the wall of the stairwell as, with the clearing of her head, she began to sob.

"I'm so sorry," she whispered between bouts of tears, to no one and anyone.

CHAPTER 13

V ESTA HUMMED, HOLDING *The Great Gatsby* closer as she walked along the lit sidewalks running from the theater to the rest of campus. After the news at practice that Cora would be taking a break from the play, and that, after a polite request from Rydar, Vesta would be standing in as Hotspur in addition to her already playing Doll Tearsheet, Vesta felt she deserved some time alone to recharge. So, when a few people had suggested grabbing food after practice, she had declined, slipping a hug and kiss to Jonas backstage before leaving the theater.

Impulsively, Vesta turned as she crested Ad Hill. She was enjoying the coolness of the evening, and she felt the sudden desire to explore and offset the lonesomeness that had seemed to creep onto campus since last semester. It was unfortunate; the campus really was beautiful at night.

Vesta considered how things had changed since September. Between Hoegren and the administration's maintaining their support of the university's theater department, the city's underwriting their support for the production, and Rydar's cunning intransigence throughout, the play looked like it would succeed, despite the growing ubiquity and asperity of the antagonism on campus blogs. The thought made her blush with shame and relief.

A footstep on dry dirt interrupted Vesta's thoughts. Pulling her head up from the book and turning around, she saw a girl and two large men. They were dressed in black; the men had their hoods up. Vesta's neck tensed; they had been following her, by the look of them—eyes focused on her, showing no intention to turn politely to the side to leave her in privacy.

Vesta turned around the side of the nearest building, increasing her step and hoping they would continue straight. She pulled her backpack in front of her and, slipping her book into it, grasped a small cylinder of pepper spray she had bought impulsively a few weeks before. When the group of three turned to follow her around the building, a third man stepped out in front of her. Hugging her backpack, she moved to avoid him, but a sidestep from him stopped her. Turning and readying herself to use the spray, she was faced by the girl, who had stepped ahead of the two men.

"You just come from the theater?" the girl asked.

"Sorry, I'm just trying to get to my dorm," said Vesta, avoiding eye contact with them and starting to shake.

"The fuck you are; answer my question, did you come from the theater?"

"She did," said one of the men behind her, who had raised a bandana over his face, "I saw her."

"I want to hear the bitch say it," said the girl over her shoulder. As the girl looked back at Vesta, Vesta felt cold stone behind her; she had involuntarily backed into the building's wall. It felt as if the building were moving, but Vesta realized it was her own body shuddering. She glanced at the other men; all had covered their faces.

"We know who you are—you're one of those fucking bigots at the theater. You're trying to put us back in chains."

Vesta knew the girl was speaking to the men as much as to her.

"Listen, I just want to go home," Vesta said evenly. Swallowing, she pushed herself off the wall to move past the girl; however, as her elbow brushed the girl's bare arm, the girl started screaming. One of the men jumped forward and knocked Vesta hard onto the ground.

"She just attacked me! The racist bitch just attacked me!" Vesta heard as she felt the scrape of her cheek hitting hard dirt. "Violence against women! She wants to attack women!"

Vesta gripped her hand; she had dropped the pepper spray.

As if their leashes had snapped, the three men approached Vesta and lifted her off the ground. She started to scream, kicking and twisting violently, but the men were too strong. They dropped her on the concrete, and one of them kicked her hard in the stomach, knocking the wind out of her. She heard a sharp, industrial sound; in the next moment the sour smell and taste of duct tape enveloped her mouth. As she tried to catch her breath through her nose—suddenly clogged from her oncoming sobs—she had to fight to keep her head clear.

As if all following the same impulse, the men picked her up by her wrists and knees. They were carrying her to the shadows of the orange trees that lined the buildings on this side of campus. The thought occurred to her that students were not allowed in those trees, and that a security guard might come. Vesta could still hear the girl screaming in the background, as if her shrieks were the fuel that enabled the men to move. The men had begun to laugh.

They dropped Vesta and started to punch and kick her, all yelling obscenities and intermittently accusing her of promoting racism and being a rape apologist. Sobbing and trying to scream past the duct tape, Vesta tried to curl into a fetal position. A boot caught her in the side of her forehead; a shock of pain and nausea turned the trees above to dull stars. No, she thought, stay conscious. You have to get out of here. You have to get help.

As she fought to stay awake and fight the pain, Vesta heard an abrupt wooden sound; a body landed hard on the dirt next to her.

"Oh fu—!"

The obscenity was cut off by a repetition of the hollow sound. The rhythm of kicks and punches had stopped. The background noise of the girl screaming slowly faded, as if she were running away. Dazed at the pain that flooded her back and stomach, Vesta rolled onto her back. She was dimly aware of the scuffling of feet, and two men fighting over a two-by-four. One of them—the one without a hood, with a red scarf tied around his face—managed to wrestle the piece of wood away and, with a swift swing, cracked it over the other's head. The hooded form dropped out of Vesta's dimming vision.

As the figure bent down above her, Vesta flinched for a moment; however, instead of receiving another blow, she felt a hand gingerly remove the duct tape from her mouth. Gasping for breath, she felt herself lifted by tender hands; no, she thought, my dorm is the other way. As the wave of pain signaling the end of the blows pushed her into unconsciousness, she had the sudden happy thought that she recognized the scarf that still obscured the man's face, as well as the attractive, desperate eyes and wavy, brown hair above it.

❁

"Breaking News: University Professor Jailed for Assault"
—Sybil Braitwaithe, University Liaison, Orangedale Daily Root

Friday, February 13:

    Last night, controversial Orangedale University Professor Rydar Colson called the police to turn himself in for attacking three male students who he alleges were assaulting a female student.

    Colson, director of the University's production of Henry IV Part 1 and Part 2 and who was present at the Fall protests against the production, claimed he acted in self-defense, saying he was walking to his car near the Hall of Letters when he saw three boys moving around a building, dragging a struggling girl whose mouth they had duct taped. Taking a 2x4 piece of plywood from his trunk, Colson ran to confront the young men, whom he alleges he found kicking the young woman, who was a member of his cast. Colson then struck the three men with the piece of wood before removing the tape from the woman's face and carrying her to the theater, where he called the police. Colson claims there was an accomplice, who ran from the scene and whom he believes was with the men, but neither the Root nor the local police department have been able to locate any of the alleged assailants or witnesses.

    Orangedale University has declined to comment, saying only that they will conduct their own investigation before making any decisions regarding Colson's position among the faculty. When asked about the status of the upcoming production, theater director Frank Hoegren, present at the police department last night, said he would be stepping in as interim director, saying "When some rabble kids shoot down a mockingbird, the answer isn't to shoot down the rest of them." He was, of course, alluding to Harper Lee's To Kill A Mockingbird, wherein it is said "Mockingbirds don't do one thing except make music for us to enjoy . . . they don't do one thing but sing their hearts out for us. That's why it's a sin to kill a mockingbird." Readers will remember a previous piece in this column two months ago covering the local school board's decision to ban Lee's classic.

    Information on the case will be forthcoming as the police investigation continues. Until then, we will wait to see who Rydar Colson is in this situation: Bob Ewell, or Boo Radley.

    —Sybil Braitwaithe
    @thebraiwai
    University Liaison
    Orangedale Daily Root

Sent: 8:17am PST 13 FEB
From: john.atwater@cityoforangedale.gov
To: fhoegren@orangedale.ad.edu

Frank,

    I hope you don't mind, I've contacted the County DA, Patricia O'Conner, about Colson. She'd already heard what happened, but I filled her in on the context of the play and how this year's gone over there. She's agreed to take care of the case, herself; apparently, off the record, she's fed up with colleges' obtuseness regarding official legal procedure. For all the alleged lawlessness on public campuses—the "rape culture," spoken of in your campus blogs, etc.—judgment and prosecution rarely take place in official legal channels. Good thing Colson involved law enforcement by calling them directly; it put the ball in O'Conner's court. I think she's wanted to make an example for a while, to show that campuses are not insulated from actual justice procedures, etc.

    Anyway, just wanted to warn you ahead of time in case others in the administration or on-campus are less keen to cooperate with due process.

    Best. Let me know if you need anything,

John Atwater
Vice Mayor for the City of Orangedale

Ermine lay back on his mattress, taking a long, Saturday-morning stretch as he reread the draft of his next post. It would build on his previous piece, wherein he had rejoiced over the arrest of Rydar Colson. Reversing *The Daily Root*'s perspective by questioning whether Colson, himself, were not the attacker from whom the group of students was attempting to save Miss Lloyd, Ermine had corroborated his exposé of Colson by referencing the so-long-anticipated scene between the man and Cora Madison, of which Ermine had taken some wonderful pictures through Colson and Ingman's office window after following Cora there the week before.

    Throughout his article, Ermine had focused on how Colson had propagated and benefited from imbalanced power dynamics, and that no man in his position could come out innocent so often without the support of a white, patriarchal power structure enabling such things. "*He got too hungry,*" he had closed the piece, "*and he thought he could stand too high on the bodies of women and other disenfranchised minorities. Happily, he was wrong.*"

Subsequently, Ermine's next piece would focus on examples of where white patriarchy had been reinforced by deferring to the social invention of due process. He began typing, adding, "*While in theory due process is the only thing that stands between the disproportionately high number of minority men in prison and the noose, it has also been one of the most insidious means whereby white men in power have avoided justice for their actions. Is it not ironic that often the same people who one day enshrine the death penalty will, when one of their own is threatened, cry for "due process?" I say this is no contradiction nor inconsistency—when your goal is to maintain your identity group's power, which it always is . . .*"

A heavy knock on the door interrupted Ermine's thought. In the next moment, as Ermine still held his laptop up in defense, Cora Madison opened the door and shut it behind her.

"Oh, it's you. How may I be—?"

"You took pictures?"

Her hard voice did not match the dark circles under her eyes. No, thought Ermine as he relaxed back, that's exactly how a girl like her would sound after having such a rough time of things. He noticed she had recently cut her hair; her head was nearly shaven.

"I saw a story," Ermine shrugged, "and I have records of my source— though don't worry, if people ask I'll paint you the victim. But I knew what I was seeing."

Mouth slightly open, Cora squinted her eyes, as if seeing something new. In the next moment, the expected realization struck her.

"You tricked me," she said, as if she should have seen it, "when I was trusting you about Elliot—about Rydar—you tricked me."

"You tricked yourself," said Ermine, satisfied to finally be able to say it to her, "long before I helped you. Oh, tut tut, Cora," he crooned, tilting his head coyly. "You were tricking yourself since the moment you laid eyes on Colson. I think you came to me for help then, too, yes? That was Colson, that day in September? You don't have to confirm it. I know you, Cora—not totally, thank God, but I understand some parts of you, perhaps much more than you do. No, not our shared race, nor our both being more open-minded than the average person on the street. No, it's both much deeper and yet ancillary than that. See, I understand how dangerous greatness—or rather, the delusions of it—can be, and how willing its disciples are to mislead themselves, especially those from the oppressed classes. This always happens to people who think they can stand up on their own and who want to prove they're not oppressed, even as they worship those they believe have done just that—and beg to be valued enough to be picked by the ones they should hate."

Cora, mouth still agape, was letting Ermine speak; he liked the feeling of an enervated audience—especially one he knew to be so rare. He had worked long and hard, he thought, to have such a personage as Cora Madison rendered captive to his voice.

"Deep down, I think they're trying to justify their own oppression—which usually takes the form of romanticizing their oppressor. Nowhere does that show itself more than in the areas of sex and desire." Ermine looked squarely at Cora. "I'd bet part of you wanted Colson to deep-dick you the first moment you saw him, and the rest of you had to justify the feeling so it would mean something uplifting or complimentary if it ever happened. You know the greatest oppression is when the victim of rape doesn't know they're being raped, but believes they want it? I couldn't sit idly by and let you believe you actually desired that man, when all you were doing was trying to paradoxically justify and deny your being merely another minority woman falling victim to patriarchal power hunger.

"But I needed you to understand it, too. All I did was push you toward seeing how things really are: that he's just using you for his play, that you're not an individual or equal to him but just a pet. Really, that's a much greater means of violating you, since he's not only using your body—not even that, but putting you onstage for others rather than in his bed for himself!—but he's subjugated your mind and your creativity, too." Ermine laughed, rolling his eyes in a flourish around the room. "He's using your desire for recognition to make you an actress, a shell, a shadow of someone else, a mere piece of propaganda!"

At that Cora focused her wide eyes on him. She squared off, her shoulders shaking as if she were holding herself back.

"You humiliated me," she said, her voice low and strained. "You didn't just cost me the respect of the man I most look up to but also all the work I'd put into prepping for this play. And you're wrong: he didn't know I thought of him like that." For a moment, tears filled Cora's eyes in a brief shade of sadness, but she covered them with a baleful look as she swallowed, flaring her nostrils. "Somewhere in your weak, underhanded shitpost of a consciousness you might really believe that you were saving me, but as much as I wanted him, you feared him. You think you know me and my kind, who believe in greatness? Well I know you, Ermine. You're a worm—worse than a worm, since you want to stay a worm. You live off of your own excrement, and you take pleasure in holding up and glorifying others'. That's why I frightened you so much, isn't it? Because I wasn't satisfied with being told I was a victim—of society, of patriarchy, of whatever. You and I might look alike, but we're completely different creatures. You were right, I am a disciple of greatness. I'm a black woman who thought she could be defined and wanted for my mind and my ability, not just my body or my potential political capital.

"But you—you're the opposite of greatness. I don't even have words for what you are; you aren't a thing, you have no substance. That's why you need to think of yourself in terms of the things you write about—your race, your sexuality. Those give you a status you could not otherwise have had. You say Colson used me for propaganda? You've been masturbating all year to the idea of my someday supporting your cause—of my someday becoming like you. I shouldn't be surprised you took the chance when you had it; you don't care about me one bit, only what I could do for you and how you could use me. But I think it's deeper: I think you wanted to eliminate me as a threat. You knew I'd never need to attack you openly. It would imply you were an actual problem. And that was the nature of my threat: I was a thorn in your victim psychology, wasn't I? So long as I was in that play, I was at least proof that Rydar and Shakespeare were not simply racist on their face, as you've tried to paint them. I was proof that you could have deserved respect but chose its opposite—need, degradation, victimhood, the oppressed and disenfranchised, whatever you want to call your mediocre creed. You aren't a victim, Christopher Jackson, and you know it. You know it and you hate it!"

"Shut your fucking mouth!"

Ermine had tried to hold his tongue, but as Cora spoke her voice had grown cold with conviction, then light and quicker with the laughter of realization. The words had made him think of Sam and, in a surprise that he hated, his mother.

In the silence between them, Ermine was aware that behind Cora's rising voice there had grown a din in the direction of the lobby, and harsh shouts had steadily come down the hall. Suddenly, there was a knock on the door. Cora, still smiling, turned to open the door.

A tall blonde woman in a grey suit stood in the doorway, flanked by two police officers, a man and a woman. Around them, though giving a

few feet of space, were several students who had apparently been harass-
ing them since they entered the building.

"I'm looking for a Mr. Christopher Jackson."

"Yeah, this is him," said Cora, motioning to Ermine, who had balked
at the second use of his given name.

The woman nodded to the two officers, who squared back-to-back
on opposite sides of the doorframe.

"Mr. Jackson, are you the blogger 'Ermine Jackson' who edits 'The
Homefront'?"

"Yes—why?" Ermine swallowed, trying to maintain an even tone as
he met the woman's cold, blue-eyed stare.

"My name is Patricia O'Conner, County District Attorney." The
woman took out a printout and a notepad. "In a recent post, you said
you were in contact with 'a witness who was with the three young men.' I
came to ask if you could give me the name of that witness."

"I'm sorry, ma'am," Ermine said, trying to smile but failing, "but I
cannot reveal my sources. The First Amendment means I can keep my
mouth shut. I know my rights."

"Really?" the woman said, narrowing her eyes and pursing her lips.
"Do you know mine—specifically the Sixth Amendment, which gives me
recourse to a 'compulsory process for obtaining witnesses'?"

Ermine shuddered, forcing himself to sit up straight in the next
moment.

"I can't," he choked out in a whisper, "reveal my sources."

After a moment's appraisal of Ermine, the woman shook her head.
"Alright, we won't make a scene here, but you'll be hearing from us. You
know if you persist it could be considered obstruction of justice, right?"
The woman held up a business card, pressing it with two fingers onto a
nearby cabinet.

The woman glanced at Cora, who had so far stood back from the
conversation. She smiled at the girl before raising her eyebrows as if remembering something. She looked at her printout.

"Also—you wrote that you have pictures of Professor Colson with
a female student. While that would be a separate charge, and not ille-
gal if consensual, the university administration would like to see them,
and, depending on their nature, they may be relevant to the case at hand.
Please submit them as soon as possible."

"Did Rydar—Professor Colson—give you his recording?" asked
Cora, stepping forward.

" . . . Yes," the woman said, evidently trying to be delicate, despite her eyes' narrowing at such an abrupt question from a mere bystander. "As I said, due to the nature of the situation, I needed to be in possession of all relevant sources."

Ermine's eyes had snapped to Cora. "Recording? What recording?"

"Colson records his conversations," said Cora, a note of triumph in her voice. "It's posted in his office. Whatever your pictures are of, they're only one side of it."

"Yes," said O'Conner, taken aback by Cora's brusqueness on the topic and apparently noticing Cora's attempt to lacerate Ermine with the words. "I'm sorry, miss, who are you?"

"Cora Madison. I was in Professor Colson's play. I'd be willing to stand as a character witness on his behalf, if you need."

"Thank you," said the woman, eyes still on Cora, "but we have several who have already volunteered." She looked back at Ermine. "I hope you reconsider your position, Mr. Jackson. If not, don't be surprised if you receive a subpoena." The woman turned and left the dorm room, followed by the two officers.

Cora merely looked down at Ermine and, scoffing, left, turning the opposite direction from the DA. A few students followed her with questions, but they were apparently silenced by a word Ermine could not hear over the sudden rushing of blood in his ears. He began to hyperventilate.

"She's just down that hall," said the receptionist, pointing. "Room 205. Her family's there now."

Elliot and Megan nodded, turning down the hallway.

Megan, Vesta, Jonas, and Elliot had taken to hanging out whenever they had free time, often studying and eating together when not at practice. Though no one mentioned it, Elliot knew he had relieved Megan from her welcome but awkward status as third wheel, which, he learned, had been made more complex by her having developed in the Fall an unrequited but now benignly latent attraction to Vesta. Megan, in her turn, had assumed a brusque presence in Elliot's life, as if to platonically fill the gap she knew to have been left by Cora, for which Elliot was grateful. Vesta's attack had only tightened and made explicit the small circle's mutual devotion. So, when Megan had texted Elliot the previous day, saying she planned to drive to the hospital in the next city to see Vesta after her Wednesday morning classes, Elliot had not hesitated to come. He had expected Jonas to join them, but apparently he was unavailable.

Shifting her bouquet of flowers to one arm, Megan knocked as she peeked around the open door.

Vesta was lying back on the bed, awake but resting. She had a bandage on her cheek but smiled in spite of it. A bright, white bandage was wrapped around her head, holding a pad of gauze just above her right temple. Following Megan into the room, Elliot saw several dark bruises on Vesta's arms. After smiling at him, Vesta looked behind Elliot, as if expecting someone else.

"Hi, Megan," said Vesta's mom, a pretty woman with a ponytail of auburn hair a shade darker than Vesta's, "and . . . ?"

"Elliot. Nice to meet you, Mr. and Mrs. Lloyd," Elliot said, putting forward his hand.

"Thank you both for coming," said the tall, mustached man who had stood upon their entering.

"Elliot and I go way back," said Vesta, wheezing slightly. "How are things going, you guys?"

"We're fine," said Megan, taking a seat next to Vesta's bed, "but how are you?"

"Alive," Vesta chuckled, trying to hide a wince. "Ends up it was just a concussion and a few broken ribs. I should be out of here in a few days, if everything goes well. They want to do another MRI." Vesta motioned up to the gauze on her head. Megan looked uneasily at Vesta's parents.

"It's okay," said Vesta's dad, frowning despite his calm tone. "You most likely read about it in the papers. Go ahead and ask." Mrs Lloyd turned and paced to the window, dabbing her eye.

"Well," said Megan, shrugging with a patient but focused expectation, "what happened?"

"Was the newspaper wrong?" asked Elliot.

"I'm not sure—things have been a bit shaky since then," said Vesta, eyebrows furrowing as if returning to a topic she had already pondered much, "I remember walking home, and taking a detour to read in spite of Rydar's warnings—."

A scoff from Vesta's mother cut off Vesta's sentence, though the woman did not turn around.

" . . . And then some people stopped me. They wanted to know if I was coming from the theater, and they started beating me up. At first they yelled about how by being in the play I was promoting violence against women, and how I was a white bitch. I think they must've carried me out of the light because I remember seeing branches above me."

Vesta paused, her face suddenly serious, as if she were forcing herself to look at something she had been considering, and in which she had a grim but intense interest. "That's when they started laughing—like they were excited, really enjoying it. Then someone else came and saved me."

"Yeah," confirmed Megan, who, eyes red and nostrils flaring, had taken Vesta's hand, "Colson saw what was happening on the way to his car and broke it up. He then carried you to the theater—."

"It wasn't Colson," Vesta said, her eyes moving to her mother. Megan and Elliot started, exchanging a glance.

"Darling," said Vesta's dad, evidently rehashing a topic they had already discussed, "he turned himself in. The police are working on it."

"Why he would put you in such a dangerous position to begin with . . . " began Vesta's mother, turning from the window, "if we had known that play would lead to this . . . "

"It wasn't his fault, Mom," said Vesta as sternly as she could manage, "he was just putting on a Shakespeare play. I was the one who went out against his advice, though it's not my fault, either. But it wasn't Rydar who saved me . . . "

Elliot could tell Vesta was saying less than she thought. He was curious about what had happened and concerned at the idea that Rydar was being wrongfully accused on campus. However, he had turned himself in; he must have had a reason to, and Elliot felt sure Vesta had thought the same but was keeping quiet.

"Practices are still going on," ventured Elliot, avoiding Mrs. Lloyd's eyes. "Hoegren's stepped in, and he's bringing in the head of the Orangedale Shakespeare Company to take over practices next week. They've assured us that they'll defer to what we think Rydar would do, until he's able to rejoin us."

"Son," said Mr. Lloyd, "I don't know if that should be your priority. Whether directly or indirectly, that man put my daughter in danger. As far as I'm concerned, you all might be better off not doing that play at all and just finishing your studies."

Elliot looked awkwardly to Vesta, who rolled her eyes.

"With all due respect, sir," Elliot said cautiously, "that play is part of our studies. I won't speak for the others, but I've read and thought more because of Colson than almost all—."

"I'll stop you right there, Elliot," said the man sternly. "You're not my child, and I don't expect you to understand. But I nearly lost my daughter. They'll be lucky if we don't bring legal action against that whole university—or against that upstart who used her as part of this vendetta of a play he's got."

Elliot wanted to explain all that had happened—how Rydar and the university had tried to prevent this kind of thing, and how all along Rydar had warned them, and how he should really be angry at people like Ermine who had fomented violence against the play. However, this was not the time, and it was not his place. There was too much to tell, and the man would not have heard what he would say. Besides, he thought, it seemed Vesta had already tried, and would continue trying.

"So," began Megan, weakly, "has Jonas come to see you?"

"No," said Vesta, her frown causing her to wince. "It's weird—the nurses said he came when I was first asleep, but he hasn't been here during visiting hours."

"That's strange," said Megan, "we haven't seen him either. He said he was busy today. You mean he hasn't come to visit you at all?"

"No," said Vesta, obviously swallowing her sadness behind whatever thought had preoccupied her earlier. Elliot realized Vesta did not want to talk about Jonas in front of her parents.

"He'll come when he can, I'm sure," said Elliot, "we'll all go out once you're up on your feet. Do you need anything? Any books from your dorm?"

"I've tried to read, but it's hard for me to focus," Vesta said thankfully, holding up a book from under the sheet; it was *The Great Gatsby*.

"You . . . " Elliot asked, "haven't heard from Cora, have you?"

"No," said Vesta, noticing his peculiar tone, "why?"

"No reason. Don't worry about it, really."

"What's wrong, did something happen to Cora?"

"I think," said Megan, placing her hand gently on an unbruised part of Vesta's arm, "this whole thing scared her, too. She's still MIA. Don't worry about it—I'm sure she's fine." Elliot saw the look the two girls shared; Vesta apparently understood she would hear more later, once she was feeling better and her parents were gone.

"We're gonna get going," said Megan, standing. "Mr. and Mrs. Lloyd, thank you for letting us visit." She deferred in what looked to Elliot as an uncharacteristic minor curtsey. He extended his hand to Mr. Lloyd, who shook it despite his frown. Mrs. Lloyd merely nodded to them, lips pursed tightly.

"That was nuts," whispered Megan as soon as they had turned the corner of the hall.

"Yeah—though I understand what they must be thinking. It was like Vesta hadn't told them anything about the play."

"I mean, it has been crazy. Have you told your parents what's been happening?"

"Some of it," said Elliot, feeling as if he were lying, "but I just tell them I keep my head down and go between my apartment, class, and the theater."

"Do they . . . know about Cora and Rydar?"

Elliot smiled simply, enjoying the irony. "They never knew about Cora to begin with—casual, remember?"

"Yeah, but . . . are you okay?"

"Sure. It actually helps me make some sense of how it all went down between us." He did not mention the past week's fight against impulsively resenting Rydar for Cora's actions.

Megan snickered. "Doesn't seem Vesta's read the blogs. That's good—whatever happened between Cora and Rydar, I'd trust the papers more than Jackson."

"He's definitely had it out for Rydar from the beginning. Cora, too, maybe, though I think after we broke up she went to stay with him—Ermine, I mean." Elliot had considered Ermine's possible involvement in the Cora-Colson scandal currently growing on campus; Elliot was finding it harder to give Jackson the benefit of the doubt, if he had ever deserved it.

"There's more to it than what they're saying," said Megan, as if voicing Elliot's thoughts. "We should talk to Cora to find what really happened, if you can stomach it. Have you seen her around?"

"No," said Elliot.

"Me neither."

CHAPTER 14

"EVERYONE, PLEASE HAVE a seat." Frank Hoegren stood on the stage, motioning to the auditorium seats. The thirty or so people scattered around the stage and auditorium moved to the seats; there were several adults Elliot did not recognize but who were smiling at him and the other students. Off to the side sat Dr. Pelton, who usually attended practice only when needed.

Elliot was already sitting with Vesta and Jonas; a few days earlier Jonas had texted him, inviting Elliot to come with him to pick Vesta up from the hospital. She was doing well, despite everything. Some yellow discolorations could still be seen as the bruises on her arms receded; despite its being cold, she had refused to wear sleeves. A bandage still graced her forehead.

"Alright," Hoegren began, "many of you have questions. I've been in contact with Rydar. All things considered, he's well. They're trying to fig- ure out what happened, beyond the hearsay," Frank glanced at Vesta, "but I have a feeling that even if he's cleared, the university will be cautious about letting him back on campus, both for students' safety and his own."

"Also, their own," muttered Jonas to the others.

Frank rolled his eyes with a nod at the murmur, resuming, "None- theless, Ry was only concerned that the play keeps going. But before we get to that—Vesta, you don't have to, but do you have anything you want to say?"

"Yes." Vesta was up before she had finished the word. Hiding a wince, she climbed up onto the stage, turning to look at the group. There was a decisiveness to her stance and an uncommon defiance to the way she observed everyone. She had only ever looked like that when standing in as Hotspur. Elliot had already noticed a quiet hardness to her glance since the hospital; now he hoped to hear what was behind it.

"I assume you've all heard my official statement—that Rydar was protecting me. Most of you didn't need me to tell you that. I thought a lot in the hospital. I don't want you to worry about me or pity me. I'm still working through it all, but please, let me deal with it. If you want to help me, don't treat me differently or try to avoid triggering me; that would only make the attack stronger, and me weaker. Instead, put it into the play. You want to really protect women? Finish this term hard and let's make it happen. That's why I was attacked: because I am part of this production." Vesta looked at Elliot. "My parents think I should stop doing the play; they've threatened to withdraw their financial help for next semester if I do it. Of course, they love me, and I think the whole event shocked their idea of what college is nowadays. But the fact that I was attacked proved to me that I have to do this thing. I'm done apologizing; I'm done giving the benefit of the doubt to those who want to shut us down—because, for all their accusations and vocabulary, they're actually the violent ones. Theirs is not just another perspective; wanting to shut down other points of view isn't a point of view. It denies the whole concept."

Elliot glanced around. While everyone was fixated on Vesta, a few "hems" and "mm-hmms" came from the group of adults behind them. Looking back, Elliot saw that a few of them were nodding, as if Vesta's words were no surprise. One man—tall and with a high-bridged, patrician nose—winked at Elliot before returning his eyes to the stage. Elliot realized he had seen the man before; Hoegren had brought him to the theater near the end of one of their discussions and had introduced him to Rydar once the group had dispersed.

"But we can't concede the morality they claim; we can't compromise to their anti-perspective, since if we concede they'll only want to shut down more things. There can be no compromise between art—between Shakespeare—and a steel-toed boot. I only find it fitting that it was with a two-by-four that I was saved," Vesta looked at the cityscape that was in the process of construction behind her, "because even that was a piece of our art. Jonas needs to keep building the set, and we need to do this play. Not just for Rydar, not just for me, not even for all the high ideals those thugs probably thought they were protecting—progress, and rights, and safety. We need to do it because it's the kind of thing those ideals are supposed to make possible, and because, whether or not their criticisms are valid, whether or not we knew it would be so serious when we signed on, it's fallen to us to defend Shakespeare—not just our interpretation of him, but his existence, itself, on campus, as well as everything that he might represent.

"In their own way, the students against us are like Hotspur; they're trying too hard to fight the wrong battle. But, like Rydar said, the answer to a corrupt kingdom isn't to just tear it down: it's to recreate what's supposedly missing. That's our job with this play. We're Harry, this is our tavern, and the performance is our coronation."

A few people started to clap, but Vesta quieted them with a hand.

"One thing I know, it's something I have to do. If the worst thing that happens to me is a few bruises and a broken rib in the name of being sure that I can do that—that I can stand up for the things I think are valuable, like Shakespeare and art—then I'll leave college proud. After today, I'm not going to bring up the attack. Like I said, let me deal with it; when you think of me, don't just think of the attack or violence against women or all that. I'm still Vesta; however all of this might change me, I'll still be the Vesta you knew, only with more experience. I'm just going to keep doing what I'm doing. And I'll do it with more understanding of what it means and what it's a defense against."

As the audience was taken up in applause, a single pair of hands sounded above the rest. Clapping, Elliot looked over his shoulder; Megan, standing and with tears running down her usually stolid face, was applauding enthusiastically. She looked relieved. Vesta was looking at her; she gave the girl an imperceptible nod. It looked like a hug.

"Thank you, Vesta," said Hoegren, stepping back to center stage as Vesta gingerly hopped down; he, too, had tears in his eyes. "That was more than I could have said. If my wife and I had been blessed with a daughter," the man's voice choked for a moment, "I would have been more proud than anything had she come out of a trauma so well and if she had understood something so profound. Let's all take that to heart and give our production a greater meaning than its perpetrators ever could have intended."

For the first time since arriving in the auditorium, Vesta smiled, mouthing a thank you to Hoegren. Two tears finally fell down her cheeks. Jonas put his arm around Vesta's shoulders, giving them a gentle squeeze.

"Now, Rydar saw much of this coming. He and I spoke last semester about what to do should anything happen to him. You may have heard that we've received the support of the Orangedale Shakespeare Company."

Hoegren motioned to the group of adults in the back. The tall, hook-nosed man stood and walked to the stage as Hoegren continued, "While I will be taking a more hands-on role in production, Andrew Severn of the OSC will be our interim director. However, don't worry: this will still be Rydar's show, and yours. Last semester I had Rydar write an explanation of theme and intent in his interpretation, in the event of just such an absence; we'll be relying on you to help us further maintain Rydar's vision. I understand you all met through last semester to discuss the plays? Or most of you?"

Several heads nodded; Hoegren was looking at those whom he had seen the few times he had stopped in at the discussion group. "Insofar as you discussed the text and developed your characters, you will help us direct you, based as much as possible on the plays and Rydar's notes."

Severn motioned his hand to speak.

"First off," the man began, smiling, "thank you for letting us help you all. We've been keeping up with your play since last semester. I've met Rydar and listened to him, and I'll try to stay as faithful to his intent as possible. Furthermore, I understand that after that protest last term and other events," the man glanced at Vesta, "a few people have dropped out. Frank has graciously opened the door for us to supplement those parts. We all look forward to doing these plays with you. While this is still your production, several of us have been doing Shakespeare for many years, and we hope to bring our expertise to your theater—as well as, perhaps, a larger audience. The city wants to support the arts, and by now many people want to see this play that has caused so much drama." The man smiled at his own pun.

As Severn spoke, the other adults had started to walk toward the stage. They proceeded to introduce themselves and what roles they would play. Elliot had noticed a small-framed man with a graying beard who was considering him with piercing, blue eyes; when the introductions reached him, the man—Vernon "Horn" Horner—confirmed Elliot's anticipation that he would play Hal's father, King Henry IV.

It was not until the students had introduced themselves that Elliot noticed Cora, seated in back row; she had not spoken, even when Vesta said she was sitting in as Hotspur. When Hoegren and Severn called everyone to circle up onstage for some introductory exercises, she stood and turned toward the exit. Before she left, she looked back at Elliot; even from the back of the auditorium, her glance unnerved him. Her head was shaved, and the confident interest Elliot had always seen on her healthy, stern face had been replaced by a stressed worry. There were bags under her eyes.

A hand on Elliot's arm pulled his attention from the back of the room. Vesta exchanged a look with him; she had seen Cora, too. Vesta smiled, as if to say she understood his worry.

"Alright everyone," said Severn, receiving a reassuring nod from Hoegren, "let's start with some introductions—two lies and a truth."

❋

The sky was turning orange as Elliot, Vesta, and Jonas walked down Ad Hill toward the dorms. Megan had left when the new group transitioned from introductory exercises to scenes wherein she was not needed; she would join them later for dinner after finishing an essay. Without having to say it, they had all felt like dining together.

The day's heat wave had cooled while they were in the theater, and Vesta wanted to grab a sweater before they met Megan at the Commons. As a breeze blew up Ad Hill into their faces, Elliot was reminded that it was still, technically, winter.

"I like Severn," continued Jonas, responding to Vesta's curiosity about the adults. "I recognize him from the Orangedale Festival a few years ago. He played a great Iago."

"Yeah, I got a good vibe from him," agreed Vesta. "Real friendly, though I think some of the others thought he was too familiar too fast."

"I got that," said Elliot, hands the pockets of his fleece vest. His eyes went up and down the street bisecting Ad Hill from the quad. "But he was probably just nervous. It's weird, it felt like I'd imagine a parent meeting their foster or step-kid would be."

"Yeah, you could tell he wanted us to be sure he'd respect Rydar's and our vision," said Jonas, arm around Vesta's shoulder, his hand rubbing her bare arm. Elliot looked away. For all the ways he felt he had changed, he still felt a heaviness in his stomach when crossing the street at that spot, remembering how often he and Cora had crossed it in anticipation of his apartment.

"Saw Cora there," he said.

"Mm-hm," replied Vesta.

"I was surprised," said Jonas. "I doubt she'll continue with the play."

"Babe . . . " Vesta intoned.

Elliot chuckled. "It's fine, Vesta—but thanks."

Notwithstanding the berth Vesta and Jonas had generally given him on the subject—for which Elliot had been grateful—Vesta had been shocked when she had learned about Cora's apparently coming on to Rydar. They had planned to tell Vesta the day after she returned to campus, but she had called Megan late that night, having heard it from Cora, herself. Vesta had understood more than just why they had kept it from her: the next day she said part of her had seen it coming, or at least understood it enough not to be shocked. Cora apparently seemed changed from the episode: she was contrite in a way Vesta had never seen. Elliot had remained quiet despite the sudden spark of warmth in his chest.

"She said Rydar was gracious through the whole thing, and that he wasn't cutting her from the play, though he was going to keep his dis—." Vesta stopped abruptly as the glass door to B-Center opened next to them.

"Oh, excus—," said whoever had just stepped backwards out of the lobby, nearly bumping into Jonas. It was Ermine Jackson.

Ermine's eyes landed on Vesta, who was staring at him wide-eyed, her hand having suddenly reached up to grasp Jonas's arm. Ermine's hand, still stretched into the doorway, was being held by a thin young man whom Elliot recognized from somewhere. Elliot sucked his teeth, thinking of Sam.

"What, who's this?" asked the young man, who stepped out of the doorway. Despite his sallow skin, Elliot noted, his eyes were intense, immediately catching the gist of the situation.

"Err," said Ermine, "these are . . . "

"I'm the 'nearly unconscious girl who ended up being a member of Colson's cast' whom Ermine here wrote about." Vesta did not extend a handshake of introduction.

"Oh," the other said as his eyes widened in recognition. Instead of joining Ermine's awkwardness—odd in itself—the young man seemed to acquire an incongruously greater control, as if learning who Vesta was had allowed him to safely and smugly comprehend the situation. Elliot had seen the look before but could not remember where.

"Well, where are my manners," recovered Ermine, turning to the group as he switched his other hand to the pale young man's. "Everyone, this is my partner, Skylar."

"Son of a . . . " Jonas began, catching himself. "So he's the one who's been writing the stuff you're scared to say openly?"

Rather than balking at Jonas's words, Skylar smiled, looking side-long at Ermine with a chuckle.

"What?" asked Jonas, looking between the two of them. "Am I wrong?"

"Oh, it's not that," said Ermine in his usual flippant demeanor, "though I wonder if that's not a case of projection—Sky, this is Jonas Templeton, of *The Praesidium*."

Despite maintaining his smile, the other young man could not hold back a sudden, brief widening of his nostrils, his upper lip shortening to reveal a glimpse of his teeth before forming back into a calm smile.

Ermine continued with a giggle, "Skylar's non-binary. 'They' will do."

"And technically," Skylar said evenly, sharing Ermine's shrewd smile, "it would be 'child of a bitch.'" Jonas kept quiet, shifting his jaw to the side behind his closed mouth as he looked away.

Skylar looked at Elliot, eyes suddenly narrowing.

Elliot's fist tightened in his pocket as curiosity turned to recognition and a flash of apprehension and anger. He had seen Skylar at the protest.

"You know who I am," Elliot said.

"Well," said Ermine, breaking the quiet and taking Skylar's fingers in both hands, "we were just on our way to get dinner. I'd ask you all to join us, as a gesture of good faith and tolerance, but . . . "

"Are you kidding me?" said Vesta, "after everything you've done and tried to do to us?"

Ermine and Skylar both raised their eyebrows, as if Vesta had gauchely broken some taboo.

"And hey," Vesta continued, pointing at Ermine's face, "do me a favor: next time you want to use me in your blog, ask me first, asshole. You're lucky I don't try to get the post removed—which I know you'd just love as a cross to die on. Too bad—unlike you, I actually believe in free speech, even for stuff I find contemptible. You want to make a gesture? Stop using us—using me—to try and prove whatever it is you want to prove. Post an unedited, uninterpreted video of one of our practices. Hell, host a guest blogger to defend our play and answer your criticism. Anything less than that and you're just a couple of cowards."

Jonas had started to slowly rub Vesta's back; he exchanged a look with Elliot. He was as surprised as Elliot by her new, fiery unpredictability.

Ermine was about to speak, but Vesta interrupted him. "Only someone who's never been beaten up could call speech violence without blinking. You two are pathetic." Her tone cooled from her initial anger to a cold contempt. When neither of the two met her eyes, she seemed to lose interest and relaxed with an exhale. Skylar did not respond, eyes still glancing as if compulsively at Elliot.

"Well . . . " said Ermine, agitated, "then we'll let you go on your way. Jonas, Elliot." He nodded tersely to the other two as he stepped forward, drawing Skylar after him by the hand.

Vesta resumed her easy pace toward her dorm two buildings over. After a step, Jonas and Elliot were again even with her. They walked in silence.

"So, that's Skylar," said Jonas after a few moments.

"For some reason I expected them—him—to be bigger," said Vesta.

"I recognized'm from the protest last term, at the theater," said Elliot, hands back in his pockets, self-consciously working out how to refer to Skylar's gender.

"He didn't like you," said Vesta, apparently not sharing Elliot's trepidation.

"Yeah. I didn't like the look—wasn't 'til then that I remembered where I'd seen Skylar before."

Vesta turned her chin to Jonas, nudging him with her elbow. "You didn't say much; why do you get so quiet when stuff about my attack comes up?"

"Well," said Jonas, "it was your attack. I don't want to speak for you."

"But I'd expect you to at least say what you think," Vesta continued, "and what about Ry? You've known him longer than any of us, but you always get quiet on the topic." Her directness told Elliot that she had been considering Jonas's reaction—which Elliot agreed had been uncharacteristically reticent—and that they may have even had words on the subject already.

"You don't think I'm worried?" snapped Jonas. Calming himself, he continued, "I haven't stopped thinking about Ry since he went away. But I need to wait until all the evidence is considered. It's the only thing that'll really help him, and it's what he wants. I gotta respect that."

"Okay, okay," said Vesta, stroking his arm. "You're right. I just want you to know you can trust me." She pulled out her keys as they approached the front door of her dorm, "Just because I was the one attacked doesn't mean you can't talk about how it's affecting you. That goes for you, too, Elliot."

Elliot smiled, still wondering about Jonas's reasons for being quiet on the subject. Elliot looked across the quad. He could not be sure, but Skylar seemed to have been looking over their shoulder at them just the moment before.

"Commons's gonna be packed," said Elliot. "How about Artisan's? I'll tell Megan." He nodded at Jonas, who followed Vesta inside; he pulled out his phone and began to type.

Soon, Jonas was driving Elliot, Megan, and Vesta to downtown Orangedale. The sobriety of the interaction with Ermine and Skylar had relaxed into a comfortable quiet. Jonas's usual album of Rush's *Moving Pictures* played in the background, Geddy, Lifeson, and Peart turning odd time signatures into rhythmic melody—"structuring chaos," as Jonas had once described it. Elliot mused as he found he remembered and could quietly hum along with the solo of "Red Barchetta." Jonas smiled, rolling up the volume knob as he nodded his head to the seven-beat measures.

"Jonas, did you check Casey's final draft covering the organic vending machines debate?" Smith Ingman asked, rereading Jonas's latest submission calling for an increased balance of critical perspective in the growing academic study of video games. Jonas highlighted a few words on the draft.

"Yeah, I just need to cut a couple of sentences of this. I'll be done in a bit."

"Good," said Ingman, returning his eyes to his screen.

"No problem. Hey, I wanted to ask: you know the girl who was attacked?"

"Yes?" said Ingman, sitting up and evidently wanting to resume his work.

"What if we let her do an op-ed? Like, let her say her piece, if she wants. She's a common subject on *The Homefront*, and she may want to give her perspective on the incident, as well as why she's still doing the play."

"Do you think she would? We wouldn't want to profit from her trauma or make her relive anything."

"Oh, she wouldn't mind."

"How do you know?"

"Well, you know . . . she's my girlfriend."

Ingman looked agape at Jonas before he removed his glasses and, placing his hand on his forehead, leaned back in his chair.

"Jonas, I'm sorry—with everything going on, I completely forgot."

"'S okay. It's midterms, and you've had a lot to deal with. However, there's already a lot of speculation about her, and *The Homefront* is using her as an argument against the plays. She wants nothing to do with the blog—she sees them as implicitly instigating the attack. I think she'd like to share her perspective."

"Ask her to come to our next editorial meeting. That's not a hard 'yes,' but I'd like to talk to her; if we can help her and others through such a thing, and set the record straight, we'd be doing our jobs. Now," Ingman returned his glasses to his nose, "finish Casey's print; we need to upload by the end of the afternoon."

Jonas nodded, smiling to himself at the pensive way Ingman hesitated in returning to his own work. The man would think about it, and by now Jonas knew that, for all his patience and self-control, Ingman did not waste his attention on things that did not matter.

Vesta bit her tongue; this was not the Shakespeare in the 1600s class she had signed up for. The interim professor—a woman named McClellan—had apparently gone through the syllabus and removed several supporting pieces Rydar had scheduled along with his list of Shakespeare's tragedies and romances. Returning to class the previous week, Vesta had found her efforts to read ahead to have been in vain.

"Professor," Vesta raised her hand, trying to maintain a polite tone, "may I ask why you removed *A Thousand Acres*, specifically?" Planning the semester to unchronologically lead up to *Hamlet*, Rydar had assigned *King Lear* before the upcoming midterm, along with Jane Smiley's reiteration of the play from the daughters' perspectives on a farmstead in the American Midwest. Vesta had enjoyed the book, finding an unexpected similitude between her reaction to her recent experience and the older sister's refusal to block out their father's abuse of her and her younger sisters. Indeed, it had been by reading the book that she had solidified why, in her case, she could not justify blocking out the attack.

"Well," said Professor McClellan, choosing her words and seeming a bit flustered by the question, "due to certain subject matter in the book, I thought it best to remove it so as not to trigger anyone in the class."

"But Colson started the class with a trigger warning. I don't mean to speak for anyone, but he would have listened if there were a problem."

"Be that as it may," said the woman, avoiding Vesta's glance, "I didn't think it was appropriate to provide unnecessary voyeurism into sexual abuse, nor would we want to risk trivializing certain subjects through discussion. Also, we wouldn't want to put anyone through unnecessary memories."

"I don't mean to sound disrespectful," Vesta pressed, not letting herself back down, "but wouldn't it be better for us to decide that as a class, rather than your just avoiding it altogether? And it's not voyeuristic, in my opinion. It's a really well-written book, I thought."

"Vesta, please, it would be too easy for someone to be intimidated from implicitly revealing trauma by speaking up. Rather than placing anyone in that situation, I've decided to nix the book. I'd expect you, of all people, to understand."

"Excuse me?"

"Well . . . " The teacher finally looked at Vesta, eyebrows raised nervously and nodding slowly. A few people shifted in their seats, looking back and forth between the two women.

"Are you referring to the fact that I was actually assaulted?" said Vesta, "Because the assumption that I'd want to avoid thinking about it—and the decision to preemptively skip a good book because it might trigger me, without even asking—is pretty goddamned patronizing." Vesta realized her voice had grown louder, and she blushed. "Sorry, I know I'm not the only one, and my experience wasn't the worst, but if you're tip-toeing around the subject for me, please," she looked at the whole class, "don't."

The professor took a breath, "Thank you, Vesta. I'm relieved that you're being so strong about it—that's good. However, I plan to stand by my decisions regarding the syllabus, and I'll ask you to respect that. I must consider others, not just you."

"That's fine," Vesta said softly, nodding, "but can I still use Smiley as a source for my midterm?"

The woman pursed her lips a moment. "I don't see why not—so long as you focus on *Lear*, itself. You're right—*A Thousand Acres* is well-written, and it gives a long-overdue feminist reading of the power relationships in the play. I don't fault Colson for including it."

Vesta gripped her scarf. Don't react; she would not fault Colson? The idea of her thinking she justifiably could was laughable.

As the woman continued to outline the readings and discussion for the next week, Vesta considered how she had spoken back to the woman. As her thoughts cooled, she became aware of her own sudden impulse to look down on the woman, which she would need to examine later; the woman was still a professor, after all. Still, Vesta would never have done that a year ago. It further added to Vesta's larger fixation on the question of what kind of teachers produced which kinds of students. Once again, she felt immeasurably grateful for Rydar's influence over the past year.

I'll do it, she decided. She would write that piece Jonas had suggested. She had felt this way in other classes—as if the discussion and even the most menial interactions were tempered to give her a cushion she had not asked for and did not want. It really would be inappropriate, not to mention exhausting, to challenge such a thing in every class, but she had felt before now the desire to scream at everyone, "I'm not a child, I'm not weak, so don't treat me that way! Don't think of it when you look at me!" Above all, she wanted to cut off the extension of comfort before she became used to it. She remembered from previous classes that, for all its uses, prolonged anesthesia could make one weak and leave them oblivious to their own weakness. So could leprosy.

Vesta quietly opened her notebook to a blank page and began to brainstorm. At least if she put her account out there, she could refer people to it. She would be damned if she did not correct the debate about her own attack, so far as she could.

"*The Real Assault on a Woman*"
—*Vesta Lloyd, Op. Ed. Contributor, The Praesidium*

One thing they don't tell you about assault: it doesn't stop with the event, and, just like the event, itself, it is those who you least expect—your supposed allies—who keep reopening the wounds.

My story is not as bad as others'. If you haven't read the official Orangedale Daily Root article, I was walking on campus when a woman and a group of men asked if I was coming from the theater and subsequently attacked me. I was then saved by a man with a 2x4". Although I was not sexually molested, my assailants certainly wanted to convey their physical power over me, which, as I understand, is the impetus for rape more than is mere physical attraction. I'm not an expert on assault, nor do I speak for other women. I can only voice my experience. Any other account—such as those of certain on-campus blogs—is unauthorized and incorrect. Yet, THAT is where the assault—the use of my body and my experience for others' gain and display of power—persists.

I have been upheld as a victim; I am not. For that moment, during the attack, I was a victim, but it was because I had already refused to quit the Spring Shakespeare Festival. I still refuse to quit it, and I will take the blows my convictions receive. I will not excuse my attackers—they should be put in jail, which would be merciful compared to what they really deserve. However, by not considering myself a victim, I must disagree with certain albeit sympathetic statements and interpretations regarding my attack which, like my attackers, would implicitly punish me for my art. I am, of course, talking about those who would paint me as a victim not of violence and intolerance against the Shakespeare production, but of that production, itself—a victim of the man now still in custody for saving my life.

The real victimization in my case is not one of physical force—again, my attackers ultimately failed to intimidate me into silence. Rather, it is one of language and intra-campus politics, and the abuse continues every time someone uses my attack to promote their perspective on the campus culture. We read in feminist literature that women should be given a voice to articulate their experience. Here, now, I claim that exclusive right, and anyone who wants to interpret my situation without my consent is necessarily impeding at least one woman's voice. To treat my perspective of it as anything less than authoritative—even under the banner of fighting a perceived "patriarchal production," as our play has been called—is to promote the stereotype of woman's inability to accurately perceive reality. Do you want to promote such perspectives of women? No? Then shut up about what my assault means.

You want to know the worst thing? When those thugs were attacking me, when they were carrying me from the light into the shadows so they could keep kicking me, and probably worse, they were accusing me of promoting violence against women. I don't know if they thought they were doing something moral (that's an abyss of self-evasion I can't begin to consider), but they made sure their language sounded moral. I think they believed they were the victims, having been told that all acts in the war against the play are defensive. As a representative of Shakespeare on campus, I was the aggressor. Such moral language provided an excuse for brutality. And they were laughing. I've thought a lot about that. In their righteous frenzy to prove themselves against the big, bad play they had been told to hate and fear, they were laughing. But no matter: whatever helps them avoid the awareness that acts of preemptive self-defense might be a sure sign of the weakness of their perspective.

Those who have used my experience to indict next month's Shakespeare production are doing the same thing: using moral language to cover their attempts to bully women and artists into silence. Filtering my attack through more seemingly enlightened viewpoints while ignoring my first-hand perspective is just another brand of duct tape. I will say here and now: you cannot be angry at my attack and also want the plays shut down; if you oppose the production's being allowed, then you are on the side of my attackers. If you really believe the assault victim's voice matters, then you must contend with the fact that I was attacked because I was—and am—proud to do this play. That I haven't quit, of course, implies I am willing to risk another attack. However, don't worry about me; look to yourself. If you want to know what's worse than kicking a girl for her virtues and art while accusing her of promoting violence against women, it's implicitly believing the virtues and art are to blame.

One thing we can't do—as individuals and as a campus—is pretend we don't understand how something like my attack could happen. All year I've always thought, 'It's just a Shakespeare play; once people realize that, they'll understand. This has all been a misunderstanding.' No. No more. Whatever people think Shakespeare represents—which they've been clear about—they're willing to use it for permission to do the worst kinds of things and count them as moral. 'Doing unto others,' is out the window when you think you're fighting Nazis; that's how they see it. My sin was not taking them at their word, instead just assuming they were exaggerating or showing another perspective that I needed to tolerantly consider. But they're not interested in discussion or understanding, nor even the tolerance they use as a mask; that's what they oppose most—because they might discover we aren't the Nazis and that we have something to say that's worth hearing. Neither are they interested in my perspective on the attack, which should be authoritative. We'll see who listens to and honors it as such after this.

This experience—both the attack and how people have reacted to it—has already taught me more than any other class has, except for maybe the books we read to help us interpret and defend Shakespeare. I'm grateful that Colson presciently had us read them because they helped me understand being assaulted for my beliefs. In that way, Colson saved me long before the attack; he made me ready to comprehend it—and, thus, able to rise above it. I can't speak for other girls who go through immeasurably worse, but, again, I must speak for myself. If that's what is at stake in keeping Shakespeare on campus—the idea that art and literature can give people the tools to deal with trauma, as it's doing for me—then you're goddamned right I'll do this play. That's why I get so angry when I read or hear my attack being used as a propaganda piece against the play; they consider criminal that of which I am most proud, and poison that which is the cure.

This will be my only public statement, which should have been unnecessary after the piece in the Daily Root. Really, my staying in the play is my statement. What happened to me was not my fault; however, my response to it will be. Rather than avoiding the attack, instead, I intend to consider it more, to look at it, to contextualize it, to understand it more than my attackers could ever know. In this way, I hope to make my victimhood shrink and my agency grow. I will heal, and I want my healing to leave me stronger, not weaker. If I can finish this production, then I believe I will have actually done something not just for the future of Orangedale, not just for the future of women, but for myself and my integrity. That is, I will not have been a victim, but a hero.

    —Vesta Lloyd
    Op-Ed Contributor
    The Praesidium

CHAPTER 15

"I JUST WANT YOU to know I'm proud of you," Jonas said as he and Vesta headed from their respective classes to lunch. "I mean, sure, I'm smelling like a rose for recommending your piece to Ingman. I think he's tired of indirectly fighting Ermine and the rest, and it was a rock in a river for him. I mean, he's in charge and everything, and he's kept an even keel, but he's been shocked more than he'll admit by everything this year. Anyway," Jonas said, ascending backwards the steps leading to the Commons, "I think you really encouraged him by defining things so clearly. That took a lot, babe."

"Yeah, yeah, watch where you're going," Vesta said, laughing as Jonas almost ran into a few students walking the other way, "And I'm glad he liked it, but I shouldn't have even had to do it—especially when I'm still trying to deal with . . . "

"Which you're doing amazingly," Jonas said, smiling and not reaching out to touch her as he normally would have. Although he had not withheld his attention, Jonas had precipitously let Vesta initiate touch more often than he had before. Vesta had told him it was unnecessary, that she appreciated his consideration, but she knew the difference between him and those thugs, that she wanted him to touch her as easily as before, and let her worry about overcoming her sensitivity. Yet, still he hesitated, at least in public, and it hurt.

"Some of it . . . I'm afraid I spoke too soon," she said, "the things we read last term and our practices are helping, but I don't want to repress anything in trying to move beyond it."

"You didn't speak too soon. It was like a thesis," Jonas said with a wink, "you're just proving it after the fact in the latter paragraphs of the semester."

"Up with your metaphors today," Vesta said, pushing Jonas in front of her as he opened the door to the Commons. He may have become a regular writer for *The Praesidium*, but he was still a cartoonist at heart. Nonetheless, for all his trite humor, Jonas had been supportive throughout Vesta's process.

Vesta stopped; a word on a bright pink flyer had caught her eye. Vesta walked up to the bulletin board.

> *Come one, Come all!*
> *An ally of Shakespeare gives his call*
> *To speak the things you need to hear,*
> *E'en as you shout, and hiss, and geer!*

> *In response to recent events, The Praesidium is proud to sponsor a year-end lecture by a person connected with the controversial production of Henry IV Parts 1 & 2. We hope his appearance will promote inclusion of ideas in a time of division while showing Orangedale's commitment to civil discourse. Space is limited, so reserve your seat on The Praesidium's Orangeware page!*

She did not need to see Jonas's face to know he was smiling. His understatement about *Praes* events was both infuriating and beguiling, since it made discoveries like this seem like a secret surprise he had saved just for her.

"It'll never work," Vesta said flippantly, resuming her pace into the Commons and not granting Jonas the dignity of seeing her smile.

"Hey, hey," Jonas laughed, catching up, "what do you mean? Ingman and I put a lot of thought into that flyer."

"You mean you wrote it and Ingman nodded a few times," Vesta said, rolling her eyes.

"At least give me credit for knowing how to ride a wave. That's journalisming, babe," Jonas said with a fierce nod as he handed her a tray.

"Whatever," Vesta said, reaching for a pair of salad tongs as Jonas continued toward one of the entrée bars. Biting her lip, she considered the event.

"But, seriously," she resumed once they were in line to pay, "I don't want you to get hurt. All that about good faith and civil discourse sounds good, but you know it's only on our end. At least I'm worrying I gave them more fuel. You're just antagonizing them—and you know it."

Jonas chuckled. "You'd rather let sleeping dogs lie, when they're not sleeping?"

"No, but we shouldn't jab 'em with a poker, either," Vesta said over her shoulder as she slid her student card into the payment slot. "We have enough to worry about, with the play and all." She mouthed a thank you to the Commons teller—an elderly woman she liked to see during lunch—and headed toward an open booth in the corner, Jonas a couple of steps behind her with a fajita plate and fries.

"The best thing to do, I think," said Jonas as he settled in, "is to boldly use the same freedoms that Ermine enjoys—even as they promote many worse things than we." Jonas took a bite, closing his eyes for a moment to hide that he had glanced at Vesta's arm, where the bruises had been. Jonas winked, waving his hand around floridly as he said around another bite, "I mean, Ermine made this situation, even if he doesn't like the consequences—when others he doesn't like discover free speech. Not just you—I know that article was tough for you, and I won't ask more of you, besides that you keep doing you—but others, who I hope are inspired by you. Still, Ermine asked for it. He thinks he's fighting people like you and me, but he's only fighting himself, all the while feeding his adversary."

"What do you mean?" asked Vesta, narrowing her eyes with interest.

Jonas wiped his mouth, leaning back to let his eyes climb up the wall behind Vesta as he thought for a moment. "Sometimes I wonder if Ermine wakes up chronically thinking of and worrying about the play and the campus discourse around it, resenting everyone he suspects of supporting it. Remember, I worked with Ermine for a couple of semesters, and I felt his revolt against Ingman coming, even if Ermine, himself, didn't. I wouldn't put it past him to resent everyone he sees, especially now that he's put himself in his little *Homefront* bubble. For Ermine, respect and love for Shakespeare—and even indifference either way—have probably spread as a vague and incalculable menace throughout the campus; that's why I don't think they're exaggerating when they say they feel physically threatened every time they hear about the production. They probably really feel that, however irrational it is. The irony would be that that's the very thing Ermine has created for everyone else—the felt threat of physical violence."

"Hey, don't need to tell me," Vesta said, skewering the last few pieces of salad with her fork.

"Yeah . . . sorry," Jonas said, smiling sheepishly as he looked away from the bright red slash above her eyebrow.

"No, I didn't mean it like that," Vesta retorted, "I think you're right. I like this—you telling me what you're really thinking." She smiled, fondling his foot with hers beneath the table. She reached up to touch the scar above her right eyebrow. She had taken to wearing her hair back to show the scar, and touching it had seemed to give her a kind of power—a quiet jolt of pride, as it were. It was the badge of a survivor—the mark of overcoming tragedy. The evening after the doctor had removed her stitches, Vesta had forced herself to look at herself in the mirror until she grew used to the bright red line. Then as now, Prince Hal's words at the end of *Henry IV Part* 1 came to her, giving her the strength of a blessing: "God forbid a shallow scratch should drive the Prince of Wales from such a field as this, where stained nobility lies trodden on and rebels' arms triumph in massacres."

Vesta was distracted by what looked like a scuffle in the entryway. A handful of students had also seen the pink flyer and, having ripped it down, were jumping into the Commons. The one holding the flyer climbed up onto a long table and held the paper aloft.

"No Shakespeare, no fear! No Shakespeare, no fear!" he yelled, crumpling the paper up above his head before throwing it down on the table and stomping on it. The others had crowded around the table, two stepping up onto its bench seats. Whooping and hollering, they began to repeat the young man's words, chanting it as they skipped around the other tables, looking at those who were seated for lunch. Many tried to ignore them, but some nodded, taking up the chant. Looking wide-eyed at the young men, the older woman joined the lunch staff's retreat from their kiosks. The manager of the Commons catering came out of his office without his customary suit jacket, pulling out his phone with a tight lipped sigh.

"Let's get out of here," said Vesta, suddenly needing to escape the growing noise and feeling cornered as the young men neared their table as they spread out among the tables, looking those seated in the eyes.

"I got the trays," Jonas nodded through the wall toward the outside walk, "you hop over the patio rail. Walk to the library entrance, I'll be there in a bit." He stood, patiently placing himself between the man on the table and Vesta. She ducked her head under her bag strap as they walked to the glass door leading to the patio. Before parting, she gave Jonas a kiss on the cheek. Beneath all the jokes, Jonas was a man of action, and she loved him in that moment for the immediacy and calmness with which he had gotten her out.

※

Elliot tensed as he saw the envelope on his doormat. It was too small to be anything official—which would have gone to his home address, anyway. Nonetheless, the continued on-campus tension made Elliot hesitate. Checking his periphery as if approaching a building as Vexxen, he grabbed the envelope and entered his apartment. He felt the key through the paper before he opened the envelope.

Elliot had only seen Cora a few times since the OSC had joined their production, and only from afar. Whenever she saw him, she would calmly but quickly turn a different direction. Her shorter hair was not unattractive, but it accentuated a new demeanor in her movements—one of unobtrusiveness, almost apology.

Unprompted, Vesta had brought her up to Elliot the previous week as they waited in Jonas's car while he grabbed something from his apartment; Cora was apparently focusing on her studies and spending a lot of time in the library and their dorm. Looking at Elliot in the passenger vanity mirror, Vesta had said, "Something seems broken in her, but something else seems as if it's getting stronger, like she's starting to rebuild in a way." Vesta had kept her eyes on Elliot a few moments longer than necessary as Jonas ambled back into the car. Her look had the quality of squeezing his arm reassuringly. For all that Jonas and Megan had or might have said to affirm the break-up, Vesta knew Elliot still cared about Cora; he wondered if Cora might still care for him.

Looking down at the brass key, Elliot grabbed his phone.

Got the key. Thanks

His phone vibrated before he unslung his bag onto his computer chair. Slumping down on his couch, Elliot swiped open the screen.

Cora Madison

Good. Was worried someone else might pick it up.

How are you doing?

Cora Madison

I'm fine. Tired. How are things?

Good.

Cora Madison

. . . I have no right to say it, but I miss you, Ell.

A wave of relief spread through Elliot; he sighed, considering what he should say. He thought of Vesta's expression. It did not have the immediate, reactionary caution of Jonas or Megan, or, Elliot imagined, Rydar. Vesta trusted Elliot. He had grown, and she knew it.

I miss you, too, all things considered.

Cora Madison

Could I . . . see you?

Elliot smiled, imagining the scene of release as, having learned what they needed to, they fell into each other's arms. It would have the kind of meaning last semester's game between them had merely simulated. A cunning thought wondered whether she might still be playing that game now; however, the look Elliot had seen on Cora's face across the courtyard adjoining the library to the Commons—a wide-eyed but tight-lipped willingness to bear whatever she had earned with humility—shook away the suspicion. Nonetheless, Elliot did not feel it would be right to see her. Not yet.

Idk if that's a good idea. Not just bc of everything that happened with us, but I have a lot I need to focus on. But I'll think about it.

Cora Madison

Ok :) I understand. I'm sorry for everything I put you through. You were worth better than me. That's why I did it all, I think. I was jealous of what I knew you might be worth.

Elliot swallowed as he reread the words, forcing himself to take them in. Tears came to his eyes, which he welcomed, not just for the compliment but for how Cora must have changed to give it so blatantly. He suddenly felt the impulse to toss his diffident self-control and go to see her unannounced, the way she often had him. No. Stay strong, kid, he told himself, imagining it were Rydar saying it.

Same.

Cora Madison

I'm sad I won't be able to join you guys onstage :') But I'll be there.

I'll look for you :)

Cora Madison

K. If we don't text before then, good luck in finals, Ell.

You too, Cora :)

He closed his phone and tossed it over to his bed, not trusting himself not to say more. Nonetheless, he found himself thinking of holding Cora again, sighing as he recalled the feeling of the length of her legs against his. Still, the image did not have the same hold on him as before—or he felt it didn't. However slightly, he felt above the back-and-forth testing of last semester; yet, that feeling, and all he had done since, only made him want to see her more. He knew he could resist her if she called, but the need to resist now seemed superfluous, or it would once they had both gone through what they needed. That she had not called—that she had given up her key and had been nothing but contrite in her texts—suggested she had grown, too.

That's how she's calling, a part of him thought; she knows you've grown. She's still manipulating you.

However, it was a small part, and Elliot found himself meeting it with an ironic chuckle. Getting up, he muttered aloud in response to the thought, "Once more into the breach, dear friends, once more . . . " He walked to the kitchenette to cook a grilled cheese sandwich.

Prince Hal—King Henry V—was only halfway finished with his story when he had said those words. If even a king could not get the girl until his mission was done . . . Elliot needed to focus; besides finishing his classes strong, the play required—and deserved—his full attention.

Rydar's words about distraction came back to him, and he wondered if Cora, herself, might still need time. Initially it had been all Elliot could do to resist resenting her for so leading him on. Was her attraction ever real, the thought had needled despite his efforts at distraction, or was I always just a stand-in, a shadow? However, in the hindsight of the previous month, his anger and despondency had given way to pity and, as he realized Cora was trying to move forward, respect. Elliot did not know what she had been going through since coming onto Rydar, but he did not want to inhibit it. "One should not dodge one's tests," Elliot had read in Nietzsche, skimming through a library copy of Beyond Good and Evil, "though they may be the most dangerous game one could play and are tests that are taken in the end before no witness or judge but ourselves."

Flipping the sandwich from the griddle onto his plate, Elliot walked to turn on his computer. However, as its fans began to whirr, he picked up Crime and Punishment. He had neglected it earlier in semester but had picked it up again because of the recent crimes on campus, as well as because of his own need to answer the question of perception versus reality, provoked by Cora, herself.

Elliot had found that Raskalnikov concretized the process, the anxiety, the absurdity, and, Elliot anticipated, the answer to the problem of having an active perception without a reliable foundation whereon to ground it. Indeed, like Rydar's reaction to Kirillov in Devils, as Elliot saw Dostoevsky laying out the clues tracking Raskalnikov's progression from ideological revolution into madness, he had more and more begun to laugh at the previous, unspoken worry that his introspection, too, might relegate him to a life of stifled, solipsistic isolation. He knew the door remained open to that version of himself—narcissistic, friendless, and resentful that none seemed to recognize his profundity; however, now he hoped he might avoid going back through it, and keep his feet on the ground. With a cunning smile, Elliot glanced over at the library copy of Nietzsche; part of him wondered whether it was always completely beneficial to keep one's feet on the ground.

With an ironic chuckle at the mixed metaphor, he took a bite of his grilled cheese and opened the Dostoevsky.

✻

"Orangedale Professor Exonerated, Charges Dropped"
—Sybil Braitwaithe, University Liaison, Orangedale Daily Root

Monday, April 6:

After a much-anticipated closed-door hearing, the office of County DA Patricia O'Conner released a statement this morning that the investigation into Orangedale U. professor Rydar Colson has concluded. After examining the facts of the case, including student testimony, crime scene investigation, and digital evidence that, despite his initial claims, Colson could not have been at the scene, O'Conner has cleared Colson of all charges. "At stake here was finding those who attacked a young girl. Not only was Colson not Ms. Lloyd's attacker: he was not her savior, either."

According to O'Conner and Police Chief Charles Winthrop, Colson was covering for another individual who used a 2x4" to save Ms. Lloyd. Having spoken to the individual—whose anonymity she has agreed to maintain—O'Conner has decided to focus on finding those who attacked Lloyd. The university has declined to aid in the investigation, calling instead for O'Conner to release the name of the individual who defended Lloyd. O'Conner has refused, saying "the heroes of the story have been punished enough already." She assured the Daily Root that any legal implications of the defender's actions will be taken care of privately—though, she believed the individual "should be praised." O'Conner has decided to overlook Colson's initial attempt to cover for the individual, citing that both cooperated with the investigation and were each defending another in different ways.

Colson, who has been put on administrative leave until the end of the Spring semester, is now home. He was unavailable for comment but has agreed to meet for an exclusive interview to appear in a forthcoming issue.

According to previous comment from Frank Hoegren, Colson's Shakespeare production has continued without Colson, though with his blessing. Andrew Severn of the Orangedale Shakespeare Company, who has stepped in as director, assured us that "everyone involved is sighing with relief. We were able to congratulate him via speakerphone . . . Frankly, I can't wait to see him in person." Apparently, although Colson has been completely exonerated, he has agreed to let Severn continue with direction. "He wants to see what we'll do," said Severn, "and whether his vision and preparation will hold up."

Orangedale U. declined to comment on the production, saying only that, "Professor Colson is not officially connected with the university's theater department and should not be associated with any ongoing university programs while on administrative leave." They also declined any comment on the minor on-campus scandal that seemed to purposefully coincide with Colson's arrest. While Colson was in custody, members of the student body who opposed him alleged that the professor interacted inappropriately with a student; however, a recording of the event has proven such rumors false and that it was the student who initiated, despite Colson's consistent rebuffs. According to the campus newspaper, the student in question even advocated on Colson's behalf, confirming that it was she who came on to Colson, and that before, during, and after the incident Colson was nothing but respectful.

We will continue our updates regarding the University's Shakespeare production, as well as any other relevant campus news. As it stands, the show must go on—for now.

—Sybil Braitwaithe
@thebraiwai
University Liaison
Orangedale Daily Root

Frank Hoegren stepped between the students; opening the wooden doors of Administration Hall, he heard voices echoing through the building's high-ceilinged lobby.

He had realized something was wrong as soon as he rounded the row of trees separating the staff parking lot from the building; it was too early for any crowd of students to be milling about on the building's altar-like steps. As he edged his way through the crowd several had turned to look at him aggressively, as if suspicious he might not be just another unnamed staff to be safely ignored.

Now, as he ascended one of the spiraling flights of stairs in the lobby of the huge, symmetrical stone building, Frank heard a din reaching down from the upper floor. He avoided eye contact with the students leaning against the stone railings of the usually empty staircases; still, they looked at him as the others outside had: with a mix of expectation and suspicion. Some even muttered obscenities at him. Several had their phones out, either texting or speaking into their cameras. Frank heard some of what one girl was saying.

" . . . and so, even though the man molested a student and was in fucking prison, Orangedale still hasn't fired him. I mean, what the hell— don't they care about our safety as students? That's why we're here today: to get the university president to finally fire Corsen and cancel the play or, if he's too chickenshit to do that, step down from his job . . . "

Hoegren gritted his teeth. So, it's finally started, he thought. He had expected it; *The Homefront* had been petitioning for Rydar's firing for weeks, regardless of the investigation's still being forthcoming. There was no way they and their followers would accept the DA's verdict. They wanted heads to roll, though Frank doubted many of the still yawning individuals waiting around on the stairs could articulate what was really at stake in the issue. The ones making the noises upstairs—the ones whom he would need to pass to reach his office—could.

Sure enough, as Hoegren reached the third floor the din turned into an echoing wave of voices. As he stepped onto the red carpet of the top floor, he saw that the usual cool, blue, morning light of the northward facing windows was obscured by bodies. Many of them were talking loudly, as if their conversation were also meant for those beside whomever they were directly addressing. Others were looking over the heads on tip-toe. Several here and there were yawning from underneath hoods and heavy eyelids while sipping from tall cups of coffee. Down the hall Frank could see students chanting, some with fists in the air. In front of the president's office a group of students lay in an inert pile, as if dead. Others lay prostrate next to each other along the hall like railroad ties. Above the many voices Frank could hear a group chanting, "No violence, no play, justice goes the other way!"

Hoegren sighed, keeping his glance down as he eased his way between students in the opposite direction toward his office. He resisted shaking his head; he had not seen the president's car in the parking lot. He did not envy the man when arrived later that morning.

With relief, Hoegren saw that Marcie was not in yet. Locking the door leading into their offices, he opened his windows to let in the light and pulled out his cell phone.

"Hi, Marcie?" he said as she picked up.

"Yes? Frank? I was just about to leave; is everything okay?"

"Yes, everything's fine. However, I'd like you to take the day off."

"Oh? Is something the matter?"

"No, you don't need to worry. It's just . . . a student element is paying our president a visit . . . "

"Well, sure. On account of Mr. Colson, I'd imagine."

Hoegren smiled. She may be old, he thought, but she was sharp.

"I think so, too," he said, "I don't want you to worry, but these kind of things can get unpredictable."

"Don't insult me, Frank," the woman said lightly, "but if you think you can manage . . . I'll do what I can from here."

"Fine, fine. Enjoy your morning. Somehow I think that'll be the best kind of defense against this kind of thing—a counter-protest as it were."

A chuckle came from the phone. "Not bad, Frank. Let me know if there's anything you need. And don't think you need to fight them. They already lost, whatever they do. Call the police if there's any trouble."

"Don't worry, I'll be fine. I'll see you tomorrow."

In the next moment he was calling Angela; his call went to voicemail.

"Good morning, darling. I just wanted to let you know I love you, and that I don't want you to worry if you hear of a protest at the college. I'll be fine—Rydar's free, after all. Enjoy today's class; call if you want, of course."

Hanging up, Hoegren thought for a moment. Marcie had been right: he did not need to fight. Drawing a sudden lightness from the blue sky and view of the mountains to the north, which counteracted the foreboding dourness he had felt on the stairs, he smiled. He picked up the phone on his desk and, taking a file from a drawer, dialed the number as he sat down.

"Thank you for calling the Orangedale City Council!" said a bright voice from the other end. "My name is Mae; how may I help you?"

"Hi, Mae, my name is Frank Hoegren, from the university. I'd like to talk to John Atwater, if he's available. He'll know who I am."

"Just a moment."

The line went to a tune of light music. Frank swiveled in his chair, stretching his legs out as he looked up at the sky through the window.

"Atwater," barked a voice on the phone.

"Hi John—Frank Hoegren, Angela's husband."

"Oh, hi," the voice brightened, "how can I help you?"

"First off, thank you for connecting us with OSC. They've been a real boon. I don't want to take much of your time. You'll no doubt hear about it on the news, but we've got another protest over here at the college. They're outside the president's office. Nothing's certain yet, but I wanted to know if that 'administrative muscle' you mentioned might still be on the table."

"Sure, whatever I can do."

"It depends on what happens here today, but I think we may need to use the park after all. I'll talk to Severn; they'll be on board."

"Of course, MacWhorter's yours whenever you need. Need me to send help over there?"

"No; oddly, I think this is something the university and the president need to deal with on their own, though we'll call the police if need be."

"Do. The university's part of our city, and your crime is our crime."

"Alright, alright, let's not jinx it. I'll let you know if anything happens." Hoegren changed his tone, smiling. "Y'know, the DA cleared Colson." He had to fight the impulse to giggle.

"Yes, I'd heard that," said Atwater. "Give him my congratulations if you see him."

"Of course. Have a nice day, John."

Frank kept his hand on the phone as he clicked it down. Despite the noise coming from down the hall, he felt weightless, as if he were on a holiday. He stood and went to Marcie's office. The students had been right about one thing: this morning called for fresh coffee.

"Breaking News: University President Cancels Play, Fires Professor"
—*Sybil Braitwaithe, University Liaison, Orangedale Daily Root*

Monday, April 6:

"We are an institution of integrity and inclusion," said Orangedale University President Nathaniel Durant tonight in a press release, "and sometimes it takes the passion and engagement of our students to remind us of that." The release came at the end of a nearly twelve-hour stand-off between student protesters and the administration. The protest was sparked by recent news that Rydar Colson, English professor and previous director of the university's Shakespeare Festival, was cleared of all assault charges in the recent attack of a student by a group of her peers, who still have not been identified.

From nearly 8:00am to 8:00pm, students blocked the entrance to President Durant's office, calling for the firing of the controversial professor and once again advocating the cancellation of his play.

Many students also expressed the desire for the university to file a formal appeal against the DA's decision, saying their safety was compromised by Colson's acquittal. "I just think that in our age of patriarchal bias and hate speech against minorities, a man like him shouldn't go free," said a student. When asked what she meant by hate speech, she said "things like 'due process' and [omitted] like that, which only upholds the oppressive status quo. They want to force us to read and learn about white male writers like Shakespeare, so of course they find a way to let Colson off. It's violence against minorities. Hate speech, I mean." "It's literally threatening our lives," said another protester, crying, "like, they wouldn't allow a gun on campus; how is letting a rapist on campus any better?" When reminded that Colson was acquitted and had never been charged with rape, the student responded, "Every man who defends himself is a rapist; accusation is as good as proof, as far as I'm concerned." The student proceeded to cover her ears, close her eyes, and join in with the other protesters.

In their press release, the university announced that while they could not break their current contract with Colson, they would decline to ask him back next Fall. They also announced that the university's annual Shakespeare Festival would be cancelled. "Despite all the work that our excellent students have put into it," said the president, "it is out of consideration for the will of the greater student body who oppose the play that we must, in the end, cancel it. Sometimes we must temper our value of tolerance with our respect for the democratic majority." When asked, the president declined to reference any specific poll of the student body showing such a majority.

When asked for comment, chair of the Theater Department Frank Hoegren merely said, "You can't kill things like Shakespeare by vote or fiat. They'll always show up somewhere else."

The Orangedale Daily Facts will continue to monitor the situation, and any new developments will be forthcoming.

—Sybil Braitwaithe
@thebraiwai
University Liaison
Orangedale Daily Root

❊

"You okay?" asked Elliot as Vesta looked up from the concrete stage, crowbar still in hand.

"Please," she laughed, sniffing as she took Elliot's outstretched hand.

"Take it slow, you two," said Severn, arms crossed in front of his chest. "Habitualize the steps before you speed up."

Elliot returned to his starting place, his back to Vesta, awaiting her line.

"If I mistake not," she said, approaching with slow steps, "thou art Harry Monmouth."

Elliot turned steadily to catch her strike above his head with his nightstick. "Thou speak'st as if I would deny my name."

Jumping back, holding her crowbar in two hands, Vesta sidestepped the slow sweep of Elliot's elbow.

"My name is Harry Percy."

"Why then I see a very valiant rebel of the name . . . " Elliot continued, allowing no pause between Vesta's voice and his and accenting his lines with the planned steps.

The previous week Severn and Maxwell had brought the group together to discuss a long-considered question: whether or not they should replace the planned document-signings-as-swordfights with a street riot, which the rebels would gin up against the king. Maxwell had taken the floor, assuring everyone that anything done to make a better performance, even if not part of Rydar's original plan, had Rydar's endorsement. He had then said that the original plan to replace swords with pens might have been poetic, and could conceivably work in a film interpretation, but that it may not work as well in performance as in thought—especially in such a large venue as MacWhorter Park.

"Ry was always unsure of having the final battle be a signing of documents," Maxwell had said. "Though often suspicious of it as sophomoric, he was trying to avoid replacing drama with action—substituting a car chase for a conflict of values, as it were. But Shakespeare takes care of that; Shrewsbury is not just action for action's sake, nor is it filler. It's where Prince Hal proves publicly whether he is a fool or a fighter. As the beginning of his public renunciation of his youth, it really should be a physical, life-or-death conflict between himself and his rival. Also, as events this year have shown, conflicts of values do not always stay abstract, even on a university campus. A physical riot would be just the thing to concretize England's metaphysical state, especially in our interpretation." Once the cast had agreed—both to the new blocking, new costuming, and to the broader idea that they would not, in fact, be betraying Rydar—they had listened to Severn lecture on stage combat, displaying upon a watermelon that there was little difference between stage weapons and real weapons.

Since choosing their weapons from among the OSC props in Mac-Whorter amphitheater's backstage building—Vesta a crowbar, Elliot a pair of nightsticks—they had been planning and practicing the steps of Prince Hal and Hotspur's long-awaited clash for the past hour and a half.

Despite covering less than twenty lines, the fight consisted of three smaller rallies and would carry them across the stage. Severn had already set up traffic cones to demark set pieces, among which would be things like cones, trash cans, and other items found in urban streets and alleyways.

"Good," said Severn as they finished, Elliot kneeling next to Vesta. "You two doing okay? Can you run it one more time?"

"I'm good for another," said Vesta.

"Yeah, my afternoon's empty," agreed Elliot.

"Great—go for it," Severn said, hopping onstage and roaming backstage to lock up.

The two of them looked at each other and began again.

Elliot was glad they had added the fight scene, and he found himself enjoying the open air of the much larger stage more than he had expected. He doubted he would have been able to swing his chosen pair of nightsticks as convincingly were they still performing at the university. Indeed, the news that the production would no longer be under the college had been a relief, a feeling shared by several of the others—especially when, on the night of the president's announcement, they had been met by almost immediate news from Hoegren and Severn that the production would continue as planned off-campus.

"Oh, Harry, thou hast robbed me of my youth—et cetera," Vesta said, foregoing Hotspur's final words as she lay her head back on her hands to look up at the sky.

"Still haven't learned your lines? Tsk, tsk," said Elliot, standing from his kneeling position.

"Shut up," crooned Vesta, relaxing and closing her eyes as she undid her bun to let her curly, red hair untwist into a splay across the grey, breeze-swept concrete.

Elliot surveyed the amphitheater; the sky was growing orange above the pine and oak trees of the park. There were a few pieces of trash here and there among the seats, but the bowl's space, framed as it was by pine, cedar, and cypress trees, gave Elliot an overwhelming sense of potential. He inhaled, enjoying the mixed smells of the park.

"Alright," said Severn, returning to the stage and waving them to the front row where their bags were. He took a seat facing them, dangling his long legs over the side of the high concrete stage. "Now, you'll get used to the place; besides, we'll have floor mics, so you won't need to worry about not being heard. Still, use whatever choices of voice and movement you need out here. I don't want you two—or anyone from the cast—to think of this as rented space. It's yours. You're all honorary members of the Company, now, and I'll need you two to already be used to the space when we resume rehearsals here next week. Any questions?"

"Are we going to have to reblock the scenes we've already planned?" asked Vesta; Elliot had wondered the same.

"We'll mostly expand them, though I'll go over doing the scenes in designated sections of the stage. We won't need to change as many of Jonas's backdrops as before; I think we'll put them side-by-side instead of rolling them on and off.

"Speaking of expansion, I got your email, Vesta. You're playing Hotspur and Doll; are you sure you also want to play Rumor, too? Of course, we'd planned to have Maynard do it, as well as the epilogue, but Rydar's original cast has precedence."

"Yeah, I think I'd like to," said Vesta, pensively scanning the amphitheater. "I've actually already learned it, and it would be interesting to do it in post-death Hotspur's suit from Shrewsbury, all torn up and bloodied." She held up her crowbar.

Severn smiled. "Are you speaking as an actress or as our costume designer? I don't remember hearing anything like that from Hoegren or Colson."

"I haven't spoken to them about it . . . the attack made me think of the idea." Vesta leaned back and turned to Elliot. "Do you think it'll be a bit much?"

"No," said Elliot, liking the idea and noticing the waver in Vesta's voice. "If you thought of it because of everything going on, I think it'd be worth trying. In fact, it'd be another jab against those who think they can ruin our play by misinterpreting it, just like . . . " He nodded at Vesta, declining to mention her op-ed.

"Yeah, that's what I mean. The women's groups on campus are already calling me a gender traitor because of my article. I think the image of me onstage, beaten up but still standing and still controlling the

conversation, only now as misinformation incarnate, might be powerful."
She looked at Severn for input.

"Hey, it's your show," the man said with a shrug, "though I think trying to form our production to displease its opponents would be as big a mistake as playing to please others. Would it make a good show, in its own right? I think it would. We could also have you give the epilogue as Doll Tearsheet, since its main subject is Falstaff in *Henry V*."

"Great," Vesta smiled, "I'll learn it. I've already got a plan for Hotspur's final outfit."

Severn laughed. "That's why Colson picked you—both of you." The man looked at Elliot. "You two have been so humble and open in this process, and I know it's kept things going more than I or any of the Company could. I hope we can do justice to your show; I think we will. Anyway, thanks for coming out here today." The man nodded a last smile and reached for his bag. "See you here Monday."

They exchanged handshakes before Severn turned toward his car.

"Hungry?" said Elliot, seeing that it was nearly 5:00 and thinking of their already being in town.

"Yeah, but I might just walk home," said Vesta as she looked past the bowl's building, toward the campus to the northeast.

"You sure? It'll be dark soon."

"Elliot, please," she said impatiently, "don't you start, too. I'm not a child, and we're not in the nineteenth century."

Elliot shut his mouth, nodding as he hopped off the concrete stage. He still did not like the idea, but he felt it must be part of Vesta's continuing fight, which he could not fully understand but did not want to inhibit. After gathering his things, he turned to her. He was thinking of what Severn had said.

"You don't owe them anything, V," he said, uncharacteristically calling her by her first letter. "Even your defiance. I'll see you on campus; text me once you're there, 'kay?"

Elliot turned to leave.

"Don't tell Jonas," Vesta said as Elliot reached the grass knoll beside the farthest aisle.

Elliot nodded, waving his hand in a half salute.

❊

"You're just finally realizing the slob you are," Elliot shouted at Blythe over the laughter, which rose to a roar. He sipped his beer, eyes on the big man.

"Be that as it may, thou whoreson mad compound of majesty!" Blythe said, pointing at Elliot with one finger, his other fingers gripping the handle of the pewter stein he had brought from home, "I never thought I'd take pride in wearing garbage bags onstage. My toast is for all of you, but especially for the apple of my eye: my Doll, my virtue, my tailor-turned-tavern-trollop—my Vesta!"

A burst of cheers and claps.

"Hang yourself, you muddy conger, hang yourself!" yelled Vesta through cupped hands over her own laughter as Blythe stood and finished his series of toasts by draining the stein.

The cast had just completed their final dress rehearsal and, at Blythe's prompting, had walked to a Downtown Orangedale pub he had discovered. As they spent the evening relaxing in shared anticipation of the next day's performance, lines from the play found their way into the good ol' time. Soon Blythe had taken their attention for a toast.

After he returned with a refilled draught, Blythe remained standing, leaning on the tall, wooden table to face Elliot and Megan on his right and Vesta and Jonas on his left.

"So," he said, the twinkle in his eye belying his serious face, "am I to gather that you've been in Orangedale for three years and never been to the Royal Man-at-Arms?"

"I've been here a couple of times," said Jonas, rubbing Vesta's back, "but it's usually people from town here, not from the college."

"The food's too expensive," volunteered Megan, taking a sip of her porter, "or, I mean, there's cheaper food elsewhere."

"Yes," intoned Blythe, nodding, "I doubt that's unintentional. I've gotten to know the owner a bit; he's from north of London—Hereford, actually," he eyed Elliot, "just like Harry's father. Appropriate for a last night before peril, no? Ha-ha!" He slapped the table. "But that's an even greater reason to come here: it's where the people, the public comes to relax, to live."

"I wonder why it's not more popular among students," said Vesta, her thoughtful tone oddly congruent with the feeling of the evening, where no honest word could be censured.

"Well," said Elliot, leaning forward, "probably the fact that there's usually a lot more adults and families in here already. For all the programs of getting students into town, I think there's an inhibition, like a net dividing those who're just staying here from those who live here."

"The more's the pity," nodded Blythe, "for you can learn much of life from such places. Indeed, that's what Hal does. It is the great leveler, the public tavern, for whatever divides us in a civil society must fall when there is need for food, drink, and companionship. It's always the first thing I do when in a new town, especially when performing Falstaff: find the local tavern or bar. It keeps me grounded in the character, as it were."

"Y'know," said Megan, "Dostoevsky often includes some kind of a bar in his books. Of course, it's degrading at first—sticky, dark, and rank—but it's real and sympathetic, and the main character often meets someone consequential there whom he'd never associate with outside."

"What did I tell you? It is not in throne rooms that culture moves, but in the monk's cell of the half-empty pint. So long as such watering holes exist, where men and women can laugh, love, think, weep, and above all, drink, mankind will not be without a future. Thank God that Shakespeare understood this so clearly, or else we might have been lost long ago. It may be on the battlefield that Hal proves he is a man, but it is in the tavern where he learns it—and proves he is human."

"Quite the philosopher," Elliot said, chuckling into his pint.

"Quite the king, if you can see that!" Blythe winked. His eyes were then distracted, and he nudged himself around the table. "Ah, you made it—to our protectors!"

Elliot saw a group of police officers quietly taking a table off to the side. As Blythe shook their hands—he had, evidently, invited them—Elliot recognized one of the officers. He had foregone giving Elliot a parking ticket while he finished practice at the park. "You're part of the play? Don't worry about it," the officer had said. Making eye contact with the man, Elliot nodded, raising his glass a few inches off the table. The man smiled, returning the nod. In the next moment, Blythe arrived at the table with a pitcher of hefeweizen and a platter of glasses.

CHAPTER 16

A S ERMINE EDGED through the auditorium's crowded side aisle toward Skylar and the rest of *The Homefront* in the front row, he observed the growing crowd, noting many with homemade placards with slogans from *Homefront* articles. There were fewer such protestors than he had hoped, compared to those apparently there in passive support of the speaker. In the front row on the other side, as expected, sat several members of the late Shakespeare production, among them Elliot Fleming, Vesta Lloyd, and Megan Armstrong.

A group of security officers stood along the front of the lecture hall, and an older man was leaning against the wall near the exit to the side of the stage. Ermine had seen him around campus, assuming from his perpetual jeans, flannel long-sleeve, and fading ball cap that he was a member of the janitorial staff. Hands in his pockets and a roll of papers tucked under his arm, his eyes landed on Ermine. A smile curled up a side of his mouth, and the man nudged himself forward, proceeding indifferently toward the podium.

Before Ermine realized what was happening, the man laid out his pages and cleared his throat. After a moment of general recognition, the crowd in the back, as if suddenly trying to climb onto a moving train they had thought inert and beyond concern, lifted their placards and met the man with a wave of noise. Ermine gritted his teeth, however, hearing how the sound was subsumed in the applause and whoops from the rest who had risen to their feet.

The man behind the podium merely stood, smiling at a few people in the crowd. His face and demeanor appeared as if he were completing a task of little consequence that, nonetheless, had had to be done that day. He raised a hand to calm the crowd.

"Good afternoon. My name is Grey Maxwell; I am the stage manager for the Orangedale Shakespeare Festival."

Cheers and screams resumed for another half-minute; still unsure how to square the speaker's unexpected identity, Ermine realized that many of the students who were cheering loudest were trying to drown out the howls from the back of the lecture hall.

A whine of feedback caused the crowd to involuntarily quiet down. The old man resumed, "There's been a lot of controversy surrounding the Festival, not to mention some hubbub over who today's speaker might be. Doubtless, I'm not the adjunct menace you were expecting." The man shrugged, attracting some laughs. "Though I'd appreciate your lending me your ears, I'm not a professor. I'm just a guy who's spent his life backstage, and I think I've seen a few things worth pointing out. If, in the end, something I say sticks, then today will have been worth it."

Maxwell's disarming demeanor perturbed Ermine. Having prepared for Colson, he now felt deflated and vaguely curious. Some in the back had continued to chant weakly, but judging from the sound's halting quality many felt as Ermine did. Maxwell had probably taken over from Colson, who had no doubt been the originally-planned speaker, Ermine thought. He gritted his teeth as the man described his background working in theaters across America.

"So, needless to say, I've seen a bit of culture, though whether it's cultured me still bears to be seen." A few laughs filled the man's pause. "Out of all, I've preferred works by the man who stands as one of the pillars of the Western Canon, and whose work articulates the trans-cultural values and assumptions about human nature that supersede any one philosophy or people that might adopt it. Whatever we call the ideals that undergird our society—classical liberalism, or the natural law, or bourgeois values—they are all, to some degree, concretized in the work of one artist, whose name is synonymous with and whose inclusion is essential to the maintenance of Western Culture: William Shakespeare."

At the mention of Western Culture and Shakespeare, chants of "Hey, hey, ho, ho, Western Culture's got to go!" had started in the back of the hall, accompanied by shrieks and curses; they knew to hate the name of Shakespeare. Maxwell had handed them a loaded gun, however much he might try to argue it away. Imagine thinking argument was the point of today, thought Ermine, smirking. Nonetheless, Maxwell had continued, ignoring the growing hum. Ermine began tapping his pencil on the top of his notepad as the old figure spoke about the various values and aspects of culture displayed in Shakespeare's work, several of which Ermine noted as actually belonging to the progressive side of history, despite Maxwell's implicitly conservative spin.

"Of course, many have accused me of—what was it?" The man looked down at his printout, "'Promoting appropriation and colonial apologia' by daring to point out how many cultures have embraced the drama and ideals contained in Shakespeare. I disagree; I submit that to do so is not to 'perpetuate white colonial prejudices,' as has been said. In fact, if I'm not being too bold—I just work in facilities, see—I believe such accusations do the very thing they allege by having such low expectations of other peoples, who apparently can't decide for themselves the merits of different ideals or art. I won't insult other cultures in that way by assuming their members are so dim, nor ours so brilliant."

The chanting portion of the crowd erupted into screams; to hear the language of prejudice used against them was a not-to-be-borne offense. However, despite his having orchestrated many of the sentiments represented in the room, Ermine felt a tinge of embarrassment on behalf of the crowd; the contrast between their growing frenzy and Maxwell's relaxed demeanor was too sharp. Also, though still wanting to scratch the self-sufficient smirk off the man's face, Ermine could admit feeling drawn in to his subject.

Maxwell proceeded to present a hypothetical girl—"let's call her Miranda"—raised on an island with nothing but a copy of Shakespeare's Complete Works. He described all the trite things she might learn from the book that, according to him, would prepare her for society off the island. Of course, Maxwell meant Western-Anglo society; Ermine found himself pitying the man's Miranda more than he did *The Tempest*'s Miranda, despite the latter's being complicit in Caliban's enslavement. He wondered if Maxwell's Miranda, too, wasn't also so complicit in oppression.

"Our Miranda would also learn," Maxwell continued, his tone shifting from its previous light optimism, "like those who knew Iago, that people are not always the way they seem, and that not all men want the good—that is, that evil actions against their fellow men are not always due to a lack of resources, knowledge, or privileged upbringing, but can be done for their own sake. She would learn that one might rather hate the dignity and greatness I've described, even degrading themselves if it meant lessening their responsibility—or harming others in the process."

Ermine grew cold as he remembered Cora's words about hating greatness, which he had been unable to forget. He leaned forward, as if to compensate for the yells and chants that had redoubled in the ceasing of Maxwell's voice. Quietly taking a breath to watch the crowd, Maxwell took a drink from a plastic water bottle before shifting around the papers before him.

"Now," he resumed, speaking to those seated but watching those standing, "allow me to speak of an island without Shakespeare. Many of you read *Lord of the Flies* in high school. The predominant interpretation of that book's theme is that man is evil. I don't think that's the book's thesis; like all common readings, it's too shallow, releasing us from responsibility by being too general. Rather, Golding's theme, so far as I can tell, is that each human can be evil. That is enormously different."

The man proceeded to explicate how this reading showed itself in the interactions between Ralph and the "little tyrant," Jack. "It's noteworthy," said Maxwell, glancing at Ermine, "that Jack initially gains power over the children by presenting himself as a protector and provider; he promises to keep them safe. However, he thereby removes their individual responsibility, then their individuality, then their humanity—and they are subsumed into feeding on his tyranny as flies do the dead hog's head."

Ermine gritted his teeth, inadvertently flexing his notebook in a serpentine manner and fighting the urge to jump up and respond. Skylar patted Ermine's knee, though they seemed as tense as he.

"We choose which island we want to inhabit, one with Shakespeare or one without. Want to lift men and women into realms of art, science, rights, and eudaimonic happiness? Believe that mankind is capable of heroism, and that the upward glance and upright posture befits our nature as rational beings possessed of a rightful manner of treatment; refuse to let our capability and godlike reason to fust in us unused, and watch as those who are willing and able transcend the material world.

"Conversely, want to rid the world of dignity and turn people into animals? Say that abstract values are a myth, that rights and duties are arbitrary contrivances, or that they must be withheld from some and allowed to others to achieve a utopian—that is, inhuman and inhumane—balance that seeks nothing above or beyond itself. Eliminate any expectation for people to ennoble their lives beyond simply avoiding suffering, and make the chief good and market of their time be but to sleep and feed, tell them they are beasts, no more, and watch them tear themselves apart in a war of disordered impulses, all the while hating you for setting them free from that which they have lost the language to name—having forgotten the author who best articulated it.

"Now, I'm not advocating we ignore the many other thinkers, peoples, or cultures that have since enriched Western Culture. However, one dramatist stands at the head of that great tradition of circumspection, of respect for human dignity, of pleasure at idiosyncrasy, of wisdom amidst ideological conflict, of nobility in the face of tragedy, and of laughter in the face of nihilism: William Shakespeare."

A few voices screamed to Ermine's right. Aware that Maxwell was nearing the end of his speech, they had ventured forward along the aisle. A couple of the guards stepped away from the front line, causing the students to retreat back.

"Enough!" screamed Skylar. Apparently seizing the moment, Skylar jumped forward, reached into his waistband, and swung something toward Maxwell; it was a gun. However, primed by the crowd and already jumping toward the sudden movement, the guards restrained Skylar, one grabbing their arm and the other tackling them to the ground. A mix of screams and applause erupted from the seated sections of the audience as they realized what had just happened. Standing only to have another guard put a palm up at him, Ermine looked from Skylar's thin, prostrate body to Maxwell. After a reflexive duck behind the podium, the man had taken a step toward the fray. His eyes met Ermine's; hard-set though they were, they were not without compassion.

Skylar's jumping to attack Maxwell had had a paradoxical effect: although those who had henceforth protested the speech were now screaming in dismay at the guards' quick action, they had stopped running up and down the aisles. Ermine knew from looking at them that despite their cries of "Hands up! Don't shoot!" they were beaten. They had not missed the greater audience's reaction, nor Maxwell's.

Suddenly, several of those in the front who had remained seated stood.

"Oh, is it time?" Maxwell asked Elliot over the microphone before checking his watch, "Sorry folks, I can't stay for questions. We have a call time to get to. Opening night—hope to see you at the Bowl." Maxwell then looked back at Ermine, tilting head forward pointedly and giving a wink.

Stepping down from the podium, Maxwell joined Elliot, Vesta, and several others who had stood as they were escorted toward the exit on the other side of the lecture hall from the now handcuffed Skylar. As the group exited, the rest of the crowd began to applaud and cheer, their sound drowning out the still combative cries of the protesters.

As people began to pick up their things to leave, Ermine grabbed the first sleeve he saw. "What did he mean, call time?"

The owner of the sleeve, a young woman, laughed and said, "The plays. They were moved to MacWhorter Park." At a look from the large man accompanying the girl, Ermine let go of the sleeve. Taking his notebook, he tried to disappear into the exiting crowd. He could not bring himself to look back at Skylar.

"Just thought I'd stop by on the way to the Bowl," said Grey, leaning against Rydar's counter. A glass of whiskey was on the table next to a glass of ice water. Behind both was an open laptop showing a paused Grey's face behind a podium. Rydar was leaning back, a yellow-white meerschaum pipe in hand.

"So, how'd I do?" asked Grey, tilting his head toward the screen.

Rydar chuckled. "You incredible bastard. It might as well have been me."

"Ry," Grey said, smirking, "I've been a stagehand for forty years. Don't make the same mistake as they and assume I haven't learned a thing or two about acting—though I meant every word."

He watched Rydar in silence; the man glanced at the laptop before turning his head as if by habit to the other side of the room, halting it mid-motion. Grey kept his eyes on Rydar, but he could see the red of Eun-ji's dress out of the corner of his eye.

"I'll never forgive you for this," said Rydar calmly and not unkindly, exhaling a ring of smoke.

"And that," Maxwell pointed at Rydar, "is why I did it."

"You shouldn't have helped me like that. I don't like people putting themselves at risk for me. I'd rather fight alone. Then announcing your retirement at the end of the online transcript like that . . . I mean, have some goddamned dignity." Rydar shook his head and took a sip of whiskey.

Maxwell just looked at Rydar, smiling. He had not warned his young friend of his previous decision to retire. Rydar met his gaze for a moment and, apparently seeing Maxwell would not look away, shifted in his chair to look outside.

"You still have a bit to learn, kid," Grey said to the back of Rydar's head. "You've already learned it, you just don't know you have." Maxwell pulled out the rolled up newspaper from his back pocket. He found the spot he had been rereading the past couple of weeks, since Sybil Braitwaithe had interviewed Rydar about covering for Jonas, even though it meant lying to the police and risking his reputation.

"'I did it because I saw a young friend who'd done something that needed doing but might ruin the rest of his life. If there were some way I could stand up in his place and take what I knew would be an unfair attack, I would.'"

Maxwell patiently folded the newspaper before rolling it back up, smiling with satisfaction. Rydar had kept his face turned away.

"I should have never given that interview."

Grey scoffed. "You're just angry because you think you broke character. You didn't; you just don't fully understand the character you've got, even now. This whole ordeal—not the arrest, but the play that led up to it, everything since Hoegren first approached you about doing a play, and probably before that—has changed you. You knew it would; you're greater than you were, something different, or more deeply the same. But that means you might do things that surprise you and that might not fit your idea of yourself. It doesn't mean you're going back on your character or values; perhaps you're just finally seeing yourself and your values more clearly. Who was it who said things like compassion and generosity are only possible to those who have something to give—those who've reached a pinnacle or greatness? Aristotle?"

Rydar exhaled a snort but turned back around.

"Yeah, he would've said that, if not in those words," Grey continued, "Maybe there's a bit of your old boy, Nietzsche, in there, too. Either way, now you've got something to give, and whether or not you believe it, you're not being a second-hander or a coddler by giving it. Whatever it is that you really achieved with this play—inside I mean, which I won't try to describe—you'll find that it's by sharing it that you'll make the world you want to live in. You've already started; you've done the 'what,' whether or not you admit the 'why.' Allow me to admit it for you. After all, that's why I did what I did. I wasn't protecting you, son; I was protecting the world I want to exist and the kind of academia I want to leave behind—which is one with you somewhere in it, not to mention Shakespeare. Really, it had nothing to do with protecting you—in the end, I couldn't have, had they really come after you—nor was I implying you couldn't take it. That's just it: I didn't want you to destroy your life in some blaze of a gesture, which I know you would've secretly loved. At least, you a year ago would have loved it. Now . . . I think you understand."

Rydar, mouth still hard set but tears in his eyes, gave a barely discernible nod.

"Alright, fine. Listen: I love you, kid. You almost threw your life away for Jonas, and you've only known him, what, three, four years? Rydar, I raised you, and I'm more proud to see you alive and free than anything I've ever done. And I don't just mean physically free, neither. I've spent my life making sure the show goes on; was there any question I'd do the same for a person my love of whom embodies all the shows I've carried to production? And not just any person, but someone I know isn't trying to escape their life—who would willingly be crushed by the weight he was trying to carry rather than give up or call for aid. We don't talk about him, but you're not your father, Rydar. You've stood up to your life and become greater for it; that's why I did that speech: because the person who would rather fail with dignity than try to avoid suffering is the one I most want to survive."

Rydar steadily put the pipe to his lips; his chin shivered for a moment. He did not wipe the tears that had begun to run silently down his cheekbones.

"Now, tonight isn't about you," resumed Maxwell, appreciating the treasure of being allowed to see Rydar cry thus, "and yet it is. I want you to go watch that play and relax. Enjoy what you made. You've earned it, son."

Grey turned, leaving the young man in privacy. As he reached to open the door, he heard the soft click of Rydar closing his laptop. Grey did not turn around.

Elliot stood behind the stage right curtain; he took a breath and exhaled slowly. Blythe, standing next to him, softly patted his shoulder. Horn, seated behind a long table center stage and dressed in a three-piece business suit, was delivering the opening lines of *Henry IV Part* 1.

The afternoon had passed in a wave of lucid half-attention. As he had prepared his makeup and donned his business slacks, open necked button-down, and loose necktie, Elliot had mused on the previous semester; it was appropriate that Grey had chosen today to step out from backstage to give his defense of the production.

As they had made their way to the bowl, Vesta had texted Rydar to ask if he would be there tonight. The man had merely texted back, "*Forget me—do your play :).*" Shaking his head slowly as he drove, Jonas had simply muttered, "Bastard." His tone articulated the quiet, grinning feeling of everyone in the car—as if Rydar, having taught them all he could, even in his absence, had already moved beyond concern for either them or the play, and that they should do the same for him. Elliot wondered which was more apparent to the others, the insult or the compliment. Like most lessons from Rydar, the text contained both—along with the message that worry, itself, was and had always been superfluous.

Now, after hearing and peeking at the crowd steadily streaming into the MacWhorter Bowl from the surrounding residential streets, Elliot felt a nervous excitement. As he yet again reviewed the key moments in his lines and blocking, he reached up to feel the open two buttons on his shirt before again checking his messily rolled up sleeves. His family had texted where they had found seats; they would be near stage right, in the section closest to his entrance. Inhaling, he felt the weight of his suspenders pressing down on his shoulders. As if knowing Elliot's thoughts, Blythe nodded, exhaling a short chuckle through his nose. Elliot could do this.

In the next moment, the lights went down. With the same breath, the fat knight and the cunning prince gamboled onto the stage.

"What, fought you with them all?" Elliot cried in mock amazement as he circled around Falstaff, who had taken a seat at the onstage bar. As Poins, Megan sat down next to him, handing him a beer. They shared a knowing glance behind Blythe's back as he began to lament.

"All?" barked Blythe, "I know not what you call all, but if I fought not with fifty of them I am a bunch of radish. If there were not two- or three-and-fifty upon poor old Jack, then am I no two-legged creature . . . "

They had done the scene many times, Elliot and Megan feigning belief as Blythe bombastically recounted robbing "a thousand pound this day morning" from a cart transporting it to "the King's exchequer," when he and his group of thieves were, themselves, set upon by men in masks—a disguised Poins and Prince Hal. The larger space of the bowl had given Elliot a feeling of freedom that had made his Hal much lighter on his feet.

At a suggestion from Severn, who had seen the development and liked it, he had even watched some ballet, incorporating elements of weightlessness into Hal's movements as he verbally dodged around Falstaff, who remained at the onstage counter for most of the scene—the longest in the play.

" . . . for it was so dark, Hal," exclaimed Blythe, waving his palm in front of his face, "that thou couldst not see thy hand."

"These lies are like their father that begets them," answered Elliot, showing his teeth in a contemptuous grin, "gross as a mountain, open, palpable. Why, thou claybrained guts, thou knotty-pated fool, thou whoreson, obscene, greasy tallow-catch—."

"What, art thou mad?" interrupted Blythe in a tone of mixed frustration and surprise, "Art thou mad? Is not the truth the truth?"

"Why, how couldst thou know these men when it was so dark thou couldst not see thy hand?" Elliot faced Blythe across the bar, meeting his eyes over a tall, glass stein.

"Come, your reason, Jack," crooned Megan as she leaned back against the bar, "your reason."

"What, upon compulsion? If reasons were as plentiful as blackberries, I would give no man a reason upon compulsion, I . . . "

Elliot had learned a lot about the play from watching Blythe over the past few weeks. Having only seen him once or twice between their first meeting in September and Rydar's party, Elliot discovered he had missed the man, despite his initial discomfort around him. In preparing their scenes Elliot had realized in action what he had not seen from reading—that, as calculating as Prince Hal might be, Blythe's Falstaff might be more so. Whereas Colson made much about Falstaff's potentially degrading effects on Hal's kingdom, Blythe revealed an extra nuance Shakespeare had included in the character: despite his bombast, Falstaff understood the importance of making the Prince look good, allowing the boy an alibi from the night's thieving gambit and letting him play his present joke at the fat knight's expense. From Blythe's interpretation, Falstaff knew he was being ridiculous and unreasonable, just as he knew he was being made the butt of Hal's prank and was playing along with it, implying an even greater game of protecting Hal from calumny than Hal was playing, himself.

However, thought Elliot in a flash as Blythe gave him a private wink from his upstage eye, such an interpretation of Falstaff might be clouded by the supporting relationship Blythe had adopted in Elliot's own life—rarely speaking encouragement to Elliot directly and relying instead on the subtle, toughening jabs and backslaps of his character. "So long as such watering holes exist . . . ." Elliot remembered how the man's words had seemed to dignify not only the place but all those in it as participating in something much greater than they might expect—that even the most abysmal, vulgar, innocuous surfaces might hold the deepest truths, the most important interactions, and the closest bonds. Elliot considered this as he readied for his favorite exchange of the play.

"I'll be no longer guilty of this sin," Elliot shouted, circling Falstaff downstage as he initiated the quick-fire exchange of insults between himself and the fat man. Right on cue, heaving for air after standing for his breathless crescendo of epithets, the man drunkenly toppled into Megan, who helped him back to the stools. As Elliot proceeded to reveal their ruse to the man, Blythe progressed through several expressions, at one point looking dumbfounded, at another circumspect, as if he had been aware of the prank the whole time.

As he had before, Elliot wondered which was the greater affect—and who was really pranking whom. Watching Blythe in the previous weeks, Elliot had remembered something Vesta had said while presenting on Mark Twain to the discussion group the previous semester: "If you think you're tricking a trickster, he's tricking you." Despite his loud shows of wounded pride and manipulative verbal evasions, Blythe's Falstaff revealed a closely held respect for and doting over Hal, even as he exerted all his energy toward testing and toppling the high-class affects of the Prince's royal preeminence by meeting the boy's jabs with insults of his own. To do any less—to make their verbal skirmishes easy on the boy—would be to risk flattering him, which, in addition to undermining the reliability of their relationship, would leave him as ill-prepared against smooth-talking sycophants as Richard II had been before being usurped by Hal's father. Paradoxically, it was only by upholding a veneer of humor, vulgarity, fibs, and offensive disrespect for the Prince's rank that Falstaff could assure the boy that he was, at heart, a trusty ally.

" . . . What trick," Elliot said, seating himself on one of the barstools as he neared the end of his revelatory speech, "what device, what starting-hole canst thou now find out to hide thee from this open and apparent shame?"

"Come, let's hear, Jack," piped Megan, exchanging a high-five with Elliot over the bar, "What trick hast thou now?"

"By the Lord," Blythe said, standing tall and putting his chest out magnanimously at the two jokers, "I knew you as well as he that made you. Why, hear you, my masters, was it for me to kill the heir apparent ...?"

The large man—made larger by the tattered, grey trench coat Vesta had clothed him in—began to step proudly around the stage, speaking how "The lion will not touch the true prince ... I was now a coward on instinct ..."

Elliot watched the man, considering the things Colson had said of Falstaff the previous semester—how the man's ability with language and thought came from his willingness to hold nothing sacred. In the next moment, as Blythe turned on his heel to cross steadily to the other side of the stage, Elliot paused. Over Blythe's shoulder, seated right in front of Elliot's little sister, sat Rydar Colson. His eyes were transfixed not on Ernest, but on Elliot; he was smiling.

C'mon, Elliot, don't pull your punches, thought Vesta as Elliot swung one of his nightsticks above her head. You had it yesterday, and Rydar's watching.

Vesta had seen Colson almost immediately when she walked out on stage as Hotspur. Her eyes had seemed drawn right to him, and upon seeing him he became the only audience member she was aware of. She had even had to resist performing only to his section. Only Prince Hal could be permitted break the fourth wall in such a way; for a moment, while watching Rydar's proud face during Elliot and Blythe's tavern play scene, Vesta had felt jealous.

Nonetheless, as she held her ground against Northumberland and Warwick, as she flirted with Lady Percy, and now, as she exchanged swings with Elliot, dodging around trash cans, wino tents, and the other flotsam of an urban setting in riot and shambles, Vesta performed for one person: the man who had inspired the whole thing, and whom she hoped had been surprised by her filling the antagonist's role. Of course, Rydar had been in contact with Severn and Hoegren, as well as Maxwell, so he would have known she had adopted the role. However, she hoped seeing her was a pleasant experience for the man—no, not pleasant: sublime, just, worth all that had gone into it. She had tried to make Hotspur her own, and now, in his final fight with Hal, she needed to make it as difficult for the prince as she could—for Elliot's sake and her own.

"Well said, Hal!" boomed Blythe, sauntering onstage from behind a panel painted like an alleyway. "To it, Hal! Nay, you shall find no boys' play here, I can tell you." The large man had just enough time to place his hands on his hips to watch the fight before being accosted from behind by the actor playing the Earl of Douglas. After a cunning shimmy by Blythe, Douglas was left holding Falstaff's large grey coat. Now, the two pairs—Hal and Hotspur with weapons, Falstaff and Douglas with fists—maneuvered across the stage. As she moved, Vesta became suddenly aware of the distant noise of yelling in another part of the park, and the sudden sound of sirens. However, ducking a swing by Elliot and rolling out of Blythe's path kept her in the scene, and she smiled, taking the clamor as a fitting background noise to the play's final conflict of urban riot.

Vesta put her arm against her chest as Elliot raised his foot, kicking her back hard against a half-collapsed tarp tent with a cushion hidden inside. As planned, Vesta fell so a metal pipe protruded between her up-stage side and arm. Blythe, finally caught and choked from behind with a sash by Douglas, lay feigning death on the other side of the stage.

"O, Harry," croaked Vesta, "thou hast robbed me of my youth. I better brook the loss of brittle life than those proud titles thou hast won from me. They wound my thoughts worse than thy sword my flesh . . . "

Elliot, wiping his brow, kicked Vesta's crowbar away before kneeling just outside of her reach. He wore a grimace, his relief and triumph at beating his rival vying against sorrow at the death of his ideal. However, a brief glance of his eyes off to the side, where the din of screams and sirens could still be heard, showed a flash of Elliot on Prince Hal's face.

" . . . No, Percy," Vesta gasped, opening her eyes wide at the stars above the stage, "thou art dust, and food for . . . " She sunk back, relaxing her stomach, which she had kept flexed through her final speech.

"For worms, brave Percy," Elliot said, assuming Hotspur's mantle as the "theme of Honour's tongue" by finishing the man's sentence. He closed Vesta's blankly open eyes before standing slowly.

Vesta held her chest steady, making sure not to breathe too heavily and so distract from Elliot's final speech. Again, she envied her friend a second time—that from behind closed eyes and the bandana Hal would use mid-speech to cover Hotspur's "mangled face" she could not see Colson's immediate reaction to her performance. However, the play was not over, she told herself; she still had to appear dead as, once the Prince exited the stage, Falstaff would stand to pontificate over the dubious honor of Hotspur's death before eventually hoisting Vesta over his shoulder to, after being confronted once more by the now changed and more honestly hard Prince Hal, carry her offstage to gain reward for killing the rash, valorous Hostpur. It's OK, Vesta thought, anticipating how she might scratch an itch on her leg unseen as Blythe lifted her; she could see Rydar afterward. Besides, she knew he would still be watching her.

"Vesta, you have a visitor," said Amanda, one of the stagehands for the OSC. Still removing her stage makeup with face cream, Vesta had to pause a moment to restrain her smile.

"Thanks, Mandy," she said, resuming and quickening the strokes of her cotton pad. In the next moment, she reached impatiently for a damp washcloth, burying her face in its rough fabric; Rydar would not care about a little makeup. Having grown used to pinning it on top of her tight bun before leaving the room, she reached for Hotspur's grey newsboy cap before leaving it hanging on the chair back; removing her button-down, its top buttons already undone in the warm excitement of the audience's long applause, she slipped a grey t-shirt over her damp undershirt. Rydar was not there to see Hotspur, but Vesta.

Passing through and exchanging smiles with the other production members in the Bowl hallways, Vesta stepped out into the sudden coolness of the evening.

Leaning against a wall, arms crossed, was Cora Madison.

"Hey," she said with a nod.

"Oh, hi," replied Vesta, crossing an arm in front of her stomach as she fought to hide her disappointment. She glanced around; Rydar was nowhere to be seen.

As Vesta approached, Cora nudged herself off the wall, reaching out a hand to offer a side hug, which Vesta met with a full embrace. Despite still being roommates, it was the closest they had been in nearly three months.

"You were amazing, Vesta. Really. You took Hotspur in a direction I never could've."

"That's not true," said Vesta, smiling in thanks. "I've . . . I've missed you." Earlier in the semester Vesta had respected Cora's prerogative to avoid direct contact, resisting the habit of initiating conversation and waiting for Cora to talk. However, as they entered the last phase of prepa-ration for the performance—and after Rydar was released—Cora had seemed to cut herself off completely from Vesta, often coming home late in the evenings after Vesta was in bed and staying away from the dorm during the day.

"Listen," Cora said with a sigh, "I'm sorry about—."

"Cora, you don't have to . . ." began Vesta, putting up her hand.

"Yes, I do. Out of everyone, I want you to understand," Cora said, closing her eyes and taking a breath. "I think I was in love with him, or at least my idea of him, and I hated him for it. I wanted him to want me—because then I would have beaten him and could disregard him. But I think, underneath it all, I also wanted him to do what he did, to reject me, because then he'd really be who we thought he was, and I could trust him. I wanted him to be stronger than me, which meant resisting me. That meant there needed to be something there that wanted me, that he'd have to resist; even if it was just in my head, I had to believe he would want me, in order to go through with it."

Cora chuckled, cutting the sound short with a sniff as she looked away. "I thought I was strong, but really I was scared. That's why I needed to test him, to see if I could break him, or he me, whatever that looked like: to see if the questions inside were justified or baseless. If he resisted, it would mean I could relax, just knowing someone like him was possible, and that all the stuff I'd been told about men by my mom or by classes wasn't the whole story, that things like masculinity, and chivalry, and honor, and pride weren't just empty covers for either weakness or lust, and that it was okay if I didn't have everything figured out. Of course, I didn't consciously know all of this, but thinking back I think I felt it. Why else would I try to tempt those things out of Rydar, and Elliot . . ."

"No, keep going," said Vesta, aware that, despite all the people congratulating each other around them, something profound and long-awaited was happening before her: a friend was transcending her own ideal.

"I wonder," resumed Cora after a shared glance, "if that wasn't why I was with Elliot, because he triggered me in some subterranean way just like Rydar, though he didn't see it. All I know is I became so obsessed with getting his attention. I mean, I think I really liked him—I still do, in a way I didn't know and wouldn't admit—but how much of last semester was really him and how much just my idea of him I don't know anymore, not to mention all the pretenses in-between. But, really, Rydar was always in the back of my mind. I think that's why things fell apart with Elliot: I was bored because he wanted me so much, I'd beaten him, and I couldn't commit because he was just a stand-in, a stepping stone."

Cora crossed her arms and looked down to hide her eyes. "That's something I've really had to face, how unfair I was to Elliot. But even he stood up, in the end. The truth was it was he who was starting to leave me behind. I think that was the beginning of the end for me; I couldn't use him as an excuse to hide from my motives. I had to act on what had been growing in me for months, or sit down and admit I wasn't as strong, collected, and inexorable as I thought."

"You are those things, Cora," said Vesta, smiling as she felt the release of months of tension on her friend's behalf, "by thinking through all this, and by trying to grow past it, you are."

Cora laughed, reaching a finger up to wipe a tear from her eye. "You probably saw it all along. I'm sorry if I was ever condescending."

"No, dear," said Vesta, reaching out to squeeze her roommate's arm for the first time in months, "I mean, sure I thought you were trying too hard, at times, and you were unfair to Elliot, who's really a great guy. But not all of it was wrong; I've always admired you in spite of those things. You have reasons to condescend, especially now."

"What doesn't kill you, right?" Cora began, glancing over Vesta's shoulder as she stepped back. "Speak of the devil."

Vesta turned; Elliot and Jonas were walking up. As they approached, Vesta stepped back and slipped under Jonas's extended arm.

The other two stood looking at each other. Where Cora had worn a hard, imperious look for most of the time Vesta had known her, there was something different in her face now, a soft, contrite upturn in her eyebrows, as if an unspoken question had passed from her to Elliot. Cora might think it was Elliot and Rydar who had broken her, but she should be proud, thought Vesta. By coming back, she had broken herself—and survived. It was right that she had come tonight.

"Hey," Elliot said, leaning forward.

"Hey," Cora sighed, accepting his hug. The movement looked like falling.

"I'm sorry," Cora whispered with a choke.

"Shhh," Elliot said, putting his hand on the back of her head and turning her from side-to-side. He kissed Cora on her temple. Vesta leaned into Jonas and looked away. Jonas felt tense at Cora's presence, but to his credit he deferred to Vesta as she slipped her fingers into his.

"So," said Elliot in a chipper tone as he eased back from Cora, "what was that racket during our fight?" His hand lingered on her shoulder and hers on his hip.

"Oh, there was a group from the college," Cora said, turning to Vesta and Jonas. "I don't think they knew the play had moved off campus. That's why they were so late in coming, and the police were ready for them."

"It was a relatively small group," said Jonas, "the only ones they could get to walk here from campus. Rioting outside their own dorms is one thing, but this is outside the school's bubble."

"Besides," said Cora, "it's the last weekend before finals, so I think most were either prepping or enjoying their last chance to party."

"Either way," said Elliot, leaning back from Cora and waving someone over from the dressing room doors, "we did it, you guys."

Megan stood just outside the hallway door, a quizzical look on her face as her eyes went from Cora to Elliot.

"Hey," said Cora, "I'm gonna take off. This is really your night."

Elliot began, "You don't have to—."

"No, I know," said Cora, smiling despite having her eyes on Megan, who was approaching the group, "but I really don't have the right. Not yet."

"Cora," said Megan, joining the group across from Cora.

Cora merely nodded, smiling without showing her teeth. Before leaving, Cora leaned to whisper something to Elliot, who nodded as the girl put her hands in her pockets and walked away.

"What was that about?" Megan asked Elliot once Cora had turned the corner of the building.

"Nothing," said Elliot.

"Really?" Megan pressed, "because it looked like something."

"Megan, relax," Elliot said, a determined layer beneath his tone. "We're just gonna talk later."

Megan looked away, biting her tongue between her front teeth as she shook her head. "Just don't be an idiot."

"Hey, trust me, I'm not going down that road again, but if she's changed, she deserves a hearing."

"We talked a bit," said Vesta, nodding, "she's been thinking a lot, and she does. But Megan's right, Elliot: don't be an idiot." Elliot frowned, but before he could speak Vesta asked, "Did anyone see Rydar?"

"He left right after the bow," Jonas said. "Shot me a text; he enjoyed the show."

"Elliot!" cried a young voice.

"Hey, kid," said Elliot, hugging the girl who had suddenly embraced his legs. "Everyone, this is Brie," he said, drawing out his syllables as if bracing himself for embarrassment, "and these are my parents."

A tall, middle-aged couple walked up to the group, exchanging a hug and a handshake with Elliot. Elliot introduced them—June and Arvin—naming everyone in the group.

"You were wonderful," said June to Vesta with a wide-mouthed smile.

"Really, really great," Arvin agreed, looking around bemused.

"Thanks," said Vesta, "It's nice to finally meet you. We've really enjoyed getting to know Elliot through this whole thing." Vesta had rarely thought about Elliot's family, but their mix of happy pride and surprise at the apparently novel setting made her wonder about Elliot's seeming preference for solitude.

"It's nice to finally meet some of his friends," Elliot's mother said jovially, patting his shoulder, "I was worried he never left his computer."

"Speaking of which, Ell," said Arvin, raising his eyebrow, "who was that girl you were hugging?"

"His girlfriend!" said the blonde little girl, scrunching her face into a pucker.

"Nobody," said Elliot evenly with a shrug, "we had a class together last semester."

"She was cute," intoned June, widening her eyes and nodding for agreement at Vesta. Megan had to turn away to hide her snicker.

"Mom . . . " said Elliot, turning red in spite of his nonchalant demeanor. In the next moment, Elliot's eyes widened with interest, "Hey, did you guys see the man sitting in front of you?"

"I think there was someone," June said, looking at Arvin.

"Blonde," the man nodded, "I liked his coat. Why, who was he?"

"Just . . . my old English teacher," said Elliot, sharing a surreptitious glance with Vesta and the others.

"Well, I wish I'd've known. He doesn't tell us anything," June said to Jonas, shaking her head with an exasperated smile. "He didn't even tell us the play's dates until a few weeks ago!" Jonas merely nodded in agreement.

"Thought it'd be better as a surprise," said Elliot, smiling wide. Vesta noticed he had his mother's dimples.

"That's Elliot," said Vesta with a shrug. They seemed like a fine family, if a bit overbearing; Vesta could imagine why Elliot, arrogant as he often portrayed himself, might be embarrassed by them. She thought of her own parents, who, after hearing the city had taken over the play, had agreed to come down for the final performance.

"Well, we'd better get this one home," said Arvin, taking Brie's hand. "Proud of you, son."

After some protest from Elliot's sister they exchanged goodbyes, June embracing each of them and giving Elliot a kiss on his cheek, which he wiped apparently without thinking, as if it were a habit.

"You're an idiot," said Megan flatly once Elliot's family had left.

"Wha—?" began Elliot, dumbfounded.

"I love you, Elliot," she continued tritely, "but you're an idiot."

"You're family's nice," said Vesta, watching Elliot put his shoulders back as he tried to repair what he no doubt considered a dashed reputation.

Jonas snickered through his nose. "Too nice." He winked at Elliot, who relaxed.

Elliot sighed. "Yeah, they can be a bit much. Too much to tell 'em; sometimes it's best not to."

"Like I said," Megan put up her hand, thumb and index finger together, and moved it as she enunciated, "you're an idiot."

Chapter 17

E RMINE SNIFFED, HIS breath catching in his throat with a painful
cough. He reached for the tissues. He could not tell what had come
first, the chill that had led to his present cold or the desire to sulk alone in
his dorm. He knew he should be working—it was the end of the year, and
they had only a few more weeks to put out articles. He knew he should
study for finals, but he dismissed them with a sneer. Now was when controlling the narrative was most necessary, when, after all they had done to
push the campus toward progress, the Shakespeare production was still
happening, albeit under the aegis of the city. Ermine would have been out
there with the rest at MacWhorter to protest the plays, but that afternoon
he had been struck by a sudden disconsolate apathy that merely took the
form of the words, "But what's the point?"

Following Skylar's attempt on Maxwell, campus safety had summar-
ily removed them from campus. Despite Ermine's initial surprise about
the gun, Skylar's sudden absence, as well as hearing about the abortive
attempt to disrupt the play's debut, had deflated Ermine's customary passion; yet, he could admit he had found a sullen pleasure in the depression
that followed.

Then, prompted by a text from Gemma, Ermine had checked *The
Praes*'s Orangeware profile. The leading article for the week was a sopping
review of the play, wherein Ingman described the production as "*a unique
phenomenon one rarely sees outside of literature: a work of art becoming
the touchstone of not only the local politics of our time but also the values
underlying them. It was not a university policy, a physical attack or breaking of laws, nor a controversial new teaching that drew a line across our*

campus, but a Shakespeare production—though, in the end, it contained and provoked all of those things. That it did should make clear to everyone that Shakespeare (and perhaps others like him) is still necessary—even to those who oppose his place in the university curriculum . . . "

Ermine had been unable to finish the three-page article, though he had noted that it was followed by a post-facto petition protesting the firing of Rydar Colson. *"We do not expect the administration to reverse course; however, we do wish to make it known that they do not, in fact, speak for all Orangedale students or faculty."* The page had been set up so that students could mark their name, either openly or anonymously, to appear at the bottom of the list. Drawn by a resentful masochism, Ermine had found himself unable to resist checking the page over the past few days; the list had consistently grown. Over the same few days a clammy chill had come over Ermine, and he had not left his room.

"I'll show 'em," he muttered as he threw a used kleenex across the room to the wastebasket. The sullied tissue fell short of the basket, prompting Ermine to roll his eyes. Everything he had done—the protests, the formation of *The Homefront*, leaving Sam, even getting the play canceled and Rydar fired—now seemed just as impotent. He had not accomplished his true aim: to change how people thought about the things he had combatted. He swallowed painfully at the feeling. He should not be surprised that a group of adults from the affluent town of Orangedale would rally to force the play—the status quo—to remain in spite of the college's decision. But to see students support it . . . Worse, Ingman's petition threatened to disprove—no, to silence—the voices Ermine had given an unprecedented platform through the year. Oh well, he thought, at least he had accomplished a few things: Colson had been fired, the university had denounced the play, and Cora Madison was no longer in the performance.

An idea flashed into Ermine's mind. He checked himself in the next moment. No, that's going too far. Then he thought of Skylar, and of campus security holding them down at the protest. Ermine had left before he could see it, but he imagined the thugs putting Skylar's lean, sensitive wrists in cold, steel handcuffs . . .

In the next moment Ermine's laptop was on the blanket before him. He typed for a few seconds, then used the track pad to open a trail of folders hiding what he sought. Dragging the final folder onto the browser, he released the trackpad and then, with a grin and before he could second guess himself, clicked *"Publish."*

After a few moments of loading, the scroll on the right of the window expanded as the pictures appeared one-by-one on *The Homefront's* Orangeware page. Ermine smiled past a sniff, stretching his arms and leaning his head back against his hands and the wall. Anyone who had marked the "Notify" setting when following *The Homefront* would open their phone or computer to find nearly a dozen pictures of the wire-crossed glass that graced all doors in the Hall of Letters, and behind the glass a young black woman sitting in an office with a white male professor. At the top of the page stood the title and subtitle: "*The True Victim: How uneven power dynamics implicit in the hero-worship of the male professoriate turns minority students into willing prey.*" Ermine had written nothing else, letting the title and the pictures speak for themselves.

Scrolling down, Ermine observed Cora progressively leaning closer to Colson before eventually standing and removing her shirt. Of course, Ermine knew Cora had come onto Colson; indeed, despite initially painting Cora as the victim, Ermine knew—he admitted to himself as he blew his nose, his head aching—that Colson had been innocent throughout that meeting. Nonetheless, Ermine had already adjusted the contrast on the later photos to obscure the fact that Colson had kept his back to Cora while standing. As uploaded, the photos seemed to merely show a dark figure against a bright window with a half-naked young woman standing before him. Whether or not the man had done anything in that moment to encourage Cora did not matter; the pictures showed something more important: not the factual events of the meeting, but their implicit significance. His favorite photograph—one where Colson's silhouette was obscured between the light of the window and the sharp image of Cora's radiantly smooth shoulders—had caught a metaphor for an entire toxic relationship, he thought. It deserved to be on the cover of a magazine.

Suddenly Ermine's laptop screen shifted; the picture had disappeared. Wondering if it was a loading issue, he reached down to click the scroll, which he found had been dramatically reduced. Tapping "Home," Ermine was greeted with a message at the top of the page.

> *Due to material deemed inappropriate by Orangeware staff and/ or Orangedale Administration involving "targeting and/or sexual harassment of a student," this page has been removed and its associated account(s) suspended until further inquiry. Please review our Orangeware Terms of Service and Code of Conduct <u>here</u>.*

"No," Ermine said, his eyes widening as his voice grew, "no, no, no, no, no!"

He heard his final shriek dissipate dully against his walls. The screen remained unchanged, and no sound answered him. Ermine held his breath. In the sudden silence he was confronted by the feeling first prompted by the sight of Ingman's petition: that he had not had the effect he had expected, that his premises were not as undeniable as he had thought, that instead of being a vanguard of change *The Homefront* had been—what?

Ermine hissed an obscenity through gritted teeth. This is how they force you, he thought in response to the feeling.

Ermine's phone began to vibrate. Unlocking it, Ermine saw that he had received several texts from the other *Homefront* writers. Gemma had texted "*Was writing my next piece and I was locked out. Said our account was suspended by admins—wtf??!*" while Carl merely said, "*They finally did it, boss.*" Ermine's phone continued to buzz with others' texts, all involving the sudden disappearance of the new posting and the shuttering of their account.

Rather than reply to any of them, Ermine threw his phone across the room and, checking his frustration just enough not to throw it as well, dropped his laptop to the floor. In the next moment he was screaming painfully into his pillow, hating his cold, his college, his world, and the inability to force things to be the way they should be.

Why can't I?

Ermine raised his head from the pillow. What happened to Skylar—both how they had been taken and why—stuck out to Ermine and began to form into an idea. Blowing his nose, he leaned back, watching his plan take shape. Fine, he thought as he encouraged his imagination to run, if they want to take what I love, I'll take something they love . . .

Frank Hoegren smiled at his screen. He should not be happy, he told himself. Nonetheless, he stood and walked over to his cabinet. Passing his hand behind the bottle of gin to take a bottle of vanilla-sweetened brandy, he poured himself a drink. Resuming his seat, he picked up his phone, dialed a number, and smelled the liquor as the tone rang.

"Well, how nice of you to call in the middle of the day," crooned Angela's voice. "Good timing—lunch recess is almost over."

"Hello, dearest. Say, do you remember that young man I mentioned who's been causing so much trouble?"

"Yes," she said, withholding the scorn Hoegren knew she felt for Ermine and his campaign against Rydar.

"I just wanted you to know, I got 'im." Frank took a sip.

After a pause, Angela's voice said, "You shouldn't be bragging, Frank. You're an administrator."

"Yeah," he said with a chuckle, "and you're an elementary school teacher, just like Rydar is a professor."

"Thank you, Frank," his wife said after a pause. He knew there was more behind her whisper than she could say, being at work as she was.

"Have a nice day, dearest," Hoegren said.

"Mm-hm," came the reply before both hung up.

Hoegren sipped his drink; the last two semesters' tension—the balancing act he had needed to play between respecting Jackson's right to speak while wanting to rip out the boy's throat for the things he said of Rydar—fell on Hoegren. He sighed as tears of release came to his eyes, mixing with the pungent fumes of the brandy. Angela was probably feeling the same release, the same tears. They would celebrate that night.

"God save thy Grace, King Hal! My royal Hal!" roared Blythe as Elliot, seated up on the back of an open-top 1940s Ford Coupe, was paraded through the cheering, onstage crowd. By Vesta's design, Blythe's enormous grey suit and red necktie, though nicer than anything the man had yet worn through the two plays, contrasted sharply with the black, white, and gold of Elliot's royal tuxedo. Despite the heat of its layers, Elliot regretted the fact that, this being their final performance, these would be his last moments wearing the costume.

"God save thee, my sweet boy!" continued Blythe, clapping and opening his arms wide.

The crowd quieted as Elliot raised his palm, marking the pause in the lines' scansion. "My lord chief justice," he said in a calm tone to Pelton, seated before him in the coupe's passenger seat, "speak to that vain man." Blythe's still outstretched arms weakened at Elliot's tone.

"Have you your wits?" spat Pelton, raising herself out of her seat, "know you what 'tis you speak?"

"My king!" pressed Blythe, a shadow of unexpected question in his ebullient tone, "my Jove! I speak to thee, my Heart!"

Elliot allowed a beat to continue, not moving his gaze from Blythe's. Blythe dropped his arms, concern now apparent on his face.

"I know thee not, old man," Elliot began, emphasizing the key words of Hal's climactic moment over the hum of the Ford's motor as he calmly leaned back and crossed his hands in his lap, "fall to thy prayers; how ill white hairs become a fool and a jester. I have long dream'd of such a kind of man, so surfeit-swelled, so old, and so profane; but, being awaked, I do despise my dream . . . "

They had been onstage for nearly five hours, including their matinee presentation of *Part* 1. The hour intermission between the plays had been effervescent; Elliot could have kissed any member of the cast without embarrassment. Finals were over, he was exhausted, and, like Prince Hal, they had nearly achieved their goal of completing their production.

Despite Severn's warning to the contrary, their audience tonight was larger even than opening night's, with the hillocks surrounding the bowl as packed as the amphitheater benches. It was a great audience, too; Elliot had watched from backstage as Vesta, dressed in a chic, sparkling, violet gown—the most low-cut dress he'd ever seen her in—strutted around Falstaff as Doll Tearsheet. Disguised as a waiter, Elliot had almost missed his cue to enter and play a final joke on the man. A swift elbow from Megan, similarly disguised next to him, had pulled Elliot back to reality. He could not relax just yet; the fat lady—or the fat knight—had not yet sung.

Now, surrounded by Vesta, Megan, and the other shocked members of their tavern crowd, Blythe stood stolidly as Elliot delivered Prince Hal's long-withheld aim of "breaking through the foul and ugly mists of vapors that did seem to strangle him." It had been early afternoon when Elliot had said those words in the second scene of the long, final run. "Presume not that I am the thing I was," he now continued, "For God doth know, so shall the world perceive, that I have turn'd away from my former self. So will I those that kept me company."

Elliot's throat almost caught at the words, which now seemed so poignant, as had the whole lucid afternoon. He had decided this would be his last semester in Orangedale. If they didn't want Rydar, he had reasoned, then they didn't want students like him. Elliot swallowed the feeling, channeling it into the present performance—the final moments of the Prince whom Elliot still could not peg as dissembling more now or more in the taverns he was presently rejecting.

Letting the thought that he might not see these people again inform his words, and directing the words as much against himself as the now agape Blythe, Elliot finished, fighting to keep his tone calm, between passion and pity, "I banish thee, on pain of death—as I have done the rest of my misleaders—not to come near our person by ten mile. For competence of life I will allow you, that lack of means enforce you not to evil: and as we hear you do reform yourselves, we will, according to your strength and qualities, give you advancement." Elliot turned to Pelton, who had sat back into her seat. "Be it your charge, my lord, to see perform'd the tenor of our word. Set on." The driver shifted the car back into gear, driving past the now stunned crowd surrounding Falstaff to disappear offstage.

Behind the bowl's building, Elliot hopped down off the side of the car. After helping her out of the car, he exchanged a look with Dr. Pelton.

"Very good, Elliot," said the woman, "you didn't break." Not knowing what to say, Elliot took her lace-gloved hand and bowed low, hiding his sudden tears from the dim orange of the parking lot light. The woman gave a bright chuckle, patting the back of his hand before proceeding toward the building.

Elliot was undoing his black tie when he saw a dark figure approaching from between the cypress trees that rounded the bowl. Elliot knew who it was before the sharp, shaven chin and impudent smile came into the light.

"You'll miss the ending," Elliot said, sniffing.

"I've seen it," said Rydar.

"It's good to see you," Elliot said.

Rydar merely stood, hands in pockets, looking at him.

"How've you been?" Elliot asked, unbuttoning his shirt to let the cool air into his suddenly unbearable tuxedo.

"I'm so proud of you, Elliot," said Rydar, ignoring the question. "You did it. You really ended up being the right man for the job."

Elliot could not speak over the sudden lump in his throat. For the second time in the man's presence, he felt tears form around his eyes. However, this time Rydar did not look away; he merely nodded, unperturbed. Reaching up a hand, the man waved Elliot over.

Elliot embraced his professor, grasping his hands behind the man's upper back as Rydar patted his shoulder. Elliot stifled a sob into Colson's shoulder, not knowing whether it was from missing the man or the awareness that he might not see him again. That would happen either way, he remembered. To his credit, Colson did not seem bothered by the show of emotion. The man kissed the side of Elliot's head.

"Hey," said Rydar, giving a final pat before removing his arms, "I'm having a little end-of-the-year get together. Just a few friends. If you're still in town on Friday night, I'd love to have you there. You've earned it." Elliot saw tears in Rydar's eyes, too.

"Are the others going to be there?"

"Some, though most of them are going home for summer. I'm trying to keep it small."

"Okay. Yeah, I'll try to make it," Elliot said, wiping his eyes with the tissue he kept in the tuxedo's pocket.

"Good. Now, enjoy the rest of your night," Rydar said, turning toward the car-lined street.

Wanting to follow the man, Elliot sighed, instead walking to the cypress trees to catch the end of Vesta's epilogue. He noted her parents smiling in the front row. They were planning to treat their group to lunch the next day. Elliot decided he would not tell the others he had seen Rydar. This moment was his.

"Wait here," said Cora as they passed Breitlinger Center. "I have to go take care of something."

"No problem," said Vesta, looking at the others. Jonas, holding her hand, checked his phone. Megan and Vesta were continuing a conversation about who they had seen in the audience. Elliot remained quiet, letting his eyes follow Cora through B-Center's glass-walled foyer.

After taking their final bows, exchanging hugs with family, friends, and several strangers, they had decided to walk back to campus. Cora, who in the post-production tide of people attached herself to Elliot's arm, had accompanied them. At a look from Vesta, Megan had held her peace, though throughout the conversation she avoided addressing the girl.

"She's held up well, all things considered," said Jonas off-hand. Elliot was grateful that Jonas had taken the lead in conversing with Cora on their hour-long stroll back to campus.

"Yeah," agreed Vesta, "and she took most of it alone." She glanced at Elliot. He shrugged, looking off across the quad as he thought of their recent text conversations.

"Good," said Megan, crossing her arms.

"We don't need to rehash it," Elliot said, calmly but firmly. Megan tisked but said nothing. Vesta nodded, her lip curling into a smile. Were it not for Vesta's encouragement, Elliot doubted he would have had the courage to try and bring Cora back into the group.

After a few moments Cora came out looking confused.

"What's up?" asked Megan, arms still crossed.

"The person I was looking for wasn't there," Cora said.

"Who?" asked Elliot, a feeling of unease growing beneath his throat. "Ermine."

The disconcerted way she said his name set the rest on edge.

"He's probably left for summer," said Vesta.

"No, he said he was staying in Orangedale," replied Cora.

"Why'd you want to see him?" asked Elliot.

Cora smiled, lowering her chin and smirking at the others. "To throw tonight in his face."

A single, hard chuckle escaped Megan.

"Hey!" a man's voice called from across the quad. In the orange afternoon light Elliot could see Sam trotting toward them. Elliot stepped out from the group, extending his hand.

"What's up?" asked Elliot as Sam took his hand. "This is Sam; he's a history teacher in town."

"Hi everyone. I just saw your show—it was great!" Sam said smiling before turning to Elliot and Cora. "I'm just here to see Ermine."

"He's not there. What's wrong?" asked Cora.

"Hm. he sent me a weird text." Sam held up his phone.

Ermie

> Sam, I want you to know that whatever happens, I'm sorry. You don't need to respond.

"Were you two texting again?" asked Elliot.

"No, I haven't heard from him in months. That's why I'm worried."

"But why apologize to you?"

"I don't know. Lack of closure? I hoped to find him here." The man's tone belied his calm expression. His demeanor matched how Cora had looked coming out of the lobby. They know Ermine, thought Elliot, and if they're worried . . .

Sam's phone started to buzz.

"Hello? Ermine?"

A woman's voice could be faintly heard.

"Oh, okay," said Sam, his eyes widening. "Thank you. Yes, I'll go over there right away. Yes, please call the police." He ended the call. "Apparently my home alarm went off. I need to get home right away." He looked at Elliot.

"I'll come with you," volunteered Elliot.

"Me, too," said Cora.

"Thanks. I'm sure it's nothing. The cat probably just knocked something over." Sam's eyes met both of theirs; he did not sound convinced.

They arrived at a small house not far from downtown Orangedale. A police car was already outside. An officer approached them as they stepped out of Sam's car.

"There are no signs of forced entry," the officer said, holding out her hand, "Do you have your key?"

"Yeah." Sam handed the officer his keys as another officer stepped out of the squad car. The two went to the front door, unlocked it, and called out. The house was silent.

After the officers had checked each room, they allowed Sam, Elliot, and Cora to enter. As they went through the house, Sam scanned the rooms. Suddenly a thought struck him, and he rushed down the hall. Elliot and Cora exchanged a glance. After a moment Sam ran out.

"He took my gun!"

The officer turned. "What?"

"My ex-boyfriend. I think he still had a key to my house. I keep a handgun near my bed in a safe. He must have figured out or seen my combo." Sam's voice grew quick. "It's not hard, just the address I grew up at. Either way, it's gone."

"Would he have any reason to use it?"

"I think he might think so," Sam said, opening the text to show the officer. Sam looked at Elliot and Cora.

"He's going to Rydar's," said Cora, voicing the same thought in Elliot's mind. "They shut down his website, and I can't imagine he'd be okay with Rydar being released."

"We need to get over there," said Sam to the officer. "Oh god, he has my gun!" Sam put a hand up and on the side of his head, running his fingers through his hair.

"You had it locked up," said the officer, evidently trying to calm Sam as the other was calling in for a patrol at Colson's house. The man turned to Elliot. "Why would the ex want to hurt Colson?"

"Too many reasons," said Elliot, pulling up the December text with Rydar's address. "Here's his house. Can we follow you there?"

"They'll send another patrol over there. You can follow us, but you'll need to stay out of the way."

Ermine opened the gate as softly as possible. Despite the warm evening, the wrought-iron hinge squealed. Already quaking, Ermine winced, pausing after he slipped into Rydar Colson's back yard. No sound came; the twilit neighborhood was quiet.

Ermine had tried to focus on the wins of the year. In the end they had defeated the play on campus, and Rydar Colson was gone. However, Ermine knew neither of these things were really true. The thought of Colson's face—the gloating, smug, superior smile Ermine had only seen a couple of times—had gnawed at Ermine from the beginning of the Shakespeare production at the bowl, throughout Finals Week, and to tonight. The thoughts had formed into a consistent daydream, which, as he ruminated on it, had turned into a plan. Getting Colson's address from Patrick had been easier than Ermine expected—a mere matter of checking past emails for a New Year's Eve party invitation. The man only lived a few streets from Sam. So much the better, if ironic; Ermine preferred not to plumb the reasons for the irony.

Skirting the neatly-kept yard along the wooden fence, Ermine saw the open sliding-glass door; only a screen door separated him from the open living room. He had seen a light on in one of the front windows, but the room he now looked into was dark. He padded up to the back door, aware of the weight of the revolver in his pocket. Feeling again his distaste for touching the thing, he remembered what he was there to do. Drastic times, he thought. It would all be over soon, one way or another. The screen door slid open under Ermine's hand.

Stepping inside, Ermine had to hold back a sudden cough as a draft of smoke hit him in the face.

"You're Ermine Jackson."

Ermine froze as his eyes adjusted. Stretched out on the couch in the dark, looking at Ermine without surprise, was Rydar Colson. His right hand held a pipe; his left hand was resting comfortably on his stomach.

Ermine stood up straight, facing Colson. The man raised the pipe to his mouth without blinking.

"So, they let you go," said Ermine, his upper lip tightening.

"Seems like it. Nice to finally meet you. Now, why are you in my house?"

"To make sure you go away—and stay away."

Colson merely chuckled, letting a coil of smoke drift unforced from his mouth toward the back door. "At least close the screen behind you."

Ermine had planned to pull out the gun immediately upon seeing Colson, not even giving him the satisfaction of speaking. However, even as it infuriated him, the man's relaxed demeanor made Ermine pause. Ignoring the door, Ermine looked around. The room was as neat as the back yard. A wooden pipe stand stood on the table behind the couch next to a large, lidded jar of something dark—probably tobacco, thought Ermine, stifling the sudden desire to retch. On the coffee table was a glass decanter; the liquid inside shone a deep brown in the moonlight. Behind Ermine was a large portrait of Colson and an Asian woman; they looked happy. Ermine had to resist smiling at how fitting the room was: wherever he looked, there were symbols of toxic masculinity.

"Son, if you wanted to contact me," the man's voice brought back Ermine's attention, "you had my university email. I'm still technically affiliated with Orangedale; we could've set something up—without the need to trespass."

It was the man's insolence that made Ermine hesitate—no, not just insolence, but that unblinking calmness. The idea struck Ermine with muted profundity that this was the first time Colson and he had actually talked; he already felt as if he knew how the man would be—arrogant, contemptuous, demeaning. Little does he know . . .

Ermine steadily pulled out the gun, allowing its weight to pull his hand down. Colson tensed but did not move, save for slipping his left hand down along his side to the couch cushion. Despite his now focused eyes, the man relaxed, as if nothing had changed, as if Ermine's presence, even with the gun, were unsurprising and inconsequential. Colson drew a long mouthful from the pipe, letting the smoke drift on its own toward the back door. Ermine was aware that his hanging wrist was shaking.

"Why couldn't you just fucking go away?"

It was not what Ermine had meant to say; while biking from Sam's house Ermine had planned a speech about how in the end he had won, how Colson had brought this on, how if he really cared about students he would have resigned long ago, how if Ermine couldn't have the life he wanted, if he couldn't be allowed to feel safe or be happy, then neither would Colson. Yet, now, even with the piece of metal in his hand that had prompted more than a little of the panicked courage of his planned speech, Colson's expression made Ermine feel silly, as if nothing he might do could make this man feel unsafe or unhappy; he, or men like him, would always remain to deflate all the work Ermine had done. The thought baffled Ermine with a long-felt but never consciously-admitted fear.

Colson merely moved his pipe back to his lips. Now that Ermine's eyes had adjusted to the room's dim light, he could see the glint of Colson's eyes flicker between his own and the gun.

"You know you brought this on, yourself," Ermine said after inhaling. "You should have just kept quiet; why did you have to fucking force your ideas on us? We didn't want them."

"When? I've never forced anyone to listen who didn't want to," said Colson; the man's lips had barely moved.

"Don't give me that! You did it by staying, by ignoring and going against what we wanted! Don't you care what the students, what the people want?"

The man remained silent.

"Yeah, I thought not," Ermine continued, gaining courage. "You're just selfish. Men like you don't care about the rest of us, not really, so long as you're happy and get to teach your bullshit interpretations of history and art—so long as you get to stay in power. You're just an ignorant, toxic bully. You don't fucking know what your happiness costs the rest of us! You don't care about the suffering of others."

The man laughed, swallowing the sound in the next moment; Ermine shut his mouth, his eyes widening.

"Ermine, there's plenty I need to learn," Colson said, pointing with his pipe stem at Ermine in the next moment, "but it's you, not me, who doesn't know what happiness costs."

"Do you really think you're in a position to talk, you presumptuous fuck?!" Ermine yelled just a second too late.

"Yes."

Ermine could swear Colson had tensed up—he could feel it in the air of the room—but the man's eyes remained steady. Ermine lowered the gun, crossing his arms with as bemused a look as he could manage; it's OK, he thought, you're the one with the gun. Humor him.

At an expectant raise of the eyebrows from Ermine, Colson spoke.

"You say I'm happy because I'm in power—I don't know if you actually believe that, but you've said it enough. You don't know a thing, kid, about me, about power, or about happiness. You're not wrong: my happiness does come from my power—over myself. I've never wanted power over anyone else, and I'd reject it if they tried to give it to me. You said I don't care about suffering, but it's you, not me, who doesn't want to hear about suffering—namely, of people like me, those who you believe are 'in power.'" The man raised his pipe in a gesture of scare quotes; he kept his left hand resting on his hip near the couch cushion.

Ermine scoffed. "Please, try being a gay, teenage atheist in a biracial Christian family in rural white America."

"Would you like to talk about it?"

"Fuck no, I'm just saying you don't know shit about suffering; you literally can't because of what you are."

"Hmph," said Colson, "try running away from a drunk dad, or working your way through college without parents to fall back on, or watching the love of your life die in front of you before your twenty-third birthday."

Ermine had not expected that. He lowered his arms, closing his mouth.

"Now, my suffering," Colson continued, "which I do not wish undone, doesn't discount whatever trouble you might've experienced. Had you actually approached me I'd have gladly listened, though not under coercion. But if you think you can come into my house and tell me about suffering . . . "

Colson cut himself off. His eyes moved over Ermine's shoulder; Ermine did not need to turn to know he was looking at the portrait of the woman. The love of his life, he had said.

"But one thing I didn't do," Colson resumed, "and it was the hardest thing, at times, was blame someone or something else for my responsibility in the midst of all of it. But I came close. You hate me for being hard—you didn't say it, but I think that's what you meant. You don't understand that it was in fighting against myself that I learned hardness, that, whatever I did, I couldn't let myself relax into and hide in resentment. Even when I most wanted sympathy, wanted someone to give me a break, wanted to wish anguish on others so they'd understand, or wanted to end it all—because why fight so hard when, so far as I could tell, there was no meaning to life—I never forgot that it was still my life, and that even pain was something real and worth feeling, that 'power' as you call it is not measured by how much suffering you can avoid at others' expense but by how much suffering you can stand for others' sake. Can you imagine what that's like, in the middle of all of it? To be both the one experiencing the loss and unfairness, of not just your wife's life being stolen but the chronic feeling that your own had always been stolen, that it had been stolen from the start, and then to be the one who has to tell yourself to get up, to stop crying, to stop hating and resenting life—because no one and nothing owes you a goddamned thing?"

"So you're supposed to just swallow it?" asked Ermine, drawn by a vulnerability he could not repress—and which unnervingly made Ermine want to listen to the man who had just named his own experience. "Just keep a stiff upper lip? Just be unfeeling and—god!—masculine?"

"Yes, and no. You certainly don't not feel it; like MacDuff in *Macbeth* says when he learns his wife and child have been murdered, before you can respond to a crisis like a man you must first feel it like one. But even in experiencing pain, you can rise above and create meaning out of it. If that's masculine, sure, though I know plenty of women who've done that same thing, in their own way. In fact, there's a decent case to be made that real happiness is impossible without such a struggle. But you're more right than you know; there's more philosophy, wisdom, and triumph in the old, British image of the stiff upper lip than in many modern books."

"That's just what I meant," snapped Ermine, recovering from his previous weakness, "you just want to keep the culture old and white."

Colson sighed, shaking his head as if he could see through Ermine's ploy to the part of Ermine that both of them knew had been revealed.

"Depends on what you mean by old, and what you mean by white. It certainly is old—goes back to Aristotle. But the concept behind it isn't racial or cultural; in fact, you might argue that more non-white people have had to manifest the stiff upper lip than have white cultures."

"Shut up!" Ermine said, putting both hands up to his ears more to block out Colson's relaxed, sympathetic tone than his actual words. At the feeling of cold metal on his cheek, he jerked his head to the side. For a moment, Ermine felt the little bar—the trigger guard?—with his index finger, making sure he did not accidentally slip his finger onto the trigger before it was time.

"So, you do understand," Colson said, narrowing his eyes as if seeing more than Ermine had meant to show.

"Shut up! Don't forget who has the gun!"

"Alright," Colson slowly put up his right palm, pipe still gripped between index and thumb, "but if you think you're the first person to point a gun at me, you'd be wrong again."

Ermine looked at him.

"Me," said Colson, tapping his heart with the pipe stem. "See, that hardness you dislike about me? I learned it with a gun in reach. Had I let myself be softer—had I blamed the world and ignored my responsibility to act in spite of the seeming death of all possible meaning—I probably wouldn't be here today."

"Well," said Ermine after a pause, "that's fine for you. But how do you know it's what others need? Why use it as an excuse to be so harsh, especially when they aren't lucky enough to have lost . . . " He cut himself off.

"Watch it, kiddo," Colson said, his mouth a tight line.

"Sorry . . . wait, no, I'm not," Ermine said, remembering the gun in his hand and why he had come here. He raised the gun at Colson. "You son of a bitch! I should've never let you start talking. It's not gonna work on me like it did the others; you won't trick me into bowing. People like you have no right to be happy any more, and your moral justification of whatever repressive shit you want to push on others is a lie."

Colson sighed. He merely leveled his gaze at Ermine. Ermine could not tell if the man was smiling. He could feel a sheen of sweat between his palm and the revolver's grip.

"Do it."

Colson's voice was calm but firm.

"What?" Ermine asked.

"If you're going to kill me," Colson enunciated slowly and deliberately, "do it."

Ermine said nothing. The guy's playing a game; he's seeing if I'm bluffing.

"Well?" Colson said, setting his pipe on the table and scratching the side of his left thigh.

Ermine pulled back the gun and pressed its nozzle against his temple.

Colson sat up a bit, but said nothing. Pressing his lips together, the man forced himself to lean back.

"Happy now?" smirked Ermine.

Colson looked over Ermine's shoulder at the portrait on the wall.

"Always." The man could not withhold his smile, despite the sad slant of his eyes. After a moment, Colson looked back at Ermine

"Well?" Ermine cried, "aren't you going to stop me?"

"No," Colson said, raising his chin to observe Ermine from narrowed eyes.

"Wha-?" Ermine asked, his tired hand wavering. "I'm going to kill myself in your fucking house, and you're just gonna do nothing?!"

"I'd rather you not," said Colson, "and not just because it's my house. You have a lot to live for, Ermine, too much for me to say here. You're a capable, smart, beautiful young man, and this world is open to you. But the decision to live isn't mine to make. It's yours; it always has been."

"No, it's not!" Ermine yelled, stifling a sudden sob. "Not with people like you in the world . . . "

"Yes, it is!" Colson shouted, startling Ermine back a step. As Colson calmed himself, Ermine again felt for the trigger guard. In spite of himself, Ermine was relieved he had not accidentally fired the gun.

Colson continued, "The moment you define your ideals, even negatively, by what you hate, you've already sabotaged yourself—and you've turned your life into an act of worship for the object of your hatred. I don't know your story, Ermine, but it's not important to me; it shouldn't even be important to you. Where you were born, who you were born to . . . none of that's important, not in any primary way; the only thing that's really, centrally important to who you are is your choices, how you respond to what happens to you. You're the one who decides who you become and how you experience your life. You're the one in control. Like you said," the man said, motioning to Ermine's hand, the shade of an ironic smile on his lips, "you're the one with the gun."

Ermine just looked back at him, stuck between tears of anger and sadness, and a curiosity that frightened him more than both. As if to fight back the emotion, Ermine gritted his teeth and moved his index finger from the guard to the trigger.

A hard knock on the front door shocked Ermine's attention to the side. As if on its own, the gun went off in his hand. Ermine's ears were enveloped in a high-pitched whine; his eyes suddenly burned. He wondered if he was dying, but he steadily realized that in his fright he had fired the gun in front of his face, missing his head. In the next few moments, he felt more than heard or saw heavy boots and hands coming in the back door and pushing him to the ground. He realized the skin on his nose was burning.

As his eyes steadily cleared to a burning blur, Ermine saw Rydar standing up, his palms out; he said something to one of the officers, who nodded. With his left hand, he reached into the cushion of the couch and lay a black handgun on the cushion. The realization hit Ermine like another shot: a gun had been within the man's reach the whole time.

"No!" screamed Ermine, his voice as a dull whine as he struggled under the knee of the officer handcuffing him.

Elliot heard the gunshot as he climbed out of Sam's car. Sam and Cora froze; they all exchanged a look.

"I'll need you all to stay back," yelled the police officer they had followed to the house as she ducked behind an Orangedale PD squad car. Rydar's door was a black shadow, two other officers having already broken through. Cora covered her mouth and looked at Elliot. A jumble of tinny syllables came from the officer's radio; she stood.

"They got him," the officer yelled to them, still cautioning them back with one hand as she holstered her pistol, "no one injured."

The three of them exhaled. Cora circled Sam's car to hug Elliot. Sam's face was contorted with worry.

Jonas's car pulled up behind Sam's.

"They got him," Elliot said as the others got out of the sedan. "We heard a gunshot, but they said no one was injured."

"Was it Ermine?" asked Vesta.

"Not sure," said Elliot.

Cora tapped Elliot's arm and pointed. An officer had stepped out of the now lit doorway; behind him, arms cuffed behind his back, was Ermine Jackson. From bloodshot eyes and across a raw, soot-stained nose bridge, Ermine looked at them. He paused for a step, his jaw going slack as his eyes met Sam's. The officer behind him nudged him forward toward the car, exchanging a tight-lipped nod to female officer.

At the sound of voices, Elliot turned to the house. Rydar stood, arms crossed, in the doorway, a police officer taking notes next to him. As he spoke, Rydar saw Elliot and the rest. He gave a small wave of his hand, focusing on the officer in the next moment.

"I'm sorry, but we'll need you all to clear the road," said the outside officer after ducking Ermine into the back of the squadcar. "We have some things to take care of here before you can go inside and see your friend."

Elliot's phone buzzed. He opened it to read the text.

Rydar Colson

> *You guys take off; I'll be fine. We'll talk tomorrow. Tell Vesta and Meg good job tonight*

Elliot looked up to see Rydar slipping his phone into his pocket.

"He said we should go," said Elliot. "And good job tonight." By their faces Elliot could tell they, too, had forgotten about the plays.

Sam stayed to give his statement about the stolen gun; the others were quiet as they went to Jonas's car. As Jonas drove them back to campus, Elliot suggested they go have dinner in town. Vesta's parents had invited them to lunch the next day, and the evening would be a pall over the meal if they all just went to their dorms. None felt like eating, but after some pushing from Elliot they conceded. He felt just as somber as they, despite the relative triumph and relief of the afternoon, but Elliot did not want this to be his final experience at Orangedale.

Eventually, as they talked, speculating about Ermine and about how the night went, they resumed their usual, comfortable modes of conversation. However, whether in the others or in himself, Elliot felt a subtle but inextinguishable gravity, as if the night's events could not be so simply contextualized, nor should they. A look from Megan showed Elliot he was not the only one who felt it.

Elliot wondered if Ermine's attempt on Rydar's life, rather than the afternoon's performance, were not the more logical end of their year-long enterprise of pith and moment. The line dividing life from literature had never been as sure as he assumed, at least not for Rydar and Ermine. Rydar had called himself a tragedian stuck in a comedy. Elliot wondered if their production had not been a history, at all, but a tragedy all along. However, the tragic ending had been averted; would that make it a comedy, or a tragicomedy? He was still not clear about what constituted that last category. Elliot glanced at the group's reflection as streetlights replaced the last hints of day.

EPILOGUE

"ANYONE NEED A refill?" Maxwell raised the pitcher of iced tea from the open fridge.

"Yes, please," said Angela.

"Thanks, Grey." Hoegren, too, proffered his glass as Maxwell stood over the others and poured. Setting the tea on the table, Grey gave Rydar's shoulder a squeeze as he resumed his seat between the man and Sam.

When he arrived Elliot had been surprised to see Sam already at the house talking with Rydar and Maxwell. Apparently, after Ermine's arrest Sam had felt the need to apologize; Rydar had characteristically dismissed the superfluous gesture, thanking Sam nonetheless. After explaining his previous relationship with Ermine and conveying his congratulations for the production, however, Sam had been invited to Rydar's dinner.

Elliot leaned back. Lunch with Vesta's family had been fun; the group's pathos had relaxed back into the pride of a completed production and relief at the semester's end. Vesta's parents had congratulated all of them, though, following Vesta's warning beforehand, no one brought up Rydar, nor the events of the semester or the previous night.

Exchanging hugs after lunch, they had gone their different ways from downtown Orangedale, Vesta back to Sonoma with her parents in their already packed car, Megan in a rideshare to LAX, and Jonas back to his apartment. Elliot had walked Cora back to campus. She initially resisted Elliot's offer to help her pack; Elliot had merely nodded, bowing his head to hide his face. However, their final hug soon became a kiss, and after a few minutes of caresses and nuzzling, she had led Elliot into the building.

In the half-barren dorm room they quietly, tearfully, made love for the first time. It was utterly unlike how Elliot had imagined it would be—and yet, in the moment, with everything that had happened between them, it seemed appropriate. Though no words passed beyond the unconscious sounds of pain, encouragement, and rapture, both understood the theme of the act; that it was unwise and would make their impending separation more painful only drove them harder against each other.

It was not, as Elliot had always anticipated, out of confident pride that he proceeded but a resigned and open-eyed desperation. Maybe that's real pride, he thought later: accepting, even desiring, what you've earned, both the good and the painful, and being unwilling to trade it for anything, even—or especially—when it hurts. Elliot had fantasized often about the achievement of seeing Cora arch her spine while on her back beneath him, but that was not the moment he found himself remembering. Rather, it was the next one, when, after he collapsed against her in exhaustion, Cora brought her arms up to hold his neck in an embrace.

Sipping his iced tea, half listening to the conversation across Rydar's table, he could still feel the coolness of Cora's tears against his temple. He had felt no triumph, no long-awaited release—just a longing more pleasurable than any trophy. They both seemed to understand the regret, forgiveness, and subtly sweet despair contained in the act. To their credit they had not attached any rash words to it; they had not hidden. "Desire without narrative defense," Rydar had called it back in January. Out of habit Elliot wondered what the man would say if he knew. However, even that no longer mattered to Elliot.

It was only afterwards, as they lay watching the light on the oak-leaves outside the window turn from white to gold, that Cora told him she would not be returning to Orangedale. George Washington University had accepted her credit transfer, and she was flying out of Ontario airport that evening to DC. Elliot said nothing; he had merely rested his lips on her forehead, running his palm along her side as she spoke into the crook of his arm. He did not stop her as she spoke about the previous months, describing what she had learned and asking him, again, to forgive her. Her tone conveyed she knew it was unnecessary—and, what made Elliot smile, that she had missed talking to him.

Looking from Hoegren to Angela's smiling face, Elliot shook the ice in his glass. His sadness had dulled from a sharp edge to a soft but heavy weight in the days since, himself clothed again and Cora standing with her sheet wrapped around her, he had hugged her for the last time. He had not told her about his own resolution, which had been wordlessly growing since Rydar had been removed from campus. However, alone in his apartment Elliot decided he would visit Cora in DC. He realized he did not want it to be over, if he could help it.

"But what are you planning to do," Hoegren asked Rydar, "if you intend to leave teaching?"

"Oh, I'll still be teaching," said Rydar. "I received an email a few days ago from the producer of an up-and-coming audio lecture company who caught wind of the plays. After following the controversy surrounding them, she flew out to see them and contacted Severn, who directed her to me. If I can prepare a set of twelve forty-minute lectures on Shakespeare's Histories, along with supplementary materials, they might consider producing them into a downloadable lecture series."

"Will that pay at all?" asked Hoegren.

"Sure," said Rydar, sipping his whiskey, "but I'll be fine. I've saved pretty well, and I think I'll enjoy going underground for a while. Besides, I think things are changing; people who want to learn aren't going to universities anymore." Rydar shrugged, knocking back his tumbler. "Maybe they shouldn't."

Angela laughed. "You're just saying that, but I don't blame you."

"He might be right," said Grey, smiling. "We might be surprised where the market takes education."

"Well, I'm just glad you're safe," said Hoegren. "Not just physically," he added at the roll of Rydar's eyes, "but in the more important ways."

"What do you mean?" ventured Elliot.

"Well, I mean Rydar succeeded, in the end. The play went forward and he wasn't crushed by all the attacks and nihilism that were thrown at him."

Rydar laughed aloud.

"I'm sorry, Frank," Rydar said, calming himself, "it's just I've thought about it a lot, and I think giving me that play in the first place might have been the most profound act of nihilism in this whole affair—since all the others were contained in and followed from it."

"What do you mean?" Hoegren asked, eyebrows furrowed in hurt shock.

"You had to know they'd crucify me. They didn't want to know what I had to say; they barely wanted to know what I had to teach! Why do you think I only talk to you all?" Rydar motioned around the table. "But, once you put me in the driver's seat, Frank, I had to take it all the way. I wonder if you hadn't given up already on Orangedale and wanted to place all your bets on a doomed horse you'd at least be proud of. I'll take the compliment, though I don't know if my faith in the heart of higher learning is so lost, wherever it relocates itself. I still don't know if I proved your nihilism wrong, though I'd concede you were right to appoint me for it. We all showed where Orangedale stands—and that its heart has been replaced. However uncomfortable that might make us, I don't consider it a defeat." Rydar smiled, taking a bite of steak.

"Well," said Frank, evidently still unsure how to take the idea, "I still wish it hadn't gone as far as it did—on the college's end, I mean. But I understand. You really showed 'em." Hoegren laughed. "And the irony is it might've been just another Shakespeare production, had they not reacted as they did."

Elliot glanced over at the living room's back wall; next to the door was a small hole where Ermine's bullet had struck.

"If things could be 'just another Shakespeare production,'" said Grey, smirking, "it might be a sign of health. But I'm with Rydar. For all the damage it did, at least the landmine's no longer hidden. I'm sorry: it's easy to say when we won't be there to help deal with the aftermath— though you know we're just a call away for moral support. That the city responded how they did was encouraging, thanks to Angela. Didn't know you'd married a lobbyist, Frank."

The others raised their glasses as Angela bowed her head in thanks. "I was only following Rydar's lead," she said.

Rydar sighed. "Yes, I was a bit more public than I usually prefer to be. However, if I'll be evangelical about anything, it's Shakespeare. I'll be his shadow any day, in the Elizabethan sense of 'actor.' In Romans Paul tells the early Christians to 'put on Christ,' like in a play or as a costume or armor. Well, I'll put on Shakespeare—and in doing so I might be putting on Christ, or Aristotle, or all the other minds that went into him. That's what's sacred to me, and what makes me not a nihilist like them, or Luther, or Marx, or our Frank, here—not to compare you to them, Frank. I believe sacred things are real and reachable by us, in this world, and that though they might change place and form, they cannot die—unless it's in death that they can most live out their natures, for a while."

Rydar stood to refill his tumbler from the whiskey decanter behind the couch. Elliot took a spoonful of barbecued vegetables, but no one said anything.

"You know," Rydar said, resuming his seat, "there's this phrase in Hugo; it's hidden in a small chapter—the smallest chapter in *Les Mis*, though it makes the whole book worth reading, as far as I'm concerned. 'In the sacred shadows there is latent light.' Of course, he's talking about the still-buried and unlit ideas that will become the future of culture. However, I've always wondered if Hugo also intended the other meaning of shadow in English, the Shakespearean meaning. I like to think so. From that reading, it's like the actors become a conduit for light that's hidden both in the past and in the present.

"Either way, Hugo caught the fact that light's in the last place you'd look; you'd think it was something up on a mountain, easy for everyone to see. No: it's hidden, shaded, muddy, filthy, almost indistinguishable from all the muck we want to avoid. 'And the light of life came to men, but they rejected it;' thus St. John the Beloved introduces the Platonic Greeks to the Hebrew Eden and its redeemer. Only the person willing to look into the shadows—into the abysses they don't even know are abysses, which they don't even know are there, they're so blind to them—will find that their preconceptions of light and dark are fallible, incomplete. Even a better understanding of darkness—I mean evil, badness, that which is contemptible in man, that which makes man less, irrational, weak, frail—is itself a form of light, in that it's a form of understanding. Thus is even evil exhumed from the abyss and integrated into truth through comprehension.

"And it's not just about the unknown: that concept might reach into the too-well-known. Taking a truth for granted, too, is a form of darkness—perhaps the worst kind, being most invisible; if one expects to survive, one must learn to look at such things with new eyes and without irony. This is why learning is the highest form of belief in values, even if it occasionally requires one to question their values: it believes something lives in the shadows and that one has the capacity to master it, even if the shadows are in oneself. The weak are afraid of chaos; the strong are attracted to it. They make order out of it, even become thankful for what it makes them capable of. That's what I find so intriguing in Hugo's phrase, and if I can put it into action by showing the light hidden in Shakespeare and the rest, then that's a hill I'm willing to die on—or publicize myself on, which might be worse!"

"So, you're just aggrandizing yourself, living out your creed?" said Hoegren with an uneasy laugh. "I swear, the lengths you go to justify helping others."

Rydar lowered his head, unable to repress a self-conscious smile.

Grey chuckled. His eyes went to Elliot over the rim of his coffee. "How about you, Ell? What are your plans for the summer?"

"I was thinking of traveling a bit," Elliot said.

"Oh? Where?" asked Angela.

"DC."

Rydar raised his eyebrows. "Why?" he asked.

"None of your business," said Elliot, leaning back to skewer the last bits of steak with his fork.

Rydar stared at Elliot for a moment before bursting into laughter.

"Okay. Fine. I'm proud of you. Say hello for me."

"Hm," intoned Grey, "and what classes will you take next year? Any plans for your senior thesis?"

"I, um," Elliot cleared his throat, "I'm not planning to come back."

Several eyes widened around the table. Grey's mustache bristled into a grin as he sipped from his mug.

Rydar leaned back, crossing his arms as he took a long breath.

"No," he said.

"What do you mean, 'no'?" asked Elliot, mustering himself for the anticipated moment.

"I mean you're not going to run," said Rydar, meeting Elliot's eyes. "You're not going to use me as an excuse to be weak."

"But you're leaving," replied Elliot.

"I was kicked out. Besides, I finished what I had to do here. You've only started. You leave, and who's going to keep the campus from going to hell?"

"But should we try to stop it? After all they did to you and to us?" Elliot tried to withhold his long-held frustration but could not. "And what was all that about looking into shadows and facing abysses—?"

"Elliot, you have not even begun to look into the abyss. But you're ready to start, and just by being there—with your implicit 'no' and 'yes'— you might make others ready, too, and hopefully preserve what's worth strengthening there."

"What's that story in the Bible?" asked Sam with a polite but knowing smile. "The one about Sodom and Gomorrah?"

"Yes," Rydar said with a nod, "about God saving the city because of just a few good people. And there's also the book of Ruth; one wonders if Elimelech wouldn't have become as rich as Boaz had he stayed to weather the famine. Either way, it's by remaining—by taking as much disease, offense, and responsibility as you can stand—that you'll survive, Elliot, and possibly end up saving a few others. In the end, this was my fight. Don't use it to avoid your own."

"I had no idea you knew so much Scripture," said Frank with a chuckle.

Rydar shrugged. "You can't read literature without Shakespeare, and you can't read Shakespeare without Scripture, whatever you personally think of it." Rydar covered his sudden smile by looking hard at Elliot. "Either way, you get the point, Ell. No one doubts your passion, but that might be the very thing you should doubt. It's the easiest thing a young person can do, to martyr himself for a cause or for his convictions, without stopping to test them. It's why I fought so hard against doing it, myself. For God's sake, it's on page one of Aristotle's *Ethics*, Elliot."

"Dostoevsky, too," Grey muttered with a chuckle.

"Yes, throughout. You really want to beat them? Take your passion and put it into your studies. Show they can't beat you, show you don't even notice their attack, that they're actually doing you some good by giving you something to refine yourself against. And then take another cue from Dostoevsky and learn to actually love them."

"Well said," nodded Hoegren. "You're almost done, Fleming. Prove yourself after, if you need to. For now, don't jeopardize your future. Although it might be tactless of me to say it as an administrator, it's not always the content of your degree that matters most but the degree, itself. Not to disagree with Rydar, but what you learn in college might be the least part of it—you'll learn that when you start looking for work. Prudent conformity, too, is a virtue employers need to see, and sometimes it's harder to learn than people think."

"And, thus, more valuable," said Rydar, chuckling, "though I'm probably not one to talk."

"We'll see," said Elliot quietly, refilling his water from the glass decanter. He looked over to the portrait on the wall and sighed. He was thinking of Cora.

Vesta Lloyd

Hey, saw you walking to class earlier with Megan. I'm glad you came back.

Yeah. I wasn't done. Plus, Cora said there's no way she'd be with a dropout :-P

Vesta Lloyd

How is she? She said you surprised her, but not really.

She's fine. Making some friends, but I think she misses us. You should text her.

Vesta Lloyd

Please, way ahead of you.

Yeah, yeah. Say hey to Jonas for me. Dinner sometime? I'm commuting this year but I can drive out whenever

Vesta Lloyd

I'll talk to him :) LMK your schedule and we can catch up. I miss you, Ell.

:) Same, V.

www.ingramcontent.com/pod-product-compliance
Lightning Source LLC
Chambersburg PA
CBHW051141030726
47504CB00004B/986